# The
# Family
# Gift

Cathy Kelly is published around the world, with millions of books in print. She is the bestselling author of *The Year That Changed Everything*, *Secrets of a Happy Marriage*, *It Started With Paris* and *Between Sisters*, and is a No.1 bestseller in the UK, Ireland and Australia. Her trademark is warm and witty Irish storytelling about modern life, always with an uplifting message, a sense of community and strong female characters at the heart.

She lives with her family and their three dogs in County Wicklow, Ireland. She is also an Ambassador for UNICEF Ireland, raising funds and awareness for children orphaned by or living with HIV/AIDS.

Find out more at www.cathykelly.com or follow her on Instagram @cathykellybooks or Facebook www.facebook.com/cathykellybooks

# The Family Gift

## Cathy Kelly

ORION

First published in Great Britain in 2019 by Orion Books,
an imprint of The Orion Publishing Group Ltd
Carmelite House, 50 Victoria Embankment,
London EC4Y 0DZ

An Hachette UK company

3 5 7 9 10 8 6 4

A CIP catalogue record for this book is
available from the British Library.

ISBN (Hardback) 978 1 4091 7922 1
ISBN (Export Trade Paperback) 978 1 4091 7923 8
ISBN (eBook) 978 1 4091 7925 2

Typeset by Input Data Services Ltd, Somerset

Printed and bound in Great Britain by Clays Ltd, Elcograf S.p.A.

MIX
Paper from
responsible sources
FSC® C104740

www.orionbooks.co.uk

*For my four rocks – John, Dylan, Murray and Mum.*
*And for Emma, whose light will always burn brightly*

# I

## Dance like nobody's watching

The boxes are going to break me – I can see that, now.

Up until this point, everything was about filling them, closing the house sale and making sure the movers got every single item, every single box, from our old house installed in their truck.

But at this moment, exhausted from being up since half five rushing round tidying and stuffing everything left into boxes, I have a sudden, horrible realisation: *I will now have to unpack it all*.

It's a Friday mid-afternoon in May: Dan and I and four house-movers, who had been looking singularly under-whelmed with the uncool and inexpensive contents of our old house, are staring at our new one.

They've stopped arguing about sports, so I think they might be mildly impressed.

Number Nine, Rowan Gardens was a tall, narrow house with on-street parking and the garden, such as it was, con-sisted of two olive trees in pots outside the front door.

Kellinch House – I *know*, a name and not a number! – is set in its own eighth of an acre, boasts several trees and is in a whole different league for myself and Dan.

Our new home, I think, looking up at it from the drive which is half gravel/half weeds.

It's a slightly run-down Edwardian red-brick that needs more than a lick of paint to dolly it up.

In fact, it probably needs a live-in handyman who works for free to fix all the wonky doors, fallen-off skirting boards and the gap between the bottom of the kitchen door and the garden which must be heaven if you're a mouse.

But – this is the important bit – it's a structurally sound, detached house with it's very own gate and, really importantly, *high walls.*

We will be safe in this new house with the big wall.

Safe.

Dan puts his arm around me and I lean in to him, determined not to let unpacking anxiety – I'm sure it's a disease – get the better of me.

'Freya, you're right. Buying this is a sound economic decision,' he says in his 'are we mad?' voice, and I laugh because Dan always makes me laugh, even when I know he's saying this to convince both of us that we haven't put ourselves into unmanageable debt for a detached house with issues.

'I don't know why they say economists aren't sexy,' I tease, to change the subject, 'because they so are.'

Dan slides one large hand up under my now-dirty T-shirt and encounters bare skin. 'We need to christen this house,' he murmurs.

'Can we wait till the movers are gone?' I deadpan back. 'Or do you want an audience, because the gravel will be uncomfortable and phone footage of the whole thing could ruin my career . . .'

He laughs out loud and we stand there, entwined, enjoying the warmth of the slanting afternoon sun, with the scent of flowers driving the bumblebees mad.

'Dan, are we starting to unload or are you going to stand there all day?' demands one of said movers, Big Brian, to distinguish him from Young Brian, who is blithely hauling boxes of china out of the van as if he was about to fill a skip.

Big Brian defers all questions to Dan because he is The Man and knows all things.

I packed the boxes and allegedly *I* know all things box-wise but Brian and his crew will be gone soon enough, so I ignore this rampant misogyny.

Dan looks at me, understanding instantly that I get irritated by men who assume women are idiots, but I wave him off.

'It's falling apart: you know that, right?' says Martin (Gaelic football all the way and driver of the second truck).

'Martin, how else would we be able to buy it?' says Dan reasonably, and he strides towards the truck. 'We haven't won the lottery yet.'

As the movers and Dan all laugh, I watch him walk towards them.

Dan is dark and sexy, with olive skin that tans, ruffled dark hair that looks as if he never brushes it, even when he has, conker-brown eyes and enough charisma for at least four normal people. I swear, women's eyes follow him on the street, watching those long legs and broad shoulders.

We've been married blissfully for ten years, together for thirteen, and adore each other but somewhere deep inside (a residue of my horribly uncomfortable teenage years and something that would make a Jungian analyst suggest years of therapy) I feel that physically, I do not measure up to his hotness.

I am too tall. Always have been. Not skinny model-tall, either, which appears to be the only way the world wants its tall women.

I don't have the permanently bent neck of many lofty women, stooping to decrease myself. My mother wisely made me do ballet for three years as a child, but I was too tall for school, too tall for dating, felt too tall for *everything*: until I met Dan.

At the age of forty-two, I am generally happy with myself, but sometimes, just *sometimes*, I wish I had been born tiny, with a retroussé nose, exquisite bones and size four shoes, instead of my canal-boat size nines.

When you're tall, you can never blend into the crowd.

The plus is that when you're tall, you have an inbuilt desire to take care of people. I mean, look at the Amazons and Wonder Woman, right? Makes total sense. Plus, I love Wonder Woman, both versions.

An hour after we arrive at Kellinch House, I'm in the hall looking at the vast quantity of our possessions and wondering how exactly we have so much stuff and why I haven't dumped half of it, when my younger sister, Scarlett, phones.

'Can I bring the children round?' she asks.

'I'm not a child, Scarlett, I'm a teenager,' says the deeply wounded voice of Lexi, our oldest daughter, fourteen and two months, who argued hotly to be allowed in as soon as we got the keys and the moving trucks rolled up.

'Getting keys on moving day is a bit chaotic,' I'd explained to her. 'With Rowan Gardens, we only got the keys at five to five. We'd been waiting since one . . .'

'Sorry, Lexi,' apologised Scarlett. 'Can I drive over with two children and one fabulous teenager.'

'Come on,' I say. 'It's ninety per cent packing boxes all over the place. I'll leave a trail of breadcrumbs in the hall so you can find me.'

I hear Lexi giggle.

'Mum.' Lexi has grabbed the phone. 'Can you come and get me? Liam is playing with Uncle Jack's computer and he says it's cooler than ours and Teddy's using Aunt Scarlett's make-up. I don't think they'll move.'

Lexi, who is not tall but is petite and so darkly beautiful that she looks like a Disney princess, has a sweet, slightly husky voice that soars in the school choir.

Unlike me, before long she *will* have boys following her around like lovesick puppies, which both worries me and makes me happy for her. She will not need to lurk in the home economics room at lunchtime because the school canteen is a place of high anxiety to those kids who are different.

'No, Lexi, honey,' I say, with regret. 'I can't leave now. The moving guys need me and Dad here because they are moving stuff in at speed and have to be told where to put things. Get Scarlett to close up the make-up shop, switch off Jack's computer and tell them I've double chocolate brownies heating in the oven.'

This is not true. Yet. But my superpower is cooking and if I can't whisk up brownies in half an hour, then nobody can.

'Love you, Mum.'

'Love you, Lexi.'

Scarlett comes back on the line: 'Message being delivered. We'll be there as soon as I de-sparkle Teddy and drag Liam away from the computer.'

'Good luck with that,' I say, laughing.

Liam, eleven and a gloriously even-tempered boy, loves the computer but is wonderfully biddable.

Teddy, four and the empress of all she surveys, needs careful handling to make her do what you want her to do. Bribery, fibbing and serious manipulation are always involved. It doesn't matter how often I read *Raising Girls*, I still can't find a chapter which deals with a child with the iron will of Teddy. I bet she'll turn up wearing most of Scarlett's make-up and clutching all the bright, shiny lip glosses in her chubby little hands.

I abandon the hall and go into the kitchen which is large, pretty, the only updated part of the entire property and is the reason I managed to persuade Dan that we needed this house, despite having an upstairs main bathroom with an original, not retro, avocado suite.

'Not that I'm Mr *Elle Decoration* or anything,' said Dan slowly when he first saw the avocado explosion, 'but I'm not that keen on the main bathroom.'

'We can live with it,' I said brightly. 'Think of the garden for the children! And the kitchen for my show.'

I am a chef, which proves that all those years in the home economics classroom were not wasted. Eight years ago, I was plucked from obscurity by a TV producer who spotted me doing a high-speed food demo at a city food festival and thought I had 'promise'. Since then, I've a new job as a chef with her own TV series and I've written four best-selling cookery books. Four books and five TV shows, to be precise.

I've even been named Sexiest Cook of the Year – once – which made me laugh and made Dan get me an apron with the logo printed on.

'At least they agree with me,' he said with a grin that was X-rated.

'And where do you think I can wear that?' I asked.

Dan grinned some more. 'In our room . . .?' he suggested.

I've always cooked. It's my thing.

In the same way Scarlett's was how to do make-up and inadvertently make boys/men drool; while my older sister Maura's was to boss people about without them quite noticing. I have a baby brother, too, Con, and at twenty-nine, I think his superpower is telling perfectly nice women he'll phone them, which is nearly always a lie.

6

Truthfully, I learned how to cook from my mother who can stare into an empty fridge, see nothing but a few bits of bacon, leftover potatoes, a rind of cheese and a shrivelled pepper and conjure up the most amazing 'throw in everything' frittata you have ever tasted, followed by a crumble made with those apples you'd forgotten about. But training at the world-famous Prue Leith culinary school in London meant I knew my stuff.

I race into the kitchen, start ripping open one of the many boxes labelled 'pantry' and finally find all the ingredients. A bit more ripping provides a brownie tin, my palette knife and the emergency hand mixer that's got me out of so many kitchen crises. You can't take a pale silver Kitchen Aid to cookery demonstrations in tents is all I'm saying.

Seven minutes later, the brownies are in the oven and I'm making tea and coffee for the masses.

'I'm an almond milk flat white man, myself,' Big Brian is saying, looking with distaste at the instant coffee.

'Ah, Brian,' I say kindly, 'we're not up and running yet. Can I interest you in a millionaire's shortbread?'

'You made them, Freya?' he asks.

I nod.

'It'd be rude not to,' he says happily, and takes two.

The men are reluctantly getting back to work, when I hear a car horn tooting from outside along with the insistent press on the gate button.

'It's me, Mum!' says Lexi's voice on the intercom.

I tear up. My babies. They might be four, eleven and fourteen, but to me, they'll always be my babies.

This house will keep us all safe.

I close my eyes for a moment and pray. I'm not much of a one for prayer but in the last year, I've been living proof that fear and trauma make you want to pray to something or someone.

I pray now: 'Keep us safe, house.'

*

It's Saturday morning and as I survey the endless boxes at the edge of our bedroom and on the landing of our new house, I wonder if I could hire a skip, fling all the contents of our old house into it, and start again?

Feng shui the whole Abalone-Conroy family in one swoop without ever unpacking a box?

People could interview me and instead of writing 'Television chef Freya Abalone tells us how she cooks nutritious food for her whole family', they could explain how the five of us live in a junk-free home where we all drift around in linen smocks like people in a Scandinavian clothes brochure.

'We just got rid of everything when we moved into our new house,' says Freya, who looks five (no, *ten*) years younger than her forty-two years . . .'

The photos would show our new house with no excess stuff in it.

Sadly, this idea is just a lovely dream. Sorting out will have to be done, to the soundtrack of my inner voice, Mildred, who spends all her time telling me where I am going wrong.

*How could you not have dejunked before you moved?*

*Yoga pants, again? Really?*

*You could fit in some exercise if you weren't so addicted to Netflix, you know.*

Yes, we all have some version of a Mildred. She lives in our head and she says things no true friend would ever say to a woman. You'd dump a friend who says you're about to be found out by the Imposter Police and fired.

But that inner voice bitching at you non-stop . . .? You listen and you believe it.

I hope that one day, with meditation, yoga, mindfulness and reading Eckhart Tolle on a loop, I will banish Mildred and replace her voice with a chorus of the lovely – deluded, possibly – people who said I was Sexiest Cook of the Year.

Just not today.

The box labelled 'first morning' is missing and all I can see are ones labelled 'shoes.'

In the story of my life, shoes take up a whole chapter. This is because I am hopeless with actual clothes but nobody can mess up buying shoes, right?

Shoes used to take up all the space in the bottom of my wardrobe in our old house.

Organising them has always been the problem.

I thought about lining them up in boxes with Polaroid photos on the outsides but really . . . Who does that?

So today, my many shoes are clogging up the landing in ten giant boxes and there is no sign of the vital 'first morning' box.

*You are hopeless,* says Mildred.

Yeah, yeah, I tell her. Enough already.

With a mere two days to go to the actual moving truck turning up, my younger sister Scarlett asked: 'Have you done lists for every box, so you know what's in them all?'

I gave her my *seriously?* face.

'Do I look like I have time to do lists of what's in every damn box?' I said waspishly. I was also considering the fact that I would never, ever be able to buy a pair of shoes again. Yes, we will be *that* broke from buying this house.

'I am too busy to do lists because I am overseeing things.

9

Did you know that Teddy is unpacking her toy boxes even when I duct-tape them shut.'

'Respect,' laughed Scarlett. '*I* can't open things shut with duct tape.'

Scarlett does not have children – a source of much pain, I should add – which is why she is impressed with the things four-year-olds can do that their mothers do not want them to do.

It is a mark of what an amazing human being Scarlett is that after years of infertility treatment, she can even be in the same house as a child. She has taken every hormone known to woman, still has no little beloved baba to show for it, and yet still takes care of my children all the time.

Today, my fabulous childminder, Angela, has had to have a tooth out, so my afternoon help is absent.

I continue my rant, albeit calmer: 'Dan has gone off to do an interview, when I've cancelled all work for four days so we can get sorted. Lexi has done her boxes and wants me to take her and her friend to the cinema, as a last treat in this house, which is not happening.'

Instantly, mothering guilt rages up in me.

You can tell me that guilt is a wasted emotion and I know it is, but I still let it have its way with me. The same way I feel bad when I eat huge slices of cake on shoots for the cake bit of my books, even though I *have* to. All part of the job.

Guilt is part of living, although I've bought several self-help books on the basis that they can help me banish it.

'Plus,' I continue, 'Liam is spending far too long every evening playing Super Mario on the Super Mario yoke because I promised it was the last thing I'd put away. Dan should be here.'

'Naughty Dan,' says Scarlett, grinning.

She loves Dan. All my family do. Con, annoying little brother, teases me that because Dan is younger than me – three years younger – he is infinitely cooler.

Which is true. Dan is the economist everyone wants on their TV and radio shows.

And in truth, everyone is cooler than me.

'Don't stand up for him,' I say crossly. 'I can't do everything myself and I'm running out of time.'

At that point, I was at the basically-throwing-things-into-the-cardbox-box stage of moving. Even my beloved shoes, which I had planned to pack like Michelangelo artefacts in tissue paper, were being jammed into boxes willy-nilly.

*You should have planned this.*

Yeah, well, the *Oprah* people should have called by now, Mildred, but that isn't happening, either.

I argue with Mildred. In my head. Doing it out loud is just plain weird.

Now, I hear a rustle in Teddy's bedroom and peek in. Teddy sleeps like a small bear who has found a duvet in a cave and decided to wrap itself up. One small arm pokes out at the top, clutching Bunny – formerly white, now grey, much darned by myself, and Teddy's favourite thing in the whole world. Her other favourite cuddlies, all twenty-two of them, are scattered around the small bear shape. I want to curl myself round her just to smell her scent, that little girl shampoo, yogurt and perfume-made-from-rose-petals scent.

Asleep, she is a cherub with the blonde curls that come from my family. All my family are white blonde, including me, and she is going to be tall, too, also like me. I am determined that she won't slouch and wish she were smaller, the way I used to do during my hideous teenage years. I have grown into my body, a confident woman of nearly six foot who is described as a Viking Chef.

Note: if you are tall, blonde, wear a plait and are called Freya, you get called a Viking in the press. People really have no imagination, is all I'm saying.

Dan is tall too. Deliciously, much taller than me. Because he's dark, together we look like a black and white photo.

Next, I peek into Lexi's room. Lexi is fourteen and is ballerina tiny with long dark hair. Asleep, her face looks so much younger than it does when she's awake and practising being fifteen. I want to stroke her but she'd wake up and on a Saturday during term time, she'd be grumpy.

In the third bedroom – wallpapered an unhappy green, but he did choose the room himself, even though he knows that it will be ages before we can redecorate – eleven-year-old Liam lies star-fished on the bed with his duvet on the floor and a pillow under his feet.

Gently, I put the duvet back on my gorgeous boy with limbs that are confusing him because they are growing too much. Liam is still a hugging sort of child, which makes me want to cry because I know that one day, he'll fight off all affection. But not today, for which I am grateful.

For a long time, I thought gratitude was an overrated, corporate invention dreamed up to keep stationery addicts buying more little notebooks.

But for the past year, since, well . . . everything, I have been working hard on gratitude. Also: a spiritual connection; mindfulness; thinking about booking a yoga class; getting round to answering my Emails of Shame and actually finishing *The Power of Now*.

'Thank you for this,' I murmur into the ether, to God/the goddess/whichever deity is in charge.

At that precise moment, Teddy appears on the landing, a small, exquisite sight in a forest of packing boxes.

Her cheeks are rosy with sleep. Her blonde curls are tousled adorably. She looks perfect. Apart from her frowny face.

Waking up in a new bedroom in a new house would send anyone over the edge.

It's done it to me at forty-two and my poor Teddy is only just four.

'How is Mummy's little pet?' I say, scooping her up, covering her face with kisses and getting that special ticklish place under her ear, which makes her giggle.

'Stop!' she commands, all suddenly right with her world again.

Mummy is here, kissing her.

She is adored. Back to normality. Teddy is in charge of our household and she knows it. I instinctively feel that when Teddy is older, there will be no critical inner voice torturing *her*.

'Peppa Pig,' she says now with an imperious duchess wave. Teddy came out of the womb waving imperiously. She was my hardest birthing experience.

Liam had been a blissful birth and I swear, if we'd had whale music, candles and a birth plan, Liam would have gone along with it and come out at high speed during the most operatic whale-singing bit.

With Teddy, I got the full works – screaming pain that went on for hours, and no sign of a person to give me the promised epidural, even though I'd have consumed a bag of Class A narcotics during the worst of the pain.

*This* is the big secret of childbirth. Not the stitches which require you to sit on an inflatable rubber ring for two weeks. No, it's the fact that one child can slip out like a dolphin, while another comes screaming into the world practically sideways (this is possible, I am telling you), having made their mother howl with pain during an eighteen-hour labour.

Lexi, my eldest, is not my birth child but I am her mother. Totally her mother.

I have been her mother since she was just over two and Dan, her birth father, brought her round in desperation on a weekend he wasn't due to have her because her mother, his ex, had left her in a restaurant by mistake. Yes, I am serious.

*Keys, handbag, yes – oh gosh, I forgot the toddler. Silly me.*

Lexi was the only child of his first wife, Elisa, a woman who was physically twenty-six when she gave birth but emotionally, still a wild, party-loving nineteen-year-old. As someone who was never a wild, party-loving nineteen-year-old because my sense of responsibility has always been in overdrive, I cannot grasp this concept at all.

'She was indulged as a kid,' Dan says now that his rage is gone over the child-abandonment issue, which is basically standing up for the stupid cow in my book.

*My* rage is not gone, I can tell you that.

'Her brothers were the smart ones,' Dan always continues.

It's well-remembered speech catalogued in his brain: he tries to make excuses for Elisa because he has somehow forgiven her and he feels that Lexi must have an unbiased version of her birth mother.

Intellectually, I agree with him.

Emotionally, it's a different story.

I had already fallen in love with Dan, but when Lexi came to live with us full-time, that was the fiercest love affair ever.

She had not emerged from my body but she was mine. I became her mother; and everybody knows, mothers are feral when it comes to their children.

Have you ever watched those nature programmes where females with their young will kill animals much larger in their defence . . .? Yup, that's me.

'Nobody knew what to do with Elisa,' goes the rest of Dan's spiel. 'She was always a bit immature . . .'

Immature? That's the best he can do?

And standing up for the woman who left our darling Lexi, innocent and defenceless, in a restaurant . . .?

*Imminent high blood pressure moment*, Mildred mutters, pretending to be a health robot from the future.

She's right.

I can't think about Elisa or I will start having arguments with her in my head – 'You left Lexi in a restaurant! What is wrong with you? Immature and indulged do not cover this level of stupidity!'

'And you, *you, Dan Conroy*, do not give me any old crapology about how she wasn't clever and her brothers got all the attention. Selfish and spoilt are the words you are looking for!'

Almost twelve years after Elisa abandoned Lexi, the very thought of the woman can still ignite fierce rage in me.

Instead I give thanks that Lexi is mine and Elisa is out of all our lives, what with her busy 'modelling' career and her exotic lifestyle financed by her current husband and possibly, her father, who appears to be remarkably wealthy.

Which suits me just fine.

My beloved Lexi is our child. After Dan and I got married I adopted her as soon as I legally could.

I love Dan more for his trying to make it all right for Lexi, but it's the one area we've always disagreed on.

Still, Elisa has been out of our lives for years, so I guess we're safe.

## 2

# *Think about what you want in life and you will draw it to you, magically*

My phone pings with my daily 'affirmation' – an app I downloaded one miserable evening and keep forgetting to delete. Every morning, I receive a daily quote designed to help me find my inner energy and release all negativity. *Puh-lease* says Mildred every time a quote pings in. *Wearing perfume in summer will draw mosquitoes to you: is that what they mean?* Mildred has not yet got with the whole laws of attraction schtick. Mind you, I'm not sure I have, either. My mind never stops running despite entreaties to the Universe to slow it down and as yet, I have failed to materialize inner peace or solutions to any of my other problems. But I'm keeping going with the programme. I mean, the app cost 4.99. I can't waste it, can I?

'Peppa Pig,' says Teddy.

There is a definite element of one of the fiercer warrior queens in her voice. In my abstraction, I have been ignoring her and this is not allowed in Teddy's world.

She will wake the whole house. Dan was up late with me shoving boxes around and trying to unpack the children's things. He's earned a lie-in.

This arrangement also means that tomorrow, I can be the one to sleep in: parental bargaining 101.

'Here.' I hand her my phone – yes, I do some bad mothering

myself but in my defence, I have never left any of my kids behind when I am out.

Still, it is a rare treat for Teddy to get her hands on any electronics. I do not want her to be able to make and upload her own vlogs before she can write all her numbers and do 'A is for apple', etc.

I make a cosy nest for her in one corner of mine and Dan's bedroom, find *Peppa Pig* on my phone's Netflix and, with the sound at a reasonable level – it is six a.m. on a Saturday after all – I tell her I am going to find clean clothes.

Teddy ignores me.

Peppa's mesmerising theme tune is already playing and I am surplus to requirements.

Technology and children are a knotty area of parenting. I have seen two-year-olds swipe iPhones with an expertise I do not have. Liam is getting a phone for his twelfth birthday. Although plenty of kids his age already have phones – and, no doubt, bookies' accounts and a string of girlfriends/boy-friends on WhatsApp – Liam is not one of them.

Lexi, who got hers on *her* twelfth birthday, has it sur-gically attached to her person at all times, except at night because I take it at eight o'clock.

Teddy giggles at something Peppa has just done and the large lump in our bed that is Dan stirs.

Speed up, I tell myself.

In the bathroom, I ignore the basic state of the place and also ignore the sight of myself in the mirror. When people – randomers in the supermarket – evince utter astonishment that I, Freya Abalone, am on the telly on the grounds that I look '. . . normal!', I agree.

After all, I see my face before the telly make-up goes on. I am a good chef known for simple nutritious food but my appeal – well, this is what Scarlett calls it – lies in my enthusiasm and passion for cooking. This is what the TV people saw when they plucked me from obscurity years ago and gave me a fledgling television series.

Dan tells me I'm beautiful. In fact, he never stops saying it.

But in real-world, non-Dan situations, I know I am not a stunning woman like my sister, Scarlett, or even classically handsome like my other sister, Maura. I am a tall, pale-skinned blonde, with an open, warm face (this is what my mother says), deep-set eyes, freckles, and generally, have a bit of lip balm still left on my lips and a wonky bit of eyeliner.

'Yes, I agree. I don't know why I'm on the telly, either,' I say to the randomers, who then sometimes helpfully tell me that they hate my cooking show and add that I'm not even a real chef because I never ran my own restaurant, which is true. Unless you are a Type A personality, running a restaurant leads normal people to nervous breakdowns or expensive wine addictions.

Mildred generally agrees with the randomers, by the way.

*Looking normal is nothing: what if they find out that you are making this up as you go along?* she likes to say.

Today, I shut the bathroom door quietly and begin ripping boxes open with a metal nail file that Dan – who has already unpacked his shaving gear, aftershave, and toothbrush para-phernalia – has laid out.

Several boxes labelled 'bathroom' have kitchen things in them.

I was so careful.

*You weren't careful. You were rushing.*

Belt up, Mildred.

I do, eventually, find my knickers, some clean T-shirts and yoga leggings that have not seen yoga since long before Teddy was born. This is immaterial – T-shirts and old yoga leggings are the casual clothes of the working woman.

I rinse my face, slather on the moisturiser I once bought Dan which he never uses but which still lives in his wash-bag, and finish off with both his toothbrush and aftershave.

Yesterday's hair elastic lies on my side of the sink so I use my fingers to corral my Arctic blonde hank into my trade-mark long plait.

I then apply a slick of eyeliner from my handbag make-up kit and a hasty pinkie-finger-swoosh of lip balm, and I'm ready to face the day.

Kellinch House is silent but the floorboards creak as Teddy and I make our way out of the room.

The stairs creak as we go downstairs and into the kitchen where I know the coffee awaits. Dan has unpacked all the things central to our well being. Pride of place is his coffee machine, which we call the Barista Baby because it's so complicated it looks as if it needs a trained barista to manage it. One double espresso and I will feel human. Meanwhile I get some cereal and milk for Teddy and install her in a chair at the table.

'Yasss,' she says joyfully at the sight of the cereal, which is for emergency use only and contains too many E-numbers and plenty of sugar.

'Just for today,' I say.

'Every day!' she chants, delighted.

'Are you going to run the country when you're older?' I add, lovingly. You have to be impressed at her negotiating skills.

Teddy beams. 'Yassss.'

I refuse to feel guilty at giving her cereal because nearly every single day, I cook for breakfast.

Because we are now broke, the only change we have made

in the house is to install the seven-burner double oven from our last house, so I stick bread under the grill. Slowly I become aware that the genius coffee machine is not working. It is making a noise, but the wrong one. I try to brew an espresso and realise it is banjaxed.

Dan will be distraught. He loses his temper very rarely. Still, if his precious Barista Baby has been broken by the movers, he will go nuts.

Big Brian will be getting a phone call, for sure.

'No coffee, Teddy,' I say, pulling a horrified face at her. 'Mummy goes crazy without coffee . . .' And I launch myself at her with outstretched zombie-tickling arms.

She giggles, then says, 'Mummy tea?'

'Tea is only for evening,' I sigh, and we eat our breakfasts together and watch Peppa and George laugh at Daddy Pig.

'I wonder if Daddy Pig could fix our Daddy's coffee machine?' I ask her.

Teddy picks up her bowl to slurp/spill the sweet milk and shakes her head at the same time.

Breakfast over, we wander hand in hand through the moving-box-strewn downstairs.

'Very messy, Mummy, very messy,' says Teddy, shaking her head.

'Mummy and Daddy will make it lovely,' I say with determination, ignoring Mildred telling me we have made a huge mistake buying this place and how will we ever pay for it?

'Do you like your new house?'

Teddy nods happily. She has the easy adaptability of the very young.

'Me too,' I say, watching the way the May morning sun shines in through the windows and how our new garden is alive with butterflies and bees, with a starling poking at the grass as if it knows a worm is hiding just a hint out of reach.

The house belonged to a widowed lady who had lived here for years but her husband was ill for a long time, the estate agent told us. I assume there was no money left because the place, though spotlessly kept, boasts decor from the late seventies and early eighties.

It's still big and detached, so we had to push ourselves to afford it, which is why Dan and I will need to do complicated curtseys to the bank manager, or even go full-Buddhist on the floor and bow our heads, for the next twenty years. I, personally, will need to work flat out with minimal childcare to pay for it all, which is going to be tricky, but once I saw this house, I knew this was it.

'It needs a lot of work,' said Dan, looking at rooms papered with wallpaper that even Laura Ashley stopped selling years ago.

'But look at the kitchen!' I said, as we admired the one modernised part of the house, that will suit for filming of my TV series in September.

The owner had it done up to help her sell the house, the estate agent added, and it has worked. This place is perfect.

Chefs who can cook in their own kitchens definitely have the edge in TV world and the redone kitchen here is gorgeous: creamy wood, a stainless steel splashback and a huge island unit.

What I don't mention, never mention, is that my actual favourite part of the new house is the high wall around it all.

A wall and a big wooden, electric gate that nobody can see under or over. Unless they are seven foot tall.

Although I have said a lot about how I'd love more space and a garden for the children, what I really like most about Kellinch House is that it's safe. And since that cold January night, just over five months ago, safety comes very high on my list of priorities.

I was . . . I hate even saying it.

OK, mugged.

I was mugged.

What a hopelessly gentle word for a vicious, shattering and terrifying experience. I was in a city centre garage late at night after doing a demonstration and Lorraine, who works with me, had helped me with all the equipment and had already driven off. I was still rearranging things in the back of the car, mentally running over what I'd said and thinking about what I *should* have said, when a man appeared out of nowhere.

In an instant, he knocked me to the ground and threatened me with a knife.

I knew he was on something – I could smell the foetid smell of despair, drugs and unwashed human, but my strength vanished. I felt as small as a child. Terrified. Cowering.

He ripped my handbag off and ran, leaving me bruised and with a broken collarbone. It was all over in thirty seconds and yet it felt so much longer.

Policemen turned up and a lovely female Garda kept saying I needed something sweet. Someone produced a non-diet soft drink from a machine to restore my blood sugar. Yet despite the kindness afterwards, the residual fear of it all has not gone away. Nobody was caught. Drugged-up muggers are part of society and the garage's security cameras were on the blink. So nobody's doing time for it.

Except me.

My inspiration for work has dried up. I'm nervy all the time. I'm taking tablets to help me sleep, and worse, the only person I have told about the tablets is Dan. And even then, I've implied that I'm getting over it because the family is dealing with so much worse.

Because compared to what happened to my father last year, being mugged is nothing.

In September last year, Dad – Lorcan Abalone, larger than life, that glorious mix of gentleman and bon viveur – was hit by a stroke. We knew about strokes – Dan's father had had one and had recovered with a mild speech defect.

But my dad – at this point, it appears as if a miracle will be required. His stroke was what the Professor called 'bilateral infarcts into the caudate heads', which resulted in a syndrome called Aboulia.

I dutifully wrote this down when the Professor told us because I knew we'd never remember. We were all in shock, anyway, and these cold medical words were mystifying in our distress.

'Aboulia,' I'd thought blankly. Sounded like a North African dish. Something with pomegranate and harissa. Not a catastrophic event.

A percentage of people with this can recover to varying degrees, the Professor explained, but over the months, it became clear that my father was not among them. The neurological damage means that while he is still alive, the man who was Dad has gone. His eyes, silver grey with a ring of blue around the irises like mine and Scarlett's, stare unseeing at us and at the world. Mum insists he recognises us. I disagree.

He can no longer happily tell people how he's grown heritage tomatoes for years; how his elderberry wine is exquisitely palatable; how his surname, Abalone, comes from Spanish ancestors who traded in iridescent abalone shells; how we and Granddad Eddie were the only Abalones in the phone book: 'unless Con gets himself a wife,' Dad would say, with a naughty grin at Con, who was – inevitably – between girlfriends.

Now he mutters, but not in any language we understand. He is not paralysed, but he does not walk or move.

He is with us and yet, gone.

The loss is so huge that none of us can get our heads around it.

And the grief is endless. It's hard to have any so-called 'closure' on continual pain.

After Dad had spent two months in hospital, and three more in a specialized rehabilitation centre, my mother brought him home, having used much of their savings to have parts of the downstairs of the house converted for a disabled person. Despite all sorts of dire warnings from the nursing home staff about how she would not be able to care for someone so utterly disabled, she *is* caring for him, with us providing both practical back-up and limited financial help.

'He is coming home with me,' she said fiercely, 'where he will be loved. He needs to be at home. So his brain can mend.'

Dan's and my fingers found each other as she told the assembled family this. Brains can mend. I now know more about brain plasticity than I ever thought I'd know but there is tragically no sign of any improvement in Dad's condition.

Therefore, I cannot talk to my mother about my anxiety/ fear/trauma following the attack.

Imagine the conversation: Your darling husband lies in bed or sits in a wheelchair, cannot feed himself, has no control over any part of his body and does not appear to recognise you – and I want to moan about having been mugged.

See? No contest.

So only Dan knows about my insomnia and sleeping tablets; but I cannot let him know how shaken I really am because he will want to wrap me in cotton wool until I get better. I cannot take time off for this to happen. I have too much to do. Besides, I believe in fixing myself. I will fill in my gratitude diaries and attract happiness from the universe, that's what I'll do. Can't do any harm?

It takes five minutes to find shoes for myself and Teddy, some clothes for her, and my purse.

We are now within three minutes of a fabulous Italian coffee shop, not to mention a deli, a pub called McQueen's, a butcher's, a SuperSpar, a fruit and vegetable shop so narrow that it looks as if only one person can fit in it at once, and a hairdresser's called Sharleen's Coiffeurs. We did a serious recce before buying and, coupled with the fact that we were actually only moving ten streets away from our old house, the presence of all these adorable shops plus a village green swung it for us.

Well, that and the wall and the seven-foot gate.

Bellavista sounds like a town perched on an Italian sea clifftop, boasting hordes of tourists, tiny but wildly expensive hotels where a coffee on the admittedly breathtaking terrace will cost you a day's salary, and where fast foreign cars complete with elegant tanned people litter the place.

In reality, it's a small part of the city with a village-y look to it because once upon a time, it *was* a village. That was in the horse and cart era.

Nowadays, it's three miles to the centre of Dublin via a traffic-riddled artery into the city.

Here, it's blissfully lovely to stroll out of our house and a few yards down the road to the little village proper and the scent of real coffee. The coffee shop is called Giorgio and Patrick's, so clearly I'm not the only one to feel the Italian vibe.

Teddy is still discussing what sort of bun she can have – chocolate, chocolate or chocolate – when we arrive at the same time as a very elderly, thin and yet not at all fragile lady with a small fluffy dog on a lead.

I open the door for her but instead of going in, she smiles a lovely smile up at me and says, 'You must be Freya.'

She smiles at my startled glance. 'You can't breathe around here with everyone knowing, so we all knew your family had bought Clare's old house. Then we saw the moving vans yesterday. Who is this little angel? Are you going for cakes? They have lovely ones.'

Teddy gazes up at the woman thoughtfully.

'I like chocolate buns,' she confides, bustling past us both.

And then we are in, dog too, which is a no-no in the catering world, into a lovely, truly Italian-style café where both the scent of the coffee and the pastries make me swoon.

'I'm Miss Primrose,' says the elderly lady, 'and this,' she looks behind her to where her dog should be waiting diligently at the door, 'is Whisper.'

'Lovely to meet you, Miss Primrose,' I say and look around for Teddy, who has pulled Whisper with her into the café.

'This is Teddy,' I say, and realise my daughter has clambered up and inserted her top half into the only bit of the pastry cabinet accessible from the customer side. Her new partner in crime is watching expectantly.

'Teddy, get down and bring the doggy back,' I mutter, waiting for an owner to emerge and have a spasm at this canine intrusion.

Teddy does, but only when she has a pastry in her hand. I whisk a plate out of a stack and hiss: 'put it on the plate.'

Teddy ignores me.

A tall, tanned man smiles at us all over the steam. He must be unable to see Whisper, I think.

'Giorgio,' says Miss Primrose, doing introductions. 'This is Freya and Teddy.'

'*Buongiorno*,' he says.

'Oh, you're Italian,' I say, delightedly. The Italian people are such wonderful cooks. Love children, even pastry-stealing ones. Possibly used to small dogs in cafés; but probably teacup varieties ensconced in expensive handbags . . .

Giorgio eyes me for a moment, working out who I am and the smile falters.

He hates my show, I think instantly. Took umbrage at my Irish version of ragu? Thinks women who weren't born in Napoli should stay away from fiddling with pizza in cooking shows? Mildred leaps into action and hits me with one of my biggest fears: *You're a fraud, Freya. No more cooking shows for you.*

And then Giorgio smiles shyly.

'George, really,' he whispers, in a voice so low it could be whispering the Official Secrets Act at me.

Miss Primrose beams.

'He only tells people he really likes,' she confides. 'George has a sixth sense about people.'

I could tell her that people tell me all sorts of mad things because I have that sort of face, but I don't.

George slips out of his Italian accent: 'I was born in Coolock but Italian coffee shops have the edge, don't you think? Giorgio and Patrick's sounds better than George and Patrick's.'

I pat George's tanned hand and his giant, rose gold watch jingles. 'You look Italian and you talk Italian, Giorgio,' I say. 'That's good enough for me. I thought you were going to tell me I was a useless chef . . .'

'We adore you!' he breathes. 'I made your stuffed loin of pork for our third date. Patrick loves it.'

'You'd never believe how many people tell me I'm useless when they meet me,' I confess.

'Patrick does martial arts,' says Giorgio, angry on my behalf. 'We'll have them all given a karate punch or whatever you call it for the sheer rudeness.'

'I only did four karate classes and it clashed with body pump night,' interrupts a beautifully groomed man with hair so black he already has a five o'clock shadow. 'I wouldn't say I'm an expert.'

Giorgio, Miss Primrose and I laugh and after that, we are bosom friends.

All except Teddy, who has been surreptitiously feeding the pastry filled with crème anglaise to Miss Primrose's small dog, who will probably be sick later, and now wants more pastry just for herself.

'Chocolate?' she says sweetly, as if nobody has noticed the creaminess/crumbs on her rosebud mouth and all down her top.

Finally, full of coffee and pastry, we are all kindred spirits, as it's leaving time.

'Whisper usually waits outside,' says Miss Primrose with a definite smile, staring down at her dog.

I smile back. 'Teddy loves dogs and she may have led Whisper astray,' I say, and I shuffle us all out the door before someone reports the café for health code violations.

Myself and a hyped-up Teddy head for home with a take-out latte for Dan.

He greets me in the kitchen, still woolly-headed from sleep, and delighted to see coffee for himself.

This morning, he has an uncomfortable look on his face.

'My mother was thinking of coming with house-warming

presents on Monday or Tuesday afternoon when the children are home from school, if you're not working. I can be here.'

'Gwanny,' says Teddy, scenting presents for herself. She has her eye on a Sylvanian family mansion that will make ours look small.

'Yes, Gwanny and she asks if she can bring Mrs Markham,' Dan says at speed.

Break bad news hastily.

I'm glad I have some quality caffeine inside me to soften the blow.

Why now?

Mrs Markham is Elisa's mother, a steely woman who runs an interior design firm where ordinary side-table lamps cost thousands and curtains could set you back the price of a small car. We see her once a year at Christmas at a neutral venue, once or twice with Elisa when the international modelling world (snort) can let her go. Elisa has a nose like a 747. Have I mentioned this?

'Why does Adele want to see us now?' I say to Dan, managing not to snap. 'It's not Christmas.'

'They wouldn't stay long,' he says, not answering my question.

'But why does she want to come here?'

'She told my mother she wants to see Lexi. It doesn't have to be here.'

'Well, she can't,' I say, fear and anger battling for supremacy in my mind.

I do not want any part of Elisa's family involved with my daughter apart from at specifically designated times. How dare Elisa's mother think she can waltz in here now and see her and us.

'She has a gift for Lexi. An aunt died, there's a piece of

jewellery for each of the grandchildren . . .'

Dan's voice trails off when he sees my face.

'The grandchildren?' I hiss. 'Where was the worry for the grandchildren when Lexi was little?'

Roughly translated, this means: where was Adele Markham when it came to installing moral values or basic common sense into her daughter so she would not leave her child behind in restaurants.

I burn on Lexi's behalf about this. Elisa handed her over and drifted off to Spain, child forgotten. *How could she?*

I know Dan also feels huge guilt over how he never realised how hopeless a mother Elisa was, but he doesn't care in the same long-range way I do. He says he tries very hard to like Elisa – 'for Lexi's sake', he always points out, lest I go into one of my 'you're sticking up for her!' rants.

'Point taken,' he says easily. 'Mum can come alone. I thought I'd mention it.'

'It's mentioned,' I say, but I feel scared. And angry. Why now? Lexi knows who gave birth to her but as Elisa married some rich Spanish guy and now bakes herself the colour and texture of unpolished mahoghany in a ritzy Mediterranean spot, she is gloriously out of reach.

Why does her mother want to come now, away from our strictly agreed Christmas schedule?

Not that I believe in novenas, but I immediately plan to get Granny Bridget saying one of her 'for hopeless cases' ones on the grounds that I need all the spiritual help I can get to keep the Markhams out of our lives.

I might stick a few rowan tree branches in a vase too, as well as finding my ancient smudging stick – Maura got it somewhere and gave it to me. It is supposed to protect your home, although when you burn it, it does smell like a music festival circa 1980 in a marijuana-ish way.

Mind you, who knows where it is. If I can barely find knickers, what odds are there of finding spiritual smudging things to ward off the evil of Adele Markham?

*You need to dejunk or your elderly corpse will be found in a mound of old clothes, magazines and wine bottles*, Mildred reminds me primly.

'Latte, no sugar,' I say, handing the coffee to Dan, who looks no more pleased than I am. 'The Barista Baby is broken.'

# 3

## *It never gets easier: you just learn how to be stronger*

At ten o'clock on Saturday night, I am comatose with exhaustion from unpacking boxes and everyone else is finally in bed. Except me.

I feel unsettled in our new house, partly because not all the windows have curtains. Outside, our slightly wild garden has transformed into a murky, dark place, full of unidentifiable shapes. But still, I reassure myself, we have a wall and a big gate. Right?

I'm sitting with a cup of valerian tea – I do try everything to sleep, nobody can say I don't – in front of the TV in the tiny den off the kitchen, a room which does have curtains. Dan, who is techy but tetchy after a long time trying to fix his coffee machine, had connected the TV early in the day, mainly because Liam had actually thrown a mini tantrum at the thought of not being able to play Xbox.

'But, but you said I could, you said, you said that, that I'd be able to and that it would be OK and . . .'

For the most easy-going child in the world, these words were the equivalent of a screaming-on-the-floor tantrum.

Afterwards, during which time Liam had said 'sorry' several times, he sat in front of it for his allotted hour before smiling and beaming.

He is such a good child. Lexi is less biddable. The Wi-Fi

is only working periodically and discussions about how it was supposed to have been installed by the previous day and how the Wi-Fi Gods are to be called out on Monday, are having no effect. She is on a slow simmer.

But still, she'd unpacked and made her bedroom as pretty as was humanly possible, with my help and some unasked-for assistance from Teddy, who felt that at least ten of her cuddly animals lined up on the bed would make anyone happy.

'They are on their holidays,' she said to her big sister with an adoring face. Teddy is Lexi's little handmaiden and secretly, though she doesn't really know it yet, wants to be like Lexi when she is older.

'They are yours and I don't want them in my room,' said Lexi, crossly, reaching out an arm and pushing a few of the cuddly unicorns and baby seals off the bed.

Like I said, Wi-Fi failure can make the best of us miserable.

'Lexi,' I said, 'don't be mean to your little sister. She was only trying to help. Say sorry.'

Teddy, however, is made of stern stuff. No crying for her.

'Gimme my unicorn seal,' she hissed, grabbing a purple sparkly thing with a twirling horn. 'You are *horrible*!'

Grabbing up her offerings, and managing to kick over a few of Lexi's books on the way out, she made a damn good attempt at slamming the door.

I'd covered up a very big grin because Teddy would make anyone laugh.

From the look on Lexi's face it was clear she didn't feel like laughing.

'She idolises you,' I told Lexi.

'I wish she wouldn't keep coming into my bedroom,' said Lexi crossly. 'It's private.'

'I know, darling.'

I hugged her for a full minute, feeling her lovely ballerina-style bones against mine and I marvelled at how quickly she's growing up.

She has small breasts now, although they embarrass her. She gets regular periods: 'Every month?' she said when I explained menstruation when she was younger.

She wants privacy too, now. My eldest child is moving further away from me and it hurts so much.

'Love you, Squirt,' I said, using Dan's pet name for her because she's such a pixie of a thing.

'You too, Mum,' she says, as I leave, but her reply's automatic. My anxiety impulse kicks in. What if she would like to see Adele Markham, who is genetically her grandmother? What if she wanted to see Elisa too? And what if they became more important to her than me?

*That might well happen.*

'Thank you, Mildred,' I say, with added sarcasm.

It will not happen.

I have been through enough.

I could not cope with that.


Dan, who is angry with me for getting angry with him, had taken two hours off in order to get his precious coffee machine fixed, because obviously, in the middle of a house move, having perfect coffee is of vital importance. I ache all over and I'm pretty sure I've ruptured something internal shoving bits of furniture around the place. I've also made a big scratch on the walnut flooring in the big living room, which will, no doubt, cost a fortune to repair.

Still, things are improving; boxes are more or less in the rooms I wanted them in. Now everyone is shattered and has gone to bed quietly, without any screaming matches from the older kids. Teddy had loved her bath in the giant old-fashioned bath in the peachy bath in our en suite.

'Pretty, princess pretty,' she'd said, admiring it.

'Yes, princess pretty,' I'd agreed.

Now I could walk around and look at the place with more of our stuff spread out and less boxes to clutter it up. Exhaustingly though, there is so much work to do. This room definitely needs to be painted, even inexpertly by Dan, who is a bit of a speed racer at painting.

It would probably be better to paint it sooner rather than later before the wall gets hidden by books and pictures and the endless supply of photos of the children that lined the walls in our old home. Still, shabby decor or not, it's ours.

I wander back into the kitchen, looking out through the dark windows into the dark of the garden and tell myself that I am safe because nobody could scale those walls and broach the murderous pointy bushes all around them. Opening the fridge, I pour myself a second glass of wine.

Earlier, Dan and I had toasted our new home, but now he's gone to bed. It's odd to be in this new house feeling so alone.

Once he'd have stayed up with me and we'd have danced around the house, as well as christening every room. In our first flat, we'd even christened the dodgy old kitchen table, whereupon Dan had half-fallen off it onto the floor and the people from the flat downstairs had banged on the ceiling because it was after midnight.

Not that many years later, we are in the house of our dreams (give or take a coat of paint and some serious work by a handyman) and Dan is in bed saying he's a bit headachey.

Headachey. Somewhere inside me a snort erupts. Women are supposed to get headaches, not men.

It's the Markhams' fault for doing this, I think, enraged.

Since the announcement, we've been doing couple-avoidance, which we almost never do.

Is that the way all marriages go, I think gloomily? You start off really close, joined at the hip, doing everything together. Phone calls full of 'I love you.'

'No, I love *you*,' and then it transforms weirdly into, 'have you remembered to buy bin liners /milk/bread.'

The mundane creeps in. Loving other beautiful, precious little people explodes into the mix and suddenly the tiny unit of two is gone to be replaced by a family.

And families mean things change.

*You've been neglecting him* . . .

I have not!

'I love you, Dan Conroy,' I say into the silent rooms, sorry I hadn't hugged him earlier and agreed that it was not his fault his ex-mother-in-law was creating trouble by changing the rules.

A cute thing I'd seen on Instagram spins into my head.

*It Never Gets Easier: You Just Learn How To Be Stronger.*

Maybe this was true. Stronger. I have to learn to be stronger.

But how? If I wanted stronger abs, I'd lay off the carbs and do actual sit-ups instead of talking about doing them with Maura, who says her waistline has left the building and is unlikely to return.

How do you get stronger inside and why do you have to learn? Why does life test us?

Why does it give us annoying inner voices telling us we're too tall, too solid-looking, an imposter in our careers, a bad mother for leaving the children in order to drive places at weekends to do cookery demonstrations? Why did I get mugged? Why do I have The Fear? Why can't I fix myself?

I should have tried harder with the Eckart Tolle book.

Sighing, I lock the front doors and the back doors, check all the windows, pull shut the curtains on any window that still has curtains on it and with my small glass of wine in one hand, go upstairs to bed. The stairs creak about a quarter of the way up. I'd have to learn all the creaks of this new home. All houses make random noises and now noises scare me.

I peek in on the children. Teddy is back to being a little bear in her cave. Liam already has half the bedclothes draping the edge of the bed and Lexi is once again doll-like in sleep, with that amazing dark hair fanned out over the pillow. I kiss them all goodnight, and murmur *thank you, thank you*. Gratitude. I am thankful. If you're thankful, nothing bad can ever happen again, right?

In our room, only my own tiny bedside light left on the floor is still on. I find my sleeping tablets hidden away in my handbag. I need to find a good place to stash them here. Its too dangerous to have kids and sleeping tablets in the same house without a careful hiding place.

I take my tablet, lie down, close my eyes and wait for it to kick in, because when it kicks in, it is wonderful. When I sleep the sleep of the tablet, I do not have The Fear.

The broken collarbone should no longer hurt. But oddly, it does. When I panic, the panic seizes control of my chest and lodges there, like something malevolent. My chest hurts. My collarbone almost hums with aching.

I breathe deeply. It's much harder now than it used to be.

People say breathing comes naturally but it doesn't always. I close my eyes.

*They never caught him – why should he escape justice for what he did to me?*

Shut up, I murmur. He wasn't caught. End of story. It's

not going to happen now. Get on with it.

Shit happens. Your sister's IVF fails continually. Your beloved father has a life-altering stroke. You have to learn to live with it.

Why doesn't anybody ever put *that* on Pinterest?

I wake on Sunday morning to the wonderful scent of coffee and the bounce of Teddy launching herself at me in the bed.

'Wake up, Mummy,' she shrieks.

My head feels as if it's been removed and put back on the wrong way round: Teddy opens my eyelids herself.

'No, Teddy,' I moan, 'that hurts. Mummy told you that hurts.'

The pulling-eyelid method used to be her favourite way of waking both of us up when she was smaller. Certainly beats an alarm clock for efficiency. I pull myself into a seated position to find Dan, Lexi and Liam all beaming at me, while Teddy, her waking duties over, dances on the bed as if testing its suitability for gymnastics.

'Because you worked so hard yesterday, Mummy, we brought you breakfast in bed,' says Dan, giving me the sexy smile I fell in love with. He hasn't shaved yet and his scratchy designer stubble and the dishevelled hair, a hint of grey at his dark temples, make him look entirely do-able.

Relief floods me. Yesterday's froideur is over. I love this man. Fancy this man, with one of his dark eyebrows raised slightly, giving me hints of what he can do to me when we are in bed alone. He can do this raunchy eyebrow thing because Lexi and Liam are behind him and can't see it, and because Teddy is now bouncing around the big bed, fascinated only by how high she can go.

'Careful, Teddy,' I say automatically. I pull her down to me and give her a hug.

Dan is carrying a tray and from the look of it, it has my favourite things in all the world on it. Croissants, coffee, unsalted butter and a jar of what looks like home-made jam. The jam must have come from a shop, I think, because my mother, who is an amazing jam maker, hasn't made any since Dad's stroke.

'Thank you, thank you all. This is a beautiful treat, but the jam, where did we get that?' I say to Dan.

'A lovely lady in the coffee shop had left it for us,' says Lexi quickly. 'It's so pretty. I had a pink lemonade *from Italy*! The man said I look totally different from you, but I was beautiful too.' This is what she is most pleased about and I smile.

'I had a doughnut,' pipes up Liam.

'Two doughnuts, actually,' says Dan apologetically. 'The lovely lady was a Miss Primrose. You met her yesterday with Teddy? The Italian guy in the café said she'd brought in some of her home-made strawberry jam as she thought you'd like it. I've got to say, they're friendly round here.'

The tears well up in my eyes: it's a combination of the tiredness and seeing my beautiful family doing something so lovely for me. Not to mention the kindness of Miss Primrose, a lady I only met yesterday.

It all ripples into a ball in my heart and makes me want to sob with happiness, gratitude and love. I really am becoming the most emotional woman on earth. What is wrong with me?

'Isn't she lovely,' I say tearfully. Dan notices this.

He puts the tray on the floor and wrangles Teddy into calm. It's like watching a TV vet dealing with an unruly calf.

'Want that,' says Teddy, pointing a finger at one of my croissants.

'How much sugar did she eat?' I ask Dan, my eyes grateful to him for distracting the children from my tears.

'More than she should have,' he says after a moment. 'I'll tell you what, Teddy, why don't you play with . . .'

'The telly,' says Lexi delightedly.

The television in our bedroom, not an enormous thing jammed to a wall but rather an old set put up on a chest, has also been connected. I do not see it getting a lot of action from me or Dan, because normally we fall into bed too shattered to watch anything. These days even the Netflix binges on Dan's laptop are over.

I will never catch up with my once-favourite shows because I have missed whole seasons.

I reach out to hug Lexi, who hugs back. Then Liam wriggles into my arms and I hold him tight, with the tears threatening to come up again.

This is ridiculous. I know moving house is supposed to be stressful but either my hormones are running amok or I am losing all my marbles.

'Right,' I say, 'I have to kiss Daddy and have some coffee. What time is it?'

'Half ten,' answers Dan. 'You deserved to sleep. I woke up in the night and you weren't here.'

'Yeah, I couldn't sleep for a while,' I tell him, as he lifts the tray off the ground and puts it onto my lap in bed. I grab the takeaway coffee first and take a deep drink.

'Beautiful. The machine still isn't working?' I ask him.

'No,' he says, 'but you know what, with that coffee shop around the corner and people leaving us pots of jam and . . .'

'I got two doughnuts for free,' adds Liam.

I laugh.

'Maybe we don't need to make so much coffee at home.'

'Coffee at home is cheaper,' I add, thinking of both the mortgage and the latest unwritten *Simplicity 5: Freya's Kitchen Jewels* cookbook.

Dan sits on the edge of the bed, puts an arm around me and kisses me on the temple. I love this man. I think I have loved him since the first time I met him, which was thirteen years ago.

It was at a party, the time when I actually still went to parties, in other words: pre-children. PC. And we'd stared at each other over the heads of so many of the other people. I was wearing my coral velvet heels and Dan, who was six-four in his socks, big of shoulders and with an intense, hot gaze that burned right into me and made me want to yell 'He's mine, girls, back off!', stared right back at me. We'd sat in a corner for the rest of the night talking and I felt as if I'd known him for ever, corny though it sounds. In the same way as you have children and instantly can't imagine life without them, I felt that my life pre-Dan was not quite right. With him, I was where I was supposed to be.

He's not just sexy: he's clever, thoughtful, brilliant with our children and I still fancy him rotten. Even better, he's a kind man, which should be on every woman's 'must have' list for prospective men and sadly often isn't.

He held my hair when I was hunched over the toilet bowl with morning sickness; clutched my hand during the first showing of my first ever cookery show episode when I thought I'd explode with a mixture of (faint) pride and embarrassment. In short, Dan always has my back. That fierce loyalty and love is immeasurable.

This morning, our children arguing over what channel to watch on the hopeless bedroom TV, Dan's eyes glint at me and I glint back. He mouths the words 'later', and I nod. We are on a promise.

# 4

## *When life gives you lemons, make lemonade*

The sound of Sunday bells from the nearby church are filling the air when the hordes begin to arrive. My mother, grandparents, two sisters, and three brothers-in-law; Dan's brother, Zed, without his current girlfriend. My brother Con is away and I know we'll miss him and *his* current girlfriend, Louise, who is unlike his usual flash-in-the-pan dates and we have all been begging him to marry her and stop fooling around.

Dan's mother, Betty, had been devastated she couldn't come, as she's such an eager grandmother. She's a complete sweetie and was probably too anxious to come after having been set upon by Elisa's bloody mother.

'She has a church thing,' says Dan.

When they all get here, that'll be eight extra people in a house where only five mugs are clean and the couches need to be vacuumed to get the house-moving dust off them. I forsee chaos.

I had pleaded a day to get the first of the boxes sorted before my family turned up and they had taken me at my word. We have been in Kellinch less than two days and when I make it downstairs, it looks far more chaotic than I had felt it was the night before.

'I don't know where people will sit,' I'd told my mother on the phone.

'We'll all pitch in,' she'd said.

We are wildly loyal, my family. Loyal, enthusiastic, determined to make a joke out of everything.

And, apart from my mother, nosy. Nosiest of all is Granny Bridget.

Despite being a fragile wisp of a thing in her late eighties with osteoporosis, a walker and hair like candyfloss fluff in palest yellow, Granny Bridget toppled three rungs off a ladder a mere two years ago while trying to see into the garden behind ours when she was 'just cutting some roses'.

'I always see her at bingo and she never talks to me. I just wanted to see what the house was like because she'd taken the net curtains down to wash them,' Granny sobbed as we got her into the car to take her to the hospital to see if her ankle was broken or just badly sprained.

'So it's entirely someone else's fault,' agreed my mother, not a word of reproach. 'Could happen to a bishop.'

'Bishops have their roses cut for them,' Granny said tearfully, a stickler for the truth.

'We need one of those bishops' housekeepers,' Mum went on, stroking her own elderly mother as if touch could cure every pain.

My mother is one of life's Golden People – these are people who emit a golden glow of kindness and decency and they wear themselves out looking after others. In my mother's case, it is three people she cares for.

Before she became a Carer – big C in there because Carers should be up there with presidents, prime ministers and people who win Nobel Prizes – my mother ran a department in the office of Social Welfare, and yes, this concept is riddled with irony.

Once, she tried to fairly distribute money and analyse the needs of people who needed help from the government.

Now, she is a carer who had to angle for voluntary redundancy from her beloved job in order to become one and as a carer, she earns less than a fast-food worker on three shifts a week. Meanwhile, she has to do the work of at least four very energetic people. All at the age of sixty-three.

I've seen her energy and life force slipping away from her over this past year but – and this is the hardest thing to bear – there seems to be so little I can do.

First up in her triad of charges is her mother, Granny Bridget Ryan, who lives in the back bedroom in the house in Summer Street along with a very old cat named Delilah who is tricky about food and clearly thinks she is in the kitchens of a Michelin two-starred restaurant. She is the kind of cat who gives decent cats a bad name and likes to sick up her dinner on inappropriate surfaces, like the clean washing in the basket or the kitchen table when a guest is just arriving for tea and cake, which is neatly laid out on said table.

Granny Bridget herself is sweet and no trouble at all, except when she is climbing ladders. Granny Bridget is Mum's mother and insists newcomers call her Granny Ryan lest anyone think she was ever married to the house's other elderly inhabitant, Granddad Eddie Abalone, my father's father. The reason for this is that Granny Bridget is a sweetheart and Granddad Eddie is a rogue of the highest order, who frightens postmen, carers and people coming to read the electricity meter. Granddad Eddie is ninety and says what he thinks. Or is wildly rude, whichever way you want to look at it.

He had been staying with my parents following a hip replacement operation, had never quite got around to going back to his own house and then, when my father had his stroke, had stayed on to 'help'.

What this help means and when it is going to materialise

is often discussed, because his presence in the house means more meals to be cooked and frequent interruptions to talk about 'the most dangerous snake on earth', courtesy of one of the Most Fascinating Facts books which he gets from the library once every two weeks. But my mother insists he's vital to her household.

'Eddie sits and talks to your father for hours,' Mum says, and, as always when she talks about my father, her eyes get wet and we both agree that if making my father happy is the price for Granddad Eddie insulting all and sundry, and complaining that he likes lamb chops on Mondays and has no truck with vegetarian recipes, then it is a price that has to be paid.

Eddie is entirely compos mentis but has developed rudeness into an art form by making vulgar hand signals at other drivers when they are on outings in the car. He is rude to the expensive carers who come to the house seven mornings a week to wash and dress Dad, and on certain days, help him and Granny Ryan too.

Comparing one sweet lady to 'a hippo – look at the size of the backside on her' has just lost Mum another carer.

'The agency rang and said they were running out of people who'd come,' my mother says, somehow imbuing this with a hint of humour, even though it is not funny at all.

'I couldn't do it,' Maura says, 'look after him, that is,' every time Granddad does some other Wildly Rude Thing.

'Does that mean you won't take care of me when I'm old?' says Pip, her husband, only half-teasing.

'I'm hoping you're going to look after me,' Maura says grimly.

The presence of irascible Eddie makes us all think about this. That and the presence of our father, who is my mother's age.

We try not to talk about this, me, Maura, Scarlett and Con. It hurts too much. Instead, we co-ordinate times to be there to help out and pool extra resources to pay for the precious carers.

Mum is coming today, as are Maura and Pip, who is known in the family annals as the worst shopper in the world but would love to cherish Maura if only he knew what perfume to bring, or what she means when she says, '. . . Oh, get me a surprise.'

When they turn up, they have brought along a pile of Sunday newspapers, a giant tin of shortbread, their vacuum cleaner and enough black plastic bags to coat the entire property.

I ask Maura if we're disposing of dead bodies, what with all the black bags.

'It's a great time to throw things out,' she informs me loftily. 'De-junk. Clear your space and your head.'

Maura is totally into the Japanese art of having no junk in your house and folding your knickers beautifully. I have tried this but just don't have the patience. Neither does Pip.

'Don't let her throw me out,' he begs me with a twinkle in his eye. He waggles a celebratory couple of bottles of wine at Dan, who grins back.

'There will be no wine until people have helped move furniture and we set up a vacuuming rota,' I order. 'We were at it for hours yesterday and I swear, it's worse.'

Dan nods. 'I think I tore a ligament moving the kitchen table.'

*I* moved the kitchen table again while he was off trying to fix his coffee machine, but say nothing.

'Auntie Mooway!' shrieks Teddy, spotting her aunt Maura.

47

'I'm hungry. Want crunchy sweetie brekkie things . . .?' she adds cunningly.

You give the child cereal one day and she's after it every day.

'Can she?' asks Maura, who is putty in Teddy's tiny little hands.

'Only if you run around after her for two hours while the sugar buzz is on,' I say.

In September, Teddy is starting school and I fear for whatever junior infants teacher has been assigned to her class. Teddy is very sociable as a result of two years of Montessori but rarely does anything she's told unless a bribe is involved.

'None of the girls coming?' I ask Maura now.

My two nieces, a scarily grown-up seventeen and eighteen-year-old, both of whom are still in school and one of which has her huge State exams coming in June, would be handy for playing Super Mario with Liam and gossiping with Lexi because the Wi-Fi is still patchy and this is a fate worse than death.

'Later,' Maura says, heading to the kitchen. 'You know they're vampires at the weekends. Alex goes to bed at one a.m., up at noon because she's internetting all night and Gilly studies at those exact hours, no matter what I say about how studying late doesn't work.'

When Dan's brother, Zed arrives, there is a lot of good-humoured teasing about the size of the place.

'Madame, or should I say, Your Grace,' he says to me, bowing low. 'The Palace of Versailles is looking lovely this morning. May I be shown to the drawing room or the red salon? I hear there is a bathroom in the fashionable shade of avocado that is worth seeing . . .?'

I whip my trusty kitchen roll from the front of my apron and bop him on the head with it.

'It's not that much bigger than our old house,' I say, which is true. But our old house was semi-detached, which is the big difference.

'She likes the wall,' says Pip, and he and Zed laugh. Clearly this is a topic which has been laughed over before.

'Keeps the paparazzi out,' says Zed.

I feel the hot sting of being misunderstood but dampen it down. Zed and Pip haven't a clue why I like my wall. I am determined to be grateful and not argue with anyone.

'It's just a wall,' says Dan, glaring at them both.

He walks past and plants a tender kiss on my temple.

'Thanks, darling,' I murmur, then I turn to my two brothers-in-law.

'You pair are hereby charged with lifting and organising the heaviest furniture,' I say with the special TV smile I've perfected to tell viewers that really, anyone can make crème brûlée. Anyone *can* but it turns out that many people find it deeply threatening.

All is soon forgotten as my mother rolls up in her elderly estate car circa 1981 and tries to do a three-hundred-and-fifty-seven-point turn in order to be facing the gate. She was never a fabulous driver but having my grandfather in the back roaring instructions at her undoubtedly doesn't help. He has to sit in the back middle seat since *he flipped the bird at a traffic policeman.*

I look at Dan. 'Will you go and—'

'Yeah, she's going to bang into that little yellow bush. What's it called?'

We both stare.

'Haven't a clue.'

'I thought you said you loved the plants here?' he asks, genuinely confused.

'I do,' I lie. Not totally a lie. I do like plants. I just don't know anything about them.

'I've forgotten the name of that one. No, it's coming: Ibexia,' I say grandly, because making anything sound a bit like Latin is very plant-like. An ibex is some sort of mountain goat, I think, because Liam likes natural history and has moved on from dinosaurs to books with other, more recent creatures in them, which he then draws.

Dan will not know I am fibbing. As an economist, he only reads books about economics and politics and he is always busy, what with the world constantly being in a state of economic flux.

Dan goes out to take over from my mother in the turning of her car.

From here, I can hear Granddad shrieking about women drivers and how giving them the vote was where it all went wrong.

My mother has selective deafness when it comes to her father-in-law. She knows he's just trying to start a row for fun. Eddie loves rows.

'I'm getting out,' she says serenely and helps out her own mother, Granny Bridget, whose fluffy hair has a pink tinge to it today.

Granny, my mother and a handbag that's nearly as big as Teddy progress towards me. The handbag is the life support system of a carer of invalids and weighs a tonne.

My mother is tall, like me, and today is wearing one of her colourful Scandinavian peasant outfits in a variety of turquoises, with wild tribal jewellery around her neck and on her strong wrists. This is all from her other life when she had some spare cash.

Her greying hair, blonde like mine not that long ago, is in a single plait down her back, also like mine. Despite having to get two people out of the house and into the car, no easy task, and to leave my father with the carer, my mother is cheerful, and has applied make-up so that her northern European pale grey eyes gleam and she has a sheeny glow to her skin that always astonishes me.

My mother's life has not been easy this past year and yet she makes it look so. She is *serene*.

'I do what I have to do, Freya,' she always says, a statement so simple and yet courageous that it silences me every time. My mother would not need a high wall and a gate or sleeping tablets, I think, shamed.

I lead Granny into the kitchen because she probably needs to sit down and she loves kitchens, the heart of the home, she says. My mother will not be lifting a finger to help with the tidying or shifting of furniture either, I tell her. She is going to rest with Granny.

Teddy is busy with her aunt Maura, Liam is playing another car racing game with his uncle Pip, who has escaped off with the wine. I turn up at the door to the room where the Xbox has been installed and give Pip a stern look, which he ignores completely.

'Pip's really bad, Mum,' says Liam gleefully as he makes mincemeat out of his uncle on a psychedelic racetrack.

'Half an hour,' I warn Liam in order to keep his computer playing limited.

Why am I the grown-up?

'Tea, anyone?' roars Maura from the kitchen.

Tea is the answer to all the family prayers.

If an earthquake hit, someone would boil the kettle on the grounds that we would think better after a pot of tea and some apple cake and that the giant earthen rift outside the house could wait, couldn't it?

'I brought fruity tea bread,' says my mother, who is one

of the few people not even slightly overwhelmed by my cooking abilities. Nobody ever brings food to my house anymore, except Maura, who does not have the culinary gene but shops for food well, and my mother, who works on the theory that I am too busy whipping up amazing dishes for work to whip them up at home too.

I have absolutely no idea how she finds time to cook.

'I have meatballs for the kids in a Tupperware container and some spicier ones for you too in another one,' she says. 'Also, I brought cheese and ham sandwiches, along with pâté and crackers because you'll never have had time to shop and this horde will want filling.'

'Thank you.' I hug her tightly, checking surreptitiously as I always do for signs of her getting too thin.

Maura, Scarlett and I worry.

Con, little brother, lost to the world of finding the perfect woman and, until this current girlfriend, working his way through the Northern hemisphere in order to do so, would not notice his mother's weight loss. With the trauma she's gone through this past year, it is a miracle she is still here.

'I'm fine, honey,' Mum says gently, grey eyes sparkling.

She is on to me. She is so empathic that, I swear, she can read minds.

Which is why I never, ever talk about the mugging with her or even imply that it has left long-term damage to my soul.

By the time Scarlett and Jack have arrived – both hideously glamorous in the manner of people from drinks' adverts on the telly: Scarlett with platinum hair in an updo and with red lipstick on her full lips, and Jack looking like he's up for a role in a Nespresso advert – Granny Bridget is installed in a comfy chair in the kitchen room where she admires the wallpaper and promises to French plait Lexi's hair.

'I had hair as long as yours once, and it was the same colour as your mother's,' she says happily, as Lexi sits with her and rifles through Granny's bag of knitting and ribbons to find something she approves of for said plaiting.

Eddie has already stomped upstairs and can be heard roaring about damp in the bedrooms.

'There's not damp, is there?' says Granny, anxious.

A trickle of tears appear on her cheeks.

Granny can't get anxious without a flood of tears. Or happy. Or even mildly entertained, for that matter. She says she cried at her own wedding, at my mother's birth and at every family wedding since. She is a danger at funerals and at bingo once, when she won the jackpot, she cried so much that an off-duty nurse raced over in case an ambulance was needed.

She's a highly sensitive person, Mum told us all years ago. 'It's an automatic reaction for her: nothing strange, nothing connected with any medical issue like Parkinsons or MS.'

'No damp,' I reassure her now, as my mother hands over a pack of tissues. 'We had a surveyor.'

'Really?' says Granny, mopping up and taking a shaky breath.

'Eddie likes a bit of chaos,' Mum reminds her mother, patting her hand where the skin is dotted with liver spots.

'He does,' agrees Granny, and blots away the last of the tears. 'He locked Delilah in the utility room this morning and I thought she was lost!'

'But she wasn't,' says my mother quickly.

Granny pauses. 'No,' she says. 'I'm going to hide his teeth when he's asleep one night. See how he likes that.' Her tiny little face lights up with an impish grin.

We all laugh.

Once her hair is plaited, Lexi decides she'll go upstairs to oversee Granddad Eddie's house viewing.

That leaves the three Abalone sisters, our mother, and Granny Bridget in the kitchen because Jack has gone off to talk to the men.

Scarlett and I have hauled one of my big pantry boxes onto the table. Mum wants to help unpack it, but I say no.

'Sit down and I'll make tea. You're having a little rest.'

The showing Granddad the house tour is going hilariously badly. I know this because I can hear the roars.

'What do you want with a house this size?' Granddad is shouting at the top of his voice, which is his only volume. 'Landed gentry are we now? I never thought I'd see the day. Far from big houses you were reared . . .'

We all grin at each other, apart from Granny Bridget, who is so used to the sound of Eddie's shouting and talking about how strange people are these days that I swear she can block his voice out completely.

'I like what you've done with this room,' she says in her soft dreamy way.

The rest of us say nothing for a moment and then I say. 'Thank you, Granny.'

We have done precisely nothing with the kitchen apart from put in the big stove, but it is lovely, with its simple cream wooden cabinets, large kitchen window overlooking what was once a herb garden, I think, and gleaming stainless steel splashbacks.

Up to now, my TV show has been filmed in a grim industrial estate in the west of the city in a fake kitchen, so the producers are thrilled they'll be able to use my home.

I wait for Mildred to tell me the modern-obsessed producers will hate the sight of the pretty herb garden visible out the window – the only sliver of weeded ground in the whole place – but for once, she shuts her mouth. My mother adores me so much that I think my unconscious cannot self-sabotage when she is around.

'You've got flowering jasmine tea,' says Scarlett in delight, pulling a tin out of the big pantry box. 'I love this stuff.'

Granny Bridget looks up, interested.

'When you add the boiling water, the blossom opens and it's just beautiful.'

Mum and I smile at each other. It's lovely to see Scarlett animated like this. I'm not sure if she's really trying her best to be happy about the new house, because I know she's so broken after the last heartbreaking round of IVF treatment. Two embryos were all they were left with after harvesting. The fertility team implanted those and she didn't even have to wait till the sixteen days were up to know she wasn't pregnant. The early bleed told her.

Still, as she said to me at the time, when she was clearly trying very hard to be strong: 'We can try again, I don't care, we are going to have a baby.'

I think of the bad things that have happened to our family over the past year: Dad's stroke, Scarlett and Jack's hideously sad infertility journey, and my being mugged, and I wonder where people get the sheer belief to think good things will miraculously begin to occur? How have humans decided that if we really want things, they will come to us? Why do we think we can make lemonade out of lemons?

I would do anything to stop Scarlett's pain, but there's nothing I can do.

With that amazing ability she has to almost see what is going on inside all our heads, Mum gets to her feet, takes the jasmine tea tin from Scarlett and hugs her.

'I think Freya has been hiding this and I think we need to have it now,' she announces. 'Have you unpacked many of the cups, darling?' she asks me.

55

I laugh.

'Five mugs, plastic beakers, cereal bowls and sundry plates unpacked.'

'Right,' says Mum. She leaves the kitchen and returns with Pip in tow, instructing him to fetch the crockery boxes, which are, of course, despite many giant 'kitchen' signs plastered on them for the movers, not in the kitchen. Once Pip, ever obliging, has hauled them into the room, he heaves the correct box onto the table and Mum starts unpacking.

'These ones will do, I think,' she says, by the time crumpled newspapers litter the floor. 'Special china for a special day.'

The special china is made up of old fragile things that I have collected over the years. For my first TV series, when *Simplicity with Freya* was born, I thought my old china would look beautiful for filming but the stylists for the production company overruled me.

'That mismatched look is so over!' they'd said, all equally horrified. 'Like, the noughties, almost.' It takes them a while to recover from this frightening image of old, cute things which are so not . . . *now*. Nowness is everything in cooking shows. In *life!* Arrive at the correct sort of nowness and you might have a hit.

'The show is called *Simplicity* and we need simplicity,' they said in unison. 'Cool. You in geometric shapes – we're thinking Cos clothes?' they said, half to me, half to the director and producers. 'You're tall enough to carry it off. No jewellery. White everything and the odd twig in a vase to lighten it up.'

I held my tongue about the concept of a mere twig lightening things up. I'm more of a fan of vast bouquets of wildflowers with plenty of blue irises, myself. I dither over mentioning that the food was to be simple rather than the

56

decor but the whole team agreed with the less-is-more approach. I say nothing. This TV lark is new to me.

I swear the whole cool/simplicity schtick started because I'm tall, blonde and have clear, pale skin and high cheekbones.

They instantly saw me as a strong, modern woman who would live in a minimalist apartment and have *no knickknacks whatsoever*, so now, every kitchen implement is Scandi modern, the plates are snowy white and even the twig didn't make the final cut. I do mourn my idea of pretty things but the team were proved to be right.

'*The sheer simplicity of the food and the set means* Simplicity with Freya *is a welcome relief after a recent TV flop in the US with a female chef trailing around in devoré tea dresses,*' said one review.

'Simplicity with Freya *is a gem. Freya is quirky and clever, cooking modern food with healthy ingredients: it gets a thumbs up from us,*' said another, from one of the most influential TV reviewers. And I was off to a good start. I yearn to be allowed to use my floral bowls and cups, but it's too late to change it all now. I am Ms Minimalist in the public's eyes and that's that.

Dan jokes that the devoré fringed kimono (pink and purple with jangling beads) that I bought in an Amsterdam market must hide in my closet forever or my reputation will be ruined.

Scarlett unearths a glass teapot with a central sieved container for tea leaves, and pours hot water on the jasmine buds.

'Isn't this nice,' says Granny Bridget, watching the flowers open through the glass. 'I don't hold with all these strange new teas, but this is so pretty to watch.'

We drink some tea, talk a little and I begin to unpack,

feeling my anxieties drift away.

All my cupboard essentials are there, the vast array of unusual ingredients that a good chef needs.

Despite my many protests, Mum insists on cleaning out the big pantry cupboard that made me drool when I saw it on the first house viewing.

'I can't sit still,' she says cheerfully. 'Let me help, darling.'

Soon, she's installing my precious things in it, while Granny regales us all with a tale of a woman from down the road who has taken up with her widowed next door neighbour despite already having several gentlemen friends.

'I don't think she's after a new beau,' Granny muses. 'She's a marvellous cook, you see. Men will go a mile for a decent meal. I told her to charge them for dinner and make a few bob out of it. Not to marry any of them, obviously. But with the money, she could go on a nice cruise with her sister.'

'I really should get you to show me how to cook, Freya,' says Scarlett idly, picking up some pomegranate molasses and gazing at the jar as if it's from Mars.

'I can always teach you,' I say. 'Delighted to, although here I have a book for just €9.99.' I plaster on a fake smile, mime holding up a book and we all laugh.

'Oh I don't know, I couldn't be bothered buying it, maybe you'd give it to me?' Scarlett teases and we all laugh again.

One of my mother's newest neighbours said this to my mother when my first book was published. Said neighbour blithely pointed out that she couldn't possibly buy it, but she would deign to read it were she handed a copy.

My mother has not said what she replied to this generous offer but there has been no mention of this neighbour since.

'You're a great cook, Scarlett,' I say. 'Ignore all the mad stuff I have. Chefs just need more ingredients than normal people because we have to start coming up with new ideas. Thinking up ten novel ways to make interesting meals requires a bigger than average store cupboard.'

I think of all my nights spent reading and rereading my cookery books, frantically scanning new ones and then I think of how I haven't thought of one single idea for my yet-to-be-written book. It's as if all the fresh ideas had been knocked out of my brain in that garage four months ago.

I'm still doing cookery festivals with my *Simplicty with Freya* demos, which is exhausting and means lots of time in the car, but my cookbook inspiration has dried up. In October, I'm due to go into pre-production for the next TV series which is to be broadcast next spring. In August, I planned to pitch my new cookery book and let's face it, we need the money.

'How's it going?' asks Scarlett. 'The new recipes?'

I cannot plaster on a fake smile because my family would be on to me like a shot. Subterfuge is required.

'Fine,' I say, pretending to search a box for something. 'Look! Moroccan spices and rose pepper. Smell it: it's divine.'

My mother looks at me thoughtfully.

'Work's going terribly and I have no new recipes!' I want to scream but I can't.

They all have such faith in me, all think I will be able to do this, that new ideas are coming, but they're not.

'How are you sleeping?' Mum asks, and I think that Dan needs to be killed when I see him.

Has he told Mum about the sleeping tablets? He promised he'd tell nobody. No, Dan is steadfast.

'Fine,' I say, brightly. 'I thought I might go to one of those victim support groups to talk about January. Just to put it to bed, you know.'

Mum looks at me with a certain scepticism.

'It's on a Thursday night,' I add.

*Thursday night?*

It appears that when I lie, I lie big.

'Darling, that's brilliant,' says Scarlett, hurrying to hug me. 'My infertility groups help me so much.'

'I want to put it behind me,' I add.

There's nothing wrong with counselling groups – just not for me.

I can't sit around in a group and let my deepest fears out, *no way José*. I don't want to talk about this, I just want to be better quickly. There ought to be an app for this: Group Therapy *on your own*. I'd download it.

I feel the flush of guilt hit my pale face and I search for diversion.

'Are you hungry, Granny? Because somewhere in the bottom of this box is a beautiful container of Turkish baklava they gave me in the office to celebrate the move. Let's get it out.'

The men arrive when they hear the clink of the teapot and the rattle of plates.

Jack grabs me in a bear hug.

'Hello, Duchess of Kellinch.'

'Jealousy, darling,' says Dan, winking at me. He pulls me out of Jack's embrace. 'Hands off my wife, you knave,' he says. 'The duchess only likes me pawing her.'

The men roared with laughter again.

'No tea bread or baklava for you lot,' says Maura. 'In fact, I am taking the cheese out of the sandwiches to punish you all.'

Somehow the cheese stays in. And eventually, we heat up the meatballs because everyone is hungry. I heat some pre-packed and part-baked white rolls in the oven, knowing my career would be irreparably damaged if such a thing were known. Chefs are not allowed to cheat the way normal people do. We must make all our food from scratch or else we are charlatans. Sad but true. In fact, I cook frozen pizzas and have eaten plenty of baked beans in my time. Real life does not always allow for hours in the kitchen.

Lexi is still doing tours of her, Teddy's and Liam's bedrooms. This time, my mother is being shown everything.

Apparently, the tour guide's spiel goes along the lines of: 'Liam's is messy. Don't bother going in. Teddy will kill you if you rearrange her cuddlies. And mine, isn't it the best? Mum and Dad say I can have one whole wall for posters. I want a big mirror there.'

Two lovely hours have passed, much vacuuming has been done, the men have shifted the furniture around and the boxes have all been installed in the correct rooms. I know it's time for Mum to go because Dad's carer is only on the clock for another half an hour.

Granddad Eddie has finally stopped his monologue about how it was '. . . far from detached houses you were raised, lassie', directed at me. The tales of his old home on the East Wall, where apparently the whole Abalone family lived in premises about the size of a matchbox and only the posh people had indoor toilets, has gloriously ground to a halt. I think Dan has given him a drop of whiskey, a known cure for Eddie's 'in my day . . .' monologues.

Mum is getting her charges ready to leave when Lexi races up to me, waving the magazine from one of the newspapers Maura and Pip brought.

I have no idea why: animal instinct? But a frisson of fear hits me at the joyous look on my daughter's face.

'Mum!' she says. 'Elisa's got a contract with Surella. It's in the papers. Isn't that brilliant?'

My mind races over the implications of this at high speed but I manage to keep smiling.

'Brilliant,' I say and hug Lexi, wishing Maura had not bought any Sunday newspapers and that we were living in a hut on an island somewhere.

My daughter's birth mother has reinvented herself as a style influencer of mild reputation in Ireland but not beyond these shores – despite the fact that she lives in Spain.

This gig, in Lexi's eyes, makes her on a par with, oh, I don't know, Lady Gaga.

I have a real job, get paid real money and put dinner on the table every night. But compared to Elisa poncing around in Spanish sunspots wearing tanning oil, minuscule alleged bikinis on her admittedly fabulous for a forty-year-old body and Tom Ford sunglasses she has bought with her trust fund, all the while rattling on about 'how juicing changed my life', my job seems to mean nothing. Personally, I think liposuction and surgery have changed her life; but that's me.

Elisa comes back to Ireland occasionally to 'model' but is thankfully never around long enough to ask to see her daughter. Astonishing, right?

But what if that changes? It is three years since she saw Lexi. Three years. And now, Lexi is interested in her.

It hurts so badly I can hardly bear it.

'So Surella . . .?' I say, stifling the urge to say that these Surella people must surely make cream for badly sun-damaged skin for women who like photographing them-selves around pools drinking cocktails.

*Careful, your bitch is showing*, says Mildred.

Ignoring this, I zip up my second-wife mouth and manage to politely ask: 'What do they do?'

Lexi rolls her eyes and the hurt locks around my heart.

'Surella are the best new make-up brand around, Mum. Ask *anyone*.'

She leans in to me and puts an arm round my waist.

'It's OK,' she says comfortingly. 'It's not your thing, Mum. They're really cool. Everyone in school loves it.'

'Oh,' I manage to say. 'An Irish brand?' I manage a bit of enthusiasm. If they're international, I will know that there is absolutely no justice in the world.

'Yes, they're Irish and they are just *huuge*! I might WhatsApp Elisa – just to say hi,' she adds, in a tone that's questioning because even though she has her birth mother's phone number – given to her last Christmas by Dan's interfering ex-mother-in-law, who needs to die horribly and who is *so* not coming to our house anytime soon – she has never till now made any attempt to get in touch with Elisa by herself.

'Why not?' I say blithely.

Be a grown-up about this, I tell myself. I knew this could come. I have read the adoption books. I know the drill but the fear overwhelms me. What if Elisa hurts her?

And, even though I do my best to smother this selfish thought, a pain of a different type hits me like a small truck.

*I am Lexi's mother. Me!*

A tiny china cup falls victim to my rage. The small handle, stuck on for possibly seventy-five years, comes off in my hand. I stare down at it.

Lexi is at an age when a girl longs for approval, and now she appears to want it from the woman who gave birth to her and then, casually, forgot her.

*That* is what I hate Dan's ex-wife and my daughter's birth mother for: not caring whether she hurts my precious Lexi or not.

Why does Lexi not realise that this woman she is now

interested in has no interest in her? Lexi was two when she came to live with us and since then, Elisa has barely seen her. *She* has not comforted a screaming and itchy Lexi when she got chickenpox or cheered her on at school three-legged races or spent hours making princess hats out of toilet roll cardboards, glitter glue and tinsel for the school play.

I did. I have been there for all the good times and the bad, and she is my precious darling.

But Lexi's not thinking of any of this.

'I'll WhatsApp her now,' she says, delightedly, and races off with the newspaper to her room.

My mother's eyes meet mine but for once, I find no comfort in her gaze.

I look down at the little china cup, broken now.

'Will you show me the garden?' Mum asks, taking the broken china out of my hands.

I shake my head. 'Give me a moment,' I blurt out.

My mother is so wise that Scarlett, Maura and I think she is a witch. One who helps, like the witches and wise women of old, rather than the made-up ones in horror movies.

'Elisa will come into your lives again in the future,' she told me once, a long time ago.

'Never,' I'd said. 'Anything could have happened that day in the restaurant. I can never forgive her for that. Besides, she's gone off to Spain.'

My mother had reached over and taken both my hands, which were shaking at the very mention of Lexi's birth mother.

'She might never come back but one day, Lexi will seek her out. Children want to see their birth parents: it's natural. You have to be ready for that.'

'Lexi won't . . .' I began, feeling my chest swell with anger and fear.

'She will, lovie. Children need to search for who they are and that's no criticism of the parents who raised them. Remember, no matter how much you want life to be simple, it never is,' Mum had said.

I didn't answer. It *was* simple. Elisa had walked away: end of story.

Except now, she was back.

The simple life was Pinterest-happy: *dance like nobody's watching*. Damn that crap. Who has the energy or the heart to bloody dance at all? And if anyone gives me a lemon, I'll hurl it at them so hard it'll take an eye out. Lemonade, my backside.

Finally, we make it into the garden: just the two of us. Scarlett and Maura are taking care of Granny and Eddie, and clearing the table after the impromptu feast.

'Why now?' I say, ripping the head off a flower viciously.

'Hollyhock,' says my mother, automatically, scanning the flowerbeds. 'I'll buy you secateurs and you can have cut flowers in the house.'

'I haven't time,' I mutter. 'I have to go back to work, try to sort out the house when I get time and be ready with plans for the kids for the summer holidays.'

'Of course, love,' says my mother, who is one of the few individuals on the planet who knows how to change the conversation when it is too painful, when the other person needs time to think. 'Eddie's probably wheedling more drink out of Dan. Time to get them both home.'

When everyone's gone, Dan and I decide that we'll order up pizza for dinner.

We sit at our old kitchen table while Teddy eats the ham and the crusts from her mini pizza, complaining that she can't possibly eat the rest because she now hates tomatoes.

'They're too squidgy,' she announces crossly.

Lexi ignores the no-phones-at-the-table rule to search up mentions of Elisa and Surella.

I can't tell her to put the phone away. I am afraid to speak about Elisa beause I am terrified that if I talk, a monster will emerge.

'Eat up, Lexi, honey,' I say instead, and Dan stares at me, dark eyes slightly narrowed.

'You OK?' he mouths.

A flood of words is waiting to come out but I can't say a thing. Lexi must be allowed to see Elisa. I cannot interfere. It is the right thing to do but oh, how it feels so wrong.

I compromise with the best fib I know: 'Fine. I'm just tired.'

# 5

## *The universe gives you what you need*

On Monday morning I wake up at six to the sound of my phone alarm. I haven't been very good at getting up during the past four months because of how badly I sleep in the second half of the night, but today it feels worse than ever.

I should have slept because orgasms at least are the ultimate in sleeping aids, but despite feeling the comfort of Dan's strong body melding with mine in bed until we were one hot, sweaty mess, and I'm moaning his name and he's moaning mine, I still couldn't drift off afterwards the way he did.

In my humble opinion, orgasms do not hold a candle to major pharmaceuticals when it comes to sleep – for women. Unless someone's doing a survey somewhere and an orgasmic sleeping tablet is being invented. Forget female Viagra – that's where the medical money needs to go.

After lovemaking, Dan curled around me, almost instantly asleep, naked except for the boxers he pulled on, his strong body spooned against me. At about four, when I had gone round in circles thinking about Elisa and how she could hurt Lexi, I finally uncurled myself from his warm skin and went into the bathroom where I stared, hollow-eyed, into the mirror.

Lexi did not choose her birth mother.

*Dan did*, Mildred pointed out, unhelpfully.

Dan and she split up when Lexi was a baby, I reminded myself. He's a good man who wants what was best for all of us, I add.

I wanted to get up because it was easier but at least if I am lying in bed, I am resting, so I head back to bed where I hope I sleep even a little.

I could not think about damn Elisa if I was working.

I would stare at recipe books in the kitchen, sit with my trusty ink pen and paper and write down foods in my wakened version of lucid dreaming.

It's how I work when I can't work: I let the foods come into my mind and the right combinations slip in. I can almost taste the sea-fresh scent of newly-caught cod and my mind skims from Asia with the delicacy of lemongrass and ginger, bok choi wilting underneath while hot sun intensifies all my senses. And then, I flip to a winter's day when I was a child, home from school, weary, and my mother stirring chowder on the stove, fresh bread baking, and the hint of dill and tang of bacon lardons fill my head.

I try to make food easier for people, to take the fear out of cooking so the love of it ignites something within them. It's how I learned to cook: watching my mother, who is the most nurturing cook ever, who effortlessly worked as well as stirring up cakes and making soups on the old stovetop, warming our bellies and our hearts all at the same time.

Good food should be eaten at a family table, whatever sort of family you are, with the cat/dog/hamster peering over the edge of the table, especially if you and your beloved animals are what constitutes your family. In my recipe books, there are just as many versions of my meals for people who live alone, as more and more of us do. Life is complicated enough without making a cookbook a judgement with its 'serves four' tagline on each recipe. I dream up the recipes and cook.

Lexi had been quiet and subdued after dinner last night and I intuited, though I didn't want to ask, that there had been no answering message on WhatsApp from Elisa. Lexi is used to friends like her best pal, Caitlin Keogh, replying instantly. Elisa is a different breed.

Instead of asking if she'd had a reply, I helped Lexi wash her long hair. Then I laboriously brushed the tangles out of it, gently brushing in the love because saying anything at that moment would have been entirely wrong. Sometimes touch is the only love that works.

'Thanks, Mum,' she said when I'd finished, and I hugged her.

I love my darling daughter so much and although she did not emerge from my body, that makes her no less my child. I want to fight for her. But I cannot hurt her in the process and if I warn her off Elisa, as I so dearly wish to do, I will do just that.

Today, house organising has to take a back seat because I simply have to go into work. Freya Abalone, the social media, wonder chef, TV personality extraordinaire has got to come out of hiding and wear something other than mangy yoga pants.

Or else we'll never be able to pay the mortgage.

Real life does not sell well on social media, for some startling reason. At least, it can – but that's 'warts and all' and my business is not sold on warts.

It's sold on the firebrand personality of me, who is both Viking Chef and calm woman of forty-two. No sniggering down the back. In other words: I carefully curate my online presence so that I appear to be calm and happy simultaneously.

I would be fascinated to find really calm women of forty-two because in my experience, women of my vintage are too busy trying to keep all the plates in the air – work, home, children, relationships, family, grocery shopping, laundry, attempting to do some exercise in case our bones crumple – to have really grasped that inner calm thing.

Nina, my social media guru, public relations genius and the slightly intense boss of her own agency at the age of thirty, explained it all to me in the early days when the production company said I needed to pay someone to handle my publicity year round, as they weren't going to be doing it.

'You are building a brand,' she said, already scaring me because it was nine in the morning and she'd clearly had a blow dry and was sipping water out of a giant bottle which she'd already half-finished. Both things I have never managed. If I drink a litre of water a day, it's in tea and coffee. Sometimes I even consume water in the form of ice cubes if Scarlett and Maura come over at the weekend, and Maura brings her beloved Baileys and makes me drink some drizzled over ice, which she says makes her feel like the last word in sophistication.

Nina drinks water and is a green juice fanatic, which is possibly why she still looks twenty-five instead of thirty. I eat too much of my own food, which has lots of green things in it but also lots of carbs, which have recently become Enemy Number One in health-junkie terms.

'Brands are built on a combination of honesty, relatability and reliability,' Nina went on. 'Nobody wants to know you had a crappy weekend, that the water heater broke and you got your period. They get that in their own lives. They want you, with a happy quote for the day, a fabulous recipe they can make without hitting the shops, a feeling that you are one of them. Plus lovely pictures.'

'Even on Mondays?' I said, having failed to switch off my sarcasm button upon entering the building.

I am so not a Monday person. I am a lunchtime on Friday person.

'Especially on Mondays,' she said grimly, a flash in her eyes showing me she saw the sarcasm and didn't like it. 'You start their week with energy. With happiness. With wisdom. You want to sell books, a TV show and later your own cooking implements and baking dishes?'

'I wish,' I sighed.

'Then get with the programme, Freya,' she said. 'This is what you pay me to tell you.'

Point taken.

She is expensive and I can only afford to use her services if I make money. Another bastion of my career is my agent, the London-based Paddy Ashmore, an utter gentleman who never raises his voice and whom I would trust with my life. Paddy does not haunt me with reminders about social media but then Paddy is old-school and negotiates deals for my books. Nina knows more about the frenetic pulse of all sorts of media than he does, so I listen to her.

In light of my absence from both the bookshops and the TV screens, I know I need to keep my media profile up there.

With this in mind I work very hard to keep the social media career moving even when I am mid-move, pre-menstrual, have flu, you name it.

Someone has posted something about difficult roads leading to glorious destinations. Once, I would have loved that – now, I am so over inspirational quotes, although I do my best to post ones every few days.

Difficult roads lead to more damn difficult roads, and road blocks, and workmen digging a hole and traffic. The universe does not give us what we need – it gives us ulcers.

I'd love to post *that* online. But Nina would kill me and as I am sure she has a deal going with the devil to make her successful and stress-free, she would have a plan to hide my body, no problemo.

In the real world, I post things on all the social media channels most days, even if it's just me beaming into the camera wearing a flour-covered apron and holding up a whisk, making early morning fruit muffins for the children's school lunches, which was one of last week's posts pre-move. It's sad that nobody viewing this lovely scene on Instagram can hear the background yelling as Teddy informs everyone that she will not eat anything with blueberries in it.

'Bunny poo!' she insists. 'Not eating bunny poo.'

'Blueberries do look a bit like bunny poo,' agrees Liam, ever the peacemaker, 'but they're nice in Mum's muffins.'

'NO!'

It is funny, so including the bunny poo story, the picture of me goes up. A chef comparing their cooking to animal faeces can never be a good thing, I think, awaiting a backlash. But hey – dark humour is good, right?

**Is that supposed to be a funny caption?**

Nina texts me about a millisecond later. That woman lives on her phone. She is not child-friendly, either. If she has a child, she will get it from a pod on the mother ship.

**I had sex last night – should I mention it?**

I type the words in and then delete before hitting the send button. Nina's odd: nothing is out of bounds for her so she might decide that a segment on 'what foods get you both in the mood' is a runner.

In her vision, I would be in a negligee (obviously, I don't have one), gazing glossily-lipped into the camera in no time.

*Write down funny lines for future,* I think. Unfortunately, most of my funny thoughts are too dark to be shared with the world.

I have a quick morning routine and I get myself done up pretty speedily. Then it's into jeans, flat shoes – the red suede trainers I adore – and an aquamarine silk shirt that suits my colouring really well. The stylist on the last show insisted I buy it and I thank the stars for stylists every time I get dressed. Pre-styling, my look was a bit chaotic. Except with fabulous shoes. Shoes I can do. It's the rest that bewilders me. I honestly don't care about clothes. Nina insists that I can't possibly say this publicly.

'Why not?'

'Because people expect you to have it all! Don't you get it?'

There's no point arguing with her. Nobody has it all.

Going quietly, I head downstairs to get the breakfast things ready. After a boost of caffeine, I race upstairs and realise that Dan hasn't woken up yet, which is unusual because he's marvellous at getting out of bed in the morning. Sickeningly a morning person, I should add. I must have exhausted him with my fabulous lovin', I think, wondering again if I could post that? Probably not. I am officially losing control of my mind.

With that sort of post, I would be invited on to some reality TV show where I'd have to expose my post-baby self in a bikini and drink my body weight in cocktails with people who think that cooking is pressing the 'on' button on the microwave.

Nina would love that. It would 'broaden my viewership', which is a vital thing.

'Wake up,' I yell at Dan from the door of our bedroom. 'You've overslept.'

'Oh, no,' he says, turning around in the bed and looking at his watch. 'Seven, no! I'm supposed to be in town for eight.'

'Unless you have a helicopter on speed dial, I don't see that happening.'

He shoots me a sleepy grin as he throws back the duvet and rips off his T-shirt.

I race into Lexi's bedroom to wake her up next. As the oldest, she needs the most wakening. It's an age thing: the older you are, the longer it takes to wake up. Liam is next, although he's not too keen on getting out of bed either and Teddy is last. On weekends Teddy can quite happily be up at half five. On days when she goes to Montessori, she is inevitably still asleep when I go in and requires much wheedling to extract her from the duvet nest.

'Come on, lovie,' I say, nuzzling into her ear, 'wakey, wakey.'

The response is Teddy burrowing further into her bed in the manner of something cute on a David Attenborough documentary. David Attenborough never has to haul said cute things out of their burrows while they are whimpering, though.

It takes twenty minutes to get everyone dressed and downstairs, including Teddy, who has a full-scale argument with me about what colour sandals she's going to wear. She wants to wear her purple ones with the sparkles and no matter how many times I tell her that we threw them out because they were old and no longer fit her, she continues insisting.

'We'll buy you new ones,' said Dan, suddenly sweeping into the room to plant a kiss on her and my foreheads. He's fully dressed and ready to go. Today's a suit day and nobody fills a suit like Dan.

Hot husband.

Is that suitable for a gratitude list? Damn straight it is.

'That was quick,' I say.

'Yeah,' he said, 'got to rush, bye, darling. Talk to you later.' And he's gone.

Even though I've been earning more money than I used to in the past few years, the job of getting the children out of the house and to their various schools is up to me, always has been unless I am away filming.

Maura, when we have feminist discussions, says Dan should do it.

I counter this by saying that I am better at it and like our morning routine.

'That's not the point.'

'Feminism is not higher-level maths,' I say. 'The rules are fluid. If the children need to be picked up from school when they are sick, Dan does it more than I do because I'm often somewhere doing a cookery demo. But he's crap in the morning with the children because his mind has already gone off to work mode, which means Teddy can totally twist him round her little finger, getting her dressed takes half an hour and everyone ends up late for school/work. Plus, he vacuums, which I hate, and he always fills and empties the dishwasher. And takes it apart regularly to remove all the gunk that builds up in it.'

'You iron.'

'Yes, oh wise sister. I am treated like dirt, you're so right. We definitely need an eighteenth-century scullery maid.'

'Scullery *man*!'

'The point is, we work it out between us,' I say wearily.

I remove the spiders in the house because Dan is arachnaphobic; he does all car and garden-related things, cleans the bath and is currently working on getting Liam to pee with more direct aim. I brush Lexi's hair, cook and make sure everyone cleans their teeth. It works, without a manifesto.

Maura teaches women's studies in university and likes manifestos. Pip is entirely happy to bow to her alpha-ness. He thinks it was the best day in his life when he met her, God help him.

Liam is a chatterbox and he and Teddy have entirely unrelated conversations as they eat breakfast. Since going to secondary school, Lexi doesn't do a lot of talking in the morning. My beloved girl no longer lets me hug her anywhere near the school. In fact I have to turn the music in the car down when we drive into the parking area.

'Somebody might hear,' she hisses at me for the millionth time.

I have given up trying to explain that, if we can't hear into their cars, they can't hear into our car.

We are working to Teenager Rules which have no basis in reality.

'Bye,' she mutters as she climbs out of the front passenger seat, then slams the car door shut in a way that makes the entire vehicle shake.

'Bad Lexi,' shrieks Teddy from the comfort of her child seat in the back. 'Bad Lexi.'

Liam, who has clambered into the front seat because he's finally tall enough, is next, little pet, and once his older sister is out of the car he talks excitedly about his day. He and Lexi aren't getting on as well anymore and it upsets me, although Maura explains that it's normal for children of different ages to get irritated with each other at times.

'We did it,' she says.

'Did we?' I say. And then I remember Con and how we used to fight with him, tease him and put dresses on his

Action Man, and I have to agree with her. Scarlett was our baby and we dressed her up like a doll. I think Con may have been dolled up and lipsticked too, and grin at the thought.

The power of older sisters is amazing.

I'm allowed to surreptitiously hug Liam goodbye before he gets out of the car in the school car park. This is the first year I haven't walked him into class – 'only little kids have their mums come in!' – so I sit there in the car waiting until he's walked along the path and in the school door. Then I wave again even though he doesn't turn round, and when I can no longer see his departing back, I settle myself into the car to deliver Teddy to her little school.

'Music,' shrieks Teddy, 'music.'

She can shriek very loudly, definitely in the bad-for-your-hearing-long-term range. So I put on some of her favourite tunes, at the moment the soundtrack of *Frozen*, which is not as nice when you have heard it eight hundred and fifty-nine times.

Sometimes I feel that I *am* Anna and Elsa.

As we pull up outside Little Darlings crèche and Montessori, Teddy's mood changes drastically.

'No go, no go,' she says tearfully, reverting to the almost baby language she occasionally uses when she's in a particular mood. Small children grow up in a two-steps-forward, one-step-back sort of way, I have found.

'Teddy,' I said, undoing the car seat straps which will cut off a finger if done too quickly. 'You love it here. Don't you want to see all your friends? Ella and Marcus and the hamsters?'

'No,' she says, kicking her heels against the seat.

There is a certain amount of wriggling, fighting and struggling but eventually Teddy and I make it into Little Darlings, whereupon she totally abandons me, rips her hand away from mine and races off squealing with delight at seeing her friends.

Koala baby to teenager outside a disco in one fell swoop.

'Tough morning?' says Babs, the crèche owner, seeing me sighing at Teddy's departing form.

'Yeah,' I said, ' we've just moved into the new house and it felt a bit chaotic this morning, not our usual routine,' I say. 'And then Teddy was doing her *I don't want to go in* thing.'

'But now look at her,' Babs finishes, as we gaze at where Teddy is delightedly holding court with her closest friends over at the little plastic kitchen.

'I know, you just always feel bad, don't you?'

'Mothers' guilt,' says Babs cheerfully. 'Tougher than titanium. Isn't that the toughest substance on the planet?'

I nod. Sounds about right. Or else that stuff that totally banjaxed Superman.

Outside, I see a gaggle of the women who make me feel totally inferior: Mums Who Exercise. They do not have saggy bits, worry about fat knees or having trouble closing the button on their jeans.

*Why don't you do any exercise?* Mildred wants to know. *You could. Because look at them with their skinny legs and perfect butts in their Lululemon leggings?*

'Gimme a break, Mildred,' I mutter.

I get back into the car, take a deep breath and start social media-ing while I'm still parked.

**Testing recipes for fabulous RTÉ Guide today.**

I then try to think of hashtags.

**#Delicious. #YouWillDrool.**

78

Is that too weird, I wonder? Drooling makes me think of those lovely dogs who drool a lot.

**#Happy. #Cooking.**

Ugh, I think. How vanilla.

But I can't think of any more. I need to get Nina to programme a few into my phone. Some of us are born with hashtaggery within us and some need it thrust upon us.

Finally, I manage to share my thoughts on each platform. Or a happy version of my thoughts.

My actual thoughts are less 'wheee, so happy!' and more 'I want to go home, get into bed, pull the duvet over my head and ruminate on plans to kill my husband's first wife.'

But I have a job and that job entails cheerfulness. Actually, fake cheerfulness.

Social media done, I lean back against the car seat, find the buzziest music radio on the car stereo and pull out into the traffic.

# 6

## *You got this*

When I was *discovered*, which is what the TV production guy, James, likes to call it, I was working a nine-to-five, not very well paid job for a company that made reasonably expensive ready-cooked meals for busy people who could afford to pay someone else to cook boeuf bourguignon or fish pie, package it into little ovenproof dishes, and sell it in delis and upmarket supermarkets. My friend Jocelyn, who'd also trained in the Prue Leith School, and I had tried private catering but the bottom had fallen out of that market pretty quickly, so we were back working for someone else. The Make Life Easier business had leapt to employ us and to be honest, after a few years, I was getting bored.

In a drive to broaden their market, which was faltering somewhat, one of the bosses had decided that Jocelyn and I should start spreading the word by doing cookery demonstrations around the country at food festivals.

First up was a prestigious Dublin city-centre weekend food festival and Jocelyn, who hated public speaking, was shaking in her chef's clogs.

It was years since I'd done anything like this, so I was a bit anxious myself.

This had not put off Kieran, boss of the company, who was very alpha male and knew nothing about cooking, but had joined his sister, Peg, in setting up the business, which made him an expert – in his eyes.

'How hard can it be?' barked Kieran as Jocelyn and I made our fears known.

Kieran didn't cook. He was the accounts/business/time and motion end of the company. He thought cooking was like making instant coffee: impossible to get wrong. He had no concept of the food industry shifting and moving all the time.

His sister and co-owner, Peg, did cook but was very keen on spending weeks in luxury spas to take her mind off work, so she was never there to discuss our concerns.

'Throw a few ingredients in a pot, like you do here – what's the problem, girls?' said Kieran.

Since he thought we were looking for extra money for the day of demos – which we weren't, but should have been – he sent us out of his office pronto.

'I guess that's Bozo's version of saying we're on our own,' I said to Jocelyn as we made it back to the kitchen.

'Shush! He might hear you!' she said.

'I don't care if he does,' I said suddenly, beyond irritated by Kieran for any number of reasons, least of all his calling us 'girls'. We were women, not girls.

'We run this business for him and he doesn't respect our work at all. We have to get out of here, Joss,' I added crossly. 'Set up on our own.'

'That's so not going to happen, Freya,' she replied. 'Our mortgage is murderous. Could we kill Kieran, piece him up in a stew, pretend he's gone on a cruise and left us in charge?'

'He'd be full of gristle,' I replied, and then we both laughed at the very idea. 'Plus,' I added, 'you'd need a stake through his heart and a silver bullet – he's some sort of Teflon werewolf/vampire combo. You'd never be able to kill him.'

'They always find out, anyway,' Jocelyn added. She loved to watch forensic crime series like *CSI* on TV. 'It's the hair transfer, the teeniest smudge of a fingerprint, a piece of car carpet: you've no idea what they can find and analyse. We'd be caught.'

And then we collapsed into hysterics in the tiny office kitchen and had to have some of my home-made protein balls and a quick coffee to recover from the madness.

On the morning of the demonstrations, we set off early. All the way into the city in the Make Life Easier jeep, we talked about how excited and terrified we were about the whole thing.

'What if nobody comes near us?' said Jocelyn, applying her lipstick again as she kept chewing it off.

I hadn't even bothered with lipstick yet. Jocelyn, who was good with make-up, was going to make me presentable when we'd done everything else.

'It's not our job to attract people,' I said. 'That's Kieran's area. He's paying for the slot. My worry is what if the hobs are terrible and we burn everything in front of paying customers,' I said. '*That's* when a crowd will gather, they'll see it all falling apart, put it up on Facebook and then, if we don't inadvertently give someone food poisoning from trying to heat it up in a dodgy oven, we'll break the internet with how hopeless we'll appear to be.'

*People can die from food poisoning*, Mildred helpfully reminded me.

'We've got the back-ups in the freezer bags,' said Jocelyn, in a voice that said she was trying to convince herself.

Stopped at traffic lights, we looked at each other.

'We're trained chefs. How bad can it be?' I said.

*

83

We were thrilled when we found our tent to discover that it had a gas and induction hob, an oven, a sink with running (cold) water and a small fridge.

'Luxury,' I said, delighted, as we examined our fiefdom.

After we'd dragged our supplies in, refrigerated everything and set up, Jocelyn went off to get us both huge coffees and I re-checked our schedule.

As newbies in the food festival world, the Make Life Easier kitchen had three demo slots that day, a Friday. One at ten, when we figured there'd be few people around, one at eleven-thirty, and one at four. None of these were hot slots: those were reserved for big chefs. People who'd already made it in the cooking world and who would draw huge crowds had weekend lunchtime slots when the crowds would be eight-deep and screens would broadcast whatever the brilliant chef was doing.

The ten o'clock demo was performed to an audience of three, which was good given that Jocelyn almost instantly burned her hand on the gas hob because it was temperamental and the front burner reared up into a fiery jet with only the slightest twist of the knob and scorched her hand badly.

'Keep going,' she hissed at me, clutching her injury.

Calmly, I ripped open the First Aid box, applied a gel-like burn bandage, hugged her and said:

'Get to the First Aid tent. Now.'

So in front of my audience of three, including one tall guy who was holding a coffee, hiding behind sunnies and looked just grey enough to be hungover, I whisked up a cream-filled chicken dish in record time, chatting away to hide my worry over Jocelyn and felt a surge of relief that at least, this mini audience wasn't expecting too much.

Mr Hangover stood well back. Probably asleep standing up.

The other two, a mother and daughter combo who told me they'd been in since nine, had already got at least half a bag of merchandise from other stands.

If they stayed all day, they'd need a wheelbarrow to carry it all around.

'Why's this recipe got so much cream in it?' asked one of the two women who made up my triad of spectators.

Kieran wasn't there so I could say what I really thought.

'In my opinion, this doesn't need that much cream or indeed, any at all,' I said chattily, deciding at the last minute that I would toast the pine nuts for the spinach side dish even though it was tricky to keep chatting, and my eye on all parts of the meal. 'Personally, I like to add a little spoonful of cream cheese if I need a creamy hint to a dish or natural yogurt if it's not going to split, as we could do with this. But cream is part of the luxury experience.'

That was Kieran's favourite expression. Add cream to everything, even though I'd told him that more and more people were experimenting with dairy-free.

'Smell the pine nuts,' I added, holding the pan carefully forward. 'I love that scent: a woody tang. Roasting them makes all the difference and lets the flavour out. No oil, no mess, just a plain frying pan and two to three minutes. Great in salads, too. Full of protein and magnesium. If you don't have enough magnesium, you're exhausted. And who needs that, right?'

We all laughed.

'I hope you don't mind me saying but I've always wanted to make pizza dough,' said the daughter, 'except it looks hard.'

'Not a bit,' I said, giving my pine nuts an extra flourish by shaking them in the pan and decanting them expertly into a little bowl. 'We can do that afterwards, if you'd like. I'm not busy and I am telling you, it's the easiest thing to do. We get scared of things we've never tried. There.'

I presented the finished dish to them all, handed out cutlery and stood back. 'Now, while you're trying that, which is available in our Make Life Easier range, I'll make pizza dough and if you come back at half eleven, when I'm making a lovely Guinness Pie, one of our best-selling dishes, I'll show you afterwards how easy it is to get your pizza ready for the oven.'

The dough took a moment to make, and both women were delighted to be so up close and personal to it. 'See?'

I would have loved to have indulged in a bit of cheffy showing off by twirling some of the dough but I was aware that I had to tidy up and get ready for half eleven, and I needed to visit First Aid to check on Jocelyn. She could not help with an injured hand. She was going home in a taxi, I decided firmly. Kieran, skinflint, could pay.

'Hope you can come back at half eleven,' I said cheerfully to the women when they collected their belongings to leave.

Mr Hungover remained as the pair moved off, waving goodbye and saying they'd be back.

I couldn't tell if he was watching me or not. Was he still drunk? Someone coming home from a night out, perhaps?

I thought I'd better send him on his way.

'I'd offer you a seat but I can't,' I told him cheerily. 'You might burn yourself too and the people who insure us would go into meltdown at two burns in the one tent on one day. But there are seats further in, in the centre of the festival area. They're set up for the bigger demos.'

He took off his sunglasses and he looked fine, if a bit red-eyed.

'I don't need a seat,' he said.

'You looked like you did,' I pointed out. 'I thought I detected a bit of a sway there and I was afraid I'd be onto the First Aid tent again when you face-planted in front of my stand.'

'I'm light sensitive,' he said.

'Right.' I began tidying up.

I knew a lot of people who were light sensitive after bank holiday barbecues, weddings and other festive events where booze was involved.

'You're very good at this,' he said suddenly.

I whirled around.

'Cooking? I'd want to be,' I said with a wry laugh.

'No, I meant cooking and explaining it to people in a way they grasp. You don't talk down to the audience, either, which is vital. You take them along with you. It's a hard trick to learn but you have it instinctively.'

'Thank you,' I said in my fake I-am-being-charming voice. 'Now you have to go. Watch someone else cook. Shoo.'

He roared laughing. 'Shoo. I love it. Have you done any television work before?'

He was beginning to weird me out.

'Only on CCTV footage on the bank robbery jobs, but I keep the mask over my face at all times.'

He laughed again, as if I was the funniest thing ever.

'What's your name?'

'Rhianna,' I said, beaming. 'Now, go away.'

I hissed this last bit because I felt sure that trying to get rid of customers at food festivals wasn't part of the deal but still. Who was this guy?

'James Kirk,' he said, holding out a hand.

'As in Captain Kirk?' I asked drily. 'You missed out the T. James T. Kirk, the T stands for Tiberius.'

'It really is my name,' he said sadly, as if he was entirely fed up with explaining this.

'My father's Scottish, which is where the Kirk comes from and the James – well, they're total Trekkies, my parents.'

'Ouch.'

'Are you Freya or Jocelyn?' he asked.

I gave him the sort of stare I reserved for Kieran in work when he asked me to stay late.

The words 'what's it to you?' hovered in my mind.

'I'm a TV producer for Slate Productions,' he said, suddenly moving forward with his hand held out. 'We film, among other things, cookery shows. I think you've got real promise in terms of television work. Real promise.'

He proffered a card and there it was on a misty grey background:

### JAMES KIRK
**Producer**

***Slate Productions Ltd***

And that was it.

Slate made a pilot for a TV show based on recipes I'd come up with, which is a lot harder than people think it is. We got the green light to film three weeks later, I suddenly had a contract as a TV chef and I was able to tell Kieran that he ought to promote Jocelyn and stop bullying staff or else he'd have no business in a year.

I'd got Dan to run the numbers and sweetly explained that the fat-heavy recipes we'd been making up till then were no longer the way forward.

'I'm doing this for Jocelyn and not for you,' I told Kieran, who had turned puce and then white once he saw Dan's financial projections.

'You could help . . .' Kieran stammered.

'I'd consult,' I said, having been heavily coached by both Dan and Maura. 'For a fat fee.'

*

This morning, I drive home to load up the car with dishes, pans, knives, you name it, and then head off into the traffic again to my minuscule base, which is situated in a soulless building and where Lorraine Ryan, my part-time home economics advisor, and I share an office.

Neither of us could afford one on our own. Nor could I afford an assistant just for me but Lorraine, who works a lot for me although also for other chefs, is a mistress of all trades and can turn her hand to anything. Including organising my computer/files/you name it. In our tiny office with its own kitchen and coffee machine area, we also have several lockable cupboards, storage for the things we both use during filming, demos, photo shoots.

There are two desks, one tidy one – Lorraine's – and one signs-of-a-scuffle one, which is mine.

Today at twelve, we're due to start shooting a cook-and-photograph for the country's biggest selling magazine, the *RTÉ Guide*, so no pressure. Lorraine and I, plus a food stylist, a photographer and her assistant are going to magic the first part of an autumnal series and photograph it so the readers drool when they read it.

Yes, I did say autumn.

They work a long time ahead in the magazine business.

By high summer, I will be knee-deep in speedy Christmas cakes and advice on how to make your own stollen without too much sugar – this is an oxymoron. Stollen's sheer glory is that it is mainly sugar with dried fruit and filaments of pastry thrown in but at Christmas, many magazine readers are also dieting themselves into frenzies so they can fit into party clothes without the aid of two pairs of Spanx, so we have to do our best for them. If cutting a sliver of almond paste out of the recipe helps (I could exist entirely on marzipan paste, but it migrates straight to my hips without even hitting my digestive system at all), then we will do our best.

Studios where food photography shoots take place are always average photographic studios – think draughty industrial loft-style rooms – with miniscule kitchens/dressing rooms/make-up counters tacked on. The resulting shots may look glamorous but the locale is not.

Lorraine and I once made an entire Christmas dinner (with vegan options) in a room not much bigger than your average bathroom. I still have the mark of a burn on my big toe from when the turkey fat went rogue. Chefs wear clogs for this reason but a hole in mine (long story) meant they were finally rendered useless.

Today would be easier. I had new kitchen clogs so the chance of oil spillage was less. Confession: magazine food shoots are often fun but always hard work.

Lorraine was meeting me there, where we'd spend probably a frantic fifteen minutes with the stylist setting the scene. But first, I had to pick up a few things from the office. Notably, one copper-bottomed pan that had been inadvertently left behind and which was more valuable to me than everything else.

Team Freya meant a certain amount of Scandi coolness. In fact I brought in quite a lot of things from home, including half of the pantry because really, you couldn't leave this stuff in the office no matter how well it was locked up.

'You love those pans more than you love me,' Dan liked

to tease me, when he spotted me carefully cleaning them so that they gleamed a rich copper, with not a hint of verdigris.

I always teased back by hugging a pan and moaning, until Teddy saw me at it and tried it herself.

'Ooooh, nice yummy pot,' she said, giving it a lick for added love.

Dan and I, when we recovered from laughing, could no longer look at my pots and pans the same way again.

I grab the precious pan, and head back into the car, en route for the photographic studio.

Today, as I drive past Bricky City – 'Buy Bricks For Half Price!' – I realise that even Beyoncé on the radio huskily telling me he should have put a ring on it isn't cheering me up.

I should be happy, I reason as I drive in a line of lorries.

I have beautiful children, a husband, new house, a career … But away from my family, my lodestones, I don't feel happy and this shouldn't be the case. *Should* is a tricky word.

I needed to look at Pinterest later, see some funnies, I decide. Pinterest always makes me happy when I have a moment to look at it.

I spend far too long looking at pictures of cute animals. Sloths – I know, who'd have thought? – are cute.

I have, obviously, gone off the inspirational quotes on a personal level but I try to pepper them into my social media for professional reasons.

I also buy kitchen bits and bobs online, which is fine as I know what I am doing there. I also – fashion police alert – buy clothes online. This is dangerous because I have, as Scarlett and Maura say, no taste, hence I make purchases with the aid of TV show stylists.

Lorraine looks like one of those beautiful but intellectually challenged girls you see in magazine photo spreads of glamorous parties. She has a platinum pixie cut, with hints of colour – today, she's sporting pale violet – and, despite her fashion-forward wardrobe, has genuine 32D breasts, not implants, and the huge, unblinking blue eyes of a sweet but slightly bewildered girl. In fact, she has a mind like a steel trap.

Chefs always need a home economist to work with on their TV shows, books and demos and when I first worked with Lorraine two years ago, I realised how brilliant she was. By her second week of working with me, she had helped me with a tricky photo shoot and with an even trickier food festival, because she is one of a breed of women who simply get things done. She'd even sorted out my inbox, organised the office brilliantly but had come to the conclusion that I should no longer throw work the way of an old friend, Geraldine, who was a stylist with amazing contacts for food purchasing.

Lorraine told me that Geraldine was purchasing bulk cheap vodka alongside ingredients. Enough vodka to have a decent-sized party in the Kremlin but not good enough quality for the Politburo, I imagine.

I had suspected this vodka-purchasing but lacked the heart or the evidence to confront Geraldine.

I am hopeless at confrontation, I should add.

'I know she's your friend but she's burning out, screwing things up and will take you and the profits with her,' said Lorraine. 'As a friend, you can stage an intervention and let her rehab her ass but as a boss, you have to fire her.'

As I said, Lorraine *looks* like a sweet but innocent young thing. Twenty-six year-olds are so much more together today than when I was twenty-six.

Firing Geraldine was a process that nearly killed me.

'I'll talk to her,' I said to Lorraine, when I was still pretending to be a tough business lady.

Lorraine was only working for me for two weeks and I had to give the impression that I had all aspects of my career under control.

'You didn't talk to her, did you?' asked Lorraine, on day five of this challenge, when Geraldine turned up at a newspaper supplement shoot reeking of booze. I was riddled with both guilt and rage, which give you a very acid stomach when combined, I can tell you.

'No,' I said. I may have wailed. 'I can't . . .'

'You're as soft as butter, aren't you?' muttered Lorraine. 'Haven't you read *Girl Boss*?'

'Nope.'

'Tonight, do it tonight. You can't carry passengers. This is a lean business.'

'But she's my friend and she needs help,' I begin.

'Think of your kids,' said Lorraine.

Magic words. Nothing works so well as reminding me I have three children to take care of.

'Plus, all this career could be over in a moment as soon as some other chef comes along,' Lorraine went on, using the second ultimate weapon

'OK, I get it,' I said.

Despite my mother having taught us all that decency and hoping for the best for all womankind is the way forward, I have a fear of being dumped in this chef-heavy world. Every time you look sideways, another chef is up on Instagram, being funny/funky/cool and doing new and exciting things with kohlrabi (cabbage-y vegetable, in case you were wondering. I have never been a fan.)

'How did you get to be so tough?' I asked Lorraine, wishing *I* was tough.

'First person in my family to go to third-level education,' Lorraine said, eyeballing me. 'It did not happen by accident. My mother pushed me. I mean push. You think I am tough, you need to meet her. Right.' She regrouped. 'We'll do it together tomorrow. Team meeting.'

Geraldine sobbed. I sobbed. She fell to the floor and did her sobbing down there. Lorraine had tissues and a handful of rebab leaflets.

'I'll write you a lovely reference,' I blubbed.

'You won't or you'll be sued,' said Lorraine, ever the businesswoman.

She had proof of all the vodka-enhanced bills and said getting witnesses to Geraldine's turning up drunk would be no problem.

'What'll I tell everyone?' It was Geraldine's turn to wail.

Lorraine hauled her off the floor and into a chair, and handed her tea. 'They already know, love. You're the last one. Do something about it. Crack cocaine's the big hitter now – you don't want to go down that road when the vodka's not taking you into your happy place as quickly.'

'I'd never touch drugs,' said Geraldine, shocked.

'Bet you never thought you'd come to work pissed but hey, here you are. Life's always surprising us,' said Lorraine cheerfully.

Lorraine had Geraldine's mother – grey-faced and red-eyed – waiting in her car outside and between us, we hauled Geraldine into it. She was a sobbing mess now, plus dirty because the lift was broken and we'd had to womanhandle her down the stairs, which was hard as she was, no kidding, already quite plastered.

'I'm so – so sorry,' I said incoherently to Geraldine's mother, whom I had known for years. At that point, it was hard to know who was crying most – me or Geraldine. Geraldine's mother just nodded mutely.

It killed me. Killed me. Still does when I wake in the middle of the night.

# 7

## *Today's the day to be the best you ever!*

Finally, I reach the studio where today's magic will happen.

'Hello Freya, hello! When do I get to see the house?' Lorraine, who lives in thick-soled cool trainers, jeans of all lengths and never a sock in sight, even in the snow, bounces over from her car, an upcycled Mini which she hand-painted to look as if Dali had a hand in it. She gets stopped regularly by the police just so they can look at it and point. The upside of this is that people in squad cars regularly wave at her and she has dated a few motorbike cops.

'It's the leather,' she says. 'I see the leather, the bikes . . . I can't say no.'

'Stop right there,' I say when she goes all dreamy. 'I. Do. Not. Want. To. Know.'

'Hello yourself,' I say now, and hug her, stifling a tear.

What is wrong with me? Have I transmogrified into Granny without noticing? Will I cry at every even vaguely emotional moment? I sincerely hope not.

Lorraine has been handling things in Team Freya for the past few days and I've missed her. She's my friend as well as a huge part of my career success, and with Lorraine you never have to ask her not to sugar coat the truth.

It's been two years since I – well, really Lorraine – fired Geraldine, and she's still working in the chef industry.

Horribly, she blanks me every time she sees me, which upsets me no end.

'We helped her,' I said to Lorraine once after one such incident when I had to run into the loo to breathe deeply. Lorraine followed

Lorraine shrugged. 'She wants someone to blame, won't take responsibility and has decided the evil person is you. Her loss.'

You see: tough. Without Lorraine, I would be doing every charity event from one end of the island to the other but Lorraine merely says no: politely, but no. She has a charity pack she can send and charities we support.

'You run a business, not a drop-everything-to-help-other-people organisation,' she says as she fires off another 'would love to help but Freya supports X charity' email.

She could write her own version of *Girl Boss* and no mistake.

We hug and I snuffle deeply, pretending I have a cold to cover up the fact that I feel tearful. Thinking about Geraldine has that effect on me.

'The house is lovely,' I say now. 'But it needs work.'

'I hope you've got pictures on your phone,' Lorraine says, opening my car boot. 'I want to see it all.'

We start moving our boxes of kitchen magic out. Photographic studios have assistants but they do not help with this type of thing.

The food stylist is already there and it is Maxwell, a man who can make a tired-looking strawberry appear so juicy on the page that you might just bite into the magazine to eat it.

He is that good.

Maxwell is outside, having a last-minute cigarette, talking to his fiancé on the phone and working a jeans, skinny white

T and white runners combo with his muscles – a hideously fashionable outfit, no doubt. He ignores us, our boxes and our struggles.

'You going to help?' I demand, as I stagger past.

'You might have told me she was going through the change,' Maxwell says to Lorraine, stubbing out his fag and blowing kisses into the phone simultaneously.

A copper bottomed saucepan nearly hits the ground.

'Kidding,' he says, grabbing it just in time. 'You look fab-u-lous, Lorraine,' he adds, 'as ever, and you look lovely, Sweetums. Love the sea-green shirt. Very now. Did Delicious Dan leave that out for you to wear?'

'No, I dress myself,' I lie. 'And keep your paws off Dan. He is not interested in what you have in your Levis, Maxwell.'

Maxwell roars with amusement, admiring his reflection in the lift door. 'Levis! As if. These exquisite jeans are Hedi Slimane for Dior Homme! Now, I've been up and the photographer has been struck with an appalling stomach bug so today we're stuck with a second tier snapper who looks about fourteen, and doesn't *do food, normally*". His assistant isn't fourteen – he's twelve.'

Lorraine and I groan.

'Suck it up,' Maxwell advises. 'We're going to be here for hours so let's smile and hope we get to go home before midnight.'

'I can't be here for hours, I've got children,' I mutter.

'You might be home in time for university,' Maxwell laughs.

Because the RTÉ *Guide* trusts us, we do not have someone from the magazine overseeing it all. I need to keep us on-theme. It's what I'm good at: gauging what is needed and delivering it.

As one review said: 'Freya Abalone knows what I want

99

before I do,' a line Dan mischievously quotes to me quite often when we are in bed. He's even threatened to have a tattoo of it inked on his lower abdomen.

'Yeah, and what's that going to look like when you need to get your appendix out,' I joked back. 'Perv.'

Three hours later, Lorraine and I having laboured over four winter warming soups, I regretfully turn the gas off the pumpkin risotto and go out to photography central where Lorraine and Maxwell are fighting with the photographer, who thinks we should do some moody shots. He's turned the lights way down and I almost stumble across a cable.

Moody is not what we have in mind today.

I know this because I have sold a lot of cookbooks and people like to be able to see what they are going to cook. They do not appreciate the camera focusing on the burnished steel of an exotic bone-handled soup spoon instead of on the actual soup.

Lorraine and Maxwell turn as I come in.

They both know me well enough to know that my approach to the photographer, who has been behaving as if a food shoot is beneath him, will be to gently cajole him into some normal shots before allowing him to have a little play with his bone-handled shenanigans. You catch more flies with honey and this has always been my way.

But I am weary. So weary that I have actually cut my forefinger, which is bound up with blue kitchen plaster, and I am cross about this because I normally have fabulous knife skills. I have a headache because the photographer's loud techno/pulse/headache-inducing mood music is set to eleven, and the oven is so temperamental, it is hard to know how long the lamb shanks will take to actually be done or if they'll be cremated. It could go either way.

'Don't tell me what to do,' the photographer is saying to

my team. 'I know what I'm doing.' His assistant, who is at the computer looking at shots, nods in agreement.

Something pings inside me in a dangerous way.

'No. You. Don't,' I say, hurling the words at him with fury.

Nobody is more surprised than me.

Lorraine's eyes widen, if possible, and Maxwell briefly stops looking fabulous to look astonished.

'This is my shoot, we're on a tight schedule here and if you want to work for *Wallpaper* magazine, go do it but today, we are taking pictures of food. Food that people need to actually see, not imagine from a distant, hazy outline. We are already running late. I know what the magazine wants. I know what I want. So cut the crap and take the shot.'

I sense I might be looking fearsome now. Dan says I can do that on occasion.

'You put your hands on your hips and your eyes – they glow. Don't know how you do it, Freya, but you can. Very sexy,' he adds.

Nobody is thinking I am sexy today. I, Freya Abalone, nice woman of the cooking industry who has been mocked – yes, mocked – for being twee because she's so nice, has lost her temper.

'B-b . . . but,' starts the photographer gamely.

'No!' I hold a hand out. '*But* nothing. Get the shot. The risotto is coming in ten minutes. Got that, everyone? Plus, we need more lighting. This is not cooking in some grittily-lit northern palace in *Game of Thrones*. And. Turn. That. Music. Off.'

The assistant jumps first. The music stops. Lights come up.

The photographer, who is definitely shorter than me and

several decades younger, appears to be thinking of arguing.

'I wouldn't,' I say and stalk back to the kitchen.

Nobody comes near me for ten minutes and then Lorraine bounces in. 'Shots are in the can. You need to come and look. I'll take over here. Are you OK, boss?'

'What?' I ask, carefully spooning risotto into a bowl the watercolour blue of a Turner sky.

'You're not yourself today, Freya, not that he didn't need telling off but you're never like that . . .'

'I'm fine!' I say, so loudly that Maxwell, who is coming in to oversee the risotto, backs out again.

'Fine,' I hiss at Lorraine.

'OK,' she says, unperturbed. 'Just saying . . .'

# 8

## *When the going gets tough, the tough put on more lipstick*

By the time we've finished enough winter warming soup to feed a small army, I never want to sweat another onion ever again. It's after five before we finish up the shoot and I know I'm going to be hitting all the traffic and going to be late home for Angela, who picks up the older two from school, having previously picked up Teddy from Montessori, and heats or cooks whatever I have already prepared for the children's early dinner. I phone her on her mobile but she doesn't answer, and I immediately panic, thinking all sorts of different things have happened.

This is my fault – my fault for summoning the Gods of the universe by being irritable and angry and *losing my temper*. I never lose my temper. What happened to me?

I drive home quite probably dangerously because I arrive at the house almost without knowing how I got there. That's got to be unsafe. All I can think of is that I let all this anger come out and it wasn't the photographer's fault. He's just young and silly. There are so many other ways I could have handled it, such as . . .?

I slump as I think of all the ways that I could have handled it and how I did handle it. And how Maxwell and Lorraine won't mind, because they love me, but, *but* there is a photographer out there now who hates me and will tell everyone that Freya Abalone is a bad-tempered bitch. All it takes in this business is for you to be mean, horrible or bitchy, just *once* and you get a reputation. I have seen it happen. Perfectly nice people who have thrown their toys out of the pram once and thereafter, everyone thinks they're either a mentaller or too big for their boots, which is a charge worse than murder.

Oh yes, this only happens to women. Men who throw their toys out of the pram are strong upstanding citizens who don't take any crap, but women who do it are either hormonal or cold, ambitious bitches.

I drive in, park the car and don't even bother getting my saucepans and kitchen equipment out. It's all I can do to haul myself into the house. And it's such a relief to have Teddy run and throw herself at me, like a little gymnast bouncing off a trampoline.

'Mummy,' she roars, landing against me with such force that I feel almost winded.

I hug her tightly. Smelling the beautiful little-girl smell of her, nuzzling her neck, tickling her, kissing her, feeling her jammy fingers all over me. Oh, she's bliss. Bliss. I hope Teddy grows up in a world where women can say what they think without being labelled negatively. Because, wow, Teddy says what she likes.

Liam comes next, showing me a drawing he did at school for geography. It's a map and I'd be hard pressed to say where it was a map of, but it's coloured exquisitely in rainbow tones that all merge into one another. Liam loves drawing and colouring in, even if cartography isn't his strong point. He didn't get this artistry from me or Dan, neither of whom can draw so much as a smiley face.

'Liam, it's lovely. You worked so hard on it,' I say, remembering to praise the work rather than tell him he is one of the most wonderful human beings on the planet, which is what I want to do. Psychologists keep telling modern parents that praising kids to the skies merely makes them think they are celestially brilliant beings and they don't know how to be normal or actually get a job later, so you have to say: you worked so hard, darling.

The rules about being a parent and raising normal kids are worse than the rules of the road and it took me two goes to pass my driving test.

I hug him, because well, he *is* fabulous and then Angela appears.

'Hello, Freya,' she says in a perfectly normal voice and I sigh that sigh of instinctively knowing everything is all right.

'Everyone's fed,' she goes on. The kitchen looks tidy and there's a pot of tea waiting on top of the stove. 'Sorry I missed your call. I texted you back,' she said. 'But I knew you wouldn't pick it up in the car.'

'The traffic was mental,' I say, delirious to be home.

I think I'm going to cry again, seeing the children, and lovely Angela with her warm open face, dark hair tied back loosely. Angela has reared her own children already, although, as she says herself, she did have her first ones when she was very young.

'Married at eighteen,' she says wryly. 'It was either that or a shotgun. My father was old school and determined I was going to be married since I had a baby on the way.'

For a brief minute, I think of Dan and Elisa, stupidly married for the same reason. How had he even liked her, never mind fancied her . . .?

I realise that Angela's talking to me.

'. . . and Dan rang to say he's going to be a little bit late and I know you had some fish in the fridge, but I went ahead and gave the children shepherd's pie for dinner because they're tricky with fish.'

Once they all ate everything – now, mealtimes are a battleground of 'I hate this!' or 'I told you last week, I don't like this anymore.'

'Where's Lexi?' I say.

'Gone upstairs to her room with her phone,' Angela says. 'She's been stuck on it all afternoon, even though I only allow her to have it for half an hour after she has done her homework.'

'It's a long-running battle,' I say lightly, knowing exactly what she's looking up. 'They'll probably have phones implanted in their heads by the time they're in their twenties.'

After hugging Liam and admiring his pictures some more, I put Teddy down and run upstairs to pull on some sweats and find Lexi. Anglea will be going in five minutes, I want to be ready to take over properly.

Lexi's door is locked and I knock on it, as per the most recent instructions.

'Yeah,' she shouts.

'It's Mum,' I say.

'Come in, come in.' She's sitting on the bed and I see she's wearing some of the make-up she got last Christmas. She begged and begged, so I said, 'All right, but only on special occasions.'

Somehow, and I don't know how, she's managed to turn a couple of pastel colours into something much heavier; did she add water? I've had my photograph done professionally enough times to know that you can do anything with the right tools, the right sort of application, but how did Lexi learn how to do this?

'Mum,' she said. 'You're not going to believe this, sit down.'

I sit down. I won't mention the make-up now, I decide; maybe at the weekend we'll have a talk about it. I think how I can bring it up and explain that she's got to stay young, because racing to grow up isn't as much fun as you think and . . .

'Elisa is all over the internet,' she says dramatically. 'It's so exciting. There is going to be a big launch next week for the Surella brand and she's going to be here. I can't wait. Her Instagram shots – look at them, look, look, look.'

I lean over, feeling sick.

Elisa's Instagram feed, which I admit to following myself, just to see what she's up to, is normally wall-to-wall pouting selfies with her by pools, sipping cocktails and gazing at the world through mirrored aviator sunglasses. Sometimes she's pictured 'out with the girls', a gaggle of women who seem to want to show the world how much cleavage you can get if you use one of those push-up bras or have had surgery performed by surgeons for whom no cup-size increase is too big.

None of the 'girls' appear to have any actual jobs, from all the pool-and-party shots I see.

But today's uploaded post is different, the amateur selfies replaced with professional-looking shots of her advertising Surella.

Elisa still looks like her spoilt brattish self (my opinion) and the 747 nose is still huge (also, clearly my opinion) but there is professionalism behind them. Lancôme it ain't, but she's clearly promoting a brand and they have proper shots of her.

'Mum, I WhatsApped her, and she replied,' said Lexi with the breathlessness of pure joy.

This cannot be happening. Not now. It's too *soon*.

'She replied?' I say, attempting to get normality into my voice.

Elisa rarely replies when Dan – with me watching over his shoulder like an angry parrot – contacts her before Christmas to see if she will be joining us and her mother to meet Lexi.

If she does deign to tap her gel nails over the phone keys, it's generally 'No, in Dubai, but Happy Christmas! Love, love, kiss, kiss.'

The sort of thing you'd say to any fan and not to a person she used to be married to, with whom she bore a child.

Still incandescent with joy, Lexi shows me the message.

**Love to see you soon, hun, kiss, kiss, love, love. I'll talk to Dad.**

My heart sinks. *Dad.* Dad as in Dan, as in bloody Elisa has a plan to talk to Dan about seeing *my* Lexi. Suddenly I wish I had that photographer there again, so I could hit him very hard with his bloody camera. Someone needs to take some of this anger.

'Isn't it wonderful, Mum?' said Lexi.

I hug her in close to me and do my best to keep the mingled fear and anger flattened down. I'm her mother: I can't let her know how I really feel.

'Yes darling, wonderful. You'll hear all about the new make-up now. So tell me, sweetie, how was your day at school?'

Dan arrives home just before seven, by which time Lexi is watching an animated Japanese show on the television, Liam is drawing, and Teddy is bathed and is sitting in bed, talking to her cuddlies and awaiting a story from Daddy.

She likes a story every night. But she has a sort of *I'm not sure who I'll choose tonight* thing going, so that generally the person she chooses is the person who isn't there. Tonight I am not suitable for storytelling duties, even though it's now late and she needs to get to sleep.

Although I have been keeping an *I am a normal mother* routine going for the evening, I have been on 440 centigrade. Truly, no lamb shank would survive that heat. Every time I'm on my own, I catch myself having mental conversations with Elisa.

*Why don't you just leave her alone? You've left her alone for a long time and now you are getting your mother to try and see her, and you want to see her and what is this all about? Do you have any idea the damage you could do with picking her up and then just dropping her?*

Worse, I begin to think about life if Elisa *is* in our lives.

'Hello, all,' says Dan as he comes in, slamming the door behind him. He can tell there's something wrong as soon as he sees me. Because normally I hug him and we have a little kiss and I say, 'How was your day, big man?' and he says, 'Ah, pretty good. How was your day, baby?'

It's a joke going back to our early days when we were first living together. I'd had a very 1950s-style apron I'd put on for cooking and one day he said I looked like an adorable 1950s housewife with my blonde hair all looped up on top of my head (I wasn't plaiting it then) and that pinny.

'That's me,' I used to say, 'I'm just a cute 1950s housewife, waiting for her big strong man to come home.'

Today there is no 'big man' pleasantry as he leans close.

I hiss: 'Bloody Elisa has been in touch with Lexi and she wants to see her. What's more, she's going to be in Ireland and, and—'

'Daddy,' shouts Lexi, swinging into the room and launching herself at him.

'Hello, darling,' he says, hugging her and giving me a slightly anguished/slightly guilty gaze. At that point I realise that Elisa has already been in touch with him. I don't know how I know. But I know. It's not so much female intuition as some sort of female Sherlock Holmes-iness that all women possess. If humans lost their sixth sense somewhere along the way, there is still an ability in most women to detect when their husbands have something they want to hide.

Maura says she has worked very hard on honing this ability. To be frank, I don't see why, because Pip wouldn't dream of hiding anything from her. Scarlett and Jack are so much in tune that they are almost the one person; there is no need for any intuitive lying or a session with a polygraph machine for them.

And as for Con – Con is never with a woman long enough to need to know if she's lying or not. *He's* the one who lies.

I rarely use my detective abilities, as Dan's a hopeless liar.

But then I used to consider myself a hopeless liar too and now look at me: lying about going to a group therapy session for my mugging.

'I have so much to tell you, Dad,' says Lexi excitedly.

'Yeah,' I say with a hint of saccharine, which leaks out. 'Lots, and Dad has things to tell us too and I'm sure of it!'

'Ah no, nothing, just the normal day at work,' he says, looking a bit green about the gills.

It seemed to take ages to get Liam and Lexi to bed. Dan was definitely delaying the moment. Liam wanted to watch his favourite programme where people fall over stuff and the camera catches them and it is, I have to admit, absolutely hysterical. I have a juvenile sense of humour somewhere, except when it comes to small children: that's the bit I don't understand. Your very small child is about to face-plant themselves on the ground and what do you do? Rescue them? No, you reach for your camera. I can't look at the small children being hurt. But some of the other stuff, like holidaymakers thinking it was wise to kiss a camel, cracks me up every time.

'OK,' I say. 'Liam, bed.'

Liam goes to bed, a full twenty minutes before Lexi. She's insisted upon that twenty minutes for quite a while and it's vitally important.

'I mean, I'm fourteen now, Mum,' she says every time I mention bed as if being fourteen is on a par with being forty-five and she should have her own credit card, electric car and apartment.

'I know,' I agree gravely. 'You are fourteen, but teenagers still need a lot of sleep.'

She loves being called a teenager. I remember I loved being called a teenager too. It spoke of being nearly grown-up and boyfriends. Mind you, I was hopeless with boyfriends.

I was taller than almost all of them. Boys do not like this, it turns out. My nicknames in school were Big Bird or Skyscraper.

How I longed to be one of the tiny girls who fitted neatly into the school uniform, the utter picture of femininity. Scarlett was tall too, but not *as* tall and the boys swarmed around her. Sex appeal, you see.

As for me, the only boy who came close to dating me was the captain of the football team (a major coup) and he and I had absolutely zero in common apart from height. Nevertheless we ended up together at a school disco on one memorable occasion. Even now, many, many years later, this date makes me shudder with horrified embarrassment. There was a bit of hands wrapping around each other and we tried to figure out where to put our mouths for the kissing. He had a big nose which got in the way. There were no explanations for that sort of thing in any of the romantic books I read. People just kissed – nobody ever mentioned anything about where you put your nose. Myself and Football Dude attempted a sort of sideways attack on each other's faces and there was some sticking in of tongues. Yuck.

But I was not to be deterred. I had a boyfriend, sort of. I could do this.

Except for the tongue thing. Seriously gross. I was waiting for the chorus of joyous angels and pure happiness flittering down from on high and it felt as if he was trying to examine how many fillings I had.

Finally, he spoke.

'D'ya want to go into a corner and shift?' As he uttered these romantic words, he was trying to get his hand up under my shirt. The embryonic magical spell, such as it was, was broken.

'Shift?' I asked, stupidly.

In those far distant days to shift meant to kiss the face off another human being. Think octopuses pressed against tanks with those suckers glued to the glass.

'Uh . . . I'm going to the ladies,' I muttered, and ran.

And that was it.

Rumours circulated that Big Bird couldn't kiss. Oh yes, and that I was frigid, still a popular stick for beating girls with.

Being a teenager was not all it was cut out to be, not for me.

I'm lost in this weird reverie of teenagerdom when Dan's voice breaks into my musings.

'OK honey, you can stay up a little bit later.'

My head swivels, sort of like that kid in *The Exorcist*.

'What?'

'I was just saying that Lexi could stay up a little bit later,' he says, giving me his *oh my God, I'm really in for it, aren't I?* look.

'Maybe not tonight,' I say, getting my careful Mummy voice out of its tissue-paper wrapping.

'But Dad said I could,' Lexi interrupts.

'Dad forgot you have an . . . um, French test tomorrow,' I said, delving deep into my brain and coming up with the facts. There's always an exam looming in secondary school. 'You need a good sleep.'

'Oh gosh, yes!' she says.

It takes another fifteen minutes before she's showered and settled in bed with her bedside lamp on and reading. For the first time, she's got the beginnings of a few spots, I notice with a pang. Spots are so horrible and they are part and parcel of the whole teenage hormone thing.

Tomorrow, I vow, I'm going to get her some really good skin products that are good for both young skin and acne.

Lexi looks at me dreamily.

'Mum,' she says, 'I feel so happy.'

I sit down on the side of her bed. I normally love these special times with Lexi, talking to her, trying to help her negotiate life, subtly give her the tools to move on . . .

'Elisa WhatsApped me! I mean wait till I tell everyone in school, they won't believe it. I bet she gets loads of Surella products. They're really, really cool.'

The happy mum bubble inside me bursts, like an acid rain cloud.

She is still on Planet Elisa and it hurts so much. Even our special time in bed is tainted with it.

'That's wonderful, darling,' I manage to say. Just because I'm jealous and enraged doesn't mean Lexi needs to know this. 'You think about it now and we'll talk more tomorrow, because I think Elisa talked to Dad.'

'Yeah,' she said happily, putting her book down on the bed. 'Maybe she could come over here and see us. She'd love the house. She's always saying she loves big fancy houses and we could do it up, right?' Lexi looks at me with those big, beautiful dark eyes that are just like Dan's.

Perhaps they don't come from anywhere: perhaps they're just Lexi.

I hug her tightly, more tightly than usual.

'Mum, you're squishing me.'

'Sorry,' I say, 'the Mum squish – it's a new type of hug.'

She giggles.

''K.'

'I'll be up in fifteen minutes to turn out the light, OK?'

''K,' she says again, giving me a little wave. But she doesn't pick up her book again as I leave the room and she lies there in the bed, propped up by her pillows, surrounded by the threadbare teddies she still loves and hasn't got rid of over the years. She's not thinking about her book, she's thinking about Elisa: I can almost see the thought bubble over her head.

I turn and go downstairs thinking, could I get away with killing Dan and do what the French do and say, 'it was a crime of passion, m'Lud' when I got to court? Would it have been such a big deal for him to warn me what was coming?

Finally I shut the kitchen door where he's sitting down finishing the last of his dinner, having been interrupted several times by Teddy wheedling for 'One more leetle story', and having to be tucked back into bed again.

'So, what happened?' I say.

Happy Mummy has gone, to be replaced by Very Angry Freya.

'Elisa sent me a WhatsApp.'

'A WhatsApp,' I said incredulously. 'Is that the only form

of communication these days? Do people not phone or do sensible things like leave a message for you along the lines of: 'I'm in Ireland and I would like to see the child I gave birth to, the child I never set eyes on anymore. Do you think we could arrange this? Or should I just randomly WhatsApp this kid and confuse the hell out of her?'

'Freya, we're not going to get anywhere if you're going to be like that,' he says. 'This is difficult, you know that.'

'Difficult?' I shriek, and then somehow, I think of my mother.

'You're not just a second wife, you're enmeshed with his former wife's family because of Lexi. Yes, she is now your child, darling,' she said when Dan and I got engaged. 'But it is not as simple as if you had given birth to her yourself. Bitterness and jealousy will not help your forthcoming marriage or little Lexi,' she said. I paid attention.

My own mother, who repurposes her clothes from things she finds in charity shops and who is now caring for one disabled and two challenging elderly people, and still has a smile for everyone, is such a font of wisdom and kindness.

I breathe. In. Out. Slowly.

I know Dan's right, I know we have to deal with this like adults. But when it comes to my children, I stop being an adult and turn into something feral.

'Will I open a bottle of wine?' he says hopefully, clearly seeing my demonic-ness disappearing as I breathe.

'You know I don't like to drink during the week,' I say sanctimoniously.

I can't help it.

A snort escapes him.

'Well, I don't,' I say.

'I think I need one,' says Dan, hastily getting up, opening the fridge and pulling out a beer.

He's not a big beer drinker, to be honest. That was another one of the things I liked about him. So many of the guys I used to meet at parties in my twenties appeared to feel that they were missing out if they weren't almost comatose with drink halfway through the night. And a really good night for these fabulous menfolk would be had by a load of them coming together, filling themselves full of beer, having a big feed of burgers and chips before letting themselves loose to chat up women. As I said: *classy*. Not.

Dan was never that guy.

He sits down with his beer and looks at me.

'What was I supposed to say?' he demands finally, and he's using that calm, measured voice he uses on radio interviews when a fellow guest is annoying him. 'Elisa *is* Lexi's birth mother . . .'

I wince.

He puts a hand on my arm but I ignore it.

'And Mrs Markham—'

'Why don't you ever call her Adele Markham?' I demand. 'Why is she always *Mrs* Markham, like, Mrs Markham, can Elisa come out to play?'

'Oh stop it. You've demonised her. Adele's OK. Plus, when the adoption went through, we agreed to visitation so that the Markhams still got to see Lexi. We knew Lexi would be occasionally seeing . . .' He pauses to find the words. '. . . The person who gave birth to her.'

There's a horrible silence.

I get up, go to the fridge and shakily pour myself some white wine. So much for the sanctimoniousness.

I don't *want* Elisa to be my daughter's birth mother. I don't *want* her seeing Lexi.

I'd been so happy to be able to adopt her, I'd have agreed to anything and look how that's backfired.

Meanwhile, Dan is into his explaining mode: his long legs are stretched out, his face is earnest, and you can see the intelligence burning inside him as he tries to help me grasp this knotty problem.

Only thing is, my instinct and not my brain is running me.

'I understand, darling,' he's saying. 'You think messaging by WhatsApp is not the most grown-up way to start a correspondence about the daughter you share but that's Elisa for you. I'm surprised she didn't try a message on Instagram . . .' he says, jokily, trying to lighten the atmosphere.

'You follow her on Instagram?' I ask, with narrow-eyed irritation.

'I'm not on Instagram,' he says, horrified. 'Why would I be? It's not my thing.'

'OK. Sorry.'

I sit down beside him. Despite my cauldron of burning rage against all the Markhams, poor Dan is stuck in the middle.

'Show it to me.'

Dan has very few WhatsApp groups. Mainly family ones: us, his family, my family, the guys he plays five-a-side football with on a Wednesday night, a few of his mates from college. Nothing that would make an irritated wife go postal. And there in the middle of all this innocence is a message from Elisa. Her tiny avatar is, obviously, a picture of her from the waist up, in a bikini with her boobs shoved up.

'She's really getting her money out of those, isn't she?' I say caustically. 'You could do a paper on that. How much money a person can make out of fake boobs.'

'I don't know if she's making much money out of them,' he says thoughtfully as if he really was considering this for a financial analysis piece. 'But she clearly paid a lot for them so she wants everyone to see them.'

My husband: the economist.

I read the message which was full of textspeak like the letter 'u' for you and 'talk L8R'.

'Honestly, considering she hasn't talked properly to you for, what, four years, you'd think she'd make more of an effort. Would a phone call have hurt? Or actually spelling whole words?'

'Freya, that's Elisa. A business like this current make-up deal is as close to an effort as she has ever come before to having a job, and I suspect that the current husband has had a bit of a financial meltdown, which is why she's doing it.'

'Really,' I say. I'm a little shocked at how bitchy I sound. I modulate my tone. 'Really,' I say again, trying to put a little bit of sorrow into my voice.

'Yeah, really. Why else would she be doing this? My mother keeps bumping into Adele in the supermarket.' He pauses while I grin at him at the very thought of Adele Markham hiding behind giant stacks of special-offer loo roll in order to jump out at Dan's poor mother, Betty.

'She's following your mother, you know. That's why Betty barely dares come here, because she's sure Adele Markham will be attached to her with superglue.'

'Surely not?' he says, in disbelief.

I ignore this innocence. Any woman who can make a business out of flogging hall table lamps worth two grand to people with too much money is not beyond lurking in the supermarket aisles to get what she wants.

Women should definitely be ruling the world: men just don't get the nuances.

'Anyway, whatever this new business is, I get the feeling that she wants to come back to Ireland, so that would imply that her marriage is on the skids.'

'Yes it would, wouldn't it,' I say, shakiness coming back into my voice, 'but she's not coming back in and messing up our lives.'

He holds up a hand.

'No, she's not coming back into our lives and messing things up, OK? Even if she does move back here. Lexi is our daughter. But you've got to face up to the facts, Freya. Elisa is Lexi's birth mother and you always knew that at some point, she'd want to get to know her properly. We agreed on an open adoption. Make it easy and quick, that was our motto, remember?'

'But it's so soon—'

I can feel the tears pooling in my eyes. Dan sees them and he pulls me close to him. Normally, his touch can soothe me but not tonight.

'On the basis of the past, I thought Elisa would never be interested and eventually, one day in the future, when Lexi was older, an *adult*, she'd want to meet Elisa properly and talk to her.'

I had all this planned in my head: Elisa would still be feckless, possibly really, really wrinkly as the sins of a lifelong aversion to suncream had caught up with her. Lexi would come back and tell me what a wonderful mother I was.

In the best version of this fantasy, Elisa looked about twenty years older than I did, reeked of cigarette smoke and desperation, and asked for a loan.

As I said, my inner bitch, Mildred, is inventive. OK, *I'm* inventive.

Dan's almost rocking me now and I can smell that end-of-day combination of the hint of aftershave and Dan's own scent.

'Lexi's just a child now and is so impressionable,' I say finally, reverting to the real world. 'Plus, Elisa is possibly the worst role model on the planet. Do nothing in school. Party your way through your late teens and have a child so you can ignore her. Have I left anything out? Exactly what did you see in this paragon of womanhood, anyway?'

I have asked him this question before and he's never been able to give me a satisfactory answer.

'You know,' he sighs, 'it's hard to say. We were young, I was a bit of a nerd.'

'You weren't a nerd,' I say loyally, 'you were just quiet, and a late bloomer. But you were always good-looking.'

He grins. 'Thanks, honey,' he says, 'but when we were at school, I was quiet and I didn't go out much. I stayed at home all the time, which pretty much qualifies you for being a nerd.'

'And now, you're one of Ireland's hottest economists,' I add. 'So if that's what nerds turn into, then, I ought to tell all our children to hang around nerds. Because nerds turn into nuggets of gold.'

Dan laughs and kisses me.

'Do you think they've gone to sleep?' he says, hopefully, a glint in his eyes.

I somehow manage a grin. 'Sex, sex, sex – is that all you think about?'

'Not all the time, no,' he says, scratching the back of his head. 'The male of the species is possibly more interested in sex than the female,' he goes on. 'It's evolution, we need to spread our seed.'

Which brings me back to Elisa. I know I'm like a dog with a bone, but I can't help it.

I've asked him this scores of times but I try it another way: rephrase it. Because I have to know.

'I still can't understand how you hooked up with Elisa. Was she different then, less pushy, less airheaded, less *look at me, I've lots of money and it's Daddy's?'*

For a second Dan stares into the distance. In fairness to him, he doesn't say, *not again, Freya*.

'It wasn't *Love Story*, Freya, I've told you endlessly. I don't know how we ended up dating those few times,' he says with a sigh. 'We were immature and I'd known her at school, well sort of known her, I mean she wouldn't have really known me, because as I said before . . .'

I interject. 'Yeah, nerd: got it.'

'Exactly. When we met up again I was with a group of guys in town. You've heard this story so many times,' he adds, exasperated.

'I want to hear it again,' I say, 'in case I missed something important.'

Dan laughs and pulls me properly onto his lap. He goes to the gym, cycles, swims, which is just as well because you need to be strong to haul me around. 'You didn't miss anything important. We just partied. Myself and the guys were on a roll then because being smart was suddenly cool. I'd written a few articles, Kevin was beginning his start-up: we were on that on-line *Ones To Watch* list and Elisa wanted to play outside her normal group. She was fed up with trust-fund babies and the jocks. We were the clever guys who were out of college then, or doing masters or PhDs, different from her normal crowd who were all suddenly boring now school was over. Peaked too early, while we'd finally stopped being the dorky kids with glasses and it turned out that having our heads in books all the time meant we were going places,' he adds with some pride.

'Plus, I had my James Dean leather jacket and that may have swung it in my favour. We dated for three weeks. OK? Three weeks. It was never serious. I guess I was flattered that she was interested in me, right? None of her crowd would have looked at me and my pals at school.'

'So you get a rich chick with benefits and date the ex-coolest girl from school?' I say.

He ignores that. 'I wasn't dating anyone and we hooked up.'

I wait for Mildred to chime in that Dan might still fancy her but sometimes, Mildred shuts up and lets my intelligent instincts take over. Dan had never loved Elisa, I was sure of that. Our marriage is rock solid.

*Really*, chimes in Mildred. *Then, why are you lying to him about how you're going to a group for victim support . . .?*

I haven't said that yet. I've said I'm going this week, I point out, silently.

'You know everything, Freya. She got pregnant,' he goes on, 'and her family went mental because her grandmother, the one with all the money, is more Catholic than the Pope. Yadda yadda, you've heard it before.'

'They must have hidden the newspapers from Granny,' I reply smartly. Elisa had been all over the papers in those days, at the opening of every envelope in head-to-toe Gucci, looking champagne-dazed.

'Her parents could have dealt with it but in her grand-mother's world, pregnancy equalled marriage or the trust fund dried up. Elisa needed hers – her family knew she was hardly going to be a career woman given her interest in school – or work, for that matter. It was wedding bells from then on.'

'You could have said no,' I point out. '*You* weren't inherit-ing the bloody money. It was hardly the 1960s.'

'Freya, you know how my mum is. She wasn't able to say boo to a goose and my dad was the same. In their world, if you got a girl pregnant, you took responsibility, whatever that responsibility took. Normally it was just an angry father – in our case, it was a religious granny.' He grinned, remembering. 'Elisa was panicked.'

*Panicked she'd miss out on the loot,* says Mildred.

'And made it the wedding of the season.'

'Oh, totally,' he groans. 'I heard some people were selling the invitations. She had four hundred on her side alone. And all the time I knew it was a mistake. Zed kept saying to me, "You're mad. Mad, Dan. Don't marry her, she's not the woman for you, but . . ."'

I finish the sentence for him. 'You did the honourable thing.'

'Yup, that's the problem with us nerds: honourable.'

'And we got Lexi out of it,' I say. 'So you doing the honourable thing, and going out with crazy Elisa, all worked out in the end.'

His face breaks into a huge smile.

'Yes,' he says, 'it all worked out in the end. Freya, Elisa has never stuck with anything in her life. But we have to give her the benefit of the doubt, for Lexi's sake. Our aim is to make sure that Lexi doesn't get hurt. But,' he goes on, 'we have to help her see Elisa if she wants to.'

*Give Elisa the benefit of the doubt?* Mildred is in my head telling me we needed a staple gun so I could go confront Elisa. *No, a nail gun like builders use! Channel your inner Robert de Niro* . . . I wonder is Mildred the worst part of me with no added filter.

'We are going to manage it,' Dan says, 'I promise you. I love you, love our family. Elisa can't harm us.'

Finally, I relax against him on the couch. He's right. We are rock solid, truly.

Only in my own head are Dan and Elisa a once-great romance.

# 9

## *Difficult roads lead to the most precious destinations*

I have the nightmare again.

I'm never in a garage on my own and it's never the garage I was mugged in.

It's always somewhere utterly innocuous like the super-market car park where in reality, you are never more than five yards from a person pushing a trolley and looking exhausted.

I'm always with the children. Sometimes, all three of them.

They're smaller: babies, wriggly as puppies, and I'm trying to hold on to them all as I run, screaming, away from a man who is bearing down on us with menace.

In the nightmare, he's huge, giant-sized.

Only I can save my babies but I keep letting them slip from my grip, keep having to stop and hoist them up again as he comes after us. The atmosphere is dark and full of dread and when I wake, I lie in that half-alert horror of not knowing what's real and what's not.

Am I safe?

Beside me, Dan is sleeping. My heartbeat gradually slows, but I'm wet with sweat and I feel the nausea the nightmare always brings.

I shove back the duvet and stagger, because my head is

woozy, to the bathroom where I shut the door quietly and turn on the mini light over the sink.

The me in the mirror looks ghostly, with huge violet circles under my eyes and my hair stuck to my skull with sweat. It's only half four in the morning but I cannot go back to sleep, not when The Fear is there in the background, waiting to pull me in again. I prefer exhaustion and relying on caffeine all day to that.

I sink onto the cold floor and cry, giant heaves where no actual tears emerge.

I hate this but how do I escape it?

I have to be strong, strong for everyone.

Once the heaving is over, I pull on my dressing gown, grab my phone and socks, and check on the children. They're safe.

I know they're safe. I'm safe, but still . . .

Downstairs, I make coffee and turn the TV on low to watch something mindless.

I used to have the nightmares in the old house but I was so sure that here, I'd be better. Except I'm not. And I've so successfully downplayed what happened to me, that I can't now come out and talk about how it's affected me. I'm so lucky! Look at all the things I have. My darling children, Dan, my family, my career. Dad's stroke, Mum's devastation and Scarlett's pain are enormous aches in my heart, and they're real aches.

Not nightmares conjured up by someone who should be able to get better on her own. I like watching car-crash TV but I don't want my life to be like that.

I especially don't want Dan to know.

The thing is, if Dan knew how traumatised I still am by the mugging, he'd go into caveman meltdown.

Behind his civilised front, Dan is *waay* more Viking than

me. All I've got is the hair: he's got the attitude.

Two years before Teddy was born, he trained for and completed an Ironman triathlon event. This means running, cycling and swimming an amount that no human should be able to do. But Dan and his brother, Zed did it because *it was there*. This is code for any number of the dense things men do.

I told him that he needed to get all that sort of bravado out of his mind with the Ironman because mountain-biking, parachuting and climbing mountains are all there and he is not allowed to do any of them. He's no use to me dead.

Zed, whom I love but not hopelessly the way I do my beloved Dan, is allowed to fling himself off cliffs if he wants as I have no power over him. I can live without Zed: I could not live without Dan.

Watching Dad has made me all too aware what can happen to people, what happens out of the blue every moment of every day.

One huge loss makes me fear loss everywhere.

But I can't tell anyone this. They'd think I was crazy.

I can't tell them I'm scared of going places on my own at night, either.

Yeah, they'd think I was crazy.

Why are we all so frightened of other people thinking we're crazy?

So I pretend that I am OK.

'Fine!' I say breezily when I have to travel somewhere on my own. 'I'm fine!'

*You're a mess*, Mildred points out.

All my combined fears, which I have linked up and called The Fear, have made me nervy and unable to sleep without sleeping tablets. The Fear has given me anxiety and has ramped up my previously quite benign inner voice to a mental torturer on steroids.

Yes, I know it's weird, but calling my inner voice Mildred does help. Honestly. It's like making friends with your kidnappers. They can't murder you if you tell them your name. Maybe . . .

My sister Maura says she totally understands what I am blithely calling The Incident.

'Obviously, your sleep's going to be a bit wonky,' said Maura shortly afterwards, 'it was a dreadful shock. But you're so strong, Freya. I said it at the time – "if anyone can get over this, Freya can."'

Maura, oldest sibling in the Abalone household and four years older than me, is dealing with the perimenopause and is at the stage where she considers ramming cars that drive dangerously in front of her on the motorway. Nobody ever mentions that stage of the menopause but all you need to do is spend half an hour driving to IKEA with Maura, and you fear for mankind and their vehicles because she drives like a woman who longs for bull bars and an assault rifle. Forget your hot flushes and thinning skin in unmentionable places – rage is clearly the number one menopause symptom.

'People who aren't going through something always say that you should or shouldn't feel a certain way about it,' she says grimly and I sense this is about herself and her rioting hormones. 'You feel what you feel, Freya. You had a terrible shock. But you're grand now.'

I practise saying this: 'It was a terrible shock but I'm grand now.'

Grand. Sounds suitably mild. 'I'm fine, nothing to see here. Move along now.'

Scarlett, younger sister, totally understands that I was seriously shocked by the attack.

Years of preparing her body for the babies who have never taken seed there means Scarlett is into candlelit yoga, writing *namaste* at the end of her emails, and cleansing vegetable juices which she and Jack drink every day as part of their fertility schedule. But even she says that after what happened to me, safety would be high on the list of priorities. With enough wine inside her, she even goes so far as to say that I ought to buy a baseball bat, which is very un-*namaste*. She did not comment on the wild speed with which we put our home on the market and bought this one or how I managed to convince Dan that this little pocket of a village close to the city will be perfect for our children.

I may have lied about my motives.

Even though I tell Dan I am fine, I know he doesn't believe me.

His chief worry is that if I am *fine*, then why do I need sleeping tablets?

'Do you think you should still be taking them?' he asked one night about two months after the mugging as he saw me popping one into my mouth with the ease of a Smartie.

'I need to sleep, Dan,' I said but I was instantly angry.

How can he even say this? I bloody need to sleep! Nought to sixty with anger is quite common in people who are suffering from . . . er, who have been victims of crime. *He doesn't understand you*, shrieks Mildred.

'Of course, I understand,' Dan said. 'But Freya, love, it's been a while and you can't go on taking sleeping tablets long term . . .'

Fury erupted out of me.

'You have to come off these things slowly,' I yelled at him. 'Plus I have a cookery book to research so there are new recipes for the TV show, and we have to pay for this house.'

This is a low blow because it's my TV career that allowed

us to put in a bid for the new house, not Dan's career. Mentioning that you might have – briefly, or not briefly – earned more than your man is on a par with giving him an instant vasectomy.

'I don't need to move,' he says grimly. 'You want the new detached house. I'm happy where we are.'

His voice is even but Stone Age men could make tools out of each syllable.

Interesting fact: we never have screaming rows. Never.

I hate those people why say fighting makes a relationship stronger. Utter rubbish, in my opinion. Fighting makes you say things you regret.

But when I think back to that evening, the car park, the feeling of someone's dirty hand over my mouth . . . I can barely breathe thinking about it. Which is why I don't think about it except at night, when I can't sleep. Cue sleeping tablets. Cue hating being on sleeping tablets. Cue not being able to stop being on sleeping tablets, but *I can't tell Dan.*

Worse, I'm nearly out of them and I have to face another trip to the doctor where he will do his best to tell me that I can't continue on a diet of sleeping pills. Or that he can't continue prescribing them.

'I'll come off the sleeping tablets when my sleep is back to normal,' I said to Dan, anger – yes, anger! – rising in me. 'As if you care.'

'How can you say I don't care,' he yelled back angrily. 'But you won't talk to me about it. You act as if you're fine most of the time, so how do I know when you're not?'

'Because . . . because . . .'

*Because you're supposed to know without me saying anything,* I said silently.

'I think you haven't dealt with it all and you're fuelling

your own stress with taking stupid drugs at night,' he said harshly, 'because you won't let go of it.'

I had the sensation of being punched in the stomach. *Dan. Saying this.* Being winded is a horrible thing and I should know.

*I wouldn't let go of it?*

It wouldn't let go of me. That was the problem.

I solved the whole argument in the most adult way possible that night. I went to bed immediately, taking my precious sleeping tablet and letting him face my back the way I've faced his so often when I wake in the wee small hours. So there.

That's the tricky thing with sleeping tablets: they hit you with their chemical cosh for a decent five hours and then, bingo, you are wide awake again.

Just thinking about how little I sleep despite the tablets, I realise that I need coffee badly.

Five damn hours. Zimovane is supposed to give you six hours but I am bucking the trend. My mind fights its way out of sleep, no problem.

Sleep comes second to peace of mind in the list of casualties in my life.

Peace of mind cannot be bought, even pharmaceutically.

I used to worry over my father and how my mother would cope, now I worry over my own fear as well. I also now worry about not being able to come up with the recipes I used to magic out of thin air. I worry over Scarlett who surely cannot face another round of fertility treatment, even if she and Jack could manage to fund it. I worry about the children, naturally.

I worry full stop.

Lorraine is on the phone first thing.

'How's Freya the Slayer?' she says, and I hear the grin in her voice.

'That's got a good ring to it,' I say, putting down my sixth cup of espresso that morning. I have the headache from hell and am blasting it with paracetamol *and* ibuprofen. 'Freya the Slayer, perhaps we could put that on the cookbooks? *Freya the Slayer has new recipes for you: photographers' intestines served en croûte.*'

Lorraine laughs.

'Yeah, you told them. I almost felt sorry for him.'

'So do I now,' I admit. 'I was thinking of phoning and apologising.'

'Don't bother doing any such thing,' says Lorraine crisply. 'I said *I almost* felt sorry for him – not that I did. He was there to do a job and he went off mission. He thought he was back in art school. You were right to stop him and you know it's good to change the old Freya sweet and cuddly image into something a bit tougher. Like I said, you have turned the corner.'

'I have not turned any corner,' I say, thinking that this corner must involve becoming Maura and getting all perimeno-pausal and a danger on the roads. 'I'm only forty-two, you know.'

'Speaking of which, we've got a request in to do a *Fabulous Over Forty* thing for one of the Sunday papers. Nina was on to me, said you had to do it and I said yes, we can fit it in, once you agree. It will be a full shoot and they wanted to do it in your house, but—'

'No,' I say, horrified. 'The only part of the house that's fit for cameras is the kitchen. The rest of it . . . Nooo. We have too much stuff, I'll never get all the boxes unpacked and we haven't painted a single wall . . .'

'Yeah, I figured,' says Lorraine, who seems to be on top or

everything without actually being told. Sometimes I think she sees my bank statements even though they get delivered to my house.

'So,' she continues, 'I suggested that because it's summer, we do a romantic picnic-style thing in a lovely hotel garden.'

'Romantic picnic-style thing,' I repeat as if I'm saying 'gastroenteritis – both ends.' 'OK.'

I hate the sort of summer clothes newspapers and magazines like you to wear for summer shoots: they're all flowy and frou-frou and if you have any sort of boobs at all, carry weight on your hips, or basically, like food, you look like a flowery sack-person who never saw a cake she didn't like.

'I would have said no, that you only like indoor photographs and sleek clothes, but they are all set on this outside shoot. And Freya, it's May.'

'Not that you'd know today,' I reply, looking out at a day devoid of sun.

Lexi's school term will be finished soon, end of the month. She's about to start her end-of-year exams and the grand meeting with Elisa and eight stone of Surella products is not happening until she's on her summer holidays. Or at least this is what I have told Dan to explain in the messages to Elisa and her mother. That's another source of great annoyance. All the messages come to Dan. It's as if I don't exist. The whole crime-of-passion scenario has shifted and I'm now idly wondering whether I'd get jail time for nail-gunning Elisa. Only most of the time it's Elisa *and* her mother.

Why are they here *now*? When everything in my life is so chaotic?

But I control the anger. I can't see there being much of a TV and cookery book market out there for homicidal chefs.

'Yes, I used this knife on my victims. So, first we dice the meat . . .' Ha!

'OK,' I say to Lorraine. 'When did they want to do it, do we have any sort of date?'

I'm thinking of my endless lists in my diary which are always full of things I have not ticked off as 'done.' Another place I'm failing.

Then, there's the appointments. Liam needs to go to the hairdresser and Lexi has another trip to the orthodontist, which I'm not looking forward to, especially since the last time when I, jokingly, remarked to the dental assistant at the outside desk that I'd have to sleep with the orthodontist instead of paying because it was all so expensive.

Something dropped in the inner office where the orthodontist worked. The nurse went whiter than her lab coat. He'd clearly heard.

'It was a joke,' I said feebly.

I mean, come on, how could that *not* be a joke?

Sometimes my mouth gets me into trouble.

I must have said that last bit out loud because Lorraine laughs.

'Yeah, that mouth gets you into trouble,' she agrees.

'Kick me when I'm down, why don't you?'

Lorraine laughed her evil cackle. It's exactly the same noise Teddy makes when she's planning mischief.

'Sorry, Freya, but you'd be lost without me.'

'I know, you're brilliant. But too sassy.'

'Pot. Kettle. Black,' she shoots back.

'Do you want to come out to the house this morning and see what it's like? There's a lovely coffee shop around the corner. So Italian, you'll adore it. It's run by these two fabulous guys, one of whom pretends to be Italian, but we are not telling anyone that. We're all just going along with it because it makes him happy.'

Lorraine isn't a bit fazed by this unusual concept.

'Sounds great,' she said, 'I can do pretend Italian as well as the rest of them. *Spaghetti alle Vongole, Frittelle di Mele*, that sort of thing.'

'Perfect,' I say. 'If you're here for twelve, we can go in just before the lunchtime rush and have coffee and one of their beautiful cakes.'

Normally, I'd bake but I am not up to cooking today. I don't say that in the last four months, my cooking brain seems to have abandoned me. I feel sure that Lorraine has already figured this out and is saying nothing. I am supposed to be working up recipes for a cookbook for which I've already been paid a signature advance. Which means I've been given some of the money up front and have done none of the work.

Stress number one.

Some of these unwritten/untested recipes will go in to the TV show I'm booked to film in the autumn, for which I have also been given a signature fee. Stress number two.

None of these projects will happen if I can't get out of the quicksand of my own head.

Lorraine keeps going: 'I'll send over all the emails and a list of what we have to do. Now we need your autograph on a few books from the publishers and we've got a demo on Saturday in two weeks with that special tasting festival.'

'Oh,' I wince.

It's in West Cork, a place I adore, but I feel a little fragile at the moment, not really able to go anywhere and it's a long enough drive.

*Stop being a wimp. This is your job and you need the money.*

Shut up, Mildred.

'OK, put it all down on the list. Will you drive this time?'

'Sure,' she says. There's a pause. 'You could talk me through the recipe ideas you have for the new book,' she says gently.

I can feel my eyes narrow. Thinking of what I need to do but haven't puts me on a stress level from hell.

'Do you have a psychic granny hidden away in the cupboard?' I ask grimly.

'No, I'm just the person who sees all the recipes you write down in the middle of the night that you send to yourself to remind you. And if I don't see them, I know they're not happening. Also Nina wants a meeting about your social media. A catch-up.'

'Oh.' I actually wince. A catch-up means Nina wants to berate me for wasting my career chances by not being a social media guru. My agent in London, the old school gentleman, Paddy Ashmore, is much kinder. I think Nina is angling for his job. As if. Paddy is a great agent because he's brilliant, understands the business and charms people. Nina is super clever but devoid of charm.

'I wish you could do more of the social media stuff for me,' I plead at Lorraine, a bit like Teddy when she's looking for more ice-cream.

'It has to come from you, be your voice,' says Lorraine. 'Believe me, I'd do more if I could. I upload everything I can but your voice is so funny. Although, you don't take beautiful pictures, it has to be said.'

'Ah well, I know a photographer who could help with that,' I say back. 'Arty, moody shots are right up his street . . .'

We both laugh.

'See you at twelve. Send directions.'

*

That night, I phone Maura and we discuss our rota over helping Mum.

'I'm just joining up some African flower crochet octagons,' she says, sounding harassed at the interruption.

Maura is a crafting person. She is always knitting, crocheting, sewing or embroidering things. She never finishes anything, mind you.

'I'm too busy,' she tells anyone who wants to know what she actually makes.

Privately, she tells me it makes her happy to sit in front of the TV and make roundy crochet bits and bobs.

She has lots of what crafting people call UFOs in the house. This means Unfinished Objects. Oh, yes, and lots of wool. She buys wool like I buy shoes.

'You finished that scarf for me and one for each of the girls,' I point out loyally.

'Never again,' says Maura. 'That wool was so thin. It was murder and I had to pay attention instead of watching *Madam Secretary* properly.'

She has now got involved in something called the slow sewing movement, which is what all my attempts at sewing have always been. Slow sewing, she explains, is when you enjoyably stick stitches into bits and bobs of fabric, attaching bits, buttons, designs, whatever floats your boat. You do not have to make anything. This is what she likes best about slow sewing – you aren't *supposed* to be actually making anything.

'I think they come round and remove all your crafting supplies if you actually finish a project,' she said joyfully, when she told me about it.

But tonight's conversation is evidence that the slow sewing is now boring her and she's back on the crochet.

I avoid the subject of what she's making because, obviously, she isn't making anything.

'I can go tomorrow in your place because Lexi starts her first-year summer exams the day after and I have to pick her up from school, can we swap?'

'Sure,' she says. 'Talk tomorrow. I have to join this bloody yoke up.'

# 10

# *The happiest people know they have to work at happiness*

My mother's house should resemble a cottage hospital, containing as it does three people who can be classed as invalids, one a severely disabled person, but it is not.

It is awash with colour and crafts. Maura inherited my mother's ability to make things, although my mother actually finishes them. The red gingham curtains in the kitchen and the adorable kitchen-themed bunting: she made them.

The tapestry cushions – mainly animals but a few interesting flowers from kits from the immensely talented textile designer, Kaffe Fassett – she made them too.

The sunflower-yellow knitted throw on the couch that Bridget's cat, another elderly inhabitant, thinks is her own, was knitted by my mother over one cold winter and it's like a spot of sunshine in the room. The hand-stitched star quilt in corals and pale blues hanging on one wall: yes, another work of art by my mother.

In short, lack of money has never stopped my mother from making her home beautiful.

'Mum,' I say loudly as I let myself in. I don't want to scare her, although with Granddad beetling around all the time clutching one of his encyclopedias or worse, his *Guinness Book of Records* and asking does anyone know where the deepest lake in the world is, she is used to constant interruptions.

Granny is easier to hear because even though she is a pixie of a thing, she does have the walker she uses at home, which bashes a bit. The skirting boards and the doors all suffer.

My mother is in the kitchen, over the stove, stirring something that smells delicious.

'Moroccan chicken?' I say, sniffing as I hug her.

'With prunes,' she says. 'Your grandfather hates prunes so I have to get them into him somehow. Otherwise, all we talk about at night are bowel movements and orange fibre drinks.'

I can smell that the dish is far less spicy than usually recommended because spicy food does not agree with anyone in the house except Mum, and she never cooks for herself. Only for other people. She is the add-on to her own meals. The carer's lot.

I pull an apron off the hook by the dresser and put it on.

'Off with you,' I say. 'I'm here. I'll see you at half two.'

Maura and I take over from Mum as often as we can, which is less often than we would like.

'I'll just finish—' she begins.

'Go,' I order. 'I can cook, you know.'

She smiles wearily and hands me the wooden spoon.

Her blonde hair is streaked with grey now, and today, she looks very tired. Rather than the massage we are treating her to and lunch with one of her old school friends, she looks as if she needs to lie down and just sleep.

I am unnerved by this. My mother is a coper. She can do anything – *has* done anything since my father's stroke, when suddenly, their life fell apart. She was taking care of her mother and she and my father were considering converting the garage into a little bedroom for his father, who was entirely compos mentis but no longer able to really look after himself, when whoosh . . . the stroke hit our family.

Strokes do that – hit a family. Not just one person.

One person takes the savagery of the stroke but all around, their family falls into the hole of tragedy, too.

Before the stroke, my father was funny, wildly in love with my mother, considering retirement from his engineering job and discussing with my mother where they would travel.

'The Trans-Siberian Railway,' my father would suggest.

'You'll be killed,' Granny would squeak.

Granny has only been outside of Ireland once, to the Marian shrine at Lourdes. That was enough for her. In Granny Bridget's eyes, Abroad is a frightening place where you will be taken advantage of and have your money robbed.

*This can happen in Ireland*, I think grimly.

'Route 66,' my mother said.

'Gone, isn't it?' said Granddad Eddie, who wants to be the fount of all knowledge but has moments where he falters because he's very keen on the information being correct. He's a stickler for accuracy.

'We could do a year-long trip involving rucksacks and Airbnb,' Dad had said, an arm around my mother, holding her lovingly the way he always did.

'Lorcan Abalone! Rucksacks indeed,' Mum burst out laughing. 'If you think I'm going anywhere with a rucksack, you've got another think coming.'

'How is everyone,' I ask now.

'Fine. Your father slept well. He's calm today. Mum had a dreadful nightmare about going into a wheelchair and she's still very fretful. Eddie says he wants an allotment.'

I laugh. 'He hates gardening.'

Mum laughs too and looks like herself for the first time since I've arrived.

'He found a mini seed catalogue in one of the papers

and he's enchanted with it, wants nothing but plants for his birthday.'

'It was his birthday in March,' I point out.

'I mentioned that,' she says, swiftly putting a few things into the dishwasher, 'but he feels that at his age, he is entitled to more birthdays than normal people.'

'Ha! At least he knows he's not normal.'

My mother finally goes upstairs to change and brush her hair, and I take stock of my charges. In the downstairs den, now turned into my father's bedroom and bathroom, he sits in his wheelchair on the highly expensive cushions that are air-filled so as to help the sitter avoid pressure sores, the bane of all invalids' and their carers' lives. My father can move – but his rare condition means he has no impetus to do so.

For a moment, I take in the smell of the sickroom: the lavender oil my mother burns in a tiny aromatherapy pot each morning to remove the scents of hospital cleansers, hand washes and the smell of the sick room. In his chair, looking out the window but not seeing, is Dad.

Dad is Not Dad. At least not the Dad I once knew. Not anymore. He doesn't talk and looks at the world with unseeing eyes. He has to be fed, as he appears not to know how to feed himself. The other great worry, as for all wheelchair-bound patients – whatever their reason for being wheelchair bound, is that he will get a pressure sore because they can lead to sepsis. Taking care of him outside a nursing-home environment is a huge responsibility, but my mother insists.

'He knows it's me,' she insists. But for once in my life, I am not sure I believe her.

It's his eyes that tell me the true story. Dad's eyes are so like mine and Scarlett's and once, they sparkled with humour and intelligence.

Not now.

I have a sudden, crushing memory of Dad on my wedding day, the two of us waiting in the tiny little porch of the very old chapel belonging to the old country house hotel where we were getting married.

I was grinning and ready for the off, and Dad – who was tone deaf – hearing the music, and saying: 'Is that our song, chicken?'

'No, it's Elvis,' I laughed, high on happiness.

The music was Pachelbel's Canon in D, which Eddie kept saying was by Packie O'Dell, because he'd wanted us to have Irish music.

My arm slipped through Dad's, and he reached with his other hand, held my fingers tightly. 'I'm always here, chicken,' he said, suddenly serious. 'Always. Dan is a great man: wouldn't have let anyone else take you from us, but we're always here. *I'm* always here.'

Dad was tall, too. Is tall. The only member of the family as tall as I am. His hair is like an old lion's mane: golden bits and grey streaks and worn too long for his own poor mother, long departed, who used to say, 'Lorcan, would you cut your hair! Or even brush it!' and everyone else would grin because Dad would not be Dad if he wasn't running a big hand through his mane of hair, making it go every which way.

Someone from the hotel stuck their head into the porch. 'Are you ready?' she whispered, a hint of the frantic about her voice.

We were the first civil wedding of the day because the tiny chapel was always fully booked for people who wanted the peace of a place of worship for their civil ceremony and also, because it has a genuine Harry Clark stained-glass window of a Madonna who looks like an ingénue 1930s movie star with smudgy eyeliner in the nave.

Dad had smiled at me and squeezed my hand tighter.

I leaned over and kissed him on the cheek. 'Right back at you, Dad,' I'd said.

The wedding party had been glorious. Fun. Not a hint of stress.

'I want it to be lovely and let nobody worry about if their daughter wants to wear her new jeans, or if their husband has to keep rushing off to the bar to look at the match on Sky Sports,' I'd insisted in advance. 'We don't fuss and I don't want our wedding to be about fuss.'

'Another reason I love you, woman,' Dan had said, burying his face in my neck. 'I won't wear jeans.'

I laughed. 'Ah now, Conroy,' I said. 'No teasing or there'll be no conjugals for a month.'

He saluted. 'Message received. No jeans, ma'm! There's no big match on, either. I'm not daft.'

Unlike Dan's first wedding, this one was non-religious, small and intimate. The guest list was short – just family and genuinely close friends. Because Dan's father was no longer alive, we had plans to take care of his mother, Betty, so that she didn't get stressed or feel left out. Watching her two tall sons, Dan and Zed (actually Ed, but he put a Z in there when he was ten and it stuck), both so full of confidence and energy, Louis Conroy had been just like them.

*We'll take care of Betty*, I mentally assured the long-dead Louis, determined that at this wedding, her needs would be paramount.

Lexi, a perfect little flower girl in pale pink tulle and silk, had taken off her shoes and played sliding with all the other children on the glossy wooden floors in the specially designated room adjoining the reception area. Liam, a stocky eighteen-month-old, was happy to be glued to his Nana

Betty because she fed him whatever he wanted.

Scarlett and I had accompanied Mum and Betty shopping to get wedding outfits.

'Tell her no second-hand shops,' Dad had roared as we whisked Mum off. 'Let her spend a few shekels, for God's sake!'

Mum had chuckled affectionately. 'Yes, Lorcan,' she said out loud. We left the house. 'That dressing-gown he loves, the purple silk one – straight out of the Vincent de Paul shop in Dundrum,' she said. 'He knows well where I got it. Loves it.'

'You could wear that to the wedding and look fabulous,' I said, 'but this is about Betty. She had an awful time with Dan's first wedding. Trying to compete with the Markham money nearly gave her a nervous breakdown, from what Dan tells me. I think the doctor gave her Valium for the day.'

Mum settled into the front seat. 'She won't need Valium at your wedding, darling. Unless Eddie asks her to dance, that is. He feels not enough people know "Doing the Lambeth Walk".'

Eddie was mad to dance on the day, but he dutifully played his role because Dad told him to.

Betty and Mum had looked stunning, although Betty kept telling everyone that it was amazing what good value was to be had in the little shops in the city centre these days. 'Less than a hundred euros for the whole outfit,' she said delightedly to all and sundry, and Scarlett and I beamed at each other, because Scarlett had hastily unpinned price labels on anything Betty liked and when she made a choice, Scarlett produced a label for €80 and said with just the right amount of surprise: 'Isn't that great? You picked one from the sale.'

Using Dan's credit card, she secretly paid for it all, far

more than €80, and Betty was delighted, dignity intact.

My first dance with my new husband was glorious – I love music and will sway to anything, but Dan, he has magic in his bones and with his arms around me, one large hand held firmly against my back, I can flow into a waltz with the best of them.

We'd picked 'It Had To Be You', by Michael Bublé, no arguments whatsoever.

'It *had* to be you,' murmured Dan as we rotated round the dance floor, all eyes upon us. But he danced as if it were just us alone, his breath close to my ear and my head resting on his shoulder.

'Right back at you, husband,' I murmured. 'Nobody else.'

When the music ended, Dan kissed me very softly on the forehead, then on the lips and the small audience whooped, at which point Dad had grabbed me. He hugged me and said 'I'm so happy for you, little girl,' which was his affectionate nickname for me because he knew how I'd once longed to be tiny.

The band, finally allowed to play, struck up a spirited rendition of 'Proud Mary' and we were off, whirling round the floor. Before long, Dad being Dad, had urged half the wedding party onto the floor and the band had been asked to play another Tina Turner classic, 'Shake a Tail Feather'. Dad was energetically demonstrating just how to shake it.

On that glorious evening, his energy was infectious.

I look at him now in his wheelchair and the memory of my wedding day seems as if it happened with another person playing my father.

Stroke guidebooks and specialist nurses tell you to treat your beloved person normally, to talk to them, tell them things as if nothing has changed. I try, I really do. Yet deep inside me, somewhere I wouldn't be able to point to on a biological map of the human body, I feel his absence. I don't see him behind those eyes anymore.

The MRI and endless neurological tests pointed to major brain damage because of the infarcts on both sides of his brain and despite the plasticity of the brain and the research on how neural pathways can improve, his particular damage is plainly irreversible. But still, we all try. Because we love him. Even this bit of him left to us.

Nobody can bear to imagine life without him.

Dan and I sometimes quietly discuss what his life is like now.

Would we want to be in that wheelchair if we were the ones lost in another world, not able to physically function in this one? There's no cute Pinterest quote for that.

'Please don't let that be me in that chair, that bed,' Dan says sometimes, when we've talked about my father and what the future holds for him. 'Find a way to end it.'

'We live in the wrong country,' I remind him, in a conversation we've had so many times before. 'We can't choose. When it's early enough to choose, people want to hold on to life. And when they've gone too far down the rabbit hole, it's too late for them to choose.'

'Hi Dad,' I say cheerfully now, 'how are you today?' and I begin the stream of chatter I have perfected as a way to make sure I am both communicating with him and not stopping long enough to leave gaps where he once would have answered back.

I can't bear that he cannot answer back. It hurts so much; therefore, chatting blithely covers it up. As a woman who can talk her way through demonstrations of how to cook an entire dinner party, I can talk blithely with the best of them.

'I want to show him this brilliant programme on Nazi Megastructures,' says Eddie, arriving in the room with biscuit crumbs sticking to the front of his cardigan.

Eddie loves biscuits and can find packets of them no matter where they are hidden. My mother usually supervises all food consumption in the house in case somebody chokes, but Eddie must have discovered the latest stash hidden for the carers.

'She gone?' he says, gesturing to the kitchen.

'If by "she", you mean your daughter-in-law, hopefully, you old rogue,' I say and brush him down gently before hugging him.

'It's only a bit of a custard cream!' Eddie says in protest. 'Imagine hiding the custard creams. It's inhuman.'

I grin and agree to push Dad to the living room where *Nazi Megastructures* is on hold. Eddie is very technologically up-to-date and controls the telly in the house. Probably why he and Teddy get on so well, I think.

Soon, the three of us are in front of the box and Eddie is pointing to Dad.

'See, you're smiling, Lorcan!' he says triumphantly. 'I knew he'd like it,' he says to me. 'Me and Lorcan love a good war show.'

I nod vigorously because I am not up to speaking.

## II

# *Sometimes bad things need to happen to inspire you to change and grow*

The next morning, I sit at my desk at home and try to ignore the fact that we have yet to tidy away a lot of the household stuff. Recipes, I think, staring at the blank sheet of heavy, unlined paper in the giant notebook in front of me.

Recipes need to be written, and now.

When in doubt, get out the serious stationery.

So to help myself out of my emotionally-blocked state, I decided that a fancy notebook with lovely, expensive paper would help.

I'd even sprung for a pretty purple ink pen to assist. I've decorated my new notebook with pretty wrapping paper and labelled a whole section: 'New Ideas'.

Inexplicably, none of this has helped. I am focusing and the magic has not happened. Bad things have not helped me to grow. They've just made me reliant on sleeping tablets.

Where are you, bloody Mildred, when I need you for ideas? I demand. Quiet now, huh? Only pop up to belittle me.

*Real chefs don't get blocked*, Mildred says.

The inner voice is right. I am not a real chef, clearly. I am an imposter. Poster girl for Imposter Syndrome. Sorry, poster forty-two-year-old woman, I amend. When I look in the mirror, Mildred rarely ceases to remind me that younger, far more talented chefs are rising up behind me in a great wave. My career could be over in a flash.

*And whose fault is that? Yours. Moping around. The world is in chaos – you were only mugged. Stop whining.*

Mildred knows how to draw blood, I can tell you.

I wish she were like Alexa or Siri or one of the computer/phone helpers and I could just tell her to shut off, but with inner voices, you can't: they keep at it.

I never had such a vicious inner voice till Dad's stroke and then my mugging, but somehow, the combination of the two have turned the normal *would it kill you to learn how to dress better?* into a critic who turns my worst fears into words and bounces them into my mind. Bitchily, I might add.

In order to distance this inner voice, I started calling her Mildred.

A name like Mildred – sweet, fond of floral dresses and cardigans she knits herself – would neutralise things.

Wrong.

Mildred is lethal. She could rip the world's self-help gurus apart in half a day.

I sigh, look at my paper and draw a flower, then a couple of badly-shaped eggs in the top corner. Then a wonky chicken. Unlike Liam or my mother, I have never been God's gift to art.

Chicken. What else can we do with chicken?

I have spatchcocked it, roasted it, doused it with lemon, olive oil and vine tomatoes. I have taught people how to stir-fry healthy, speedy foods for when they race in from work tired and need good food for their families. I have made it with Asian and Indian influences, bashed lemongrass into it and shredded it for healthy grain salads complete with bulgur, quinoa and jewelled pomegranate seeds. I have done everything with bloody chicken except serve it raw, which is never a good plan.

Once upon a time, the ideas for recipes flooded in without me having to make an effort. I could magic a new chicken twist out of my head with half an hour of meandering in my pantry and some glorious cookery alchemy. I did not appreciate that at the time. Now, when the flooding-in bit has gone, I am like an icing bag with all the icing squeezed out.

I fiddle around a bit with ideas but I am borrowing from other people and I know it. That is the kiss of death for my career.

I have to phone my agent about this.

Paddy, who runs a big agency between Dublin and London, has time for all his mainly non-fiction clients, and disproves all those jokes about agents being tough as old boots. He would give me a kidney if I asked, never mind giving me sound advice.

But if I phone Paddy, if I actually say: 'I have no recipes: my mind has dried up,' then I would be making it all real. I would be saying that my career is in trouble. That I am not going to be able to fulfil either of my contracts, TV series or book. And I can't do that. I have a family, responsibilities. I need to sort this out on my own.

That's how I do things. On my own.

Still, when the phone rings, I drop the pretty purple ink pen like a shot and answer it.

It's Dan.

'Hi, love,' he says and I can hear the gulp in his voice. 'Adele Markham was on to me this morning. The make-up, whatchamacallit, launch is this weekend and that's when Elisa would love to see Lexi.'

'Well, she can't,' I rage. 'She's doing her end-of-term exams.'

'Elisa WhatsApped Lexi, apparently, and it seems she can.'

I would sweep my fancy notebook to the floor with irritation if the desk wasn't so chock full of stuff that it would take at least two piles of mail with it.

Elisa, with her peanut-sized brain, has outfoxed me. This explains how jellyfish are still a species.

'I will kill the bitch,' I hiss.

'Freya,' says Dan, clearly startled.

'Meet Freya the Slayer,' I say. I am sounding unhinged.

*You go, girl,* shrieks Mildred. *Bet you'd get a nail gun in Lidl! They have everything. We should go now!*

'Freya, we have to do this, for Lexi's sake.'

'Yes, I know, for Lexi,' I say and I grind my teeth. My teeth-grinding is increasing too. At this rate, I won't need a nut cracker. I'll be able to crack any nut myself with my teeth.

That's the recipe thinking session over for this morning, I decide. I will worry about it next week. Now, I just have to worry about Saturday.

*

I haven't seen Elisa in the flesh for some time and when I do, the whole early Saturday morning of Lexi trying on every item she owns gets pushed to the back of my mind. Because Elisa is, and there is no other way of saying this, a green-tinged tan colour. I don't mean her clothes. Her clothes are perfectly OK if you like that sort of *I'm a twenty-four year-old going to a night club* look (Elisa is not twenty-four and is not going to a night club, but I am not here to be bitchy, oh no).

However, Surella appeared to have created, among their other products, a new high-speed fake tan that turns the wearer bronze with an unmistakable hint of green. I had the same problem myself once with a very famous tan that made other people a glowing brown and made me look like I was a troll's love child.

I wonder if it's a trick of the light, because these Surella people are clearly spending money on the marketing and launch. Would they have let Elisa out if she was channelling Shrek? Or have the chemicals in tan affected their minds? Too long in the lab, and all that . . .?

The launch this Saturday morning (*for brunch with Prosecco!!!* as the invitation gushes) is in a very glamorous hotel called The Mercer where a large and achingly trendy room has been rented out.

And then Dan moves closer to me and whispers: 'Is she, like, green?'

I love him fiercely at that moment. We are a team again, which we have not been for the past few days since he broke the news of this meeting.

'It could be the lights,' I say, trying to be someone kind and nice. I mean, I *have* to sometimes.

We both look up.

The lights in The Mercer Hotel are a subtle off-white, perfect for the launch of a new product. The lights are not at fault.

From the lack of other non-Surella people and the scurrying around of two assistants putting neon-pink Surella bags on a long table and adjusting the flowers alongside a big cardboard Surella stand, it is obvious that we are not there for the launch as such.

It appears that Elisa has organised this so that Lexi, Dan and I are there for the pre-launch. In other words, the bit before anybody gets there. Her mother isn't even there yet, for which I am grateful.

The thought of Adele Markham descending upon me

like a designer vulture, all clattering genuine Chanel pearls and diamonds that would take the sight out of your eyes, is enough to give me a headache.

Elisa has invited us along early so that Lexi can look around, marvel at how terribly beautiful and glamorous it all is and then leave.

I figure that this scheduling plan is because of two things: one, which I have always suspected, is that nothing will age the endlessly 'youthful' Elisa faster than having it made obvious that she actually is thirty-nine and has given birth to a now fourteen-year-old daughter. And two, she doesn't like sharing the limelight and I'm a lot more famous than she is.

None of this is apparently affecting Lexi, who is looking around the way she used to walk around Santa's grotto at Christmas in those early childhood days when there were sometimes real reindeer, or sometimes just fluffy big ones that she wanted to bring home with her.

Once, memorably, there was an over-refreshed Santa who reeked of whiskey. It didn't matter – it was all magic. There is a lot less magic today in watching Elisa wandering around with big heated rollers still on the top of her head to get that ever-important crown lift. She is shoehorned into a lizard-print stretchy fabric that would be a dress if there was more of it, and it has to be said, she's thin.

Not-eating thin? Liposuction thin? Vodka, cigarettes and cocaine diet thin?

'It's all beautiful,' Lexi breathes.

Finally, Dan and I chance another glance at each other. We are on the same page on this one. We don't want our little girl to get hurt. That's all that matters. And if Shrek hurts her, the bitch inside me will emerge pretty quickly.

*You never used to be this aggressive before the parking garage incident,* says Mildred.

Oh, shut up.

We have been standing there for five minutes, having been let in by a tall, leggy blonde also wearing distinctly nightclub clothes, who then ran over to Elisa and told her, but beyond a limp wave in our direction, Elisa is still glued to her phone and has not come over to greet us.

To my mind, she's looking amazing despite the subtle greeny gold of the tan. Up close, the thinness looks like yoga-muscled thinness, which makes me feel envious. *I want muscles from holding Warrior Two for five minutes and a belly that is definitely not held in with suck-it-in undergarments. But I have no time in my life for yoga and—*

*You could do yoga yourself in the morning, the way you pretend to when you talk to journalists.* As ever, Mildred is helping. Not.

'Perhaps Elisa's too busy today.' As soon as I say it, I regret the words. This is about Lexi. Not me.

Not me being jealous of where this other woman will fit into my daughter's life. Or jealousy over where she once fitted into my husband's life.

'But we can wait—' I begin.

Too late.

I have pushed Dan's buttons and he's irritated with Elisa.

'Come on,' he growls, steering our daughter in the direction of the woman he once married.

Dan does not have a 'let's pretend' voice – another reason I love him. He is straight as a die. Honest. While I feel spectacularly dishonest because I hate being here for a variety of reasons, I can't say a thing. This is my stuff to deal with.

'Lexi, let's go and say hello to Elisa,' Dan says.

Lexi, ballet trained and walking like she should already be in the corps de ballet somewhere, glides excitedly over with him and I follow.

Instantly, as if she was waiting for this all along, Elisa beams in our direction and hangs up her phone.

'Darlings, I'm so glad you could come, and early too because we have all the press and it will be terribly boring for all of you.'

If I'm not mistaken, Elisa is nervous.

Her eyes flicker towards me and I realise that something has clearly changed with her. Before today, I've only met her five times but there's something different now.

Gone is the perpetual party girl who thought that the ultimate in cool meant designer clothes, fast cars, never having an actual job and counting many sub-celebrities among her 'friends'.

In her place is an extremely attractive dark-haired woman approaching forty. To my mind – to my mother's mind – forty is just the start of another decade.

To the Elisas of this world, forty is Armageddon.

The time of reinvention or a major facelift unless you have married extremely well or have a career.

I feel a hint of pity.

'You look wonderful, Dan,' Elisa is cooing and I zone back in to realise that all this time, Elisa is addressing Dan and hasn't spoken to Lexi or me at all.

The hint of pity vanishes.

'Elisa, hello,' I say cheerfully, because you can't be on TV for a few years without learning a few skills, notably how to sound pleased to see someone when you're not. 'This . . .' I gesture with my hands, 'is all great fun. Well done you. Say hello, Lexi darling, you haven't seen – er, each other for a very long time.'

I stumbled there but I am not calling Elisa 'your mother'. *I'm* Lexi's mother. Even if I don't have abs of steel or a beauty contract.

'Hi,' says Lexi shyly. 'Nice to meet you. I can't wait to see the products.'

Elisa smiles and bends to hug Lexi, the child she has seen perhaps seven times since she officially gave Dan full custody and allowed me to adopt her.

I am standing behind my daughter and I instinctively tighten my grip on her shoulders.

'Mum!' says Lexi, wriggling free.

It's like letting her go off on a gap year.

They hug, and I watch with breath held.

'You've grown so – uh, grown up,' says Elisa finally.

'I was fourteen in March,' says Lexi.

'OMG, really?' says Elisa.

There is a pause. Dan and I look at each other.

'But you know that,' he says easily, although to me, I can hear the steel in his voice. 'Obviously, you wouldn't forget that.'

'Of course not,' says Elisa. 'Silly me. It's just that, well – you've grown so tall . . .'

Elisa still looks startled at this. Did she think Lexi was still in pigtails and little girl sweaters with fairies on them?

Lexi beams at her. How could anyone resist this exquisite girl who is kind, funny and so talented?

Both myself and Dan put a hand on each of her shoulders but she shrugs them off.

'I follow you all the time, Elisa,' says Lexi, who clearly doesn't plan on calling this woman 'Mother'.

Small mercies.

'You do?'

Safer ground here. Elisa can do fans.

Fans, but not daughters?

'I should give you my autograph.' Elisa is all perked up now. Bet she has a pink pen and puts hearts on the 'i's in her name. Fine until you're twenty-five; worrying afterwards.

'Not an autograph,' I say, attempting my 'isn't this fun?' voice. You do not give someone you actually carried in your body an autograph.

'The girls in school would love it!' Lexi says.

Nobody in her school ever wants my autograph, I think glumly. But then, they see me picking Lexi up in a dirty car with my hair a mess and Teddy screaming things at us all from the back seat and tossing her small box of raisins around. That does take the glamour away, somewhat.

'You're right, Freya,' says Elisa. 'Instead, show them this!'

She walks, in a rippling movement, over to one of the tables where she picks up a neon pink bag left to one side and tied with a white bow.

She repeats the rippling walk back and I wonder if she's had an eighth of an inch removed off one shoe, the way Marilyn was supposed to have done, in order to keep that exquisite hip movement going.

'I picked all of this myself for you,' she says, handing the bag to Lexi, who flushes with pleasure.

'I've even signed the compliment slip inside,' Elisa adds, 'but it's not an autograph.'

This last bit is to me.

'I'm not really famous yet and just so you all know, I'm using Elisabetta from now on. The Surella people love it. It's classier.'

'I love it,' says Lexi happily.

'Now, I know you came to see this, but it's probably not a good idea this morning,' Elisa – sorry, Elisabetta – says. She gives me a look that I instantly identify: anxiety over me being here.

Elisa has decided she wants to be somebody – and that

somebody does not want another better-known somebody in the background: i.e., me.

Just to make a point about being a somebody: fame means nothing other than the fact that more people know you. That's the way I've always figured it. I make more money by selling my books and my recipes on TV and going on radio shows and talking to people around the country and doing demonstrations. It's my business and even though I love what I do, it's a job, not a calling that places me on a higher plane to the rest of the planet. I'm not better or more special than anyone else because I am well known, so I don't buy into celebrity. Except I have seen plenty of people who do. And it looks as though Elisa might be one of the converted.

Fame on my level is limited. I get recognised on the street.

But I still have to buy toilet paper and scrub the bath when Lexi's used one of her colourful bathbombs and the bath gets covered in sparkles. I still haul groceries from the supermarket into the car, still have to put them all away when I get home, still realise I forgot the milk. In short, I have a job that means plenty of people know me but that's all.

There *is* a level of fame that includes murderous amounts of money so that people are insulated from all of this, but few people reach that level. I haven't and I'm not sure I would want to.

My other celebrity factoid is that fame maximises who a person is. If you're grounded before it, you'll be grounded afterwards. If you're an adult who has never had a proper job and thought it a good plan to get her only child adopted, well, your chances of normality are limited.

'Everyone tells me that to keep it professional, family gets in the way,' Elisa adds and all sympathy for her vanishes.

'Let's meet for coffee soon,' she says to Lexi, who beams and says 'Yes!'

'Then, I have to rush because this is starting soon.'

Someone is waving at her and her attention has waned.

*Stab her now*, says Mildred.

Just whose inner voice were you before you became mine? Vlad the Impaler's?

*Since you mention it . . .* Mildred, if she could, would be rocking with mirth.

A man in an expensive suit appears. Definitely one of the people who are putting up the money for this bash. I know this because he is not green.

'Elisabetta, people are going to be coming in in the next fifteen minutes, so are we ready to go? We need some shots beforehand and I want everything to start on time.'

'Of course, Gavin,' she says, and there is a hint of the old Elisa in that pussy cat purr.

'I don't think you've met Dan, my ex-husband and . . .'

She turns to me as if she can't bear to say my name, which is OK because I'm pretty much the same with her. 'Freya, his new wife and . . .'

Dan and I stop breathing for a moment, and then it comes: 'Lexi, their little girl, isn't she just adorable?'

I can feel Lexi stiffen and the guy, Gavin shakes hands with everyone, smiles and tells me he loves my shows, and will I stay for photos, which does not please Elisa because she calls loudly for the hairdresser to come and de-roller the crown of her head.

'No, they can't stay,' she coos.

I can't see Lexi's face because I'm standing right behind her and I think of all the things my darling daughter could have said, like, 'You didn't say you were my mother once upon a time.'

But our darling Lexi is not like that: she's thoughtful, sometimes anxious. I wonder if I could possibly stand on

Elisa's unshod sandalled foot, put my heel through a few vital bones. It would make Mildred happy. Me too.

'We'd better be going, Elisa,' says Dan definitively. 'We can see you're busy.'

'Of course. Talk soon!' She hugs Lexi again and then waves, and rushes off in the direction of a woman with a comb in her hand.

Somehow we whisk Lexi away carrying a carrier bag with Surella written on it in gold lettering.

'Why didn't she say that she was my birth mother?' Lexi asks as we head to the hotel car park.

'It could be because I was there,' I say suddenly, desperately wanting to take away the pain.

'Exactly,' says Dan picking up on the cue instantly. 'Mum has raised you, she's your real mum, so Elisa was being tactful there.'

We both know that tactful is probably down the list on Elisa's mind, but she's back in Ireland and she's going to be back in our lives on some level, so we need to manage this.

'How about we have a milkshake to celebrate a fun morning?' I ask, knowing I'm at the shallow breathing point – very bad, according to all mindfulness Apps – and not caring.

In the milkshake place, I examine the goodies from the Surella bag and feel even more upset. *Hot Lips Honey* is not really the correct name for any sort of lip gloss that a fourteen-year-old is going to wear, I think primly. Although maybe it is among our social-media obsessed youth and I don't know. But still, I don't want Lexi going out and trying to copy Elisa and saying: 'I'm a Hot Lips Honey.'

But Lexi looks so upset when I say that perhaps all the products aren't suitable for girls her age, that I don't quite know what to do.

My instincts feel off. Do I hate this stuff just because I hate Elisa? But I don't really hate her, do I? I just think she's a bit superficial and desperate. I definitely hate that years ago, she insisted she wanted to stay in touch with Lexi – it was part of the adoption agreement – and then didn't. Not with any proper routine, anyway.

Lexi has a plan herself for what to do next – planning is a skill all fourteen-year-olds learn effortlessly: 'I texted Caitlin and can we go by her house so we can pick her up? Her mum says it's OK. We want to try the make-up – uh, and do our homework . . .'

Caitlin Keogh is her best friend from school and her family are like ours: careful with their kids, not the sort to say 'sure, off you go' when older daughters head off to discos wearing belts for miniskirts, little skimpy tops and no coats, no matter what the weather. Caitlin is a lot like Lexi: both lovely dark-haired would-be ballerinas who practise end-lessly and walk with grace.

'Great plan,' I say.

In Caitlin's house, while our daughters scream with excite-ment at all the products, I manage a ten minute conversation in her kitchen with Kathleen, Caitlin's mother. Kathleen is the sort of person I'd like to be when I grow up. She knows the whole story about the dreaded Elisa. And when I tell her about the contents of the bag, she raises her eyes to heaven.

'That's a tricky one,' she says, 'but listen, in my experience, with Sarah and Mairéad, I found that the more I forbade them to use anything, the more determined they were to use it.' Sarah and Mairéad are seventeen and twenty-one. 'Give her a little leeway on this, but how about we tell Caitlin and Lexi they can use the make up in your house but they can't go out wearing it. Does that sound all right to you?'

'Yes,' I say, 'but will you say it because I'm afraid it will come out wrong if I do. I'm all at sea with this Elisa stuff and I'm terrified Lexi will realise it. I'm torn between wanting to kill Elisa and wanting to tell her to get a real job.'

'Right,' says Kathleen in a matter-of-fact voice. 'I'd feel the same, but keep the lid on it, Freya – always a mistake to let your kids know that you have murder on your mind.' She laughs loudly. 'I'll tell them that there is no way in hell that they are setting foot outside your door looking like they are nineteen and about to go to a nightclub. Simple.'

'Yes, simple,' I agree, relieved.

At home, my head aching, I hug Maura for taking care of Liam and Teddy, whisper that I'll phone later to tell her all, then put my fake smile in place.

'Pizzas for lunch,' I say brightly.

I take out the pizza dough I have resting and make pizzas for everyone. Lexi and Caitlin barely touch theirs. They're dying to get upstairs to try out their goodies and they are already on Instagram looking up Surella ideas.

Kathleen's talk seems to have worked but I still feel anxious. Elisa coming back into our lives is bad luck. I can feel it.

*

In the middle of the night, I wake in a frenzy of sweat and fear; the sensation that someone is in the room is so powerful and terrifying that I cannot move. This happens a lot: sleep paralysis. It means you are not quite awake but the dream you're having is so powerful, it literally makes your body unable to move. Fear grasps me, every muscle straining because I want to move but . . . And suddenly, I can. Still fearful, I sit up and I look around but there is nothing, nobody. There was someone here – I feel it!

I could wake Dan, but I have to get through this on my

own. I leap out of bed and walk around the room, poised, ready to hit someone as hard as I can. I open all the wardrobes, stumble over the few as yet unpacked boxes. I just have to check to make sure there is nobody here. When I have done our room and the bathroom, I race out onto the landing and staring around, hurry into Teddy's bedroom. Safe. I look under her bed; nothing. In her wardrobe and behind that pile of teddies we still haven't sorted out. *No, nothing.* Into Liam's quickly – it's all OK. Chaotic, but then any bedroom of Liam's is always going to be chaotic. I know there is no one here but still I open the wardrobes and I check, look under his bed. *OK, nothing.* I should have brought my phone so I could see, so I crawl around the other side and look under there too but there is nothing, not even a dust bunny. The woman who owned the house before us had vacuumed the place within an inch of its life before we moved in and the dust hasn't crept back in yet.

I'm beginning to calm down a bit, but there's still Lexi. My Lexi. Into her room; I repeat the routine, opening cupboards, wardrobes, checking everywhere. She's safe, asleep. I look quickly into the main bathroom, dark in its avocado-ness and still nothing. At the top of the stairs, there is some ugly award that Dan got years ago, which has bewilderingly been left on the top step, probably to hold a door open because it's heavy and bronze. The perfect weapon. I grab it and creep downstairs quietly.

I am calmer now but still, I'm going to kill whoever it is. Because if any mugger dares come after my family the way he came after me, I will end it all for them.

I race into every room and there is nothing, nobody. Finally, I look out into the dark garden and wonder if it was a good idea to move into the house with the now-unkempt garden and the walls because now I can't see anything in the garden. It's just a black mass of nothingness. A person could be hiding there. I want lamps outside, lamps that light up if anything moves, anything: a bird, a fox, a mouse, a spider, one of those big ones: I don't care.

I switch off the alarm, go to the back door and open it. I stand there menacingly, wielding my ugly bronze statue like a weapon.

'Come if you dare', I hiss into the night but nothing answers. All I can hear are the noises of the cars from the road and the low mumble of the wind. Maybe the wind woke me, but probably not.

The wind isn't the thing that frightens me or wakes me up. It's the paralysing fear that I'm in the car park again, a simple underground car park, but with corners where people can hide, jump out and hit women on their own, knock them to the ground, stand over them, laugh, stand on their hands, kick them. My collarbone and contusions took a while to heal, but the rest of it, will it ever heal?

When am I going to be normal?

*Normal's a setting on the dryer*, mutters Mildred in my head.

Things must be bad, I think, if even Mildred's on my side.

It's half four now, and I can't even bear thinking of going back to sleep. I'd be afraid I'd go back into the dream again. So instead, I turn on Dan's blasted coffee machine.

I admit it: I love it too. I never used to. Too much coffee is bad for you, I used to say cheerfully. Drinking herbal tea, determined not to become a hyped-up chef. But now, I drink a lot of coffee: coffee in the middle of the night when I wake up and I know sleep is not coming again. I could take another sleeping tablet but then I'd be like a zombie at seven o'clock in the morning when I have to actually wake up. So I sit and drink my coffee and turn on the TV. Middle of the night TV is not particularly good, but with the curtains drawn and all the lights on in the cosy little den just off the kitchen, I turn on Netflix and find a chick-flick, something gorgeous and funny. *The Other Woman* with Cameron Diaz, I love her.

I want her golden skin and her beautiful hair and that wonderful face. So I sit there and I watch it again, hugging my knees in to me. I don't know how many times I've watched this film, but it helps. Because right now nothing else does.

## 12

# *What would you do if you knew you could not fail?*

On Monday morning, I look at my stash of sleeping tablets. Only four left. So it's either brave my doctor again or enter a life of crime where I try to buy them illegally.

*You're not cut out for a life of crime*, says Mildred.

She is, naturally, right. I've never even got so much as a speeding ticket.

Dr A.J. Grant's waiting room is full of people either coughing and sniffing or scratching. Must be a bad cold doing the rounds or the 'strange insect bites' time of year. I sit beside a tall man who is clearly unfamiliar with either deodorant or the shower. On the other side of me, a young mother is holding a very wriggly, very annoyed small baby. I attempt to smile at the young mother but she's not in a smiling mood. Probably been up all night with the screaming baby: that never makes anyone happy.

Morning surgeries are always busy. I have been here over an hour and I have looked at my phone, sent a couple of emails, some texts, checked news and I'm fed up of blinking at the little screen. AJ, whom I have known since we were kids in primary school together, always has the worst magazines in his waiting room. He is interested in fishing, while his wife is interested in crafting. If Maura was here she'd be delirious but since I had no interest in either of these things,

I just look gloomily at the pile of magazines and wonder if I should pick up the children's Beatrix Potters and read them to myself.

A door bangs in the distance and suddenly AJ himself sticks his head round the door.

'Ms Abalone,' he says, nodding at me.

I leap to my feet, pick up my stuff and follow him post haste before anyone else can grab him and complain that their leg/lumbago/small child is in dire need of help. I have got to get out of here soon. The door to the surgery is barely shut before I say so.

'Sorry, I don't have a lot of time, AJ,' I explain, 'I'm just in for, er . . . a renewal of my sleeping tablet prescription.'

AJ looks over his half-moon reading glasses at me. We are pretty much the same age and yet AJ has much more gravitas than I have: it's probably the half-moon glasses and the fact that he is 150 per cent bald.

'A repeat prescription,' he says, looking at my file on the computer.

I wince. I knew this was going to be hard.

'I'm still not sleeping.'

He just nods.

'And I'm having nightmares.'

'Still?'

'Yes, still. It's terrible . . .' I think of filling him in on my hideous dreams but there's no time. 'I need to be awake during the day and not crash the car with the kids in it and—'

'How's the victim support group meeting going?' AJ asks, entirely ignoring me, which is pretty much what he used to do all those years ago.

Others used to try and set us up on dates but we were always just friends. I feel something brotherly for AJ, although not at this exact moment.

I change tack. 'You know what happens to people when they have a traumatic experience?'

'I do,' AJ says, and removes the glasses to massage the bridge of his nose, which lets me escape the laser version of his gaze. 'Is the victim support group helping?'

My eyes slide around somewhere and land on the wall behind his head.

When I came in to see AJ four months ago, looking for something to help me sleep, he knew I was serious. But he told me that sleeping tablets can't be a long term solution.

'I still can't sleep without them,' I say wearily, although I only try for half an hour at most on rare occasions. I can't bear lying in bed, thinking, remembering.

He says nothing.

'OK,' I snap, 'I haven't gone to the victim support group, happy now? I'm trying to help Mum with Dad, and Scarlett's going through so much, plus . . .' I pause because this is the worst: 'Lexi's bloody real mother has come back into her life and that's stressful on a whole different level. I've got three young kids, a job, a sick parent, I just don't have time to go to some meeting with a lot of people who are all going to sit there and cry.'

'I don't think that's precisely what they do,' AJ says mildly.

'I'm sure it is and it's not going to work for me. Besides,' – this is a cheap shot and AJ will know it – 'you know they might talk about me to someone else and it will get in the papers. You know I don't want that, you know I've worked hard to keep it quiet. I don't want to be "TV chef who was mugged". That'll be my job descriptor forever. No matter what I do, I'll be Freya Abalone, who was mugged traumatically and . . . God knows what else they'll add in for fun. These stories take on a life of their own.'

AJ picks up his pen again and begins writing.

'You possibly need to see a psychiatrist then about other drugs, perhaps antidepressants. I would prescribe them myself but I think, given your experience, you may need more expert advice, and then a psychologist to help you work through your issues'.

'I don't want to talk,' I explode.

'Freya,' says AJ cosily, 'the Zimovane is drying up soon.'

'But I get nightmares,' I say desperately.

'Freya, you've got to come at this from another angle, meet me halfway. I just can't keep doling out sleeping tablets forever, that's not the answer. You have to deal with what's stopping you sleeping. You think talk therapy or group therapy is a load of old rubbish, but it isn't, it's worked for so many other people who have come into my surgery.'

'People who are mugged?' I say crossly.

*You give it to him girl*, shrieks Mildred.

'Oh, shut up,' I say. Out loud.

'Shut up?' says AJ.

'Not you,' I say, mortified. 'You know the horrible little voice in the back of your head that tells you you're useless at your job and should have got up half an hour earlier to get working on your to-do list and not to have that toffee-filled muffin if you want to have a flat stomach? She's working overtime at the moment.'

'You were saying "shut up" to the voices in your head?' says AJ.

'Not voices!' I shriek. 'It's the classic inner critic, nothing else. I'm distancing myself from the inner critic by calling her Mildred: that way I can tell her to shut up when she's annoying me and it works, because the voice says nasty things and undermines me, the way all our inner voices do.

When that happens, I say *shut up, Mildred*. I know it sounds mad but it helps.'

'I understand but why Mildred?' says AJ.

'It seemed innocuous,' I mutter. 'Come on,' I add desperately, because even with a doctor I'd known for years, this could sound bad, like I was having a—

'It's not a psychotic breakdown,' I said urgently. 'I'm as sane as you are, AJ. Just stressed and talking to myself, which we all do. If Dan thought I was truly losing it, don't you think he'd drag me in here and make you section me to a mental hospital?'

AJ eyed me.

'Suidical ideation?'

'No.'

'Other voices?'

'No.'

'Times when you can't remember what you've done or where you are?'

'No.'

'If it was anyone else sitting here,' he says, 'I would have them in hospital seeing a psychiatrist as soon as I possibly could. But it's you, Freya, and I understand the way that weird mind of yours works, so I'll give you a pass. Yes, many of us talk to ourselves but giving your inner voice a name is not one I've heard before.'

I shrugged. 'Keeps me happy. Mildred is bad tempered but I can cope with her. Look,' I stared down at my hands. 'Not sleeping is hideous and I have bad nightmares. It is affecting my work in that I'm not coming up with new recipes, but creativity does slow down with anxiety. However, I am working, doing cookery demos, taking care of the children, helping out with Dad. I have no history of mental illness, no depression, nothing. I'm not hiding some big disaster or . . .'

I'd run out of reasons to prove my sanity. 'I get sad; that's not a crime, right? It's normal human behaviour. Humans get sad, AJ. My sadness is made worse by a variety of things and no, I don't want to be on sleeping tablets forever. But I need them to function right now.'

I eyeball him fiercely.

AJ sighs. 'Fine. We'll keep going on the sleeping tablets. But I need to see you next month to see how you're doing. I'd be neglecting my duty if I didn't. We need to set up a plan not too far in the future to get you off them, which will take a while. You've got to come off them gently, detox. But I've one stipulation: you've got to go to a group for help with this, Freya.'

'You won't tell Dan?' I say. 'He thinks I'm already going to a group.'

'I can't. Confidentiality, remember. But you've got to do something or I will. You can't live on sleeping tablets for the rest of your life and I won't prescribe them. If I didn't know you, I'd be worried.'

'No, OK.'

'Support group or counselling. Have it set up by this time next week. I'll phone.'

I feel like a chastened child sitting in the headmistress's office after she's been given a telling off.

'If I didn't have ten patients sitting in the waiting room, I'd take you out for a coffee and a talk. We'd work through this. But I don't have time, so help yourself, Freya,' says AJ. 'You have serious issues but you need help and perspective. There are people in here who are dealing with cancer, are watching relatives sink into dementia, are terrified their child will die, you name it. Not everyone can get through these things. Some crack because the burden is too huge but so many, in unbelievable circumstances, get through. You've got to get help, other than pills to make you sleep, Freya. Obviously, if you feel in crisis, come right back in. You have my mobile number and I'm always available for you. Unless Carla is cooking up something completely amazing, in which case you'll have to wait till I'm finished.' We both laugh. Carla is an amazing cook. 'But deal with this, I know you can. Find a group, phone one of those therapists I recommended.'

"K,' I shuffle out of his office, clutching my Zimovane prescription and feeling like Gollum muttering: 'my preciousss'.

The small baby, whose crying has reached a crescendo, is called next as I wait to pay.

I suppose I'm going to have to do this bloody group thing, because I'll never sleep without the tablets, but how do I sit down in front of people I don't know and tell them stuff? Tell them about the nightmares, discuss it all?

I can't. But AJ says I must.

I'm sitting at home, reluctantly looking up victim support groups when I'm supposed to be spending the rest of the day working on recipes, when Scarlett phones.

'Hi, sis,' she says.

She sounds as if she's been crying.

'What's up, honey?' I ask.

'I've been asked to a christening and I need advice on whether I have to go or not.'

The baby being christened has been born to her old school friend, Charlotte.

'Alfie,' she says, her voice low and sad. 'That's the baby. He's Charlotte's second baby, and she's having a big day out because she and Mick have been trying for another baby for so long. You know what they call it when you have one child and you can't seem to have another baby?'

I say no, although I do know what this is called, but

Scarlett wants to tell me, *needs* to tell me. I let her.

'Secondary infertility,' she says. 'So you've one baby and you want another baby, and you can't have that child: that's called secondary infertility. It must be horrendous. I, I can feel their pain but . . .

'They have one child.' She's husky with pain and weeping. 'That's all we are looking for. *One child*. We'll stop at one. We don't care, we're happy, but just one.'

'Scarlett, can I come round to you? You shouldn't be on your own.'

'I'm like this so much of the time,' she says wearily. 'Trust me, nobody can live with me twenty-four/seven. Even Jack can't cope. But I just can't help it.'

I'm silent on the other end of the phone. Scarlett's pain is another ache in our family, another reason nobody should have to know what I'm dealing with. Because I'm strong but this has weakened my beloved Scarlett so much.

Before I can start comforting her, she gets there: 'There's nothing you can do,' she says simply. 'I feel like such a bitch for hating Charlotte. No.' She corrects herself. 'I don't hate her, I just . . . but she has two children now, and she knows how hard it's been for me and she hasn't given me an out for the christening. She could have said, *look, don't come if it's too much for you*. But she hasn't. So I have to go and smile, hold the baby and pretend . . .'

The pretending is the hardest, she told me once. Seeing other people's babies – because they are everywhere, Scarlett insists – and then pretending to be happy for the new parents.

'They don't see how hard it is for anyone else.'

And now in two weeks she's got this christening and I honestly think, for the first time ever, that this battle is going to break her.

I glance briefly at my notebooks which are empty of recipes and I close down the computer with its support group details.

'Look,' I say, 'I'm coming round to you now, OK?'

'I'm at home,' she says dully. 'I called in sick, I'm not going to have a job soon and I need one because we are so in debt, but who am I kidding? I don't really care anymore.'

I hop in the car to drive to her house and want to cry myself. Scarlett is three years younger than I am, closer in age to me than I am to Maura. And Maura is always giving out about Scarlett's name.

'It's so much fun,' she wails, 'Scarlett O'Hara it's the best name ever. Why is she called Scarlett and I'm called Maura?'

Mum called Scarlett and me after wonderful characters' names in books that she was reading.

I like to tease Maura by saying she could have been called Amber after *Forever Amber*. And then she straightens up a bit, and you can see the steel coming to her spine.

*Forever Amber* was the sort of book that we stole out of Mum's bookshelves when we were teenagers in the hope that there would be lots of rocking goods in it. It wasn't really that sexy in our day; although it was probably considered the height of sexiness when it was written. By the time we were growing up, it was positively tame. Maura had a friend whose mother was addicted to Harold Robbins, and we read plenty of those.

We all agreed that once you'd read Harold Robbins, you didn't need the non-existent Catholic schoolgirl sex education classes.

Scarlett is so used to her name that she doesn't think about it, but it does make people look up. She looks like a blonde Scarlett: her hair is the same striking blonde as all of ours, for which we thank many deities all the time, because really it requires no time in the hairdressers, and she is prone to smoky eyes and the odd bright red lips that drive men wild. But the only man she's wanted to drive crazy, ever, is Jack.

Jack is an amazing man, although not as amazing as my darling Dan.

Con, my brother, says Jack's amazing for putting up with Scarlett at all, but the women in the family – myself, Maura and Mum – all make faces at Con when he says this and say 'shut up, Con.'

Jack is all the things that Maura half wishes her husband Pip would be. Jack is romantic, given to public displays of affection and buys the right presents.

'He knows how to cherish,' says Maura, mournfully.

Jack gets hold of impossible-to-find foreign perfumes for Scarlett for Christmas or buys her sea glass necklaces encased in filigree silver. Pip trots down to the shop of Maura's choosing and follows instructions: 'enter the shop, turn right, take two paces to Clarins stuff. Talk to nice woman there who is already prepped on what I need: that new serum to stop my face meeting my chin.' Said gift is then wrapped for him and he pays. Done.

Since Jack and Scarlett met ten years ago, they have been like twin souls who navigate the universe together: voyagers on a difficult journey across the oceans. For them, the difficult journey has been trying to have a child.

Dan says he's lost count of how often they have gone in for infertility treatment, but I know. Five times. Five times that has put them into debt.

Not only do I love Scarlett, but I admire her so much because I don't think I'd have been able to cope with what she has gone through. First all those years of trying to get pregnant, then the endless tests, then having been told there was a great chance in one clinic and two full cycles and one frozen cycle, and nothing.

'I can't understand it,' Scarlett said to me the second-last time, sitting at the kitchen table in our old house and resting forward with her face in her hands, so that her hair covered her face. 'I don't think I can stand it anymore, the pain, the emptiness.' Her hands slid down to her empty belly, almost in disgust. 'Why is it that it's women who have to bear babies? Why did bloody evolution put this one on us?'

'I don't know.' I sat beside her, so I could pet her head the way I used to when she was little.

When people say that sometimes there is nothing that you can say, it's true.

Sometimes there is literally nothing you *can* say, nothing that will take away the pain.

Somehow, Jack and Scarlett managed to pull themselves together, go to a different clinic and do it twice again, which brought them to their fifth and latest failure.

Don't let anyone tell you that infertility and infertility treatments only affect the woman. Jack was devastated each time. He didn't cry to me or Dan or anyone in our family, but to his brothers, all of whom had big glorious families: the types made up of three or four children, a scattering of dogs and cats, a ferret and two parrots even – their houses veritable menageries of creatures while Scarlett and Jack had nothing.

I nearly hit Dan the day he said, 'Do you think that's the problem? That they keep trying. They need to accept it's not going to happen, not now, not at Scarlett's age – what is she? Forty soon? It's not happening.'

I rounded on him with rage. I never got angry with Dan, not properly angry.

'How dare you say that,' I'd hissed. 'How can they give up. Would we have given up?'

I'd rarely felt such anger towards him, not even when he was dealing inadequately in the early days with stupid Elisa, when Lexi was just a little girl, used to a neglectful form of mothering and my rage against Elisa had burst its banks and washed over him.

But he held his ground this time.

'I'm just saying,' Dan said calmly, 'that I don't know if I'd be able to keep going.'

'You don't know because we have three beautiful babas. Our lives are so full, but Scarlett and Jack – it's a totally different situation. Plenty of people choose not to have children and more power to them but Jack and Scarlett are not among them. They want a baby. More than anything.'

'I suppose,' said Dan.

Scarlett and Jack's house is a slender house in a terrace: pretty and with a murderous mortgage. It's not far from Summer Street but while Mum and Dad's house is a bit rambling with higgledy piggledy extensions added on over the years, Scarlett and Jack's home is a small two up, two down.

Inside, it's ironically the sort of house you'd imagine could never welcome children: all white wooden floors, off-white couches with pale throws draped across them. Yet Scarlett loves having children there, adores it when my three are visiting, and she just laughs and says 'It's a washable cover,' when Teddy gets the inevitable bit of chocolate/ice cream/raspberry juice on the couch.

We all have keys to each others' homes and she's upstairs lying on the bed in her and Jack's bedroom, which is equally white and yet still cosy with its nubbly curtains and a soft grey throw made of mega-chunky wool on the bed, an item

Maura insists she could have made.

'Well, I could,' Maura says when we look at her.

'If you ever have time, I'd love another one in cream for downstairs,' Scarlett said kindly, even though she and I both know that finishing craft projects is not what Maura does.

'Mum is addicted to buying wool,' her daughter, Gilly, says naughtily. 'Not making anything – just buying wool.'

Even Maura laughs at this.

'Touché,' she admits.

Today, Scarlett is wrapped up in the chunky grey throw and is watching daytime TV, one of the sadder shows about people who are genuinely trapped in their houses by hoarding.

*Mildred, please don't*, I beg. I am not going to be that person. I'm just not good at throwing stuff out.

*No shit*, says Mildred caustically.

Scarlett's paler than usual and her hair is unwashed.

'Hello darling, let's talk,' I say.

Scarlett hugs me back and then says: 'No, let's not talk. I might cry and when I cry, I can't stop. Let's go shopping.'

'But I thought—'

'We're going to the damn christening,' she says fiercely. 'I want something fabulous that makes people not even *think* of asking if we're ever going to have children. I want them to imagine us with a glorious life full of holidays and fun, and no desire to be parents whatever. I don't want naked pity on anyone's face.'

She showers, I make coffee as per her instructions and I decide she must be taking some anti-anxiety medicine. It would explain a lot.

'Are you taking something?' I ask straight out when she arrives downstairs, back to being Scarlett, beautiful, albeit with sad eyes.

'Yes,' she says almost defiantly, 'and they're helping me cope. They make me tired, though. I don't want to talk about it: I just need a hit of coffee.'

Worryingly, I almost ask what she's taking. Maybe AJ will give me those? I won't sleep, but I'd be happy.

'Will we talk or shop?' I say, handing her a cup of something so dark that it's even black-looking when a smidge of almond milk has been added.

Scarlett puts a slender hand on mine.

'No talking. I'm all talked out. Let's get this done,' she says, her voice wobbling. 'Love you, Freya.'

'Love you too, Scarlett,' I say.

It takes two hours to get an outfit she can bear. Scarlett is a fabulous shopper. I am hopeless. Sometimes I take photos of me dressed in clothes the show's stylist has picked in order to remember how to hang the scarves properly or what way to tie belts. Yes, I am that bad. But buying the clothes that the TV stylist on my show finds for me is how I finally have a decent wardrobe.

Mum has such great style and an eye for stunning colours that make her glow, while Maura has a particular look, made up of neatly fitted skirts and colourful blouses. Scarlett has exquisite taste and can wear anything. I am the one that style forgot.

*You can't be good at everything*, Mildred remarks.

Mildred? What gives? Are you listening to my mother telling me how great I am? Mildred keeps schtum.

Now that Mum is in my head, I have to say it.

I'm driving Scarlett home and then I'll work on recipes.

'Have you seen Mum this week?'

'No, going over tomorrow evening.'

I pause; saying this is going to make everything more real,

but I have to. If I said it to Maura first it would be like ordering DEFCON 4, so saying it to Scarlett is sort of the easier option.

'I'm a little bit worried about her, I dropped in the other day and she looked tired . . .' my voice trails off.

'Well of course she's going to look tired,' says Scarlett, stirring sugar into her coffee.

'Not just ordinary tired: tired in her eyes. I mean, Granddad would drive anyone to drink and Granny, though she's a complete darling, does require a lot of petting and minding, it's . . .' I stop for a minute. 'It's Dad, it's taking care of him – it's looking at this man she loves and knowing he's in another place. That's heartbreaking.'

Scarlett looks me in the eye. She doesn't say it but I can tell what she's thinking: people with heartbreak recognise it in other people. That she and my mother are on one side of the tragic divide. They both deal with huge pain.

I can't compare mine to theirs.

So I need to fix myself in order to be there for my beloved family. That's my job.

# 13

## When you can't find the sunshine, be the sunshine

In the evening, Dan takes one look at me and can tell I'm upset.

'Babe,' he says, dropping his briefcase onto the kitchen floor and reaching out. I go into his arms and rest my head on his shoulder, breathing in his scent, feeling the solid muscle underneath his jacket.

'What's up?'

'Scarlett,' I say, still resting my head against him.

I want to stay here all evening: to not cook dinner, but just stand in this warm circle of comfort and feel healed. No matter what's going on in the world, Dan can make me feel better.

'Right. Did you go over to see her?'

I tell him the story of our shopping trip, and eventually, we migrate to the kitchen table where he sets me in a chair, makes me tea, finds my hidden stash of chocolate and puts four squares in front of me so that I can eat them quickly before the kids come in and want some. Eating chocolate secretly is a risky business in our house.

He then looks into the oven to see the progress of dinner.

'I know you hate when I say this, Freya,' he says, look-ing marvellously domestic with gingham oven gloves on as he checks the home-made fishfingers we are all going to eat because I was too exhausted to make grown up *and* kid meals, 'but you can't take Scarlett's pain. It's like you think you're the family's bomb-proof chamber and all bombs can be detonated inside you because you can deal with it. You can't.'

'I can,' I say wearily. 'I'm like Dad: he could take it all and now that he's gone, I do it. So? You and Zed mind your mother because she has nobody else.'

'It's not the same.'

'It is!' I protest.

'No,' says Dan evenly. 'We look after Mum but we don't think we can fix her. Nobody can fix another person. You, on the other hand, try to fix everyone: Scarlett, your mother, everyone. You can't . . .'

He sits back down again, pulls off the oven gloves and takes my hands in his big ones. '. . . we used to talk about this stuff. We don't anymore. You don't tell me how you're doing.'

'Fine,' I say, and I am lying. I never used to lie to Dan – apart from that one time I secretly got Botox and hated it, but couldn't bring myself to tell him, so said I had laser hair removal instead.

'If you'd let me come to one of your meetings,' he begins. 'I'm sure they let family members of people who've been hurt in?'

'They don't,' I say.

Another lie. They might only let single-celled amoebas in but I don't know. Dan knows me inside out. *Please don't know I'm lying*, I pray. I love him so much and I couldn't bear his reproach, but I can't talk about a meeting I haven't been to yet.

'The sleeping pills . . .' he tries again.

I decide to come at him with a big lie: 'I went to see AJ

this morning and I'm coming off them. Slowly, obviously—'

Dan doesn't let me finish. He's beside me, on his knees, holding me close and he's muttering: 'I was so worried, Freya. Any pills are dangerous. It's so easy to get addicted, and you take such good care of everyone else, I wish you'd let me help you.'

For the second time that evening, I lean against him only this time, I feel like crying.

'Thank you,' I say and I feel utterly appalling. Another lie. Worse than before. What's wrong with me?

Dan hugs me lovingly in the morning in bed before we get up.

His early morning beard growth nuzzles my neck and despite everything, I arch towards him, responding.

'We've got a few minutes,' he says softly, and his body covers mine, allowing me to feel exactly how ready he was for me, as he maps kisses along my neck and down my breastbone.

'Mummy!' roars a small voice. 'Ambulance!'

Teddy.

Dan rolls off so quickly he nearly falls off the bed, and we both giggle hysterically, so that when Teddy comes in, un-characteristically up early on just the wrong day, she stares at us.

'Wendi the Dolphin has run away,' says Teddy in a cross voice. 'It is not funny!'

'Wendi was there last night,' I say, getting up, because I know Dan can't at that exact moment. 'We only say ambu-lance when we're hurt. Wendi is just missing.'

Teddy stops and puts a dramatic hand just above her stomach, which is where she has always figured her heart is. 'It hurts here!' she yells.

Dan tries to smother a laugh.

'Daddy!' she growls at him.

'A hurt in your heart. That's different,' I say, figuring that at least the other two would be woken up by the Wendi incident. Teddy sure can scream.

Wendi turns out to be under Teddy's bed and will require medicine to get better, Teddy announces.

Out of the mouths of babes.

I'd slept my full six hours last night thanks to a Zimovane but I tell Dan, when he asks, that I'd been restless because I was cutting back.

'I'm so proud of you, Freya,' he says before he goes and I feel about as low as I could get. 'But there'll be other side effects, I looked them up.'

I blink. Lying takes practise. 'I'm doing it slowly,' I say, hating myself.

That morning, Lorraine is over as we test and cook recipes for a corporate food gig the following day where I'm doing two different demos at a conference.

Lorraine is speedily making a tarte tatin for tomorrow and at the same time, packing away all the ingredients for the one we'll begin to make at the conference. She's better at tarte tatins than I am: she has the patience for the fiddly placing of caramelised apple slices.

I have asked her why she sticks at what she does and doesn't try to get her own TV/cookbook thing going.

'I can't stand up in front of the camera,' she says. 'You either can or you can't.'

'But you could,' I always say back.

'That's why I like you, Abalone,' she shoots back. 'You genuinely think that what you do is nothing and that anyone can do it. You'll never get a swelled head.'

'Not with you around,' I laugh.

Finally, we've finished, the catering fridge is full and bags are packed with all our goodies. We'll travel together, as we always do. Lorraine's insured on my car so that we can share driving on long trips. I have an hour before I have to pick up Teddy and on a whim, I decide that a few moments with other people is a good idea.

*So you don't have silence and have to think about all the lies?*

Yes, Mildred. Precisely.

I wish she wasn't always right.

'I want company,' I say out loud. To be among people. Apart from the fabulous walls that Kellinch House provided, I'd figured moving to Bellavista would be good for all of us because it was a beautiful village within a city.

Community – I love that. Why not take advantage of it?

Grabbing my purse and a carrier bag for any groceries I might find en route, I set off. First stop is Giorgio and Patrick's. I'm no sooner inside the door before I'm hailed by Giorgio himself.

'Freya, my darling,' he says, in an exaggeratedly Italian accent. 'We have not seen you for so long. I must give you a kiss, *carissima.*'

He emerges from behind the counter and kisses me Italian style, three times on the cheeks.

'Afternoon, Giorgio,' I say, feeling the tight knot in my chest melt. 'Thank you, I needed that.'

'We could do it again,' says Giorgio and he does it again. Lovely!

'Giorgio, sweetie, I think she came in for coffee,' comes the sardonic voice of his partner, Patrick, who's the tall, businesslike member of the pair.

'No, Patrick,' I say. 'I needed that,' I add, feeling myself tear up. I wish I wasn't so hopelessly receptive to kindness these days.

'I was only teasing,' says Patrick instantly, clearly seeing my tears.

Weirdly I am not embarrassed and Mildred keeps her mouth shut.

Being sad is not a hanging offence, I realise. Excellent!

I do not have to be Freya The Viking at all times, after all.

'Sit down over here.' Patrick bustles forward and finds me a seat, where I am adjacent to the kitchen.

'This is our quietest little nook,' he says. 'Now what will it be?'

I think about it for a minute because my mind has gone blank.

'Junior moment,' said Giorgio, abandoning the Italian accent briefly. 'Like a senior moment but you are youthful and beautiful. I hate that phrase, *senior moment*. Youth is in the mind. You just sit there, sweetie, and we'll bring something out.'

Giorgio races off and I sit there and look around. They've put me in absolutely the best place in the little café, because from here, I can see everything. I'm far enough away from the window not to be in full view of passers-by and yet I can see everything. People walking outside, mothers pushing buggies with small children, a couple of teenagers who are probably bunking off school early. A tall and thin old lady making her way slowly but with great determination towards the café . . .

*Miss Primrose*, I think, delighted. A moment later she comes in, and even though Whisper is the most adorable white fluffy dog, I'm thrilled to see she's on her own, because that means she can sit with me and not linger at the door ordering her coffee, which is what she normally does, I now know.

'Miss Primrose.' I stand up and wave to her.

'Freya, my dear girl,' she answers, in that lovely, slightly posh voice. I never realised it before, but Miss Primrose sounds decidedly upper class. There is something of the old-fashioned grande dame about her. And yet my idea of a grande dame is that they are always isolated and looking down upon the rest of us. There is nothing of that with Miss Primrose. She comes to sit beside me and Giorgio goes 'tush' and helps her out of the way while he organises a little throne of cushions behind her.

'Really,' he says, 'you know better, with your lower back problems.'

She pats his hand gently.

'Dearest, how kind you always are.'

In moments, we have food and drinks in front of us. Neither of us has ordered but it appears that Patrick and Giorgio not only run a café, but they operate a psychic ordering system as well. I have a mocha and I can smell the blended chocolate and coffee and feel myself salivate, which is weird because I don't like mocha normally. Yet this smells delicious and just what I want. I also have a heated berry scone with raspberries bursting out of it, a little mound of butter in a tiny delicate dish, and some juicy jam.

'Sometimes I give them my jam,' Miss Primrose remarks, 'but I don't have enough fruit or the energy to make it these days, I find. I need to sit a little bit more than I used to when I was younger. And one must listen to the body, I always think, don't you?'

She looks at me with those pale grey eyes and I realise that there is nothing of the faintly dizzy old lady about

Miss Primrose. She has the clear, penetrating gaze of a headmistress.

'Yes,' I reply, because I'm not sure what else to say.

Miss Primrose has a couple of very plain biscuits and a beautiful china pot of what smells like Earl Grey tea.

'I do love the cakes that dear Patrick makes but, unfortunately, when one gets to my age, what one wants and what one can actually consume vary greatly. Whisper is the same. She is older than I am in dog years, I think. I rescued her, so I'm not entirely sure. But she has an old soul.' Again she looks at me with a penetrating gaze.

'How lovely to have saved her,' I say.

'You look a little tired, child,' she adds. And one papery-skinned and delicate finger, slightly cool, touches my cheek. The hopelessly receptive to kindness thing goes into overdrive and to my absolute horror, I find the tears are rolling down my face.

I've lied to Dan. He might hate me if he finds out. Scarlett is so sad. And I can't help. And Lexi – right at the back of my mind, in the place I am trying to avoid, are thoughts of Lexi and whether I'll lose her to her birth mother or not.

'Turn your chair a little so you're more hidden, my dear,' says Miss Primrose as if nothing is happening. 'Don't want the whole village coming over to have a gawp. Rubber-neckers, I think they're called.'

She deftly rearranges the position of her chair so that she's almost blocking me from view, because she, too, is tall, although her height has clearly somewhat diminished because of her age. She reaches into a beautiful little black leather handbag that looks as if it came straight from 1950 and hands me a sweetly smelling, freshly pressed handkerchief.

'Use this,' she commands, 'much better at drying tears than those tissues.'

'Better for the planet, too. Lexi would be impressed,' I say, sniffling. 'She's very into saving the planet.'

'Clever girl,' says Miss Primrose. 'It often astonishes me how the human race has lasted so long when we rape and pillage this beautiful land, but we can only do our best. Do you take sugar?'

'No,' I say.

She pushes my mocha towards me. 'Take a little bit, it will help. There is a little sweetness in the chocolate that's very healing. Patrick always knows what's best.'

'I thought it was Giorgio who figured out what people wanted?' I say somewhat confusedly.

'Oh no,' she shakes her head. 'Giorgio is an exquisite creature who enhances all our lives, but Patrick underpins it all. Don't mind that slightly gruff exterior, he has a heart of gold.'

I take a sip of my drink and find that Miss Primrose has sliced and started buttering my scone. She adds jam and cuts it neatly into tiny little squares as if feeding a child.

'Have some,' she says.

And I do. Not even Dan talks to me this way. Nobody talks to me this way, but it's nice.

'You're terribly sad, my dear. Do you want to tell me about it. I shan't be offended if you don't. However, I am a vault of secrets, so anything you tell me is safe.'

For a second, anxiety flares inside me and I look up at her, but her gaze is steady. She must have been movie-star beautiful in her youth because her face is a perfect oval and the wise eyes surrounded by map-lines of wrinkles are still large.

'No, everything is fine really, it's just, you know, some days are difficult.'

'Lots of days are difficult,' said Miss Primrose. 'So many

days in fact, but we get through them. I sensed you had a sadness in you that first day we met.'

'You see things?' I said suddenly, perking up. What if she was psychic: she could tell me everything and explain that I was going to feel fine soon the way horoscopes did in magazines. *Wear green and Tuesday is going to be your lucky day. By the end of the month everything is going to be fabulous. You won't have nightmares, Scarlett will get pregnant, Dad will recover, Elisa will go back to Spain, you'll think of amazing recipes and write the book in record time . . .*

I love horoscopes, I often read quite a few magazines until I get one I like.

'No, I don't see things in that way,' she says and pours some of her aromatic Earl Grey. 'I just notice things. I'm terribly old, you know. If you're terribly old and you pay attention, you do see things. Sort of like Sherlock Holmes if he got to be very, very old and perhaps spent less time in 221b Baker Street experimenting with unusual medications.'

We both laugh.

'You're not what I thought,' I blurt out and then I feel embarrassed.

'Nobody is ever what anyone thinks they are,' says Miss Primrose. 'Now do you want to talk about it, because I'm a very good listener and I don't discuss.'

'Well,' I take a nibble of my scone. 'There's so much going on with my family right now and I can't fix it all.'

Miss Primrose eyes me. 'No,' she says, 'tell me what's making *you* sad, not what's making everyone else sad.'

'It's just something bad happened to me,' I say once I've consumed my mocha. 'You know when you are going along and everything is fine and then *pow*, this litany of problems spring up out of nowhere and change everything.'

'Ah,' says Miss Primrose gravely, 'I know exactly what

that's like. I'm eighty-five, have lived through some of the hardest times of the twentieth century, I understand that absolutely. So tell me, are you keeping this particular pain of what happened to you all to yourself or do other people know?'

'My family know.' I backtrack. 'I mean, it's not all about me. My sister is going through so much, for a start. You won't talk to anyone about this, will you?' I say, suddenly anxious.

'Not a word,' she insists.

'My sister and her husband have been trying for a baby for so long and it keeps failing and I don't know why, because they deserve it so much.'

Miss Primrose's hand finds mine. Her fingers are very long and strangely, I imagine them playing the piano, coaxing delicate music out of the keys.

'Did you ever play the piano?' I ask.

'Yes,' she says, 'I wasn't taught to play it as a child though, not the way I was brought up: no money. In later years I had the chance and I did.' She stretches long fingers untouched by arthritis. 'I took up the piano when I was sixty and I have to say, I did adore it. But now my stretch is rather gone, you need the stretch in your fingers you know.'

'I understand,' I say.

'Your sister,' she prompts.

'They deserve a child so much. She's brilliant with my children. You met Teddy and she's such a little pet but she can be an absolute monkey. Scarlett comes over all the time and helps me with the children at the weekend if I have to go down to the country and do a demonstration and if Dan has got work. We have a lovely childminder, Angela, during the week. But our work is sort of strange, doesn't come at ordinary hours of the day.'

'What I have found from my time on this green earth,' Miss Primrose says, putting down her teacup, 'is that we don't always get what we deserve but we have to learn to live with what we get.'

'I know,' I agree, taken aback at this approach. 'I know, but I keep seeing people who shouldn't have children but they have them and Scarlett and Jack don't.'

'They may never have them,' she adds calmly.

I stare at her crossly.

'I'm just telling you what you know in your heart,' she goes on.

And the anger dissipates. She's right.

People don't always get what they want. There's no law that says they must. If they did, there would not be people starving all around the world, parents who couldn't look after their children, diseases that killed parents and children. Those things wouldn't happen because everyone would have what they want.

We have to learn to live with it. The truth of this is so overwhelming that I cannot quite deal with it right now, so I shove it into a corner of my mind.

Taking a deep breath and another sip of the mocha, I continue.

'Last year my father had a huge stroke: he's there but he's not there, if that makes sense. My mother takes care of him. She takes care of his father and her mother as well, and that's hard work but taking care of my darling Dad is slowly killing her. She has to do it, she says, because she loves him so much and . . .'

'Then you must let her do it.'

This is not how I want this conversation to go.

'But she's wasting away,' I insist, 'watching him not being there and mourning what they had, what they never will have now. I worry so much about her.'

'Still, it is her choice to make,' Miss Primrose continued.

*We have to learn to live with it*, I think again, unearthing Miss Primrose's words.

That can't be right. What about '*the universe will send you all great things*' or whatever the hell it is?

I snuffle some more into her handkerchief.

'As if that wasn't enough, I was mugged in a parking garage and it was horrible. I was pushed to the floor and I broke a bone. But that wasn't the worst thing; it's The Fear. That fear coming back. And my daughter has a birth mother, and she's sniffing around my daughter now, causing trouble.' I finish with my voice suspiciously high.

'How can I live with any of that?'

This is the first time I've said any of this out loud to another human being. I had skirted around this when I spoke to AJ, my doctor, but that's all.

If I had been going to the putative counsellor or attending some sort of a victim support group, I might have spoken of The Fear there. But I wasn't doing any of those things. So here, in this little café, I was telling this woman I barely knew about The Fear.

'Tell me what this fear is like, how it effects your body,' said Miss Primrose, all pretence at drinking her Earl Grey abandoned. And I began to tell her.

# 14

## *Laugh and the world laughs with you*

Now that the idea is firmly set in my head, I can't wait to do it. At home, inspired by Miss Primrose, I do more internet surfing. I hate the idea of sobbing in a room with strangers. That is not who I am.

But maybe this will help me learn to live with it – as well as the guilt from all the lying I've done about my putative 'group'. The guilt is like a living, breathing entity for every half-truth to my family. Lying to my beloved Dan is worst of all. How can our marriage have come to this? Me being untruthful about the things that matter? Me hiding this inner rage against Elisa, the terror that she'll somehow take Lexi away from me?

I have to deal with this pain and for that, first, I need practical help and preferably a victim support group that takes place on Thursdays.

*You're not asking for much.* Mildred is predictably acidic.

I ignore her and continue my internet trawl. Only one victim support group fits the bill.

They might all be weirdos, I think, as I click 'contact', but this is it.

Then I just have to wait.

An hour later, my phone pings.

My contact turns out to be someone called Ariel and via

text messages, she sounds dreamy and young, peppering her text with words about 'healing energy'.

She's on the message board but full access is only available to complete members of the physical group, so I have no idea what her story is. I wish I knew. Wondering if I'm being absolutely crazy, I agree to meet Ariel outside a coffee shop in the city centre at a quarter to seven on Thursday.

'I've got this long brocade sort of Chinese thing I'm wearing at the moment,' Ariel writes: 'it's black, so that's how you'll recognise me. I have a rucksack. It's orange.'

I think Thursday will never come – now that I've made the decision, I can't wait to do it. I've messed up everything with my lies. Why couldn't I tell Dan and everyone else that what happened to me in January left me feeling broken? Why can't I let myself be vulnerable?

\*

I get there early on Thursday evening, scanning the passers-by anxiously.

And finally, just on time, a girl shows up wearing a long brocade Chinese coat and with a shabby orange rucksack. I think that Ariel probably should have mentioned the jet black hair with the purple extensions. I mean, that would be the way you could recognise someone. But maybe she changes them all the time. Surprised at how anxious I am, I go over to her and say, 'Ariel?'

'Hey,' she said, 'Freda, you came, I'm Ariel.'

'I love your hair,' I say.

She idly twirls a bit of purple.

'I'm getting bored with the purple but I'm keeping the black. My mum doesn't like it but she doesn't mind, it's whatever makes me happy, isn't it?'

I put Ariel at about twenty-five and there is something

so sweet and beautiful about her heart-shaped face and yet her eye make-up is as dark and her lips are a purplish-black colour. I feel really guilty for calling myself Freda, but I'm so terrified I'll be recognised, although it's not as if I'm the President or a movie star or anything. It's just that the weirdest people recognise me and I don't want anyone knowing who I am tonight. To that end, I've tied up my hair in a scarf which mainly makes me look like I'm auditioning for a part in a play about Rosie the Riveter, but still. I'm disguised. This is *my* secret. My pain. I have to be in charge of it.

As the secret-me, I can sit in a room with a group of people who have been scared and perhaps, just perhaps, I can talk about it. Feel something, get something out of my system quickly because that's what I need.

Like having a tooth pulled. Extraction. Clean and simple. One trip should do it. Right?

If it's awful, I can run and never go back. I'll sit near the door.

'There's time for takeaway coffee.' Ariel insists, dragging me into a small café, her girlish charm still so appealing. 'We do have tea and coffee but they always forget important things like sugar and if I can't have sugar, I can't relax because there's something comforting about the sweetness . . .'

She talks in a stream of consciousness, as if nothing bad ever happened to her but her eyes are sad. Again, I think, *what happened to you?* It must be like being in prison where you are afraid to ask what someone is in for, or maybe you do. Who knows.

But apart from her sad eyes, lovely ethereal Ariel does a good job of pretending as if nothing bad could have happened to her. It's as if this is a project she's taking on and it's nice to meet wounded people on a Thursday evening every two weeks. Once we've got the coffee, she brings me to an ancient, unloved mobile phone repair shop. Beside the shop is a shabby door left open to the stairs above and we climb them.

'Not the most beautiful place,' she says, 'but it's free. It's a community centre during the day.'

'And how does it work?' I say, my speech speeding up as we climb.

What if they want names, details? I need to know exactly how this works because otherwise I'll get anxious.

'I don't want to say the wrong thing or start talking when I'm not supposed to.'

We stop outside a door that's ajar and Ariel shines me a smile of such sweetness and kindness.

'There's no wrong way to do it,' she says.

If only that were true.

The room itself has three couches, all utterly threadbare, along with uncomfortable-looking school chairs and one very ornate armchair that might have come from another century. There are all sorts of community notices and posters on the wall and it's clear that this room is used as a meeting place for lots of different groups. There are eleven people in the room, all ages, men and women, and I walk in self-consciously, keeping my bescarfed head down and trying to appear invisible, which is very difficult when you're my height.

'This is Freda,' says Ariel in her soft breathy voice.

Everyone says hello cautiously.

I'm on edge. I immediately don't like it. Strangers sitting here to talk about stuff. No, this isn't for me.

'Give it half an hour,' says Ariel beside me, as if she knows what's going through my head. She drags me to a couch, takes off her boots and sits crosslegged beside me, utterly at ease. 'I felt the same at first. Just listen.'

So I do.

One elderly man was mugged too but even though I can feel empathy for his pain, I have nothing in common with him. *Nothing.*

I can't engage with his story because he's so frail and it hurts to imagine him being beaten, so I do my best to stop listening and look around the room, surreptitiously, in case everyone thinks I'm judging them. The room is horrible, I decide. The others are all listening keenly, drinking their tea or coffee, relaxing into what's obviously a safe space for them. I don't belong here.

A woman talks about her home being burgled. I feel my heart race. I don't want to listen. What if *our* home gets burgled? I couldn't cope.

The Fear roars up in me. I can't take any more.

Suddenly, I'm on my feet, swinging my bag onto my shoulder.

'Sorry,' I whisper at Ariel and I'm out the door, rushing down the stairs and out into the street. I half walk, half run away, expecting Ariel to come after me, to beg me to stay. But she doesn't: nobody does.

*

Melody Garot's honeyed voice and moving music has accompanied me all the way from my house to Kilkenny. Normally, driving and listening to music relaxes me. Today, the hatchback – a vehicle with too many miles on it and too many hopes and dreams pinned to it – has suddenly developed squealing brakes, which sound as if some enormous, long-necked bird is putting up a fierce fight while being strangled right beside a loudspeaker. People stand and look at the car as I pass whenever braking is required. That is to say, at every small town and traffic lights.

With my vast mechanical experience (almost zero), I know that this shrieking means my brake pads need to be replaced. But I have to be in Kilkenny for lunchtime, I have no clue how long actual brake-pad changing takes (an hour, a day?) and I know, from a previous experience of this, that I can drive with shrieking pads as long as I crawl along and get them fixed as soon as possible.

Possible is tomorrow.

Lorraine has driven her own car for once because she has family in Kilkenny and is going to stay over. I am not. Brake pads or not, I may just propel myelf home with the force of my rage/anxiety – who knew they were so similar – because Dan phones me when I arrive in Kilkenny for the corporate event to inform me that Elisabetta – we are, clearly, now calling her that – rang asking if she and Lexi could meet up that evening for coffee.

'Coffee?' I yell into the phone. 'Lexi is fourteen: fourteen-year-olds don't go out in the evening for coffee! They do their homework, have showers, and get into cuddly pyjamas before reading Harry Potter books with a few precious teddies lined up on the bed!'

'I told her that but it's a quick thing – half an hour in Giorgio and Patrick's at seven. Maura's coming over to take care of Liam and Teddy, although if Teddy gets wind of it, she'll want to go. She's passionately attracted to their cake cabinet.'

'I won't be home by seven,' I say, stricken. It will be closer to nine and I start to run through scenarios in my head where I drive at death-defying speeds so I can arrive in the café to make sure Elisa doesn't say anything cretinous and hurt my precious Lexi.

'I'll be there,' says Dan, really trying to calm me. 'It's going to be fine, Freya, love. Elisabetta won't hang around:

you know that. But Lexi has to be allowed to get to know her.'

'Yes,' I squeak, knowing this is the moral thing to do but still, the ache inside me makes me want to beg Dan to keep Elisa away from our daughter.

What if Lexi prefers her as a mother? What then?

Lorraine, who could take her pick of any spy job should the opportunity arise, figures that I am in a towering rage from the way I am slicing carrots when she enters our catering area.

'There's something frightening about the way you're doing that,' she remarks, standing well back as she puts down the rest of the stuff.

'I had to do something!' I hiss, slicing with a fierce intensity.

'We haven't got all the equipment in yet. We don't start the voodoo sacrifice for ages.'

I glare up at her and her face, concerned and wise, makes the anger dissolve into tears in an instant.

'Elisa wants to take Lexi out for coffee,' I say miserably, snatching up some kitchen roll and wiping my eyes.

'When?'

'This evening.'

'Lexi's a kid. Kids don't do evening dates, do they?' says Lorraine.

'No. Dan is going too, it's only going to be for half an hour but I swear the bloody woman picked a day when I wasn't around.'

'She doesn't sound bright enough to be that manipulative,' says Lorraine and I glare again.

'She might be!'

'Think this through, Freya,' says Lorraine, removing the

knife from my hand, dragging up one of our stools and shoving me onto it. 'Make-up launches hardly last forever. It's not as if L'Oreal have signed her. It'll be over in a few weeks and she'll go back home to Spain. End of. Just hold your nerve.'

I get home, screeching brake pads and all, by a quarter to nine, to find a candle burning on the coffee table. Two glasses are waiting for me and Dan, some cheese and crackers are ready with napkins and my home-made chutney, and a bottle of red wine has been opened and being allowed to breathe.

Dan, who likes wine but has no time for any of the associated carry-on that so many men immerse themselves in, is clearly doing it all for me.

Not that I'm a wine connoisseur myself but as a chef, I understand a fair bit about it. I still get swayed in the off-licence by bottles with pretty labels, though.

I ignore the set-up and race upstairs, taking two steps at a time and collide with Dan on the landing.

His strong arms grab me.

'All asleep,' he whispers, and I let out a huge breath of rage.

Lexi cannot be asleep. She's so often awake at this time, in half-sleep but still awake.

'I'll keep my eyes open till you get home, Mum,' she always says when I'm out on a job.

'Damn,' I say, and he hugs me into him but my body is too stiff and angry. I pull away and step quietly into her room where I swear, the scent is different from normal. Lexi normally wears a light flowery perfume she got from her aunt Scarlett for her fourteenth birthday, something entirely suitable for a girl of her age. But her room now smells of something sexy and grown up.

*Elisa's bloody perfume*, I think, furiously.

In her bed, Lexi is lying the way she always does, dark hair fanned out, her teddies and old cuddlies still there on the bed but on her bedside table is something new: a publicity shot of Elisa propped up against the lamp: all glossed lips and hair tweaked to within an inch of its life. I can't read the writing at the bottom, so I take the photo onto the landing and look.

'To darling Lexi, to lots of fun, love and hugs, Elisabetta.'

If AJ was there, he might think I was psychotic at that moment because I want to rip the photo into shreds, then set fire to them. I want to ring bloody Elisa and tell her to stay away from us but I can't.

Dan is suddenly holding me and at first, my body is rigid with rage, and then I lean into him and let myself cry. We stand there for several minutes, and while I always get such solace from my husband, tonight I cannot. He can't understand this. He doesn't hate Elisa the way I do.

Finally, he moves, takes the damn picture and replaces it, then leads me by the hand downstairs and into the den where he pours me some wine and sits on the couch with me, holding me.

'I'm sorry, baby,' he says. 'I know it's so hard. I know you can't bear her near our daughter but we have to.'

'Why?' I say, sobbing, pushing the wine away. 'She can't want to be involved now. She can't. I don't want her here. We're a family, not bloody Elisa or Elisabetta which is stupid, because who changes their name at her age? She's so fake, and who says "to lots of fun . . ." to a child? Who does that?'

Dan takes a slurp of wine and winces. He really is a beer man. Despite my pain, I feel huge love for him because he's carefully organised all the things I like for my return.

'You bought this because you liked the picture on the front, didn't you?' he says.

I nod.

Golden leaves with a background of hills made me buy it, along with delicate writing redolent of ancient times. A Chianti.

I take the glass from him, drink some and wipe my eyes with one of the napkins. Dan unwraps his arms from me and almost automatically, I cut some cheese and eat it.

'What happened?'

'The three of us sat and Elisa talked about the make-up and what bloggers she'd been talking to. It's a whole new world out there, darling,' he said, 'but she seems to know what she's talking about and Lexi certainly does.'

'Did she ask anything about Lexi, though?' I rasp out.

'Yes. She wanted to know about school, although she doesn't have much of a grasp of the educational system, given that she went through it herself. But then . . .' Dan looks into the distance '. . . Elisa and her gang were great ones for bunking off school. Lexi said she's doing her Junior Cert exam next year and Elisa said it used to be called the Inter Cert in our day, and she asked what subjects Elisa liked.'

I could feel fear rise up in me, different yet worse than The Fear that comes in the middle of the night when I relive my mugging.

Elisa was interested? What did this *mean?* I would not let her take Lexi from me.

'Why's she so fascinated now?' I ask flatly.

Dan shrugged. 'Don't know.'

My fear coalesces into one lethal spear point.

'You need to find out,' I say to him and my voice is cold. 'Or I will.'

Leaving everything where it is, I head upstairs again and into our room. Within moments, I am in bed, sleeping tablet swallowed. I cannot face this right now. Dan is ignoring the danger Elisa poses to our life. She cannot ruin what we have. I won't let her.

I have to pretend I have a cold the next morning: it's the only way to explain my reddened eyes and the hollows underneath them.

I can't cope with Dan at all because I feel that he's brought all of this on top of us.

I pretend to drink a lemon and paracetamol hot drink during breakfast and blow my nose a lot as I ask Lexi how she got on the evening before.

'It was wonderful,' she says, eyes shining. 'Elisabetta's got this plan for what she's going to do next: she wants to build a . . . What was it, Dad?'

Dan looks at me from under hooded lids. 'Lifestyle blog,' he supplies.

'Yes! Isn't that cool! She wants my advice too because she says younger people are the way forward.'

I'm sure that's a song lyric but say nothing narky. 'Lovely,' I say, dredging up some enthusiasm from somewhere.

'She wants to see me again soon but we don't know when we can fit it in,' Lexi adds and that's when I look at Dan, stricken.

This is one half of what I am afraid of: that Elisa's friendship is casual and therefore will destroy Lexi when she realises it. If, on the other hand, it's a real attempt to connect with her long-lost child, I will be destroyed.

Dan and I keep gazing at each other. In the grand scheme of things, Lexi is the one who must be taken care of. I know that.

She is mine but not a possession. She is entitled to have this relationship with her birth mother.

Under the guise of tidying, I pass Dan and hug him briefly.

'Sorry,' I mutter to him. 'It's just . . .'

He puts a long arm around my waist. 'We can manage,' he says in a low voice. 'Our family can get through this.'

After I drive everyone to school, I sit in the car and search for victim support meetings. There are lunchtime ones, helplines. I need something now. In two days, Lexi will be off school and will be starting her ballet camp, which is shorter than the school day. The summer is a tough time for the working mother, so I need to get myself organised now.

I don't want to spill my guts to anyone but if it helps, if I am calmer and able to sleep like a normal person, then I can handle all the rest of my life better. I search up another victim support meeting and make myself go.

STRENGTH meets in a church parish hall at 1 p.m. and as soon as I enter, I feel out of place. I am easily the oldest person there and while I don't know the exact statistics on crime, I do not think that only older people are victims.

'Don't pull the chairs: lift them,' says a lady with a blonde cap of hair and some sort of flowing outfit.

I put down my chair and go up to her.

'This is a victim support group?' I ask.

'We support everyone,' she says with the benign gaze of a woman who has been on many committees. 'Fiona's a widow and poor Harry is only buried a week. We got her to come, didn't we girls?' she says to her assembled ladies.

Poor Fiona looks shell-shocked, as if she'd rather be at home in bed with her TV remote and a big box of tissues while she tries to begin the painful negotiation of life without Harry.

'It's for widows?' I ask.
'Oh no, it's for everyone.'
Everyone except me, I think.
'Sorry,' I say. 'Wrong meeting,' and I run back to the door.

# 15

## *Be happy – it drives people crazy!*

The week trundles on. I stare at my recipe books but don't go into the office.

I make Lorraine cancel a demo for the weekend because I know, without a shadow of a doubt, that I will not be able to manage it.

I stop looking up sleeping pill withdrawals online and jump like a nervous small dog every time Lexi's phone pings with a WhatsApp in case it's Elisa asking her for another 'coffee'.

Worse, I can barely speak to Dan.

In bed every night, he holds me and we lie there, cocooned under our duvet, while he asks me what's wrong and tells me he's worried about me.

'I'm fine,' I lie. 'Just tired.'

Which is not a lie at all. I *am* tired. My guilt at lying to him has turned into something heavy that lies in my heart but I feel too shattered to fix it.

'Maura can take care of the children on Thursday,' he says. 'I can drive you to your support group meeting.'

I shake my head.

I still don't know if I can go back to the first meeting. The threshold for pain in my heart has been reached. I don't know how any meeting can help that. And another session with fragile old men who've been hurt, or Ariel with her sad eyes and her pretend-happy voice . . . I can't take it.

But I know I must.

That dingy room might be all that stands between me and falling apart.

I don't ring Ariel to say I'm going. Instead, I climb the stairs beside the dilapidated phone repair shop on Thursday evening at five to seven and close my eyes before pushing open the door.

The crowd seems different tonight but Ariel is there, this time with hair that's blue-tinged.

'Freda!' cries Ariel delightedly, standing at the tea table stirring sugar into a cup of herbal tea.

'Sit here,' says a white-haired woman of my mother's vintage and pats a sofa on the far side of the room. There goes my plan to sit near the door again. 'We've got cushions and everything for your back, this is the best place to sit. And Ariel, honey, you go on my other side.'

Ariel squishes in beside her, takes off her shoes and sits cross-legged like a Yogi.

For the first ten minutes I can barely listen. My breathing is incredibly shallow and I'm just trying to concentrate. A man called Steve announces how this group has been set up to help people recover from the pain and suffering resulting from crime. It's a bit of a broad brief, I think to myself. It'll take more than this place to unlock all the pain inside me. And then I realise I didn't even hear this bit the first time round: I must have been so anxious, all I heard was noise.

'Who wants to go first?' says Steve.

'I will,' says the cosy lady sitting between me and Ariel. 'I'm Eileen and this has been a really hard week. Last week was so good. I was walking and doing my garden. I did my

Daisy rituals, obviously: went to the grave, put flowers on it, prayed. But this week is different. Sometimes it comes and goes like that – you'd think I'd be used to the ups and downs. I know you all know it you have heard me say so before. This week is difficult. It's the twentieth year school reunion and she'd have loved that. Daisy was brilliant at school, brilliant. She wasn't wildly sporty or terribly academic like that but they loved her, they all came to the funeral, everyone in her class. They were genuinely heartbroken. But that wasn't what made me think of it,' said Eileen and out of the corner of my eye I can see she's starting to cry wordlessly.

Equally wordlessly, Ariel opens her backpack, finds tissues and hands a handful to Eileen who mops her eyes. 'There was a car death on the news the other night and I don't know why it hit me but . . . The person was a teenage boy not a girl but I just kept thinking of Daisy and how Daisy had so much life in her and now it's gone. I don't know if I'll ever get used to that. I'm sorry,' she holds up a hand, still crying silently. It's like the tears are such a part of her that she just lets them flow out. 'I know I'm trying to say the right things and convince myself all the time that I can get through, that we can get through. I mean Ken just goes into these silences sometimes, for weeks on end, but we manage. We have the dogs and, and . . .' Eileen's voice trails off as if she can't think of anything else to say. 'I miss her,' she says finally.

Reaching across me, Ariel's hand is now clutching Eileen's larger, older one and I think I might cry myself but I can't. I've never heard anything like this except on the TV when people talk about children dying. I can't even allow myself to think about it. There are so many questions I want to ask Eileen, like: *what age was your daughter and what happened and did they get whoever hurt her in the car because if the person responsible goes to prison that must help?*

But I can't ask anything. Because she's in so much pain and to ask would be to add to that. And even if the culprit is in jail, so too is Eileen. There is nothing simple about this pain: it's layered. It can't be solved. Eileen lives with it, day by day and this room helps.

I feel ashamed to think I imagined this room would be full of nuts. It's a room of healing. Ariel was right.

Nobody speaks for a while: it's as if we are all in silent communal prayer, the type of spiritual prayer that's sending love and hope towards Eileen. A young guy with a shaved head and quite a lot of tattoos has got up and he brings a cup of tea over to Eileen and swaps it for her existing one.

'That'll be cold,' he says gruffly.

'Thanks, Shane,' she says, 'thank you, I feel better. Needed to get it out – better out than in.' She sighs. 'I wish Ken had come with me but he doesn't see the point in this raking it over, talking about it again.'

This time, I pat her hand. I have no wisdom to offer but my presence.

Eileen smiles. 'That's me done,' she says and everyone looks around, waiting for the next person to speak.

'I had a good week,' pipes up Ariel. 'It was a gift. I didn't feel sad or scared. Imagine, I didn't feel scared,' and she beams round at everyone. I wonder briefly if Ariel is not quite all there. But when she starts talking again I realise that she's every bit there, she's just suffering.

'There was another of those syringe robberies in town. I just saw it on the internet and I didn't let it get to me, I said no, not going to happen.' She says that in a sing-song sort of voice and I'm not sure I believe her. 'So I went to my friend's house, the one with all the cats.'

Everyone laughs. This is clearly an in-joke.

'I stayed there for a few days. We even went out and I stayed late, till nine o'clock.'

'Hey,' say a few people, 'way to go, Ariel.'

Ariel looks at me. 'I know nine is not very late in the real world but it is for me. It happened after nine and I just keep trying to get past that barrier. Like nothing bad will happen before nine o'clock and after, I have to be scared.'

She turns to me, clearly finished.

'Everyone, this is Freda. Do you want to talk, Freda?' she says. 'You don't have to. It's totally up to you, you can just sit in and see how you feel.'

Suddenly I know I can't lie to these people.

'My name isn't Freda. It's actually Freya and I'm sorry I lied.' Nobody looks shocked or angry. Their faces are still warm, interested. 'I – I feel so stupid. I have this job that puts me on TV sometimes and so some people recognise me and I just wanted to be able to come in here and be normal.' I laugh with a hint of bitterness. 'Or try to be normal.'

'Hey,' says Steve, 'none of us are normal, why should you be any different?'

And there's more laughing.

'I was mugged over four months ago and I can't sleep at night.' The words spill out of me. 'I'm angry and stressed and I'm *different*. I don't know how else to explain it, it sounds really stupid but . . .'

'It's not stupid,' says Eileen.

'That's it,' I say. 'I want to stop feeling different from everyone else.'

I'm waiting for someone to give me some wisdom but they don't. They're silent, and I can feel them, their love and kindness. They understand.

And then I allow myself to cry because I've been bottling it up for so long and it wants to come out, now.

Eileen's arms are around me, Ariel is patting my back and I feel safe.

Lorraine and I had made three trips back to my car in the underground car park.

'We need one of those old lady shopping trolley yokes,' said Lorraine on the last trip, when our arms were killing us both and I could feel the ache in my neck from setting the whole thing up, prepping, then an hour-long demo and Q & A afterwards, signing books, talking about recipes to people who wouldn't go home, then packing it all up again and schlepping it all back to my car.

'We need a weightlifter to join the team,' I grumbled. 'Why does nobody ever understand that we have to get all the stuff into the venue and then get it out?'

'Life of glamour, huh?' said Lorraine.

We finally slammed the boot shut.

'I'll do the parking ticket for you,' said Lorraine, who wasn't coming with me but was going on to meet someone in town because she was still in her twenties, still had energy.

'No, go off and have fun,' I said. 'I can still move.'

We laughed, went to the stairs together because the lift was slow, and made it up to the ground level where we hugged goodbye at the door and I went to pay for my parking at the automated machine.

My mind had gone into that other land of being tired and not paying attention. We'd been up and down the steps so many times that evening: the garage felt familiar, friendly.

I shoved open the door on my floor, finding my phone because I could stick some relaxing music on as I drove home and let the stress of the demo flow away. I was at the car, bag still open, searching yet again for my keys when he struck.

I don't know how he got there without me noticing. But

then, I'd stopped noticing. Somewhere in my gut, the fear alert was probably pinging frantically, but I'd overridden it by the sheer familiarity of the place.

The first blow went to the back of my head and in truth, it wasn't hard but the shock – nobody tells you about the shock. I fell to my knees and then he hit me again, still weakly, so that if I'd been thinking at all, I'd have turned around and screamed, scratched him with my keys, yelled blue murder, run away.

But no, the second blow made me fall to the ground, my arm slamming into the ground, my collarbone breaking as nature designed, my face following suit so that I felt the sharp abrading sensation of the cement on my cheekbones.

I saw the glint of the knife as I lay there and pure terror meant I was unable to move.

'Gimme your bag,' he said, his voice croaky and I shook, unable to do anything but smell the dirt of the street, of long unwashed clothes, the pungency of drugs.

'Your fucking bag!' he hissed again, and I moved, wincing at the pain of my body.

He ripped it off my arm and ran, leaving me lying on the ground with fear.

'It made me scared,' I say now. 'Really scared. I moved house because I wanted walls to hide behind. My daughter's birth mother is back and it makes me terrified. My father had a stroke months before and now I see illness everywhere. We're so vulnerable,' I cry out loud. 'I can't stop any of it.'

Ariel hands over the tissues, I murmur thanks and let the tears flow.

'We don't give advice here,' says Steve, 'but we talk about what works for us. Anyone got any wisdom for Freya,' says Steve.

Nobody says anything for a full minute but the silence is OK, not weird.

'I come here because nobody judges and because here, I know that I'm not alone. Nobody tells me I should be "over Daisy", or that if I take up a hobby, it'll help. Here, I learn to live with it,' says Eileen, and puts an arm round me. 'That's as good as it gets.'

I nod and still cry, but there's more relief in my tears now. Living with it.

I've no idea how to do that but if that's what works, then that's what works. Because anger and avoidance don't.

People talk and I sort of listen until a very quiet woman with long, mouse-coloured hair begins to speak. She looks at me as she does so.

'I'm Farrah and I was attacked by a couple of teenagers. They stole my bag, kicked me, scared me,' she says. 'It was four years ago and the police told me there wasn't much hope of finding them. I don't know if it would make any difference if they did,' she says. 'It made me jumpy, I jump at the slightest thing and sometimes I get really angry and I don't know why. I'm on antidepressants but I'm still scared. It took me ages to come in here. I still don't know why I'm not better. That makes me angry.'

I stare at Farrah, shocked.

'You just said everything I feel,' I say. 'Like I should be over it and yet my temper is on hair trigger and I never used to be like that and, and I do jump at everything. We moved in to a new house and I'm scared when I look out the window at night because all I can see are these black dark shapes and I imagine they're intruders. I never used to be that sort of person. I keep thinking we could get a better alarm or . . .'

'You want to be safe,' says Farrah, shrugging, 'but safe doesn't come from the locks and the alarms. I know that because I did it and I still don't feel safe. Safe is an inside job.'

I grin.

'That's brilliant,' I say.

'Yeah,' said Ariel, 'it is, isn't it? Helps me.'

The meeting goes on for another forty minutes and stops when someone comes round with tea and some very nice biscuits with coffee icing that I'd never have looked at before in the supermarket. But now in this cosy, safe, place they are delicious and I eat six of them in a row. I love sitting here in this dull little room with these people I hardly know, but there is a connection between us all. Steve works in a bank and the bank was held up by armed robbers. There was coun-selling but not enough for him and he still feels scared. He can't tell anyone, not his wife, his kids, his bosses. 'Everyone else is fine. Except me.'

He's afraid he'll lose his job and he needed something else. He started the website and I can understand its quirkiness the more I listen to him, because he's pretty quirky.

'I don't think anyone else understands it unless you have been through it,' he says, 'and we all have different stories. But somehow they brought us together and we try to get better,' he shrugs. 'It's simple. If I'm feeling stressed during the week I hit the chat room and send out a message. Someone always gets back. I'm not alone. There's loads of us around the country and not everyone can get here, but when you can get here you feel good, a bit more normal.'

'Speak for yourself,' laughs Shane, the shaven-headed guy.

We end by holding hands and saying we are here for each other and we are here for ourselves.

'Do come back,' says everyone, as Ariel and I walk out the door.

Even though I hadn't wanted to go, now that I have, I

almost don't want to walk away. I'd had visions of a crowd of people telling me to 'get over it' and 'be strong, you can do it!' like my old gym teacher yelling at us all to get out onto the basketball court on days when the rain came down like shards of glass.

But this had been nothing like that. We'd all shared stories and nobody had commented that one person's tale was less important. There was no scale of fear. No points system for our pain. And after comparing what I'd been through with the tragedy of Dad's stroke, and the ongoing agony of Scarlett desperately trying for a baby, it felt good to talk about what I was going through.

'Eileen lost her daughter fifteen years ago,' Ariel says, as we walk down the stairs.

I can't even comment on what Eileen has gone through – since having children, the concept of losing a child means I cannot even look at news of war on the TV.

Copping out? Definitely. But right now, I can't. Still, what's happened to Eileen is hideous and my mind turns to Lexi, Teddy and Liam: what if this happened to them? I feel weak. I don't think I could continue to exist if they weren't in the world. But nothing *is* happening to them – except that Lexi's birth mother is back in Ireland and really, is that the end of the world . . .?

'And you were mugged too,' I say to Ariel.

'Yeah,' says Ariel, 'but I have had that other stuff happen to me too, it's just this group, I sort of like this group best because we talk about all different sorts of stuff. I go to another group too. They all help.'

I want to ask her what other stuff but I'm afraid to in case I hurt her or insult her. Down on the street she looks me in the eye. She really is so young and pretty and I can imagine some mother going out of her mind at Ariel's insane ugly clothes and the hair that does nothing for her beautiful little pixie face. But it's clearly a way of hiding herself.

'I was raped,' she says, really quietly as we leave, 'so I go to a rape support group and that's great, but everything leaves a mark you know, lots of marks.'

'Raped?' I repeat.

Ariel shrugs and doesn't meet my eyes, as if she's used to this reaction: the reaction of people who suddenly realise they have nothing they can say because how can two terrible things happen to a person, one far more soul-destroying than anything that's happened to me.

'Can I hug you?' I ask.

Ariel's face brightens.

'Yes. It's men I have a problem with. But I like you, Freda/Freya/telly person.'

There is a points system for pain, I think: Eileen and Ariel win. If they can function in the world and smile, I can too.

*Be* the happiness? It's worth a try, I guess.

# 16

# Many people are in pain – you just can't see it

Watching my mother laying out the lavender hand cream for my father hits me in a way nothing else does: the hospital bed, the scent of the invalid's room, all of it.

It's my day to give her a break and she has a new routine, thanks to a lovely organic cream a friend brought.

'I know he feels it,' she says, sitting on the edge of the chair beside his wheelchair and patting his hands as if she cannot bear to leave him. 'I have this little routine going since I got the cream. It's far nicer than the oils I used to use. His skin gets so terribly dry,' she adds. 'Maybe his system doesn't operate the same way since the stroke. Or maybe it's the heat of the house since the dry spell, I don't know. But at night I rub cream into his legs and massage them a little bit, do some lymphatic massage, helps them not be swollen from being in the wheelchair all the time. But I love to do his hands too, makes them soft, and you know how your father never looked after himself like that.' She smiles affectionately at him as if he's listening to every word. 'So I like to do it for him now, just a lovely treat and touch is so very important, isn't it?'

The first time she explained the whole leg massage system to me, I had nearly fallen apart. My parents had loved each other so much and my mother still loved Dad. Here she was taking care of him and there was no glint of recognition in his eyes, no awareness that he knew her or any of us, bar the fact that he was generally calm. Although, as the doctor said when he came on his visits, a lot of that could be down to the medications. Nobody knew the answer but my father had no anger or rage or frustration. No obvious emotion at all. Not since the stroke.

'Will I bring you a cup of tea?' Mum says as I take her place beside Dad.

'Oh, that will be absolutely lovely.'

I don't want tea but she hates leaving and I've discovered it helps her to slow down her departure. Make her feel as if she isn't a woman racing out the door for freedom – a concept she hates – but merely a woman who is taking a little normal 'me' time while her daughter visits her father.

She is, I think, trying so hard not to think about the reality of their situation, even if she handles the logistics of it all so well.

'I'll make a cup for your father too,' she says cheerfully. 'Just in the last few days, his swallow isn't so good so we'll just go very slowly with the little sippy cup.'

I should have made the tea and not Mum, I thought as I sit down beside Dad and begin to talk to him. It was, as ever, a one-way conversation, but I have learned to be good at it because Mum has taught me.

Con still finds it hard to sit and talk to Dad, because he needs that response. But Scarlett, Maura and I are better.

'Talk to him as if he's still listening to every word you say,' Mum had said fiercely in the beginning. 'Maybe he can hear you, maybe he can't move anything but he will find comfort in listening to us and we will be there.'

I tell him about my day, about how that naughty little Teddy had got into the shoes and had decided that several of mine were much better off in her room. She'd painted quite a few of them, both the inside and the outside with nail varnish. It's Lexi's nail varnish and she's supposed to keep it up on a high shelf away from Teddy's reaching arms. The colours, because they're Lexi's, are all terribly delicate and pretty, but still there are quite a few pairs of shoes that will never be worn again. The nail varnish did not come off with remover or any sort of kitchen cleaner.

'Look what she did,' Lexi said, furious at her things being purloined.

I tell this story, then move on to Dan and me piecemeal painting the upstairs of our new house, which my father had not seen and probably never would.

Dan and I are almost back to where we were before Elisa returned to Ireland but not quite. She's still here, Whats-Apping him and Lexi, avoiding me and with Lexi at least, I have to pretend that this is all right.

With Dan, it's between us, a subtle wall that exists because I don't trust Elisa and he feels he must let her into our daughter's life. Yet I have moved a millimetre away from my rage against Elisa. My children are all alive. Healthy. In the grand scheme of things, as per my Thursday night support group, I can live with Elisa's presence.

'Teddy's bedroom is closest to ours and I have managed to paint the walls a subtle pale pink, and not the Peppa Pig colour she wanted, and put up very nice curtains. She still has one of those little princess net yokes over the bed. Remember it, Dad? She loves that thing. It's a complete nightmare because if she wriggles up in the night the whole contraption is in danger of falling down. I'm going to try and move it back a bit so it's less over the bed and more of a decoration that shouldn't be pulled around.

'Anyhow, my shoes were all over the bed and the smell of

nail varnish was unbelievable. And poor Angela who minds them for me in the afternoon, well, she was in bits at this having happened on her watch. As if she could stop Teddy when the child moves at the speed of light. If you take your eye off her for a minute, she's into some mischief. Angela kept apologising: to me, to Lexi, then to me some more. Then she kept saying, "Teddy, I thought you were being good having a little rest with your teddies where I left you." And you know me, Dad?' I say. 'Well, I laughed, I can't help it, laughing gets me into trouble in the worst situations. So then Teddy laughs and Lexi's not impressed and Angela finally laughs and I have to warn Teddy that nail varnish is for big girls.'

Mum arrives with tea in an ordinary cup for me and in what looks like a child's cup, but is really a special invalid's cup for my father. She brings it over to him and carefully helps him to some tea.

Another sight that makes me want to cry: he's young, he shouldn't be in a wheelchair being fed, staring into the great unknown.

'This hand cream is lovely, Mum,' I say, as I open the tube and take a sniff.

'There's lavender in it,' she says. 'I love lavender. I know you're not such a big fan of it, Lorcan,' she says lovingly to her husband. 'But it's so calming.'

Dad doesn't react either way.

Can he smell the lavender, can he hear my voice?

It doesn't matter. He will be talked to and have his hands stroked and caressed as I rub the cream into his skin.

'You go and have a rest now, Mum,' I say. 'I'm going to sit here for an hour and you just lie down on your bed.'

'I have things to do, pet,' she says.

'No, I'm here for the morning. You're going to lie down

and then I'm going to make sure the baby monitor is turned on and I'm going into the kitchen to do some cooking. Because what's the use of having a trained chef for a daughter if you don't get a bit of good out of her?'

For a moment, I think I see tears glitter at the corners of my mother's eyes, but I must be mistaken because Mum doesn't cry, not anymore, not since the early days in hospital. Which is unnatural. Maura, Scarlett and I all agree on this.

'You're dead right,' she says with unnatural brightness, 'what's the use of having this fabulous chef if I don't get the use out of her. I'll go up and have a little lie down, sweetie, but I won't be that long.' Smiling brightly, she twirls and is gone.

No, I thought, she couldn't be crying.

An hour and a half later, with the ingredients I've brought, I have twelve shepherd's pies made and in the oven, all in separate little tinfoil containers, so that they can be defrosted. A single portion each. I was making chicken soup now as well as a lamb stew. The freezer will be full, even if I can do nothing else.

'Women's work,' says Eddie, appearing in the doorway and sniffing the air. 'Any tea and biscuits going?'

'Sure, Eddie,' I say cheerfully, 'as long as you sit with Dad.'

'Sit? We have an Alaskan adventure taped.'

'I'll wheel Dad in, then,' I say.

'I am perfectly capable of wheeling my son—' begins Eddie but I cut him off deftly.

'Someone has to carry the biscuits,' I say.

Eddie's face lights up.

'I made them myself,' I add.

'You're a great girl to have around the place,' Eddie says, which is high praise indeed from him.

Once he and Dad are installed in the living room, and Eddie has his snack, I give Dad a little of the liquid protein drink he gets two cans of every day.

'Awful muck, that,' says Eddie balefully.

Our eyes meet.

'But, sure, he needs it. Never thought he'd be in one of those blasted chairs before me, Freya,' he says hoarsely.

'It is what it is, Granddad,' I reply.

With all this pain around her, how does my mother not cry, I think?

*She can't let herself. What good are happy thoughts here?*

You're on the money, there, Mildred.

Once all are sorted, I go back into the kitchen, to my soup and stew.

Granny Bridget comes in carrying Delilah, her tricky and elderly cat, who instantly clambers out of Bridget's arms in order to cough a bit near the vegetables.

'Bridget, you need that walker and you shouldn't be carrying the cat,' I say gently, and race off to get it for her. 'Delilah will manage.'

'What if she goes before me?' Bridget wails.

*How is your mother not on the gin by ten in the morning,* Mildred says now.

Because she's strong.

*There's strong and there's avoidance.*

I prescribe strong tea for Bridget, check she's had all her medication, then give her a piece of fruit cake, which she has always loved. I tune the radio to Lyric FM because she likes it when they play waltzes sometimes and she reminisces about how she and Granddad Leo used to dance at the Classic Ballroom.

After an hour of telly, Eddie moves on to reading one of his 'most horrible animals ever' books and Bridget and I grin.

'He loves those daft books,' Bridget says, fixing her pinky blonde bouffant. 'Mad as a bicycle, he is. Always was.'

By the time Mum comes downstairs, I hear her first go immediately into Dad and Eddie.

Via the monitor, I can hear her chat to Eddie and kiss Dad, all the while talking to him gently.

Mum comes into the kitchen smiling, and she smiles even more when she sees that I have made a comfy bed for Delilah on a big old kitchen chair.

'Granny and I decided that Delilah only gets onto the table because she's nosy and likes to see what's going on, so this nest means she can be safe, closer to the floor, less close to the food, and not break anything getting down.'

'Isn't Freya clever?' says Granny delightedly. 'And sniff. She's been cooking. There's enough food to feed the multitudes.'

'All of this smells wonderful. Freya darling, you're just fantastic. What would I do without you?' She plants a kiss on my temple. 'What can I do to help?'

'Sit down,' I command. 'you do enough.'

'No really, I mean—'

'No, just sit, or go out and potter around the garden for a little while with a cup of tea to wake you up.'

Mum loves the garden, although she hasn't much time for it lately. But I know it's a place of great refuge for her, where she can walk slowly through the quite often overgrown bits where weeds grow frantically, strangling all her beloved plants. But neither Maura nor I know anything about gardening, so we're afraid to go out in case we pull up the wrong thing and besides, we keep hoping that Mum will get a chance to go out and do it.

'Weeding is terribly therapeutic,' she'd always said, although I couldn't see it myself. But she sits down on the kitchen chair. We listen together to Eddie's voice coming over the monitor from the living room as he reads his latest grisly 'true facts' book with great relish.

Bridget chatters as I cook but Mum says nothing, which is unusual because normally when we're together we always have a million things to talk about. But she is tired today – that much is obvious.

Bridget goes off to sit with Eddie and my father, and Mum hovers until she's safely installed in the other room.

'Call if you need me,' Mum says.

She never stops. She does not have one of those fitness watches but if she did, I imagine her step-count per day would rival a marathon runner's.

'Will I make you a snack, Mum?' I ask when she comes back and I turn away from the stove top so I can really look at her. This time there's no mistaking it, the glitter of tears in those beautiful eyes and one solitary tear sliding down her cheek.

'I never thought it was going to be like this,' she says. 'I knew exactly what it would be – that's not what I mean, but the grief, Freya . . . the grief is so hideous. It's as if I'm grieving and he's not gone because he's there in front of me but I am anticipating grief. Waiting for it. And living it at the same time. I'm so busy taking care of him and Mum and Eddie and yet, I look at your father and there's nothing there. He's still there physically but he's not there and I think of what it's going to be like when he's gone.' Her voice breaks.

I pull my mother into my arms and let her sob. Then, with one yell into the other room to say we are going into the garden, we head for the back door: the garden is the only place I think we can go and not be interrupted.

Outside, it's gloriously sunny and under normal

circumstances, Mum would be out here in it if she had a spare moment. But there are no spare moments in her life now.

I get her to an old bench seat that's been there my whole life, from where we can see the now defunct vegetable garden – an old project of Dad's – and the stalks of plants that should no doubt have been pulled up, cut back, whatever.

I'm ready to deliver my speech, the one that's formed in my head in just a few moments, but she beats me to it.

'Freya, darling,' she says, sitting upright, wiping her eyes with one hand. 'Forgive me. I'm tired. You know how hopeless I am with naps. Some people can do it and wake up refreshed. I wake up feeling as if I've been bashed by a couple of heavy books.'

Her smile is bright, she's breathing deeply, determinedly.

'But Mum—' I begin.

'No.' She takes my hands. 'I'm fine. Honestly. I feel so guilty at all the cooking you've done.'

'But—'

'But nothing, darling. Go. It's time you got home to work. That book won't write itself!'

This is all delivered with a beaming smile.

My mother has pulled up the drawbridge.

On the way home, I think about my social media feeds and the much worked-upon 'happiness' I am displaying with every photo of me making muffins, bashing the stems of lemongrass, having coffee in Giorgio and Patrick's. None of us feel we can be honest anymore. My mother is hiding her pain and so am I, from behind the screen of my so-happy life on Instagram.

What if I posted something totally different?

'Devastating day – my father's so ill and it's destroying my mother.'

I could illustrate it with a picture of hands: four pairs of hands holding on to each other – my father's limp ones, Eddie's and Bridget's elderly ones, my mother's thin and veiny ones from overwork. That would be real.

Not 'aspirational' as bloody Nina would call it. But does Nina know everything, I think?

*Does she know anything at all?* asks Mildred.

'Good point, Mildred,' I mutter, as I pull up outside our house and prepare to get out to open the gate.

Dan is working late because there is a big economics conference in town and he's one of the speakers. It's a three-day thing and to be honest he adores these conferences. It gives him a chance to sit in on other people's talks in ugly conference halls and have animated discussions with others for whom economics is their very life.

'Economics is not my life, Freya,' he always insists in a wounded voice when I say this and I grin back.

'Not your life, sweetie,' I say, 'but you know if it was a toss up between me, say, losing a limb and you having to miss all these conferences forever, I'd probably have to learn to do things with just one hand.'

'I am hurt,' he says, pretending to be wounded.

'I'm only kidding.'

I know stuff like that isn't his life but he does love it. So tonight it's just me and the three children at home. Teddy is in bed and for once she's tired and appears to be going to sleep without asking, 'Why isn't Daddy reading me my story tonight, I want Daddy,' because Daddy of course isn't there.

But she's gone to sleep, miraculously.

Liam is reading on the couch in the kitchen because I've said he has to cut down on Super Mario to half an hour on school days. He really is such a good kid – I must have done something right, I tell Mildred bitchily. There is no comeback. She must be having her dragon wings resprayed or something.

Lexi is in her room, possibly doing something with make-up. I know this because when I run up to tell her to turn her music down as her little sister is in bed, Lexi's dressing table is covered with Surella products. At this point, she hasn't actually applied anything and I manage to rein in my temper, an irrational temper I fully agree, and hope that she is just doing a little bit of messing around.

Lots of girls practice with make-up and do crazy things with their faces that freak their mothers out. I didn't but Scarlett, at age sixteen, was a great one for traffic-stopping lipstick and enough mascara and eyeliner so that she could barely blink.

My mother, typically, never batted an eyelid and would say: 'That's interesting, honey,' whenever Scarlett emerged from her room looking like she was about to go on stage on Broadway. If any of us thought we were going to get a screaming: 'You will not leave this house looking like that', lecture from my mother, we were mistaken.

It was, my mother told me later, a little bit like hearing small children say rude words.

'If you sound shocked, they say it again one hundred times, possibly in front of their teacher. But if you largely ignore it, then the desire to shock goes. Scarlett usually rubbed most of it off in the cloakroom under the stairs before she went out.'

Mum had taught me well.

So I am ready for this phase. Or at least I think I am.

Now that Lexi has a bag full of appalling Surella products, I am no longer as primed as I'd hoped to be.

I go upstairs half an hour later to say that she only has

233

twenty minutes more before bed.

'Lexi, honey,' I whisper, giving the lightest of knocks on her shut door. 'Can I come in?'

'Sure.'

Her voice sounds different, as if she's practising a part in a play. The lights are all on and I stare at my Lexi in horror. She looks unrecognisable from my beautiful little girl.

She'd borrowed a skimpy silver camisole of mine, which is far too big and falling down off her shoulders. She's clearly used all the limb-bronzing gel so that now she is a bizarre golden shade all over. Her face, her beautiful face . . . it's caked with base. Literally caked.

She's managed to put on false eyelashes, although I don't know how they've stuck with the amount of positively glittering eye make-up on her delicate eyelids. And her mouth is outlined into a parody of a mouth, a mouth that looks as if it's been injected with chemicals to make it swell up.

She's tried contouring and while her artistic skills can't be faulted, she's given herself cheekbones that gleam and hollows in a still-baby face that shouldn't be hollowed. Worse, she's tried to contour her narrow collar and breast bones, creating shadows as if she's inviting people – boys – to look down.

She's trying to look sexy and it's that bitch Elisa's fault, all of it.

All my Thursday-night-calm goes out the window and though we're standing on the landing, mere yards from Teddy's door, I can't keep my voice down. 'What have you done to yourself?'

'I'm wearing my make-up. I thought I'd try something new, I am fourteen, you know,' says Lexi defiantly.

'But you just look . . . it's not good, you're hiding your beauty and it's . . .' The words come out of my mouth before

I can stop them racing out like an express train. 'It's cheap. I can't believe you've done this to yourself.'

Lexi's little chin gets higher.

'I sent Elisa a picture on Instagram,' she says, 'and she replied right back and said it was fabulous and maybe they'd use it in their marketing.'

'What!' The explosion that comes out of me now must surely wake Teddy and possibly the whole street, but I really don't care. 'You did what? Give me your phone.'

'No.'

I try to breathe.

'Give me your phone.'

'No.'

'Lexi, I want that phone right now so I can WhatsApp that stupid Elisa and tell her that under no circumstances are any pictures of you to go up *anywhere* as part of her marketing campaign for that shit make-up.'

'She's not stupid and you can't do that.'

'I can, because I'm your mother.'

'But she's my mother too,' she hisses back at me.

There's absolute silence apart from some half-waking wriggling from Teddy in her bedroom.

It's like being knocked to the ground in a car park all over again.

I don't know what to say and I'm afraid of hurting Lexi.

I can't believe what I've already said, so I go for a different approach.

'Honey, you're too young for all of this—' I begin.

'Elisa says I could be a model,' she hisses.

That old canard, I think.

*You could be a model. You too could be a thirty-nine-year-old woman without a proper job to her name ever.*

Stop! Somehow, I come back to earth. What have I said?

'I'm sorry,' I begin, the mother part of me rising up out of the shock. 'I should never have used the word cheap. It's horrible. I apologise. You're so beautiful, darling. You don't need all that make-up and you need to grow up a little bit more before you use it so heavily. I just got upset—'

'You think I'm a baby,' she yells at me. 'I'm not. Elisa doesn't treat me like a baby.'

'She doesn't know you,' I say, unwisely.

'She does!'

I think of all the things I should say and of all the articles I've read about teenagers, about independence and moving apart. This doesn't have to be so brutal. Why have I messed this up so much?

'Can we talk?'

'No.' She turns from me. 'I'm going to bed now. Goodnight.'

'Darling—'

'Goodnight. I'm tired.'

A hand snakes out and she switches off her light.

We've never ended a day like this, not ever.

But I can't grab Lexi and make her hug me, make it the same way it always was.

'Please forgive me, Lexi,' I beg. 'I didn't mean to hurt you. I got a shock. You know how much I love you—'

I'm saying this to her back but she refuses to turn around.

I decide that the best thing I can do is go downstairs.

'Oh God, oh God, oh God,' I whisper to myself as I take each step.

*You really screwed that up*, Mildred says.

I don't answer. If Mildred were not in my head, were not *me*, I would rip her out and dismember her for stating the bloody obvious.

Liam is still sitting in the kitchen, reading.

'Liam: bed,' I snap.

'But it's not time.'

'Liam, just go to bed, right?'

'OK,' he says crossly and hugging his book to him, he turns and stomps upstairs.

Great. I should put myself up for Mother of the Year. That's two of my three children I've upset.

Cheap? I called my beautiful Lexi cheap – what kind of a mother am I? So I open the fridge, find an opened bottle of white wine, wrench the cork out of it and pour some into one of those filament-thin enormous glasses that they only half fill in expensive restaurants.

I really don't drink during the week because it's a slippery slope and besides, I like my tea at night. Jasmine, proper jasmine.

But this is perfect for now. I curl up on the couch in the tiny study and wonder how I am ever going to make up for this. Where do we go from here and how do I get my Lexi back? Damn you, Elisa, I think, damn you to hell for coming into all our lives and screwing it up again.

*You need to think of an alibi*, says Mildred helpfully. Unhelpfully.

*And a way to kill her. Remember all those thrillers you read when you were younger, pre-kids? Ground-up glass? Digitalis? An injection containing air to hit her lungs? Arsenic? Only fifty per cent of the population can smell arsenic, you know.*

Thank you, Miss Marple, I say. No to glass. Where do you get digitalis? How, precisely, am I supposed to inject the stupid cow, and arsenic, really?

One of us needs to think straight, and where were you when I was running my mouth off?

*Inner voices interrupt after the fact*, Mildred explains unhelpfully.

As if I didn't know.

*Mildred, I need help and so help me God, I will do mindfulness all the time and you'll be out of a job!*

Mildred is silent.

*Tell Dan immediately,* she proffers. So I do.

Dan is clearly having a world-class discussion over the dinner table with a group of economists, so he doesn't answer my text till very late, when I am just slipping into Zimovane world.

**I'll talk to Lexi tomorrow, Freya – I totally get what happened. We'll fix it.**

We'll fix it, I think sleepily. I do love that man. Me and him against the world.

# 17

# 'Normal' is just a setting on the dryer

We are all late to school the next day. My head hurts from the combination of two giant glasses of white wine and from the tension surrounding me and Lexi, who is refusing to speak to me.

'I'm really sorry, darling,' I say, standing outside her door which was firmly shut when it was time to tell her to get down to the car as we were leaving. 'I just . . .' I search for how to say this. 'Mums can overreact too and I was worried about how you looked. I shouldn't have said what I said.'

From the other side of the door, there is no reply.

I stand outside the door listening, knowing that Lexi can hear me standing there because the landing in the house is very creaky. I've just been such a stupid cow, inadvertently hurting one of the people I love most. That's not normal. Then I think of what Mum always said whenever one of us moaned as teenagers that we weren't a normal family.

'Normal's just a setting on the dryer,' she'd say calmly.

This might be true but somehow it doesn't cheer me up as much as it used to when Mum said it.

She wouldn't have done this: lost the run of herself and let her rage at another woman come out in that way.

Somehow, my mother was always calm and together as if being a mother was the centre of her universe.

At least Mildred is keeping schtum.

Upset, I then shout at the other two for dragging their feet when it comes to brushing their teeth. Liam looks stunned but Teddy blithely ignores me.

'Mummy cross,' she says with a sweet smile as if this is ammunition that she is saving up for later. 'Mummy very cross, I'm going to tell everyone in skool.'

Everyone 'in skool' will know that I screamed this morning. I have no idea what the other things are that people hear in there.

Once Babs from Little Darlings confided that she could write several books on the details given out by the small children in her care.

'I have had children tell me that Mummy hits Daddy with a frying pan regularly and if only for the fact that Daddy generally does the drop off and never seems to have any suspicious dents or bandages on his head, I'd believe it. There's a fine line between make-believe and the real world with small children.'

Liam is suspiciously quiet, so I go into his room and he says: 'Are you and Lexi fighting?'

I bite my lip.

'Yes, and it's my fault but I have said sorry, and I'll fix it,' I say, hoping I can.

'She's not coming out of her room,' he adds, 'and we're going to be late, Mum. We do sums first. I can't miss sums.'

I feel the pang of knowing it's my fault and there was no need for it. I sit on the bed.

'I'm really sorry, darling,' I say. 'I want to apologise for being so grumpy this morning. There was no need for it and I love you so much and I'm really sorry. I've apologised to Lexi. I'm going in to Teddy now.'

At this he giggles.

'Teddy is going to tell everyone you hit her over the head with something,' he says, grinning, sounding a bit like his old self.

'I dare say,' I agree gravely, 'or that I locked her up in the dark cupboard with all the spiders.'

'Oh yes,' he says, perking up. 'She'd like that.'

In the car, we go, as usual, to Lexi's school first and then drop off Liam. I want to go in with Lexi but she's not talking to me and as far as I know, she hasn't eaten any breakfast.

At Liam's school, I womanhandle Teddy out and we go in together because, as we are so late, some explanation has to be given. We get to Liam's classroom, he goes in and I motion to the teacher that I need to talk to her. Teddy, wandering around beside me, is fascinated with this big school because she both really wants to go to big school and doesn't want to go to big school.

As she says to herself: 'Does big school have a kitchen in the corner where I can play?'

Liam always says no, at which point she decides she doesn't want to go there.

'Ms O'Reilly,' I say to the teacher who is young, fresh-faced and looks as if nobody ever threw her to the ground in a horrible garage: 'I'm really sorry we're late, it's my fault, bit of a family emergency and just keep an eye on Liam today to make sure he's OK. He's so sensitive.'

'Of course, Ms Abalone,' says Ms O'Reilly. She has my phone number, my email, the house number, Dan's number. I check just to be sure she has all these things.

'I'll talk to you if there is anything we need to do and I'll talk to the headmistress too. But he seems all right.'

We look through the glass-paned window at Liam who is sitting in his seat smiling, talking to his friend Jake. Jake and Liam are quite alike – both quiet children. Jake hasn't been round to see the house, I realise, except that one afternoon when his mum dropped by. I should organise more play dates. I haven't been thinking.

'Ms Abalone,' says Ms O'Reilly, 'just . . . er, your little girl is going into another classroom.'

'Blast,' I say and run off and grab Teddy, who has decided that she will go into one of the bigger classes because that's where she's obviously suited to be. I carry her giggling out of the school.

'I know there's a kitchen for playing,' she said mutinously. 'They're hiding it somewhere, I know they are. Liam said if I go in there he would be able to be with me in the playground and we'll have loads of fun and you can swap lunches.'

'Swap lunches?' I say, shocked, thinking that I make such an effort with the school lunches.

'Liam says your lunches are the best, but everyone swaps, so you have to swap.'

Pride restored.

I bring Teddy to Little Darlings, semi-explain the circumstances and leave her delightedly in the care of Babs where she happily explains about being screamed at and how she had to hide in a shoebox *with beetles*. Back in the car, I ring Lexi's school and explain why she was late in or a limited version of it.

'Just a little mishap in the house this morning, really sorry she's late, all my fault,' I say. And then I sit in the car outside Little Darlings and sob because it's half nine and look at what I've managed so far today.

*'You really hit that one out of the park,'* says Mildred, *'go big or go home.'*

Listen Mildred, I say, just shut up. Why do some people have inner voices that tell them they are fabulous and wonderful. Why am I stuck with you, who bitches at me the whole time, tells me I'm not good enough and makes me think I am a prime candidate for imposter syndrome?

Mildred does not answer this. Your inner voice doesn't really answer. It's only there to tell you that you're useless, unless you have been doing shedloads of mindfulness in which case it tells you that here and now is precious; you are a wonderful spiritual being whose very presence on life gives light to other human beings. Oh yeah, and that when life gives you lemons, make lemonade.

'Mildred,' I say out loud, 'why couldn't I have gotten one of those inner voices?'

*You never did the mindfulness,* she says. *Don't blame me. Why do you think Buddhists are all so happy?*

Damn it, she's right.

Dan is on the phone to me almost as soon as I get home.

'What exactly happened?' he said.

'I don't know,' I said, 'I, I just, I just turned into the bitch from hell, I don't know why,' I say and as I say it, I know exactly why. It's because I'm so stressed and anxious and I haven't let anyone in and I'm lying to my husband whom I don't lie to. Have been lying non-stop. I hate myself for this.

Sure, occasionally I'll buy another pair of shoes – not expensive ones – and I'll secrete them in my big shoe library and not mention them to Dan. But neither of us lie over the big things, that's not the way to have a marriage. You need kindness, respect, truth – my mother would always have said that's what it took when we were growing up, that's what she had with Dad.

She gives him kindness and love now, but truth . . . there's no truth to be had in sitting beside a man whose mind may or may not be there and saying, 'I don't know how long you're going to last, darling and I don't know how long I'm going to be able to look after you.'

No, truth is sometimes kinder left unsaid.

But in a living breathing marriage between two living breathing and aware people, truth is important; I know that and yet I can't bring myself to tell him. So I lie.

'I'm trying to do without the sleeping tablets,' I say. And even as the words come out of my mouth I feel like a heel.

'That's great, darling,' he says and he sounds so hopeful.

'I can't stay on them any longer,' I go on. Once you get started on a lie, it just grows and grows, but I am beginning to hate this version of myself. 'I was tired last night and I snapped because Lexi was all made up . . .'

I can barely finish telling him exactly what happened because I am so ashamed.

'Lexi messaged me,' he said, 'and told me she'd sent a photo of herself to Elisa . . .'

I can't help it: I shudder.

'She told you?'

'She told me,' he said 'and she's really upset. She thought it was OK, that you didn't mind her seeing Elisa and now, now she knows you do.'

'It's more complex than that,' I say, and explain. 'She wouldn't talk to me afterwards. I put some lunch in her schoolbag this morning but I don't know if she'll eat it. What if she gets an eating disorder and it's all my fault because I said something stupid and—'

'Calm down, honey,' says my husband. He hasn't berated me or told me I'm a moron or shouted at me. He's been loving and kind and I don't deserve any of it.

Maura and Pip have taken a long weekend away when all hell breaks loose.

First, Granddad Eddie takes a fall against the jamb of his bedroom door on Saturday morning and Mum thinks he might have seriously damaged his wrist.

When my mother phones to ask if I can come over to take care of Dad and Granny Bridget, I can hear Eddie roaring in the background that he is not, repeat *not*, going near a hospital.

'They get you in there and you come out in a box!' he's roaring. 'Crowd of quacks. No way. I'm not doing it.'

'You think he'll keep saying that when he's in the hospital?' I ask, mentally working out what I need to reorganise.

'Definitely,' says Mum. 'We'll be the most popular people in the whole place, I should imagine. I might draw up a sign that says: "We are related but I do not agree with anything he is saying. I love doctors, nurses and everyone here."'

'I'd add a bit to the sign,' I say, laughing. 'Write: "The sooner he gets out of here, the sooner the noise level will drop." And say sorry a lot.'

'I spend my life saying sorry for Eddie,' Mum sighs. 'To the police when he makes V-signs at them, to the carers, to my mother's poor innocent cat because he shakes his stick at her all the time. I love him and he's so good to your father but he's tricky.'

Dan is put in charge of taking the kids bowling and on the off-chance, because who knows how long Mum will be with Eddie in casualty, I fire off a text to Scarlett asking if she and Jack are around to add fun to the weekend.

Dan's perfectly capable of looking after our three children but the gap in ages means that what Lexi wants to do – meander by the clothes shops en route to the bowling alley – will not be what Teddy or Liam want to do – buy ice cream/have a go on the shopping centre's mini carousel.

Plus, Lexi is not her usual sunny self because since the

245

make-up debacle there has been no contact with Elisa and she is blaming me. I have not contacted Elisa but Lexi doesn't believe me.

'She thinks you told Elisa to back off,' Dan reports back to me.

'But I didn't,' I say. 'Did you?'

'No. There was no need. Elisa just says whatever she thinks people want to hear. She never acts on it. I knew nobody would contact us from Surella.'

'And you told her this?' I ask.

'I told her that neither of us stopped Elisa from contacting her but she doesn't believe me, either,' he says sadly.

I can think of nothing else, so today's emergency has come at a bad time, hence me phoning my sister.

Normally, Scarlett replies instantly but today, she doesn't, so I tell Dan he's on his own.

'I am not an idiot who needs assistance with my own kids,' he says, definitely affronted.

*You could tell him that normally, you do more child-minding than he does, even though he's good, but just sayin'. . .*

Mildred, shut up, I tell her.

'Course you're not, honey,' I say, hugging Dan, 'but it's easier to handle three in the bowling alley/shopping centre with multiple pairs of hands.'

*Copped out?*

He's a brilliant husband, and stop causing trouble, Mildred. I swear, I am taking up Buddhism if only to get you off my back.

I concentrate on my here-and-now husband. 'And Lexi is still not herself,' I say to Dan. 'A bit of retail therapy with Scarlett might cheer her up, and you hate shops.'

'Fair enough,' he admits grudgingly.

*

Eddie is clearly in a lot of pain when I get to Mum's in fifteen minutes' flat, and the pain is not making him any happier.

'Painkillers,' he pleads. 'You've got a box of strong pain yokes somewhere, I know you have,' he says to Mum.

'You need an X-ray and stop shouting at me, Eddie. I'm not giving you anything stronger than paracetamol until someone with medical training sees you.'

*I'd hold on till I got some Hillbilly Heroin in me,* Mildred says.

My mother does not have Oxycontin lying around, Mildred. You are so low rent, I tell her.

*And which one of us is using sleeping tablets like sweeties, huh? Bitch.*

Mildred knows how to hurt me. Besides, I'm seriously low in my stash of precious sleeping tablets. I have not been tailing off gently the way I'm supposed to be doing. At this rate, I'll be coming off them cold turkey and that's going to be fun – not. I have googled the side effects and they all sound terrible.

With Eddie grousing and his arm in a sling, my mother and Eddie head off.

Dad, Bridget and Delilah, the cat, are all watching *The Waltons*, which is one of Bridget's favourite programmes.

Poor Dad, I think – he never gets to choose his own telly anymore. Someone always does it for him: Eddie and his WWII shows and Bridget with her 1960s and 1970s classics.

Everything appears to be fine on Walton Mountain and I lean against the door jamb quietly, thinking back to those days when I was a child, when *The Waltons* was always on TV and everything was fine.

Delilah scrambles off the couch – her days of leaping are long behind her – and makes her way to me, whereupon she weaves her body in between my legs, tail aloft.

'Freya!' says Bridget in delight, even though I can see her face is streaked with tears along with the make-up she carefully applies each day. High-emotion crying, I assume, thanks to Eddie's accident.

'We were going to have tea and watch some episodes of *The Love Boat*!'

'I'll make the tea,' I say, going over to hug Dad and make sure he hasn't slipped down in his wheelchair. I kiss his warm forehead and suddenly, I want to cry too.

It's that damn Waltons theme tune. It whacks me over the head with thoughts of earlier, happier times. Mum loved it. She never appears to watch television anymore – she reads. Non-fiction only. Biographies and autobiographies. Nothing later than the 1930s.

'I tried that wonderful biography of the Romanovs,' she told me once, 'and I cried too much. So I'm beginning to think that 1900 should be my cut-off point. Before that, I can distance myself.'

I make tea and sort out Bridget with some hidden biscuits before feeding Dad some lukewarm tea very carefully. His face never changes even though he's facing the TV and I'm talking quietly to him. Sometimes, he gets facial tics but that's all they are: not emotions darting across his face, as we once all hoped. His face is now a mask and I always think how strange it is that we assume our faces are who we are, and yet they're not. We are the emotions behind the face. Nobody shows this more than Dad.

By six, I've made dinner, fed Dad his meal and am waiting for the arrival of Kevin, one of the best of Dad's carers, who will stay with him and get him into bed by half eight.

Mum has rung at intervals but it seems casualty is jammed

with serious cases and Eddie's wrist is not high on the list of priorities.

'I think we might be next but that's only if nothing else serious comes in.' She sounds exhausted.

'I'll get Scarlett to race over here and take over, in case this goes on longer,' I say decisively. 'You can't sit there all night. Mind you, neither can poor Eddie.'

I phone Scarlett and she answers when I've almost given up hope.

'Hello, finally!' I say and while I don't mean to sound narky, it comes out that way.

'Hello,' she replies, sounding as if she has the worst cold in the world.

'You're sick?' I ask, seeing this plan disintegrate. A sick person cannot help in the house of invalids.

'No,' she says.

'Thank goodness,' I say, and race through chapter and verse of what has gone wrong and how I need her help.

'OK,' she says flatly.

'Really?' I ask. 'You sound – a little off.'

'Just a bit,' she says, with a hiccup. 'Jack's left. But I'll be right over.' And she hangs up.

In twenty minutes, Scarlett arrives at the house and while she is still Scarlett, she is also not. This woman has hollowed eyes, is dressed in very warm clothing, even though it's late June, and neither hair nor make-up were a priority before she left. In short, she looks nothing like my beloved sister.

'Don't.' She holds a hand up as I rush up to her to hug her, ask what happened, comfort her.

I stop.

'Please. Don't. I can cope if you are not nice to me or don't ask anything. You didn't tell Bridget?'

249

'Heck, no,' I said. 'She'd cry for a week.'

'Great.'

This automaton of a sister walks into the house and manages a reasonable performance for our grandmother, who is now into her Saturday evening viewing of *Miss Marple*.

I follow Scarlett into the kitchen like a dog and she holds up the hand again.

'Freya, I can't talk about it.'

'But when did he . . .?'

'Yesterday,' she says tightly. 'We started to row and he just packed and walked out. That's it. I can't say anything else. Go to Mum. Don't tell her. Not yet. Please.'

I sigh. 'Fine.'

Gathering up some bottled water and a couple of the energy bars my mother uses when she's truly exhausted, I text Dan to check in and to tell him that I'm on my way to the hospital to take over and head off.

It's midnight before I get Eddie back home with his broken wrist in a cast and plenty of medication to be doled out by someone else.

'He asked could he double up on the tablets if the pain was really bad,' says the lovely nurse who's been taking care of him, and is one of the few people he hasn't been rude to because she got his measure pretty quick. Plus, he appears to fancy her.

'That's very Eddie,' I murmured back at her. 'If in doubt, take two.'

'And no whiskey, Mr Abalone,' she adds sternly, after he's already offered to take her out for a drink to say thanks, but only hard spirits, none of that girly shite with cocktail umbrellas in it.

Eddie, who is definitely slightly in love, but that could be the painkillers, smiles a very naughty smile.

'He lives with my mother and she will be in charge of the drugs,' I say.

'Did you write down your phone number?' roars Eddie to her as we head out the door.

'Eddie,' I say, 'you've got fifty years on that woman.'

'Plenty of tunes to be played on an old fiddle,' he laughs.

I hope it's the painkillers. It's not that I'm even slightly against nonagenarian romance but I fear for any poor woman Eddie lusts after.

I finally fall into my own bed at one in the morning and my mind, free of Eddie and his problems, swerves right back to poor Scarlett. It's so unfair, so sad.

If Life were to give my family any more lemons right now, I'd throw them right back and keep at it ferociously until Life got a black eye, serious bruising and a few broken ribs.

*Atta girl*, says Mildred.


Over the weekend, news of Jack's departure filters through the whole family.

Mum, Maura and I, via phone, discuss it endlessly.

'I would never have seen it coming,' says Maura. 'They love each other. They're like that couple in *Love Story* – I swear it. Nothing could break them, nothing.'

'Something did,' I say and I think that sometimes, the pain of life can just be too much. Look at Eileen in my support group. She's getting on with life but something has certainly died in her soul with the death of her beloved daughter.

Con does none of the phone discussions but says he's putting all his mates on the job of finding Jack, who has gone missing.

'That's no help,' says Maura crossly. 'What are they going

to do if they find him: handcuff him and haul him back home to Scarlett?'

'Well, I'm only trying to help,' says Con. 'I could reason with him . . .'

'If he's gone, it's because he wanted to go, Con,' I point out gently. 'All the reasoning in the world won't change that.

Jack's family, just as mystified and all anxious to descend on Scarlett to support her, have heard nothing from him.

Scarlett refuses to talk to anyone but me, Mum and Maura, and makes me deal with them.

'I can't talk about it or have Jack's entire family land up here sobbing and saying they'll make him change his mind,' she says in a monotone. 'His mother keeps phoning me and texting, saying he'll come to his senses, she knows he will. But he won't, so I can't talk to them.'

I am now the UN Secretary General of Scarlett's in-laws' family talks – and am coping with a weeping Lexi, who is upset at Elisa leaving the country without talking to her.

Lexi arrives into our bedroom at seven the morning after Eddie's late-night hospital jaunt and sobbing, holds out her phone: 'She's gone!' she says, and she falls into bed beside me and cries her heart out.

Somehow, a sleepy Dan retrieves the phone from the bed and finds his ex-wife's latest Instagram shots: at a party in Madrid.

'Why would she go and not say anything?' sobs Lexi and there's nothing I can do but hold her, stroke her softly, and tell her that we'll never leave her.

Dan tries to undo some of the damage: 'Elisa isn't used to telling people what she's doing, darling,' he says, but his words only make Lexi sob harder.

I shake my head at him, and keep stroking Lexi until she calms, then I suggest we clamber into her bed and watch *The*

*Gilmore Girls* on my iPad with some hot chocolate.

'With marshmallows?' she asks, her little face tear-stained.

'Marshmallows and chocolate swizzle sticks,' I say.

'Mum, you're the best,' Lexi says, snuggling into me and I close my eyes and sigh with relief. I have her back and I vow, I am never losing her again.

I'm also getting ready for a big interview Nina has lined up for me, and, when the children are at school, spending a lot of time sitting at my desk staring at old recipes and worrying about work.

I've done some cooking demonstration work for big stores, which pays well, but the book and TV show money won't be long trickling away if there isn't more coming soon. This is the wrong time to give up sleeping tablets so I take my life in my hands and visit my friend, Dr AJ again.

'Two more weeks of tablets. But that is it, Freya,' he says.

'AJ, look at my life right now,' I beg. 'If I can't sleep, I certainly can't work.'

'You've got to consider going to a psychiatrist. And a therapist.'

'I have my group,' I say smugly. 'It's made a huge difference.'

'That's not enough.'

'It is,' I reply.

Scarlett is scarily calm.

Thanks to Con, reports keep coming in of Jack: he's been seen in a bar in town; seen walking on Sandymount Strand in the rain – a sign of his brokenness?

Seen with a woman, not his sister/sister-in-law/any other female friend that could possibly be helping out and not be attached romantically – seen as appalling behaviour.

Nobody tells Scarlett any of this but everyone in the Abalone clan is that strange combination of wounded, mystified and utterly enraged that he would hurt Scarlett. The mystified bit comes from the fact that they are like one person. Have been since they met. Jack and Scarlett. Scarlett and Jack. It's like one word. And how they have coped over the last few years – Jack has been quite simply the perfect husband, perfect man.

'He's my best friend,' Scarlett always used to say. And I have always believed her.

I ring every day and meet her every few days for lunch or a cup of coffee.

Maura, Con and I are team-tagging this. Mum phones at night, but she reports that Scarlett won't stay on the phone for any length of time.

None of us, Scarlett has insisted, are to come to visit her.

'I am not an invalid,' she says fiercely. 'I will manage this myself.'

And then, on an evening when it's so warm that Dan fires up the barbecue and we eat in the still-overgrown garden, and Teddy, Lexi and Liam are blissfully at one with the world, my phone pings with a text from Scarlett.

**Sorry, sorry, Freya. But I need you. Can you come?**

# 18

## We are all works in progress

Scarlett's usually perfectly tidy house is in a mess as I let myself in. Bad sign – she is wildly house-proud.

The mail is piled up on the tiny hall table, and Scarlett's jackets hang on the newell post. She's standing in the kitchen and I've never seen her look this way before.

She looks broken.

'Thank God you texted,' I say, racing to hug her because I am suddenly really scared for what would happen if I leave.

'I know where he is,' she says.

I let her sob into my shoulder, holding what turns out to be a frighteningly thin body close to me and thinking back to when we were children and she was my little baby sister. When Mum got pregnant, Maura and I were both desperate for a little sister, but me even more so, because I didn't want to be the baby anymore. I wanted a little doll to dress and play with. I got all those things with my beloved Scarlett.

'I know where he's gone,' Scarlett sobs, 'he's had enough, he wants a child so much. You have no idea, Freya. We have spent everything we have ever had on this and now there is nothing, there is practically no more money and no point and I kept thinking there was no more point, but we wanted this so bad, I want this so bad.'

'Where is he?' I ask, wondering if I should kill him or send rescue.

She pulls away from me and looks at me with beseeching eyes: 'Where else could he be, but going out to get a baby with a real proper woman, not this husk like me.'

She scrapes her fingers over her non-existent belly as if ripping at herself for her lack of fecundity.

I'm stunned to silence.

'No, he isn't, Scarlett, I say earnestly, although if he was, I think I'd kill him myself.'

'You've got to stop thinking like that. Jack loves you: I know it's true, you know it's true.'

But I stop. Because even though I know he loves her desperately, I know that sometimes even love can't overcome the pain of life. What if Jack really had just had too much and had gone away? Not to find another woman but just to get away from the pain of their failure.

'No, you're wrong. He needs a baby,' she sobs. 'It's all I can think about: he'll find someone he loves more and have a baby with her.'

She really seems to think that Jack is out looking for women to impregnate. Because she couldn't get pregnant, it was therefore all her fault and he would find someone with whom he could have a baby. I could understand it, for sure. Understand how her mind would go off in that direction, but it was crazy—

There it was: that word again.

Crazy. Sometimes I felt crazy and now it looked as if Scarlett was going crazy.

There really needed to be a new word to describe what happened when huge emotions overtook us.

What was wrong with huge emotions?

Everyone has them. The person with them shouldn't be

given a shroud and a bell and made to chant 'unclean'.

But in our Instagram-filter-happy world, we aren't allowed to be sad.

Like I have been.

Like Scarlett is now.

I stare at my sister sadly. She is so tall and thin that she could possibly walk the catwalk, but her face doesn't have that lush fullness of the usual young, beautiful girls who step out for the designers. Her face is that of an adult, a hollowed mask of grief.

'He's always been there with me. Friends of mine used to say, they couldn't understand that he was such a part of this, that it wasn't just me wanting a baby and him going along with it. No, he wanted children, like his brothers, wanted everything I did. And I can't give him that. This stupid bloody body of mine has failed.'

She grinds the words out as if she's ready to take a kitchen knife to herself and start cutting into her flesh.

I know how easy it is for people to hurt themselves when they are this devastated. When their world has fallen apart, the need for physical pain to block out the emotional pain can become fierce. I immediately think, would she start doing that now? Cutting herself? I have never seen Scarlett like this before and she's not unhinged – that's not the word, that's a cruel old word, but she's suffering so much grief that I honestly don't know what she's going to do.

A phrase from my support group comes at me: *you have to learn to live with it. Because stuff happens and life goes on.*

'It's another woman,' she insists. 'I don't know who she is, I don't know what woman, but that's where he is: with someone else. I can't give him what he wants, so he's gone to find someone who can.'

Mildred says nothing, mercifully, so I run through the

options of what I can do: take Scarlett to the nearest psychiatric hospital or bring her home to our mother?

Our mother, I think. The golden woman who can heal all – except her own pain, I admit.

But then, healing other people is easier than facing yourself.

'Come on,' I say briskly to my sister, 'upstairs.'

I manage to gentle her along in front of me without even making the normal detour to the kitchen for the all curing cup of tea of the Abalone family.

I can't see Scarlett being able to drink anything, anyhow.

Somehow, we get upstairs.

She's weak, like Granny Bridget is weak and that scares me.

I sit her down on the bed in their bedroom and take on the brisk persona of Chef Freya cooking in *Simplicity with Freya*.

'Let's get you organised.'

'Freya Abalone could command and control an audience of thousands,' said one reviewer and boy, have the whole family teased me about this. Zed calls me Commander when he's in the mood. Today, I channel this talent because I think it's the only way to get Scarlett out of this house and somewhere safe where we can reassess.

I know where she keeps her suitcases: neatly stacked on a wardrobe in the spare bedroom.

Because Scarlett is very unlike me, almost on the verge of OCD with her organisational abilities, it's very simple to find knickers, bras, sloppy T-shirts, comfortable around the house sweat pants and cosy sweaters because even though it's summer, I know she'll be freezing. The shocked, thin and elderly are always cold and Scarlett scores two out of three in the trifecta. I throw in her trainers, a pair of jewelled thong sandals I know she loves, and her fake Ugg slippers.

She doesn't have my shoe thing: she has a comfy-around-the-house thing. I find little nightie sets and in the bathroom just sweep toiletries into another small case.

Beside the bed there's the usual tangle of cables and I unplug a whole load of them and plop them in the top of the case too.

What else? What else do I need to bring? There are pictures of all of us everywhere: the Abalones; Scarlett with Jack's family complete with endless children, photos which must crucify her when she sees them every day; beautiful holiday pictures of the two of them; that gorgeous one of them on their honeymoon at the Indian elephant sanctuary.

I carefully put that into the suitcase. I was grabbing a fluffy dressing gown, have stuffed it in and am about to close the bag when I realise that Scarlett is barefoot and shivering in a little T-shirt. I hastily extract the dressing gown and her slippers, wrap her in her dressing gown, shove her feet into her slippers and say: 'Come on, we're going.'

Downstairs, I rush around making sure all is safe, while she sits mutely on the couch and I very quickly text my mother.

**At Scarlett's, she's in a bad way. Mine or yours? You have enough on, but I think possibly being with you and Granny Bridget would help.**

I don't want to burden my mother with too much when she's dealing with so much already, but I have this instinct that being with my mother is the right thing for Scarlett. Despite all the people my mother cares for and the craziness of each day, the text pings back within seconds.

My mother is at the door when we drive up. We'd driven in pretty much absolute silence and I'd kept the radio on low on a talk show, so there was some sort of indistinct mumble in the background. Scarlett had sat and looked out the window like somebody who has witnessed something absolutely terrible and can't focus on the real world anymore.

Maybe bringing her to my mother's wasn't enough, I panicked as we drove. Maybe she needed to go to the doctor immediately.

But as we turn up Summer Street, I suddenly feel an imperceptible shift in the atmosphere in the car. It's as if Scarlett's breathing has deepened from her shallow, anxious breathing before. I knew that feeling. Just being close to home calms me.

'Oh, darling,' Mum says as she hugs Scarlett. 'I'm so glad you're here. I need you, it will be so lovely to have your help. Eddie has been so tricky with his wrist and he wants the cast off *now*, and poor Bridget is getting upset each time he roars, which she never used to do. I don't like leaving Dad on his own so much, so I really need help with all three of them. Can you do it?'

'Of course,' says Scarlett.

It's like a miracle: the first time since Jack left that she is like herself.

'I've been hopeless,' Scarlett apologises. 'What with Jack—'

'Oh, that'll sort itself out,' says Mum, still holding Scarlett. 'Jack adores you. You adore him. You'll get through. We'll talk about it properly later when you're in the mood. Dr Phillips might have a few ideas to get you through it too, but for now, I need you, darling.'

Scarlett actually smiles as they walk, arm in arm, into the house.

'Has Eddie been an absolute nightmare?'

'Worse than ever,' says my mother, holding Scarlett tightly. 'First, he's decided that he needs to get married again and wants to join a dating site. He keeps trying to download Tinder on my phone. Tinder! I've had to change all my passwords. I've never heard of a broken bone affecting a person that way. Normally, they get a bit depressed.'

Scarlett laughs.

I realise again that my mother really is the wisest person on the planet. If she'd just grabbed Scarlett and said, 'I am here to fix you,' Scarlett might have fallen into pieces on the floor, shattered like a precious piece of glass. But no. My mother had said, *we need you*. And a sliver of Scarlett's self esteem had been returned to her.

Food, I think, instinctively: I'll cook up some meals. If Mum is taking care of four people, she won't be able to cook. Even though I've cooked meals recently, four people and a multitude of carers go through meals very quickly in this house. And cooking makes me calm, even cooking by rote like making soups and shepherd's pies.

In the kitchen, I can hear all sorts of chat coming from the house: Bridget giggling with delight as she realises Scarlett is here for a visit; Eddie explaining how Tinder is just what he needs and could she help him because she's young and there's some wiping or swiping involved, and how would you go about that? Adverts in the newspaper are very old fashioned, Eddie goes on, causing a certain amount of mirth.

No, says Eddie, no Good Sense of Humour or 'mature lady' nonsense – he wants photos.

And from Dad, nothing.

*It is what it is*, says Mildred.

Have you got a magic eight ball in there and are using it, I ask her?

*Just saying.*

I open the fridge and have a look inside. There's the makings of all sorts of different dinners inside and some lamb: Granddad Eddie adores it, hence the shepherd's pies.

Right: a lamb casserole just to ring the changes, I think. No fat, some rosemary from the herbs in Mum's garden, if it's not totally overgrown. I think briefly about prunes. Eddie will complain if he gets too many prunes in absolutely everything. I take the lamb out so that it can get up to room temperature and open the kitchen door to go out to the remnants of the kitchen garden. There are all sorts of herbs: the feathery light dill, fat mint taking over the place, a giant bush of parsley, sage hidden by an encroaching weed, and some lacklustre chives, looking like every tender stalk needs its own bamboo cane.

I head towards the big, woody rosemary bush and realise that I know enough about herbs to know that it has to be trimmed back in winter. Rosemary bushes turn to wood without help, like humans, I think.

I pull off a handful, strip the leaves and smell them, glorying in the aromatic scent that sends me to a Greek island holiday with Dan and Lexi when she was small, when we rented a tiny apartment in a little village and where goats wandered in the fields nearby as we strolled down to the beach, walking up to us and staring with their strange yet beautiful eyes. The Greek lamb served with yogurt floods my senses, and I can almost smell the sun on the whitewashed little houses, feel Lexi patting my belly, where Liam lies, the calmest baby ever, sparing me even morning sickness.

I breathe deeply, images and scents rippling through my brain. There's bound to be some wild garlic here too with its ripe, powerful smell. It would be wonderful if Scarlett ate a filling stew but I know she's barely been eating; so eggs, I think.

An omelette with a hint of cheddar in it, and some wild rocket. A Greek salad, with good feta and those rich tomatoes that taste as if you are in Greece.

Holding on to the herbs, I wander around the garden. Mum never has time for it anymore. But she still keeps a hat and her old secateurs on a string outside the door, just in case.

Flowers, I decide, taking the secateurs and stalking around for something blooming. The roses were suffering with black spot but one bush, an old climbing French damask rose, is untouched and even though it needs severe pruning, the flowers are plentiful.

Granny Bridget loves them, I think, determined to get plenty for the kitchen table, for Bridget, for Mum and for Scarlett. It's wildly prickly though, thorns all over it.

'In order to get the joy of the scent you have to put up with those terrible little thorns,' my mother used to say years ago.

*True*, sighs Mildred.

I stop cutting for a moment.

Mildred is either unwell/has left a kinder replacement as she goes back in time to slip into Vlad the Impaler's head or is softening up.

Which is it?

*Duh? For a smart woman, you can be very dense*, Mildred says.

Dense how?

*I'm your inner voice, honey. Not some randomer. Keep picking herbs and roses. Think about food, not about how you can't come*

263

*up with recipes. Lord help me for saying this, but stop running. You've been running.*

Have not!

*Oh, puhlease.*

Shut up, I say crossly. I have not been running. I have been worrying myself sick because I have been terrified of my beloved daughter being taken away from me. Furthermore, I have a career which could slip away because since January, my mind has been set to 'high anxiety', not a setting conducive to anything but irritability and insomnia. And, Mildred, I add: I have had to cope with my mother killing herself to look after Dad when it's plainly impossible; not to mention trying to keep my business on the road by social media-ing myself to death. Lying by social media, I add. Pretending. Faking.

And lying to my darling Dan.

Take that, Mildred, I scowl.

But Mildred has vanished.

Bitch.

Muttering to myself, I hold the roses and pass the herbs again. Just like a quicksilver bird flying across your path, some forgotten part of my mind comes alive.

The scents begin to swirl around inside my head. It's how I've always cooked: smelling things and imagining what they'd be like together, having visions of mixing entirely different ingredients to create food that nourished, comforted. Greece is replaced by southern France, where we ate too much boullabaisse because we simply could not stop, mopping it up with bread made in the café kitchen that morning. For breakfast, Lexi and Liam had hot chocolate in bowls first, and I made comfort food of lovely French toast with a hint of good quality cinnamon grated in and just the smallest sliver of nutmeg, because nutmeg made such a difference.

*Stop running.*

I allow myself to wallow in my memories of how I cooked before and suddenly, I feel the wall of pain burst and the woman who cooks is back.

In the kitchen, I lose myself chopping and searing, washing vegetables, rinsing the wild garlic and then bashing it with Mum's pestle and mortar, letting the crushed leaves perfume the air. Scarlett isn't up to anything with meat in it, no. Scarlett needs something simple and filling and nutritious.

We eat dinner early in the house on Summer Street and it's nearly six when Granny Bridget comes in accompanied by a stomping Eddie.

'You're here,' he says. 'Nobody ever told me, nobody ever tells me anything around here. I'm just forgotten. Once you get old, people totally forget about you. I was only saying the other day—'

I interrupt him.

'I came in with Scarlett and I haven't been around to see anyone. I dropped in to do a little bit of cooking.'

'I thought you were a chef,' Eddie snorts. 'In my day we called them cooks, I don't know about the new words you young people have.'

'Cook is a lovely word,' says Bridget thoughtfully, 'but I like chef too and I've never seen you wear one of those funny hats, Freya: you know, tall with a floppy puffy bit on the top.' Bridget smiles, happy in her own world.

'She doesn't want a hat like that,' says Eddie.

'She might. Ooh, roses,' says Bridget, who has noticed the flowers on the table, sprigs of lavender and rosemary threaded in amidst the blooms for added scent. 'I love these ones.'

'I know.'

I pat her hand and help her sit in her place, with Delilah

on a be-cushioned stool beside her. Delilah has plenty of food in her bowl but has already turned her adorable pink nose up at it and is looking wistfully at the human food.

'That cat's ruined,' said Eddie.

'She's an assistance cat,' I say. 'She sits on Dad's lap and he likes it.'

'He does, doesn't he?' says Eddie, smiling suddenly.

'He likes *Miss Marple* too,' says Bridget.

'The *Battle of Britain* series is his favourite,' Eddie retorts. 'That Marple woman's always got her nose in other people's business . . .'

Nellie, a carer from Uganda, has arrived and refuses dinner because she is about to feed Dad.

'You eat,' she commands the others and even Eddie takes up his fork.

Now Nellie is a woman who'd be able to command armies, I think with a grin.

'I'm just running upstairs to see if Mum is coming down. She was doing something upstairs, organising, tidying or something,' I say. I heard her slip upstairs with Scarlett an hour ago when Nellie first got here after a hasty phone call from Mum. I imagine they've been talking and I want to see if Scarlett is able to face the family downstairs.

*You're a fabulous liar,* says Mildred, as I rush up the stairs.

Why is it, Mildred, I say, that the only time you ever said anything nice to me is when you are encouraging me in badness?

*That was a covering-up lie.*

'I'm only putting up with you until I train you to be nice to me full-time, and stop telling me I'm too fat in certain outfits, or that I'm no good as a chef.

*You always look good. Plus women have bellies because that's where their uteruses live,* Mildred said. *Basic biology.*

At that exact moment, I'm passing the hall mirror. I look at myself and think that a) Mildred has a point and b) I do look good.

Mildred, I don't know what drugs you're on, but you're making great strides with the being kind to me thing. By the time I've managed to erase you altogether and replace you with some harmonious angel who only tells me I'm wonderful, I'm going to miss you.

Scarlett and Mum are upstairs sitting in the tiny spare bedroom. Scarlett looks more at peace, but I'm still shocked again at how thin she is. How did this happen so quickly?

'Come on,' I say, putting my arm through Scarlett's. 'I dithered over an omelette or French toast but went for the toast. We have to fatten you up somehow. You look like you've been doing one of those crazy juice and nothing else for five days diets.'

'Oh, French toast: I love it,' says Scarlett.

'Yes, food for the broken hearted,' I say and instantly want to kick myself.

'Well, that would be fine,' says Scarlett with a hint of the old Scarlett in her voice, 'except I'm not broken hearted. I'm here to help for a couple of days.'

'Eggs, then,' I say. I have just the recipe.

## Break-Up Scrambled Eggs

Use free range eggs because they have the richest, yellowest yolks and they will give your immune system a boost when you need it. A broken heart has many physical manifestations – this is not pseudo-science: it's real. And we've all been there! So go free range for this.

A good quality wholewheat toast is a must, too. Forget about giving up gluten for this meal – unless you are a card-carrying coeliac or happen to be on the gluten intolerance spectrum. We all try so hard to do the right thing that we forget to feed our bodies the right way. Stick your wholewheat toast under the grill, whisk the eggs, add a hint of milk – I like a smidge of grated parmesan but that's just me – a pinch of salt and pepper and stir into a heated pan already hot with a smearing of butter all over the bottom.

Keep stirring. It's simple, rhythmic, comforting.

Think of nothing but this. Stirring. Making these eggs beautiful. From a happy hen straight to you.

Once the eggs are in delicate lumps but still have a sheen upon them, take them off the heat. They'll cook in the pan for another minute while you butter your toast.

Pile on and feed your soul. Right now, be your own best friend.

# 19

## *If you put everyone's problems into a bowl, you'd probably take yours out again because everyone suffers*

This time when I wake in the middle of the night, I feel utterly awake. And hungry. I have again fought through the Zimovane to have only four hours' sleep, so I think that tonight, I will try half a tablet.

I fear this concept because I've looked up the whole withdrawal from sleeping tablets thing and I could turn into a raving lunatic (withdrawal may turn you into a werewolf) or else have headaches, nausea, depression and sweats. Not to mention damn all sleep.

But it has to be done. From now on, half a sleeping tablet a night. They'll last longer too. I might get the summer out of them before I have to give them up and learn to sleep on my own again.

Plus, maybe if I'm very tired, I will sleep.

And yet that's not first and foremost in my mind: chocolate is.

Chocolate helps people sleep, like hot milk and valerian, which does admittedly smell like lettuce at the botton of the crisper when the fridge has gone feral. But chocolate . . . I yearn for the lush, velvety taste of chocolate cake. Right now.

I slip from the bed, quickly check on the children, and then pull on yoga pants and a sweatshirt.

Moonlight lights up downstairs with squares and rectangles of light in through the windows but it doesn't scare me.

Instead, I head for the kitchen, grab my pen and laptop and begin to research. I feel strangely like myself again.

By morning, I think I've cracked it. There are two chocolate cakes sitting on the counter, and I've swept all the offcuts into the compost bin. I sit looking at them with pride. This glorious confection has a name:

### Fear of the Dark Chocolate Cake

If you can't sleep after eating this, then at least you'll lie there with a sense of wellbeing in your heart. No bad dream can get past it. Like warriors guarding your heart, you can take comfort in that one glorious thing today because sometimes that's all you can focus on: one glorious thing. Everything else might be dreadful, but you've got mouthfuls of your chocolate cake to give your courage.

As I run upstairs to wake everyone, I think of telling Dan about my plan with the sleeping tablets but . . . I've already told him I'm trying to cut down, so he'll know I'm lying. And what if I do sweat and go nuts during it all? But I have to tell him the truth. Just when?

It's weird how I look forward to the Thursday evenings and my victim support group. For a start it's cheaper: I had been going to shopping centres and idling around, trying on bits and bobs and then having to leave the shop without buying them because we really are broke. But I had to buy a coffee, right? And even a bun. Cream.

*You might consider exercise,* Mildred points out mildly. She is definitely kinder lately.

And for a second thing, the group is so comforting because there is some magic in this not particularly beautiful little room with other people, talking. Honestly. My family has always been brilliant – we discuss everything. But I know that's not necessarily normal and that for a lot of people, talking about their deepest inner fears is really unusual. Here, I can talk about my fear of January and what I still call The Fear, although I am considering downgrading it from capital letters to just the fear.

'Progress, right?' I say to Ariel on the phone.

'Progress,' she agrees.

One day, I think, I might be able to talk about January, the garage and The Fear with my family. I might not feel that I have to protect them from it. It's not as if we haven't had a lot of talking about our deepest inner fears this last year, what with Dad.

And now Jack's leaving is out in the open, we can talk – cautiously – about that. Scarlett is doing marvellously at Mum's for a whole week now.

'She's eating, she's tidied out Eddie's room and she dyed Bridget's hair,' Mum reports on the phone. 'Of course, she's treading water but right now, that's a result. It's better than drowning.'

Lexi and Caitlin are involved in a ballet camp for a lot of the summer, so Caitlin's mother and I are organising pickups and drop-offs, a complex system because it also involves taking Liam to soccer camp and getting Teddy to a small children's play camp that includes art.

Anyone seeing Teddy after a session would think it entails redecorating the interior of a bordello because she comes out every day covered, and I mean covered, in paint at the dark purple and red end of the colour spectrum.

She has paint in her hair, on her clothes and another pair

of shoes are totally ruined.

'Don't they wear old shirts or aprons for the painting bit?' I ask one day, when we are laundried out of clothes because none of the stain removers appear to be working and Teddy's wardrobe has been seriously depleted.

'Teddy is such a natural artist,' says Carly, the teacher in charge of the camp, an enthusiastic woman in her thirties who wears – no, not making this up – loose dungarees and has hair as curly and red as Little Orphan Annie's. She could audition for a children's TV show right now. With her beaming face, dusting of freckles and all round good-natured loveliness, I know she is exactly the right person to run a camp for someone as energetic as Teddy. I just wish they didn't paint every day with such abandon.

Carly holds up Zoom, her own tortoise, who is one of the camp's pets. 'Today, we're having a nature day,' she says happily. 'We've got Zoom and Fluff, the guinea pig. And some ants.'

I have a vision of Teddy holding Zoom upside down and shaking him to see if he falls out of his shell. Fluff had better look out for herself. But, guineas can bite. Only thing is, if anything bites Teddy, she tends to bite it back.

And if she comes home with any ants she's secreted in her lunch box, I am going to euthanise them with my shoe.

Elisa is due back in Ireland at the end of July for the second round of Surella publicity blasts. Summer is fake tan madness, apparently, or so Dan says to me that evening, when the day has gone well for everyone and no ants have made it home.

'You *have* got Instagram?' I say.

'No, Con's doing it for me. He says it's brilliant. There's make-up, underwear, all sorts of gorgeous women showing you their outfits for the day. He says it's the new way to hunt for girlfriends.'

'Con is like a fourteen-year-old boy with a hormonal surge,' I say sternly. 'You are enabling him. I can follow her myself but—'

'But you can't bear to let her see you follow her?'

'Exactly. Would one of Maura's girls do it, do you think? They could tell me what she's up to without me having to actually look.'

'Good plan. Ask them. See you later, babe,' he says, as I leave.

I head off for my support meeting in cheerful form.

Talking helps, I tell Mildred.

*No shit*, she replies.

And there was me thinking you were kinder lately, I tell her.

*I speak as I find*, Mildred says.

Speaking as you find is code for being rude, I remind her.

This evening however, when I walk up the stairs above the phone repair shop, I see a newcomer sitting beside Eileen on the couch. Her hair is a wonderful dark auburn colour and she's wearing make-up, lipstick and really elegant clothes. I walk over to introduce myself to her because that's what everyone does here and I realise with absolute shock that it's Farrah. Farrah of the mousy hair who almost hides in her chair during the meetings.

'Farrah,' I say, actually taking a step back with astonishment, 'you look . . . just . . .'

'Amazing,' says Eileen enthusiastically. 'You wouldn't recognise her, would you?'

'I certainly didn't recognise you, at first,' I say and sit down on the other side of Eileen. 'Not that you're not always lovely but this—'

*Foot in mouth. Stop talking,* Mildred points out judiciously.

Farrah touches her hair self-consciously.

'I thought I needed a change,' she says.

'Change,' I say smiling. 'It's wonderful, it's not a change, it's a . . .'

I search for the words.

'It's a transformation.'

Farrah grins.

'I used to have this hair colour years ago,' she said, 'when I was younger.'

'Oh, and you're one hundred now,' I say with amused irony. Everyone laughs at that.

'I just got out of the habit of making an effort, I thought if I didn't draw attention to myself that—'

Ariel has come into the room and she interrupts.

'If you didn't draw attention to yourself, then nobody would know it was you and it wouldn't happen again,' she says in her light little fairy voice.

'Exactly,' Farrah says wryly, 'but that's not going to work, is it? I was walking to work the other day and somebody bashed into me, by accident. They were running for the tram and *bam*! It shocked me, frightened me, and then I realised they didn't mean to hurt me. They even yelled sorry. But I was shaking because it brought it all back and then I thought, I'm going to keep shaking forever if I don't do something. Walking down the street is like being in a war zone when your head's in this place. That's no way to live.'

'You're coming here,' I say carefully, because just coming here was helping me.

'I think it's not enough just to come here,' says Farrah with determination, 'I think you have got to really try to make a difference. Do things in another way, because I'm different now. A different Farrah. I don't know if I'll ever be that person who can walk down the street entirely without fear *but*,' – she looks at all the faces who are nodding, understanding the way people on the outside can't. 'I could completely lose myself and try not to let it happen again, but I'd have to live in a tower and get food delivered. How real is that? Stuff happens and I've got to keep on living.'

Eileen, who is so affectionate and wise that she reminds me of Mum, reaches out and hugs Farrah.

Steve comes in, apologising for being late, and we start the meeting. Ariel says she has had a good week and she'd gone to a friend's party. The friend's brother had walked her home and she had felt pretty safe.

Steve had gone to see the counsellor at work again. He'd been nervous of doing it, nervous it would affect his promotion prospects in some way, although everyone kept saying, 'Don't be ridiculous. You can't be penalised because your bank was held up.'

'I know,' he says. 'It's just the voice inside me telling me I will be. That I have to pretend.'

*Mildred, you got relatives?* I ask.

She doesn't deign to answer.

Eileen is still Eileen, smiling, making an effort but I can always see it in her, that huge loss. How could there not be a huge loss. Her daughter Daisy is gone. I'm sure I'd never recover from something like that.

But even as I think of how much Eileen has lost, my mind is working on another level – dancing around as people talk.

And then the thought begins to trickle into my brain. Farrah had done something different, she'd changed the narrative. She was refusing to get stuck in this one. Yes, she'd been coming to the group for two years and I had been coming for such a short length of time but she'd said something that resonated with me: *I want to live my life.*

275

'I've changed, for sure,' she says, when it's her time to speak in the group, 'but I have to live with that change and make it work.'

Her family and friends all know that she came to a victim support group, they know about what had happened to her, they know when she could or couldn't cope. Mine didn't.

I didn't tell Scarlett because she was dealing with the loss of Jack, and all her hopes and dreams of being a mother. I didn't tell Maura because she was trying to coax Gilly through her State exams and deal with a busy job and besides, she worries enough about Mum as it is. And I don't tell Dan because . . . I don't tell Dan because I don't want to be different. I don't want our lives changed by this thing and yet they *have* been changed.

*Shit happens,* says Mildred in my head and I smile.

'Yeah, shit happens, Mildred,' I say and everyone looks at me.

'I said that out loud again, did I?'

Everyone nods.

'Sorry.'

'No, go on,' says Farrah, 'you need to speak. I was done anyway.'

'You sure?'

'Sure.'

'I was just thinking that I have all these little compartments in my life and one of them is being mugged and the fallout of what that's done to me. I keep that compartment away from my family because I don't want to upset them. There's my Mum and how she takes care of my Dad, you know that. My sister's husband left her and I think he couldn't cope with the pain because they've spent years trying to have a baby. And finally . . .' I stopped. Did this hurt the most without me realising it? 'There's my daughter's birth mother coming back and having the power to hurt my daughter—'

'I don't know what that woman is up to,' interrupts Eileen fiercely. 'She truly is the most selfish person ever.'

I grin. Eileen really is the sort of person you wanted in your corner.

'I happen to agree with you on that, Eileen' I say, 'but I have to deal with it. I can't change it. I worry about what it's going to do to my daughter; what infertility and now marriage breakdown has done to my sister; I worry about my mother; I worry about my career and if we'll be able to pay the mortgage; I worry about *everything*.

'Then I'm presenting this happy front to everyone in public. *Look at me doing some cooking in the kitchen. Aren't my pancakes beautiful?! Happy!* I spend half an hour a day doing social media to prove how happy I am. Sick or what? Do you know, until I had to cook for my darling sister, I hadn't come up with a single recipe since I was mugged. Not one. I was just broken. But now, now I am cooking again except I'm being honest in a new way with this work.'

Nobody speaks. It isn't a silence of shock or horror. It's the silence of people giving me the space to talk it out.

'Do you think sharing more of your life with the people in it would help?' says Eileen, 'Because you can't keep all this pain inside, otherwise it just eats you up. I tried that and it doesn't work.'

'I know you're right,' I say, 'I've got to share it, I can't keep it in the box, because the box is never big enough. I'm different now and that's fine. OK, total disclosure: I have this voice in my head.'

Shane looks alarmed.

'I know a few lads who've had that problem after they

have done too much really strong skunk,' he says, 'or taken a few too many mushrooms. It wrecks them, sometimes for years. You . . . you haven't done anything like that? I could tell you who to talk to but it takes a long time to get over it—'

'No, Shane,' I say. 'This is not lots of voices in my head telling me I can fly after an acid overdose – this is that critical voice that says you're an idiot or why did you do that? You know that voice?'

'*That* voice,' say Farrah and Ariel at exactly the same time, and they both laugh.

'Well,' I go on, 'I've given my voice a name, I call her Mildred, because it makes it easier and when she's been very negative I say, *shut up Mildred*. So Mildred was just telling me that shit happens.'

'Mildred has a point,' says Eileen. 'Shit happens.'

'I've never heard you swear,' says Ariel, astonished.

'I have been known to swear on occasions,' says Eileen primly, 'but as everyone in this room knows, shit happens and you keep going. You have no choice. I don't know if I'm the best or the worst person to demonstrate this because I can never, ever get back to who I was. I've lost too much.'

Farrah cries. She often cries when Eileen talks.

Eileen continues. 'I'm not saying my losing Daisy is worse than anything else in your lives, but I do think you have some chance of going forward. You're changed now, for sure. But you go forward, changes and all. I come in here once every week and I cry and I can tell you all exactly what I'm feeling. And then I go back out to my family and I try to get on with my life as best I can. There's a Daisy-shaped hole in it and that will never be filled. But I have other people I love and I need to be there for them. I need to be there for me. So, if I pretend everything is OK, then I'm lying to all of us and I'm lying to me.'

We all sit in silence.

'I think that's what Mildred was trying to say.' I agree. 'Shit happens to everyone.'

'And it's how you pick yourself up that matters,' chimes in Farrah. We all looked at her.

'Somebody really said that to you after you'd been mugged?' asks Steve.

'Yeah,' says Farrah, and we all laugh with recognition. 'It's amazing the platitudes people come out with. This person hadn't been mugged but they *thought* they knew what I was going through.'

'*You create your own happiness* or some rubbish like that. From a guy I work with who's never had anything happen to him,' she adds.

'But nobody knows what you are going through,' I say crossly at the notion of some do-gooder saying exactly the wrong thing.

'It's taken me a long time, but I now tell people,' says Farrah. 'I say, I'm going through a difficult time and if they try and say, I understand and try and compare it to oh, I don't know, getting a flat tyre when they were late for work, I say, no that is *not* the same thing.'

'Farrah is right,' says Steve, 'maybe you should tell the people you love how you feel. It helped me.'

'Yes,' Ariel chimes in, her face lit up suddenly, her eyes sparkling. 'And you could tell people on your social media accounts – it would be brilliant. *Stop the fake,* stop pretending everything is OK. That's what I do, my friends know what happened to me and that's why my friend's brother walked me home from the party. He knows I'm scared. He doesn't bang into me when we walk. He's kind, gentle and knows I'm scared of noises and being touched. That helps:

that people I care about know.'

I rolled the idea over in my mind. Imagine if people really knew, what would it mean? Imagine if I told Dan? Imagine if I told everyone? Imagine if I stopped trying to pretend I was happy Freya Viking Chef and said 'shit happens'.

*Hey*, said Mildred irritably. I don't think Mildred likes these meetings. *What's the worst that could happen?*

## 20

# *Sometimes people with the biggest smiles are struggling*

On Monday, Angela is having the day off, and I'm picking up the children from camp.

First up, it's Teddy who insists she is not sitting in the back of the car in her special seat and wants to sit in the front. She is covered in paint again but clearly the reds have been put away and she is very yellow. I idly wonder what colour Zoom the tortoise is.

'I'm sitting here like a big girl,' she says.

'You are quite a big girl,' I say choosing my words carefully because every battle with Teddy is a bit like fighting with a senior counsel in court. 'But you are still not big enough to sit in the front seat or to sit without your special seat. What if Mummy bumped into . . .' I search around for something suitably non-threatening, 'a tree. Imagine we banged into the tree and the poor old branches got a bit squished and the front of the car got squished and you hurt your lovely head.'

Teddy looked at me. 'Don't bang into any trees,' she said. Like, duh!

'Correct answer,' I replied, controlling my laughter, 'but you still have to get into the back and into your seat.'

It takes about three minutes to achieve this and Teddy screams and shouts quite a lot. To any onlookers it would appear as if I am trying to strangle a small child, but the people outside the camp are used to this type of behaviour. Other parents nod with understanding as they try and attach small wriggling people to car seats with those small wriggling people shouting, kicking or demanding treats. To outsiders, it looks like a mass kidnapping.

'Want sweeties, want buns from George and Patch's bun shop!' shrieks Teddy. She ardently wants to go to Giorgio and Patrick's and have buns. They would have to laugh at having their exquisite café called a 'bun shop'.

'We are going to go home first and have a lovely snack,' I say, using my Calm Mummy voice, which has a failure rate of about 75 per cent with Teddy, 'and then maybe if you are very good we could go to Giorgio and Patrick's.'

'No!' she shrieks.

'How about I put on the soundtrack to *Frozen* and you can sing along to Elsa and Anna?' I say in my happiest voice.

'Yes,' says Teddy delightedly.

Thank goodness small children can sometimes be easily distracted.

I can now tune out *Frozen*. That's progress.

We get home and I manage to get a snack into her.

'Don't want the rest of it,' she says, looking at her home-made fish fingers with a tiny can of baked beans that has cartoon people on it.

'Now darling, you like fish fingers,' I say, crossing my fingers behind my back. She always has up to now . . .

'I want a dog. A dog would eat the yucky fish fingers. Timmy in school has a dog and when he doesn't want to eat his food he gives it to his dog and his Mummy can't see.'

I know Timmy's mother. Should I pass on this bit of important intel or should I let it ride? I dare say Timmy's mother has already noticed the dog delightedly eating half of Timmy's dinner. And indeed when Teddy was younger we could have fed a whole fleet of dogs from what she threw on the floor around her high chair.

'We can't really look after a doggie but maybe when you're older,' I say, which is what I always say. Teddy slams down her cup.

'George and Patch's, now,' she demands.

In the end I give in. I am writing recipes again but I'm slooow doing it and besides which the only way I could get any work done would be to park Teddy in front of the television.

'OK,' I sigh. I know when I'm beaten.

We head round the corner and into the café which is mercifully empty. There is no sign of Miss Primrose, Patrick or Giorgio and one of the stand-in baristas, a handsome young Argentinian student named Matteo is behind the counter. His English is flawless, his skill as a barista amazing and he's even patient enough to carefully help Teddy choose her favourite bun, which requires the patience of Job.

'Half now, half after dinner,' I say fiercely. I have to win some battles or I will lose my Mother badge altogether. 'Won't you cut it up into two bits, Matteo, because Teddy and I have an agreement.' Teddy eyes me like a hawk watching a mouse it's about to kill.

I eye her back.

She realises that this is not going to work because I'm wearing my steely face. So she turns to Matteo, giving him the small child version of an 'I have not been fed in a very long time and I'm beaten' look. Given that she's still a bit paint-splattered, this is very effective.

'Vewwy hungry, Mattie,' she adds.

'Go on,' I said to Matteo, sighing. 'Give it all to her.'

I'm just not strong enough. At four, Teddy has broken me. I will have to hire Supernanny for her teenage years or else the house will be full of unsuitable boyfriends who sneak in late, stay overnight and I will be able to do nothing apart from be a Granny to quadruplets.

An hour and a half later, we are on our way to pick up Liam, who is delighted because he scored four goals today. Dan has been helping him with football because this is definitely not my area of expertise.

'Aren't you brilliant,' I say, then follow this up quickly with 'and you worked so hard!'

He's sitting in the front seat because he's tall enough now and says he's not moving when Lexi gets in.

I sigh. Despite the front-seat rota, there is a constant battle between my two eldest for the shotgun seat and Lexi might get a little irritated when we roll round to the hall where she and Caitlin do ballet. For a long time, she was always the person who got to sit in the front seat: the eldest child's prerogative. I remember the arguments when I was growing up and I, Maura, Scarlett and eventually Con were old enough to sit in the front seat. There was an actual rota stuck on the dashboard and we had to mark everyone's goes off in pen. It was that bad.

How patient my parents were at going along with this. But they did, and eventually at some point they put us in charge of the rota, so we had to make sure it was all fair and square.

By the time we make it to the ballet school Liam and Teddy are chattering away to each other, Teddy discussing her bun and how a dog would be very helpful around the house for eating yucky things like scrambled eggs, and Liam explaining how one of his new soccer friends got a puppy and it can already offer up a paw.

There's a lot of dog in this conversation, I think, wondering how I'm going to nip this in the bud.

I like dogs but I just don't think I could cope with an extra soul in our currently-complex world.

And then we pick up Lexi and Caitlin. I can instantly tell my daughter's angry or upset from the way she walks out to the car. You notice stuff like that about your children: their walk, their movements. They don't have to say a thing but you know when there's something wrong.

'Hi, darling,' I say cautiously, as she opens the back door of the car and lets herself in, shooting Liam an angry glance at the very nerve of him for sitting in the front seat, her seat this time round.

'Fine,' she snaps. I wait until she and Caitlin have put on seatbelts and Teddy resumes the conversation about buns, dogs, Peppa Pig, Mattie, what she did in camp today and how tortoises look nice painted orange. Lexi sits there in stony silence, staring out the window.

'How was it, Caitlin?' I ask.

'Fine.'

OK. Monosyllables. Never good.

'Did you have an OK day, darling?' I ask Lexi, knowing that whatever happened it was not an OK day.

'Fine,' she repeats.

'OK,' I say. Two fines from two girls. Not good.

I drop Caitlin off with a mention to her mother that something happened in ballet camp but I don't know what. Then, I head for home.

After I unhook Teddy, the three of them escape into the house and Lexi races upstairs to her bedroom and slams the door so hard that I wonder if we have ever checked the hinges on the doors in Kellinch House. Knowing I'm relying on the television babysitter, I plonk Teddy in front of it, turn it on to something she likes, stick a load of Sylvanians on the floor in front of her in case the TV isn't interesting enough, give her two biscuits to add to my parental guilt, and belt upstairs at high speed. The house is pretty much child-proof, but still you have to keep an eye on four-year-olds or else give them things to amuse them totally for the five minutes you look away. One moment for catastrophe is all it takes.

Lexi's door is shut and I knock.

'Lexi, honey, you OK?'

'Fine,' says the voice again, only this time it's shaking.

'Darling, what's wrong?' I ignore all the recent rules about knocking and privacy and just push open the door. My beautiful little girl is sprawled on her bed face down and she's crying. Her face is stained with tears and the look of utter misery in her eyes makes my heart break.

'What is it,' I say with horror, 'what happened?' I sit beside her and gather her to me. 'Tell me, tell me, Lexi, did somebody hurt you, were you bullied, what, what is it?'

'No, none of those things,' she says, 'none of those things.'

'You have to tell me, Lexi, it's really important. Did anybody hurt you?'

The things that are going through my head are horrific. There's rage boiling up inside me. Someone has hurt my daughter and I just want to find out who they are and rip them apart with my bare hands.

'It's, it's nothing,' she says.

'It *is* something because you are lying here sobbing,' I say.

I hold her close to me and let her cry until she's cried out. I stroke her hair the way I used to when she was little and I croon her name and kiss her head until the shuddering stops.

The joy of motherhood is exquisite but the exquisiteness has an equal match in pain and the pain of being a mother is sometimes just too much to bear. I'd be mugged ten times over, I think at that exact moment, as long as Lexi goes through life without pain. But everyone has pain and I have to teach her how to cope with it.

Right now, I need to know what happened.

Finally, she straightens up and looks at me, her lovely face tear-stained and blotchy, her eyes swollen.

'Just one of the girls in the class, she knows about Elisa and that I have . . . that she's . . .'

'Your birth mother,' I fill in before it gets even trickier.

'Yes,' nods Lexi. 'She showed me this thing on an entertainment site and it's got Elisa on it and some guy she's going out with and . . .'

'Yes . . .?' I say hesitantly. What has Elisa done now?

'And there's an interview with her and she's so happy, she said, she's never ever been happier in the whole of her life. It's the best thing that's ever happened to her,' Lexi is saying and the tears start to flood again.

'What's the best thing that's happened to her?' I ask tentatively, having a sick feeling that I know the answer to the question.

'She's having a baby.'

My heart stills.

Instinctively, I pull Lexi back close because she's sobbing again and I think that if I had Elisa right here, right now, I would carve her up with some of my ultra-lethal kitchen knives to make her understand the damage she is doing to my beautiful daughter. How can I undo this?

My baby in in pain and all because of a woman who clearly can't have a relationship with anyone except herself. Lexi was so determined to have some sort of rapport or friendship or *something* with Elisa, and now Elisa has just destroyed it all.

If only she'd told us this. Let Dan and I tell Lexi: let Lexi be ready for it.

What do I do next? I just don't know.

And then Mildred speaks up.

*What do you mean you don't know what to do next? You're a mother, a good mother. Cop on to yourself. You know how to handle this.*

It's slightly startling to have my own inner voice stop bashing me but I realise that Mildred's voice is giving me courage – I *do* know what to do. I *am* a good mother. I have raised this beautiful child for twelve years, have given her huge love, care, courage, self-belief – everything I can think of. I have two other wonderful children for whom I've done the same, even if Teddy is on the way to breaking me.

Dan and I have built a family.

We manage. And I always know what to do. I sit up a little bit straighter.

'Now, darling,' I say, ultra calm as if we are discussing what to have for dinner. 'That's lovely for Elisa that she's going to have a baby . . .'

'But, but, but . . .' sobs Lexi 'I'm, like I'm her baby.'

She says the words as if she's been afraid to say them to me before.

I realise that even though I will always be Lexi's true mother, there is some part of her connected to the woman who actually gave birth to her.

It's part of life, part of the great tapestry of one woman giving birth and another woman taking care of that child.

I think I always knew this great fact but I was so caught up in rage against Elisa that I forgot it.

I reach into that universal mother lode inside me and come up with the goods:

'Darling Lexi, when Elisa gave birth to you, she was very young and immature and she wasn't able to look after you. Giving you to your dad and me was the most selfless thing she has ever done in her whole life, the kindest thing, the best thing she could have done for you.'

'I know all that but aren't I special to her? This new baby thing is on Facebook and Instagram and everything, where she talks about this baby as if she's never had a baby before and . . .'

Again I try to choose the most careful words I can.

'Lexi, sometimes girls in your school get pregnant and sometimes they have lots of support and bring up the babies.'

She nods. Lexi knows that teenagers have babies because her school is very hot on sex education and the reality of what youthful sex really is.

'When they have those babies very young, they haven't matured. Do you know, the human brain does not fully develop until you're twenty-five?'

'No,' she looks at me astonished. 'I thought once, you know, you left school, you were officially a grown-up, and you could go out and vote and do stuff?'

'You can vote, you can get married, you can drive a car, you can do lots of things,' I tell her. 'But until your brain is fully developed, you're liable to make a few mistakes. We all make mistakes, at all ages,' I add. 'Adults make mistakes all the time. But the responsibility of having a child is huge and when Elisa was pregnant with you, she wasn't ready for that responsibility, because she was very young.

'Now she is. It doesn't change the fact that *you* are the first beautiful little baby she gave birth to. But, it might be hard for you to see it that way when she's telling everyone about this new baby.'

'She never told anyone about *me*,' Lexi says in a rush. 'Me

289

and Aisling talked about it at lunch break. I was nowhere, nowhere on any of her stuff or her posts or her Instagram or anything. It was like she just appeared from Spain and had no children. She lied. Do you know, she says she's thirty-two.'

'Really?' I say, doing my best to sound surprised. 'Lots of women try and pretend they are younger than they are and in Elisa's world maybe that's very important. So how about you show me some of these messages and posts and we can talk about it again, think about it again. Now we have a different prism to see it through. You have me and Dad and Liam and Teddy. You have six grandparents if you think about it: my mum, Dad's mum, Great Granny Bridget, Great Granddad Eddie, and Granddad Lorcan, though he's not well. Plus . . .' A brilliant idea occurs to me but I have to plan it.

'Elisa has a mum and dad too, and brothers, so you have other family.'

Lexi ignores this.

'Granny Bridget cries a lot. And Granny Betty's nervous,' says Lexi as if she wants to find flaws in this excess of relatives. The relative she wishes would care, simply doesn't.

'I know, but if you had Dad and Zed as sons and they always wanted to do triathlons and things – you know how Zed is into parachute jumping – you might be a bit nervous, too.'

Lexi manages a small laugh.

'I'm telling you,' I add, now that I was on a roll, 'I will be stressed out of my head if you decided that you want to do rock climbing or parachuting when you are older.'

'Ugh,' she says with a shudder. 'I don't want to do anything like that. I want to dance.'

'Perfect, lovely you want to dance. And don't forget you've

got Scarlett, Maura, Pip, Zed, Caitlin, Gilly and everyone.'

'Why can't Scarlett have babies?' she asks me suddenly and I'm taken aback at this sudden *volte face.*

'Because not everyone gets what they want in life,' I say 'and for poor Scarlett and Jack, they tried so hard and they haven't been able to have babies.'

'And people like Elisa who had me when she was young, they get babies but they can't look after them?' she questions.

Out of the mouths of babes.

'Life is very strange, darling,' I say to her, 'never quite works out the way we want it to. But when we have people who love us and when we know we can talk to those people, tell them all our fears and know they will always love us no matter what, we can get through most things.'

She throws her slim arms around my waist and squeezes as tight as she can and I bury my lips in her gleaming dark hair. I can't cry, not yet, although I want to. My beautiful girl is having to deal with so much.

'Now let's think about what you might say to Elisa next time you see her and—'

'I don't want to see her again,' says Lexi suddenly, pulling back from me.

'OK,' I said.

*But she needs to,* says Mildred.

Mildred is being surprisingly helpful.

'I think it would be great to see Elisa. In fact,' and I don't know where this idea comes from, 'I think we should visit your other Granny and Granddad, her mum and dad, have them to dinner. Nothing fancy and she can bring whoever she's going out with.'

I'm still not entirely sure who the baby Daddy is.

'He's a musician,' says Lexi.

'OK,' I say, vowing then and there to seriously cut down

on Lexi's time on social media. I know it's going to be like fighting against the sea, but still. She needs a little bit more childhood before she has to face up to the weird and wonderful world of the internet. 'So let's organise that. I'll ask Granny Adele.'

'Elisa says they're nice, really rich though. They have a dog, Coco. We could get a dog.'

I grin. 'Have you and Liam been planning this?' I say, suddenly feeling my feet on very familiar territory. 'It's a plan isn't it? Everything that's going on, just to get a dog.'

Lexi laughs and suddenly she's back, my beautiful girl, not so little anymore, growing up, facing difficult things, but her eyes are shining as she looks at me.

'We could get a small dog. I promise to walk it.'

'I'm not so sure about you walking it all by yourself,' I say, 'but certainly you and Liam can be involved in,' I grin, 'picking up the doggie poo.'

'No,' she shrieks.

'Yes, doggie poo, it's the only answer,' I say. 'Now, don't look at any more Elisa videos – in fact, text Caitlin to say that everything's all right and I might hold onto your phone for the rest of the evening? We'll figure out how we're going to invite Elisa over and say we're pleased for her news. And Dad will be happy that she's happy.'

Lexi looked at me with a sceptical gaze.

'I don't think Dad likes Elisa very much.'

This time I burst out laughing.

'Why do you say that?' I ask, trying really hard to make my voice sound normal.

'Mum, I can tell,' she says. 'Hello! I'm fourteen. I'm not a baby, even if my brain isn't grown up yet.'

'Uncle Con's brain isn't grown up yet and he's nearly thirty,' I point out and she giggles. 'OK, you're not a baby, right, got that. And we can talk about the dog thing.'

'Really, Mum?' she says, sounding like Liam.

'Yeah,' I said, 'but not just yet. We've still got a few hurdles to jump over. We need the right dog. We have to plan this. Have discussions but yes, let's get a dog.'

While the children screamed with excitement about the dog and Liam got out an animal book to look up exotic breeds that Teddy would no doubt terrorise within their first five minutes in the house, I hid in the pantry, rang Dan and I filled him in on the details.

'I'll kill bloody Elisa,' were his first words.

'No,' I say.

'What do you mean, *no*,' he growls. 'Stupid cow was the one who wanted to talk to Lexi and now this—'

I interrupted him.

'Let's face it, Dan,' I say. 'Elisa has never been exactly emotionally mature and we should have expected something. *We* just have to be grown-ups in all of this and I have a plan.'

'A plan to blackmail Elisa to go back to Spain and never darken our door?'

'No, a more grown-up plan than that and possibly one that will keep us out of jail, because we have three children to take care of and a mortgage and it would be handier if we weren't locked up.'

'I don't know,' he says. 'I could put up with jail for a little while. Stupid, stupid cow and it's all my fault.'

I could practically hear him running frantic fingers through his dark hair.

'Young guys are totally led around by their—'

I interrupt him again. 'When it comes to your ex-wife, I do not want to know what part of your anatomy was in charge, but I can figure it out. Let's deal with what's happening right now.'

It's strange but I feel totally in control.

*'You can do this,'* Mildred keeps saying in the background.

There was something cheering about having Mildred on my side. Even Mildred knew I was a good mum and could work things out.

Getting bashed to the concrete floor of a parking garage had rattled me more than I could ever say. But, I was handling that and I was going to handle this.

Stuff happens, as Mildred says. You've got to live with it. Somehow.

Energy surges through me.

I think of my mum and how she'd dealt with some unbelievably hard things – Dad disappearing into the dark caverns of his mind and being there only in body; witnessing the pain of Scarlett going through years of infertility treatments and then falling apart. Mum had been able to cope and I was made of the same stuff.

## 21

*Ask someone how they are really feeling.*
*Not how they're pretending they're feeling.*
*The result will surprise you*

Adele Markham sobs on the phone when she hears my voice.

'Freya, I was waiting for you to phone. It's Lexi, isn't it, she's heard the news?'

This is a million miles away from the tough, hard as nails woman I've always felt her to be at our brief Christmas meetings. Funny at how you can look at people and have one impression and then find out they are something totally different behind it all. Another useful thing to put in my bag of tricks. Don't judge a book by its cover.

*Now you realise this*, Mildred says.

'You've got it in one, Adele,' I say.

I decide to cut the small talk: 'Unfortunately Lexi found out through Elisa's social media and she's devastated.'

Adele starts crying loudly now. She sounds as if she's talking through a tissue.

'I didn't know until one of the women I work with told me. I don't keep up with Instagram. Elisa never told us. She never tells us anything. I thought we had time to figure out what to do – please, Freya,' she begs, 'let us see Lexi. Don't stop us now. I love her, even though I've seen her so rarely.'

At this, I feel guilty.

'William says a year between meetings is so long and her uncles are dying to see her. She's so special. I'll never forgive myself for letting Elisa try to take care of Lexi . . . when I think of what happened in that restaurant . . .' She's almost incoherent now. 'I never told you this but I wanted to raise Lexi myself—'

'You're not losing Lexi,' I say, surprising myself.

'Thank you, thank you,' sobs Adele. 'I've never known how to make it better. She has a trust fund, we set it up and my aunt died and there's this seed pearl necklace left to her that she'd love and—'

'Lexi needs family, not money,' I say firmly. 'When she's a grown-up, you can hit her with trust fund stuff and Teddy will probably play her at poker to win it off her. You need to welcome Teddy and Liam too – we have to be a family.'

I had thought this out.

'Dan's father is dead, mine is . . .' I pause. 'He had a stroke, he's not coming out of it, so Lexi's missing a grandfather, although they have their great-grandfather, Eddie, who is both fabulous and eccentric at the same time, and a great-grandmother too. You'll have to meet them all. You already know Betty, Dan's mum. But now – Elisa and how to make things right for my daughter. Are we on the same page, Adele?'

'I'll do whatever you want,' she says tearfully. 'I don't know what to say to you, Freya, except that I'm so sorry. You must have thought we were the worst parents in the world to bring up Elisa the way she was but the boys are great, they have families, they have responsibilities. They are such fine men except that Elisa was always wild and—'

I interrupt her.

'Adele,' I say calmly, 'I'm not ringing to fight with you or to demand to know why you didn't do x or y so that Elisa would turn out in a particular way. Let's just deal with what we have got to deal with. Lexi is a very young fourteen. She is having a very hard time with Elisa never admitting she had another child first. Now Elisa is saying this pregnancy is the most amazing thing to ever happen to her. I tried to explain to Lexi that when Elisa got pregnant the first time she was very young, very immature and now she's ready to have a baby and that feels like the first time for her.'

'I understand.'

'Adele, I don't know if I can ever trust Elisa, but let's try and make this as right as we can.'

'OK.'

She is definitely crying again, I realise.

Adele insists we come to her for lunch.

'Please,' she says. 'I want you to see us here, let Lexi know that she is our beloved granddaughter, not just an hour at Christmas in a restaurant.'

'That sounds good.'

Elisa, who has been busy with her social media and posing, sticking her skinny belly out, for society shots in newspapers, has not been in touch with Lexi since news of her pregnancy broke.

Lexi is tearful sometimes so we're spending a lot of time together. She's missed a few days of ballet and she's helping me with my new cookbook.

*Pain in Your Heart Vegan Quiche!*' she says, finally coming up with the name for our newest dish.

'I like *I Wish I Hadn't Done That But Hey, What's Done Is D*one salad,' I say, checking my quinoa to make sure it's fluffy enough.

'Thank you for helping me,' I say to Lexi, 'it's so much more fun when you're here.'

She beams at me. 'I love being here,' she says. 'Can we have *No, You* Don't *Understand How I Feel* chicken nuggets for dinner?'

'How about *Insomnia Salmon*, I say?' and feel the familiar ache of guilt.

I'm still sleeping thanks to half a sleeping tablet but I feel so guilty about them. I need to tell Dan, I can't keep this secret from him any longer. Speaking truth in my support groups makes me aware that I need to speak it to my beloved Dan too. But what if he hates me for keeping it secret? Dan barely takes a painkiller if he falls off his bike: he hates drugs. He's been going on about the sleeping tablets for a long time and I now make sure he never sees me take them, so I am more or less pretending I no longer do.

What will happen when he finds out I still am?

'Mum,' roars Lexi up the stairs, 'come on, we'll be late!'

*God forbid you're late to the lunch of the century*, coos Mildred. Teddy has packed a small rucksack of cuddlies in case she's bored and Liam has his drawing things.

We drive along the city towards one of the poshest pieces of real estate in the whole country. Houses here regularly sell for sums that involve more digits than I can possibly count. But since I'm quite bad at counting, that isn't hard.

'Wow,' says Lexi, looking out the car windows. 'This is so cool, it's like lifestyles of the rich and famous.'

'Yeah,' I say brightly,' but it's not about the big houses, it's about the people inside . . .'

'Hungry,' shrieks Teddy at the top of her voice, 'hungry!'

'Give her some raisins, maybe,' says Dan, who has a hint of strain in his voice. I look at him.

'Raisins are so over,' I say.

'Ice cream, cereal,' shouts Teddy. Liam giggles. Teddy

then kicks the back of my seat.

'Stop it, darling,' I say, knowing she is bored.

I lean closer to Dan, who is driving.

'Do you think this is a good idea?' I whisper. 'I was trying to give Lexi a sense of family . . .'

'Brilliant,' he says.

I grin at him.

'OK, thank you.'

'You're a genius,' he says. 'Lexi needs this.'

We turn into the biggest, most fabulous house on the street: a massive red brick Victorian, flanked by two gates with – I kid you not – stone lions on top of them and from what I can see, an actual fountain in the front circle of lawn. The driveway runs like a horseshoe around from one big gate to the other, in and out. I'd bet a lot that the gates were electric.

Wow. This is certainly not what we are used to. I felt very glad Adele hadn't come to our house. I love it but we haven't done anything with it yet and then, I stop myself.

Dan and I have brought up Lexi, taken care of her, made sure she slept at night, was safe, loved, adored. *We* went to her dance recitals and brought her to ballet classes, not Elisa, not any of the Markhams. We'd taken care of her when she had vomiting bugs, had nits, had laboured over homework. We'd done it. So I wasn't going to be intimidated by all this money.

If I could deal with life after a mugging – well, thanks to my support group, which was proving invaluable – I could deal with the Markham family's obvious wealth.

'Want ice cream,' announces Teddy. 'Oh, swimming pool!' She'd caught sight of the fountain.

'That's a special swimming pool only for fish,' I say. 'People are not allowed in it in case they stand on the fish.'

Being able to fib at short notice is a very important skill for a mother and I have the imagination for it.

Dan keys in the number to the pad at the electric gate and it swings open seamlessly.

'It's amazing,' says Lexi, awestruck, and I feel a shiver of alarm and annoyance. I thought we'd taught her that stuff like that doesn't matter, that who you were was what was important. And yet here she is with her mouth open, looking at this house.

Instead of having to wait to be let in by a butler, Adele Markham and her husband, William, whom I have always thought is straight from central casting from a Ralph Lauren advert stand at the open door. A coppery spaniel is at their feet, sitting perfectly.

For once, unlike the times we have met her over the years when she's been all done up, Adele has clearly dressed down – or her version of it. She's wearing chinos and a white shirt with actual pearls around her neck. She looks anxious.

She and William come forward, with the spaniel bounding up happily, ears and trailing dog fur flying.

'A dog,' cries Lexi and gets to her knees.

'Welcome,' says William.

I think there are tears in his eyes but I don't know him well enough to be sure.

'This is Coco, who loves licking people. Hello, my dear Lexi. And you,' he turns to Liam, 'must be Liam.' He holds out a polite hand to Liam.

Liam, who has not done much hand-shaking, gives it a try.

'And this delightful little girl must be Teddy,' he says finally.

'I'm hungry and I want a go in your swimming pool,' says

Teddy winningly, and she takes his hand and reaches over to his other one to examine his watch.

I need to work on her 'don't talk to strangers' thing but then again, we have been selling this visit as a 'fun time'.

Adele hugs Dan and approaches me before Lexi.

She looks worried, I realise. Her eyes are a little red and there is a faint tremble in the hand she puts forward. 'Thank you for coming,' she says. 'I do want this to work.'

I allow myself to smile at her. Mama Lioness being cautious.

Then she puts her other hand over mine. 'Elisa's not here.'

*She's afraid*, I think. Afraid that Elisa will ruin this fragile meeting and she will never see this precious granddaughter.

'This is for Lexi, Adele,' I whisper. 'Elisa is only a small part of it. Lexi needs to see she has a family outside of Elisa.'

Once Lexi and Liam have been hugged, we all follow Teddy into the house, where she is opening every door and blithely picking up every no doubt priceless ornament.

The house is beautiful but the first thing I notice is all the pictures.

They're all over the walls, some black and white, some colour and they're all beautifully arranged in a way that must have taken many hours to organise but comes naturally to interior designers. There are ones of two good-looking men from boyhood to adulthood, complete with their weddings and lovely shots of gorgeous boys who are older than Lexi. Then there's Elisa in all sorts of various guises from her early days as a schoolgirl to even ones of her marriage to Dan.

'Look, look there's Elisa and Dad.'

'Family's important,' says Adele, standing behind her granddaughter and looking as if she wants desperately to touch her but dare not. I feel the guilt of having kept this woman out of Lexi's life for so long apart from an hour every Christmas.

'But there aren't any of me,' says Lexi.

'There are when you were little,' says Adele evenly and she leads Lexi over to a part of the wall where there are many baby pictures and some toddler ones which we have copies of. After that, the pictures of Lexi are a few school ones, ones Dan must have sent because I refused to have more than the barest contact with these people.

'We need more pictures of you up there, Lexi,' I say, meeting Adele's eyes. 'How about we start with one today. We could get you and . . .' I don't know where the words came from but they did, 'your Grandma and your Grandpa and you can put that on the wall then.'

'That would be lovely,' says Adele and William is at her side, squeezing her hand.

'We should have Teddy and Liam in there too because it's important to have everyone together,' he says.

Definitely tears, I think, smiling at him.

'And Coco,' says Liam, 'Coco has to be in the picture.'

Coco, who is now surgically attached to him, wags her tail, apparently agreeing with this.

'Bring food,' William says, smiling. 'Coco loves being in pictures as long as someone is feeding her at the same time.'

'Brilliant plan,' says Liam, looking around. 'Where's the food?'

Once dog treats have been found, we sit them all on a couch and put Coco beside them.

Then Adele and William sit in at either end. Dan takes the pictures because I think my hands might shake too much.

Lexi looks so happy and I feel utter shame that it has taken so many years to reach this point. I should have organised this years ago. I'm Lexi's mother and I owe it to her to know *all* her family properly even if her birth mother isn't my favourite person.

Somewhere deep inside me I heard Mildred go '*But*'.

'Shut up, Mildred,' I say mentally, 'you really are surplus to requirements.'

Lunch is fabulous fun. Adele, typically, turns out to be a wonderful cook but I do not hold this against her. Instead I ask her about some of the recipes.

'I have two sons,' she says. 'Elisa was the last baby and possibly a bit spoilt,' she adds, looking down. 'But the boys: they ate so much. One minute the fridge would be full and the next minute it would be empty. I just couldn't keep the place full of food. You have to learn how to cook but I'm a simple cook. You're the proper cook. Chef, sorry,' she corrected herself.

We were there about an hour and a half when Lexi suddenly enquires: 'Is Elisa coming?'

'Do you know,' said William easily, 'I don't think so. This is about us, not just Elisa.'

'Family,' Adele and I say at the same time.

We have tea in the garden where Teddy, Lexi and Liam play with Coco, and Liam keeps up his running commentary about how we need a dog.

Finally, it's time for us to go. So we reluctantly get up and have discussions about what we'll do next time so we can all meet up with Lexi's cousins, uncles and aunts. There are hugs and lots of little chats going on in the kitchen where Liam and Teddy have discovered Coco's stash of treats.

'She'll be sick,' I say to William, who beams at me.

'I don't care,' he says, smiling, and whispers, 'thank you so very much, Freya.'

Suddenly Teddy lets out an eldritch screech.

'I never got to go into paddling pool with the fishes,' she hisses, now catching a glimpse of it again and realising she's been duped.

'Next time,' I say, and take Dan's hand.

## 22

# *You create your own happiness*

I can't work but not because I have no ideas – I'm full of them – but I want to grab a lovely special coffee from Giorgio and Patrick's first. Just one moment in there makes me happy: that's down to them.

I run upstairs to check that my hair isn't too wild, slash a bit of lipstick on and I'll do. Patrick and Giorgio don't care what I look like. In five minutes I'm at the café door and I push it open, letting the glorious scents hit me: *nutmeg*, Patrick must have done something with nutmeg today, I think. And I look around the cabinet to see. There they are: his Portuguese tarts, and he puts an unusual dash of nutmeg into the custard/crème glaze which gives it just a little something extra. The place is half full, buzzing along nicely and there is no sign of either of the men. Instead, Josie, another of their part-time staff, is behind the counter.

'Hi, Freya,' she says, 'the usual?'

I'm a big fan of the flat white. Extra dry and fluffy.

'Yes, Josie, thanks a million,' I say. 'Can I just run in the back to see the boys?'

'Er . . .' Josie says, which should have been my first warning.

There's a tiny kitchen but it's fitted out beautifully and even though Patrick buys in most of his stock, he still makes some of the beautiful goodies he sells. He trained in patisserie and met Giorgio when they were both working in a big hotel in London.

'Hotels are hard work,' said Giorgio, 'and then when we fell in love, well, it seemed natural to come home.'

There's no sign of them there either and I'm a little confused.

'Josie,' I yell, 'where are they?'

'They might be upstairs,' she says, sounding harassed. 'There's . . . uh . . . a visitor.'

'Oh, well I won't go up then,' I say, feeling embarrassed at my being here at all. They're my friends but I don't know them that well and I've never been in the upstairs apartment and—

'Freya, that you?' yells Patrick from somewhere upstairs.

'Yes,' I say, going to the door which separates the kitchen from the stairs to their apartment. 'But Josie said you've got someone with you. I was just coming in for a natter,' I say quickly. 'It's fine, I'll talk to you again another time.'

'No, no,' chimes in Giorgio's voice. 'Come up, come up! She'll know what to do, Patrick!'

I briefly wonder about not going up. Is there a dead body upstairs and Giorgio saying I'm practical merely means he thinks I'd be good at cutting up a corpse because I know my way round butchering?

But I'm nosy, so up I go.

Even the walls up the stairs are typically Patrick and Giorgio: classy, arty, beautiful. They've created a fantastic gallery wall with wonderful old posters of food and drink from the twenties and thirties with prints of peacock-feathered girls sitting on top of coupes of champagne alongside Art Deco adverts for hot chocolate. It's bliss.

'Keep coming,' says Patrick and then I hear this strange noise, a squeaking.

A dying pig, I think, with anxiety.

I'm not *that* practical. They need a vet. Then Patrick appears at a door wearing his apron, his sleeves rolled up, and not looking his usual immaculate self.

'It's all going fine so far but we're hardly experts, you see,' he says.

'OK,' I say, wondering what exactly I have gotten myself into.

I walk into a beautiful kitchen-cum-sitting room with a marvellous dining table and exquisite club chairs in front of a genuine thirties fireplace, but in the middle of the floor is a mound of cushions, fluffy blankets and on that lies a smallish white dog of indeterminate breed who appears to be giving birth.

'Oh,' I say. Not what I expected.

'Look,' says Giorgio, turning to show me. 'Two already.'

'I didn't know you had a dog,' I said, bending over near the dog.

'Oh, we don't,' Giorgio says, 'but we found her in the back yard and we couldn't leave her because, look, she's so thin. You can see her ribs. I went out to feed her and whoosh, a baby started to come out. Well, I called Patrick pretty sharpish and we got her onto this,' he indicates the blanket, 'which was very difficult because she growled and then we carried her upstairs. Although, I think we should have brought her to the vet.'

'I don't know,' says Patrick, sounding uncharacteristically anxious.

'Farming or animal experience, anyone?' I ask.

'No,' they said.

'We had cats when I was a child,' adds Patrick.

'How many pups do dogs have, do you think?' I say.

'I don't know,' says Patrick. 'Giorgio is looking it up on the internet. Some dogs have eleven.'

Giorgio looks as if he's saying a prayer to some deity.

'Her figure will be ruined,' he says.

I get down on my knees and look at the dog who isn't wagging her tail or looking particularly happy to see me. She's concentrating on birthing another small little puplet.

'But we should ring a vet.'

'We did! They're busy. Said it should be fine. It's natural, they said. Does this look natural to you?'

'Not if I was having eleven, no,' I reply.

'These ones seem OK,' I say as I look at the two little ones lying beside her.

'They came out with film on them, so she started licking the film off one and we got the film off the other and they are breathing. We've put them up close to her because that's what it said you should do,' says Giorgio, holding an iPad. 'But what if there's more and something goes wrong and, and you know we aren't qualified for this.'

'I'm not qualified for this,' I say.

With a huge sigh the dog groans and another little bundle comes out of her wrapped in a milky film.

'Oh wow,' I say. 'This is amazing.'

Despite the fact that I have never done this before, I reach down, take the tiny little puplet up and place it in front of the mother.

'She'll know what to do,' I say with some strange instinct and sure enough, the mother licks away the film from the pup's mouth and then the tiny creature begins to make a little mewing noise. I realise the other two are mewing too.

'Food, they need food. Women put babies on the breast

as soon as they are born and that helps with the afterbirth,' I said suddenly.

'Ugh,' Giorgio shudders.

'It's natural,' I hiss.

Patrick and I are on the floor, the world's two strangest midwives who really know nothing about this, but with Giorgio on the iPad as well, we begin to think we are in control.

'Do you think she needs a drink?' says Giorgio.

'I need a drink,' says Patrick. 'But Freya, what do you think? Does she need water?'

He looks at me. I, as a female, am apparently the expert in all matters of childbirth, including dog birth.

'Let them feed first.'

I remember that puppies are born blind, so I take each tiny creature and put its miniature little face close to a teat. In an incredible act of magic, the little mouths open, close on the teats and they suck.

'You *do* know what to do,' says Patrick as if he had expected nothing else.

One more tiny little creature is born, this one smaller, a little all-black puppy, and the dog is tired, too tired to lick the membrane away, so I remove the film from the puppy. It feels still and I hold it close, smelling an indescribable smell of tiny new little creation just born into the world. I don't think it's breathing and without thinking, I gently open its tiny mouth and blow in. Then I rub the little back, trying to get the lungs working. I blow again. I have no idea if this is right or wrong but it feels right and then suddenly, this tiny little thing begins to mew. I cuddle it close, wet fur and all. 'You're mine,' I say, and check to see if my family are getting a girl or a boy.

'Magic, Princess Magic,' I announce, and put my little

darling beside her brothers and sisters where she begins to drink energetically.

Patrick finds some ham in the fridge and brings it to the dog, along with a bowl of water. She drinks but doesn't eat for a moment, waiting to see if she's safe. We retreat to give her space and she finally wolfs down the ham.

We all sit there, lost in admiration.

'Oh.' Giorgio looks at them and I can tell he's crying. 'They're beautiful, let's keep her, let's keep them all,' he says. 'Except for your one, Freya.'

'We don't have the space,' says Patrick running his dirty hands through his normally immaculate hair. 'But we can,' and he looks into Giorgio's eyes and the two of them melt.

*

I swear that as soon as Lorraine hears my steps outside our office, she's got the machine on to make a cappucino.

'Hey boss lady,' she says, 'how's it going with the taking over the world and taking no crap from anybody?'

*I really like her*, said Mildred. *She takes no prisoners, you should be more like her, why are you not more like her?*

Because I'm not, I say. Deal with it.

*Fine.*

'Something bad's happened?' I ask, as I take the coffee and drink.

'The cappucino was a giveaway, right?'

'Yeah. What gives?'

'Nina has been on the phone and because she thinks I'm some sort of answering machine so she doesn't have to keep anything secret from me, she wants you to know when – what was the word she used? Oh yes – '*when the bloody hell you were going to have something fun to say about your new series-slash-book-slash-any bloody thing.*'

'She is a little bluebird of joy,' I say sarcastically.

Somehow, and it might be because I'm feeling stronger than I've felt for a long time, I decide to ring Nina and tell her it isn't that simple but it's all coming together. Finally.

Lorraine groans.

'You don't trust Nina, do you?' I say. 'I do, I think she's brilliant.'

'You trust everyone,' says Lorraine. 'You trusted bloody Geraldine when she was robbing you blind by drinking the profits.'

'True,' I say. 'Sometimes there are people who aren't your friends: they just work with you and they don't mind ripping you off.'

'Nina doesn't mind ripping you off and she would if she got half a chance.'

'Nina has been with me longer than you've been with me,' I say hotly.

'Fine, but keep her on speaker. I've better instincts than you.'

'When did I start to rely on you for all my business judgements?' I grumble, even though I know she's right.

'When you realised I was nearly always right,' says Lorraine as if she can read my mind.

*Wow, you have so got to be more like her,* says Mildred. *You're just a wimp, a total wimp and besides she works for you, she shouldn't be able to talk to you like that.*

Mildred can be funny that way, one moment she's praising somebody, the next moment she's giving out to me because I'm not tough on them.

With enough coffee down me and a little dish of chocolate-covered raisins in front of me to give me energy, I phone Nina. I've written down several possible reasons why the book is late. I can't tell her that I've been broken for a while

311

but am up and running again, with my new, quirky recipes. Honest new recipes, I think.

'Hello,' Nina says in that slightly faux posh voice she uses all the time. It doesn't sound right to me and Lorraine insists Nina's just normal, but is desperately trying to hide it.

'Never trust people who hide where they're from by using a fake accent' is one of Lorraine's mottos.

'I was just going to ring you,' I lie. I am getting good at this lying.

'That's good,' says Nina, 'because I was just going to ring you too. In fact, we need a meeting because I know one of the producers of your TV show. We bumped into each other and he's saying he hasn't heard a peep out of you in months. Which is disastrous for your career – and mine. You're one of my top clients, obviously, and I have to look out for you—'

I interrupt this diatribe and immediately make a mistake: I go off message. I'm looking at the bits of paper on my desk that explain how I'm trying something new and it must be right and suddenly I feel emotional, misunderstood. If only Nina knew anything about me she'd understand what's been going on in my life and that the stress of the past four months has been intolerable.

'I was mugged and I'm only just limping my way out of the anxiety and of course I had to hide it because nobody wants to hear my problems, as you always say and . . .' Suddenly I realise that all this mental chatter isn't mental chatter at all, and that I'm actually *saying* it. Out loud.

'Mugged?' gasps Nina. 'Like mugged where? What happened? Held at knife point?'

There's a definite change in her accent, I notice, despite the mounting fear that I have just done the stupidest thing on the planet and actually told her.

Lorraine is making *are you nuts?* faces at me but I keep going. I have to now.

'It was in a parking garage, I'd done this cooking demonstration in town and I had just paid for my ticket when this guy mugged me.'

'Mugged? Not just bumped into? Properly mugged? The police came?'

'Thrown to the ground. Broke my collarbone, had bruises on my temple,' I say. 'He had a knife.'

'A dangerous criminal had a knife to your throat and you never thought to tell me,' roars Nina and the posh voice is totally gone now. This is the real Nina, I realise.

Lorraine is looking at me with a combination of pity and *I told you so* written across her face.

'This is . . .'

I wait for her to say 'terrible. No wonder you haven't been able to work. I can't imagine the stress you're under.'

And then she says: 'Fantastic, you have no idea what this can do for your career. Oh Freya, you're such a novice sometimes. I have no idea how you have got this far in life, because you can't see the wood for the trees. There you are, going along with your little happy pictures and saying that blueberries and muffins are like animal poo which is ridiculous. And then, this unbelievable thing happens, this will have you on every paper, on every talk show in the country. This will give you an in into the UK because you finally have something to talk about. I mean, who wants to talk about bloody recipes? There's got to be more of a story to you . . .'

I tune out and look over at Lorraine who is making cutting noises with her fingers across her throat to imply that I should hang up.

'You said people didn't want to hear my problems,' I say anxiously.

'Yes but I meant small problems. This is *big*!'

'Oh, Nina, there's something wrong with the line,' I say and I stab my finger on the end call button.

There is a horrified silence in the office.

'I won't say I told you so,' Lorraine says and she goes to the cabinet where she keeps the chocolate which we only take out in emergencies. Very expensive chocolate that costs an absolute fortune, but makes an enormous difference in food. And frankly, we've been going through it in the office. She breaks both of us off a few big lumps. My stash is bigger.

'For the shock,' she says and hands it to me.

I sit back in my office chair, shaking. The phone starts ringing again frantically, then my mobile starts ringing, all Nina.

'Ringing from two phones at the same time,' I say, 'that's a trick for sure.'

'Yeah, when she's really excited all her alien flippers come out and she can make phone calls with them,' Lorraine snaps. 'You know she's an otherworldly being and I don't mean a *nice* otherworldly being. She's one of those aliens who come here to take over the world and you just happen to be caught in the way. She has no empathy and she will walk on your grave if she thinks it will get her a sale of some sort.'

I grin at Lorraine.

'Tell me what you really think,' I say.

'Freya, if you want to go the *My Secret Hell* in the papers route, that's fine but I know you and you don't. So ring her, tell her you've been on to your agent and if she spills a word of this, you'll sue her. You're doing that big interview of hers tomorrow and if she breathes a word of it, then she is dead.'

'Dead? Is that legal?'

'Say it the posh way,' Lorraine grins. 'Say you'll sue her clothes off her back, then.'

'That's the posh way?'

'Yes.'

'Right.' I sigh. 'I wish I hadn't done that. But I thought if I had said what had happened, she'd understand.'

'She understands cash signs,' says Lorraine sombrely.

The next day, I'm getting my make-up done in a proper make-up chair, with a lovely woman discussing the right sort of base for my skin and I'm only *half* listening.

This means I'm stressed out of my head.

You see, I do want to know the right foundation for my skin: I'm obsessed with it, actually. When your hair is this pale it's very easy to look like the undead without the correct base. Finding a colour that suits is vital, so on every shoot I have ever been on my first question has been: 'What colour base do you think will suit me?'

We are having exactly the same conversation but my mind is almost entirely elsewhere – on Nina and her promises that we have a secret and she will go 'to the grave, dahling' before she tells anyone about my terrible experience.

I feel anxious.

I'm nearly ready to go. Nearly, in that my hair is beautifully styled and held back with little clips to give the make-up artist room to do her work. Hair first, make-up afterwards, then clothes.

The shoot for the interview Nina has been talking about for months is taking place in an elegant country hotel with an exquisite spa, fabulous gardens, and two championship golf courses round the corner. But Nina clearly doesn't want Lorraine here and she's taking tiny little bitchy swipes at her. This is a clue that Nina's angry that Lorraine knew all about my mugging – and she didn't.

Lorraine drove me to the shoot, which had Nina raising

her eyebrows and saying. 'I could have picked you up, darling, if I had known you wanted a taxi.'

And suddenly I know we have a problem.

First she has Lorraine running up and downstairs getting all the coffee orders which, with the two hair stylists, a make-up artist, someone from the magazine, a photographer and his assistant, and a stylist there, means a lot of up and downs because people keep changing their minds and the cappuccino with almond milk suddenly becomes a skinny flat white, if they have it. I don't ask Lorraine to get me coffee, I can get my own coffee thank you very much.

Then it's the tone in Nina's voice when she speaks to Lorraine.

A bitchy tone.

Then she's insisting Lorraine sits outside while I'm being made up.

I rise out of the chair to say something but Lorraine catches my eye and shakes her head. Lorraine is keeping everything on an even keel by not tackling Nina full on. So she's going and getting the coffee. She's staying in the other room. She's not ripping Nina's face off when Nina is incredibly rude to her. But as I look at Lorraine's eyes this last time, I realise that something has to change.

I call Lorraine in when Nina's on a call. 'She's being a bitch and I am terrified of what she's told the reporter,' I say.

'She doesn't want to be sued,' says Lorraine soothingly. 'Let's keep it all nice and calm so that by the time the journalist gets there you'll be a calm, relaxed version of yourself. We'll have beautiful pictures and you know that you're doing what you need to do.'

I wince.

'You're doing it, aren't you?' she says.

'Doing what?' I say.

'Imagining how it could all work out if Nina had her way.'

'Yeah,' I sigh, 'I don't want to be that person, I don't want that following me everywhere as if . . . as if I'm nothing more than a victim, because I'm not a victim.'

That's one thing the group has taught me, I'm not a victim. People call people like me victims of crime and I suppose we are, but I don't want to consider myself a victim. Something bad happened to me, but I can get over it. A lot worse things have happened to other people.

Like Ariel, who was raped. Like Eileen who lost her daughter.

'Look at my parents,' I say to Lorraine, 'and my mother grieving every single moment of every day as she takes care of my father lovingly, wearing herself into the ground because she still wants to show him how much she loves him. These are much worse things and I don't want my case turned into some enormous deal just because I'm famous. It shouldn't be like that.'

'Just stop going over it in your head!' says Lorraine, 'and if you get really stuck in the interview, just think of . . .' she pauses. 'I can't think of anything,' she says finally. 'I've been trying, but if you break down and cry and say you're working so hard on all your new recipes . . . shit, that doesn't work either.'

'Yeah, I know,' I say, 'it's a tricky one. I have to try and give people what they want: the happiness, the fun.'

'Exactly,' says Lorraine, back on track. 'Talk about the new house and how it's nice even though it needs a teeny bit of work. Not a lot, mind you, because you don't want to upset the lady you bought it off and if you say it has a hideous avocado bathroom, she might not like it.'

I turn and grin at Lorraine.

'You're a real softy at heart,' I say. 'Girl boss indeed! But you're soft as butter.'

'No, I am tough,' she protests.

'You're thinking about the lady I bought the house off and you don't want to upset her.'

'You said she'd been looking after her husband who was ill, too and things had been difficult and maybe she wanted to make the house all pretty and couldn't afford it. I don't know,' mutters Lorraine. 'Just try not to hurt anyone, well that's what my mum says.'

'That's what my mother says too.'

We nod in agreement, thinking of strong women who hold the world up.

'OK,' I say, 'I'm ready for this.'

We take endless pictures.

'Just one more,' lies the photographer constantly, as I lean against the tree in the garden and try and look deliriously happy, and as if it's not the five hundred and fiftieth picture of the day.

'That's it, that's it. Now look off into the distance, give me that misty-eyed stare.'

'Do you know,' I say, turning to look at him, 'that misty-eyed stare thing does not make me look nice. I look deranged. So let's just do more smiling.'

'OK,' he says.

I'm getting the hang of photographers, I think and I wink at Lorraine.

Finally I'm back in my normal clothes, everyone is clearing out except Nina and Lorraine and the journalist is waiting. We've talked before, she's a nice woman: Stephanie Robson, clever, one of those people who treat your words with respect and quote you accurately because she tapes everything. But she works for a tough newspaper which takes no prisoners.

Neither of our jobs are easy here.

'You guys don't have to be here, do they?' says Stephanie.

'No, no,' I say as if I'm totally relaxed. 'I'll tell you what, ladies, why don't you go downstairs and grab a sandwich in the bar and I'll be down when we are finished here.' I smile at both of them, a slightly insincere smile because I know that Lorraine wouldn't even want to get into the same lift as Nina. But they exit anyway and I'm left alone.

The interview rolls along swimmingly for a while. And Stephanie asks one of those questions I always find impossible to answer.

'What keeps you going, Freya?' she says. 'You've moved house, you've got small children, you've got a daughter in secondary school, you run a business, you travel. How do you manage it all?'

This time I have practised.

I say, 'I'm grateful in the morning.' I look her straight in the eye, because it's true. And I almost hate myself for saying this, 'I do yoga in the morning. It's completely fabulous.'

*Well, it might be if you actually did it.*

It's over, I think, glancing at my watch. I've nailed it.

But I haven't.

'And Freya, I hate asking you about this as I know you haven't spoken about it before, but you had a horrible experience this year, can you tell us about it?'

Nina.

*That bitch. You should fire her. No! Kill her.*

Relax, Mildred, I sigh, thinking: if it has to happen, it's got to happen my way.

I get up and go to the coffee thermos that's been there all morning and that everyone has been ignoring in favour of flat whites and Americanos. The stuff's probably awful at this stage but I don't care.

'Want one?' I ask Stephanie.

She nods cautiously, probably wondering if I'm going to bail on her and not answer.

I get us two coffees and take a deep drink of mine.

'I didn't want to talk about this and I'll tell you why,' I say. 'In the past four months, since I was mugged, I've met people who've been victimised in every way and they are doing their best to get on with their lives. Compared to some of what people on this planet go through, being shoved onto the ground of a parking garage is nothing. Yes, it was horrible. Yes, I was scared.'

Stephanie is watching me now, fascinated as her story unrolls before her.

'But I kept it to myself.'

'Why?'

I smile. 'You ask all the right questions. Because I didn't want to make my experience on a par with what some people put up with just because I'm "famous".' I make air quotes with my fingers. 'Also, if you make a career in anything that involves the media, I've been told . . .' I pause. This one's for you, Nina, I think. '. . . that happiness sells. I've been told that people don't want to hear about problems but when I was devastated and couldn't work, I got fed up with all the "happy" Instagram feeds and blogs. I felt so awful that I could no longer look at people who might be pretending to be happy because I had to pretend to be happy too.'

'Can you tell me about the attack?' she asks.

'I got shoved to the ground, got my collarbone broken when I tried to stop my fall, I got contusions, and yes, I was terrified. I think he was on drugs, No, nobody's been caught and no, I don't want all addicts hung, drawn or quartered. I imagine the person who mugged me was broken too. He broke me for a while but my family and some really good friends and my support group put me back together.'

'And . . .'

'That's it, Stephanie,' I say, getting up and collecting my stuff. 'I honestly didn't know you knew this. That's all I've got to say. Don't make the headline "My Mugging Hell – Viking Chef Flattened". Please.'

Suddenly, we both laugh. We know that's pretty much exactly what it will say.

'What's next, then?'

At the door, I turn. 'I'm working on recipes for helping you when you're down, for when your family is down, for life. Because it's not all happy. Social media likes to pretend life's fabulous, but it's not. I hate fakery. We should try to be real, because when life's really good, it's marvellous.'

I give her the beaming smile I'd given to the photographer scores of times earlier that day, but this time it's real, and leave.

I go downstairs to the bar where Nina is at one end, not eating a sandwich but tapping away on her laptop and Lorraine is sitting down the other end nursing a Coke and looking as if she really wishes it was a very big glass of wine. I sneak over to Lorraine.

'Come with me,' I say.

We walk to Nina together.

'You told her,' I say.

'Wha—?' Lorraine roars.

'It's publicity gold,' begins Nina.

'You're fired and I'm suing you,' I say and I drag Lorraine out before she can punch Nina.

'Let me go! I'm gonna get that bitch!' she shrieks.

'You can't put the genie back in the bottle,' I say calmly. 'From now on, we do it our way.'

# VIKING CHEF FREYA'S SECRET MISERY

A terrifying city centre car park mugging plunged TV chef Freya Abalone into depression – and her attacker has not yet been caught.

'I can't get it out of my head,' says distraught Freya, forty-two, one-time winner of the Sexiest Chef of the Year award. Leggy, blonde Freya, whose cool good looks mean she's known as 'Viking', was knocked to the ground and had several bones broken and insists that if it wasn't for a victim support group, she'd be living in terror.

For the first few days after 'My Secret Horror: Viking Freya Mugged', Lorraine is on the phone all the time. Crisis management, she calls it.

'I'm fed up of crisis management, Lorraine,' I say. 'I want non-crisis management, what's that?'

'I think that's what happens when you go out on a Friday night and get scuttered,' says Lorraine, straightforward as ever.

Uber-agent Paddy Ashmore in the UK has put us on to a fabulous publicity team who work with Lorraine because I am not discussing anything again until I want to. Saying no to people is a full-time job.

Dan hugs me a lot and says: 'I don't know why we trusted Nina in the first place.'

*I always thought there was something wrong with her,* says Mildred.

No, you didn't, I tell Mildred. You thought she was fabulous. You were entirely taken in by her and wished you were her when you grew up, even though she's at least, I don't know, fifteen years younger than we are, or a hundred years older if she's made a Faustian pact, which is a possibility.

*OK*, Mildred agrees. *She dazzled me a little bit with all the 'you can have the universe if you just learn how to do social media' stuff. I was taken in by her.*

We both were, I say. Actually, you and me are really the same thing. You do realise that? You are my inner voice.

Mildred says nothing. She knows she's my inner voice. She just does this to amuse us both.

I think the crisis management is just about managed.

But what's amazing to me are the emails and messages and tweets of support from real people who say they understand how I feel.

**I was attacked and I didn't leave the house for a year. You made me feel normal, Freya, thank you.**

**My daughter was mugged and she has never been the same again. She's terrified. I showed her your story and she wants to write to you. If you can get through it, she can.**

**Tell us the real story because that's what we need, Freya, not the pretend stuff on social media.**

**I've had body issues my whole life and it got much worse two years ago when I became obsessed with having lovely Instagram pictures. I pretend I eat loads but I don't. I weigh six stone. My doctor says I'm anorexic and I need to go into hospital.**

There were hundreds of them and once the story began to move on social media, it grew and grew. I was sent stories of pain and suffering; stories that people hid because who wants to hear about the pain of real life in the 'happy insta-world'? And all of these people said that my story helped because it was a real story in the celebrity world where everything was supposed to be perfect.

I wanted to answer them all and could see a whole new job for me opening up: one where I allowed myself to be who I really was, because that seemed to help people.

I wrote to everyone, posted, Instagrammed and then one day, I told my growing number of fans about my new recipe book and my Fear of the Dark Chocolate Cake, and everything went crazy.

# 23

## *Do one thing every day to make yourself happy*

My mother isn't one of life's texters – when she needs to talk, she phones, but today, when I'm doing the final checking of book lists for the children for going back to school in September, just two weeks away, she texts.

**Freya, can you come round later today, this evening perhaps, when Dan's home. I need to talk to you.**

**Of course,** I reply instantly and follow it up with **What's wrong?**

**Nothing is wrong,** my mother texts back quickly.

And that's it, radio silence.

Dan is home late. Teddy is in bed or in other words, Teddy is getting up and out of bed every five minutes demanding stories, glasses of water, glasses of milk, that she needs to go to the toilet and would somebody please come and tell her another story. Liam is drawing and Lexi is reading. She does a lot more reading these days and it's been helpful in the light of my 'terrible trauma', as she didn't read all the rubbish, and we were able to tell her that I was fine and that making things sound much worse is a lot like making things sound fabulous when they're not. Fake.

'I might be late,' I say, kissing him goodbye. 'It's the tone of her text. She's the only person I know who manages to get tone in her text and she just sounded off.'

I drive quickly to Summer Street and let myself in. I call quietly to Mum because I don't want to frighten her. There's no sound of Eddie stomping around, thank goodness, so he might be watching one of his military TV programmes. Scarlett, who hasn't gone home since she moved here, is at her dance class, so the person sitting in the kitchen must be my mother.

I listen and hear loud battle noises emanating from the tiny sitting room. Eddie's watching something about the Second World War and the taking of a bridge or something that requires lots of blowing up things. Granny's probably still reading. She loves novels, although she's on to the big print novels these days and she has a special stand for the books so she doesn't exhaust her poor hands holding them up.

'She's very gone on those romantic ones,' Maura once said to me. 'I don't understand it, how can you be her age and still think the prince is going to whisk you away?'

Mum had smiled. 'Aren't we all twenty-five somewhere in our hearts,' she says.

'Mum,' I say now.

'Here, darling,' she says, appearing at the door of the kitchen. 'Come in.'

I go into the kitchen and for once it feels cold and unloved. It's a little untidy, which is quite unlike my mother who tidies up as she goes, and is a great fan of lighting the odd candle in the kitchen in the evening.

Mum looks, I realise, absolutely shattered. I can see the hollows of her eye sockets as if she is about to paint herself for a fancy dress Dia de Muertos.

Her hair, once a beautiful white blonde, just looks white

now, and with her pale face, she's beginning to look old. Old before her time.

I want to cry and that's before I notice she's not wearing any of her lovely jewellery. Mum loves jewellery – she'd go to hell and back for some old turquoise bit of a necklace with a feather attached to it and a few little bits of crystals dangling off it. Tonight, there is not so much as an earring on her person.

'Do you want herbal tea?' she says.

'You sit down,' I say. 'I'll make tea.'

She sinks into the big chair at the head of the table with a sigh so big it sounds as if she might never get up. I wait until I have made the tea and sit down beside her, taking one of her hands in mine.

'What's wrong?' I say.

'I hate laying this on you, Freya,' she says, 'it's not fair because there is Scarlett, Maura and Con, but you are the person I go to first. It's not really right, is it? But parents sometimes do that and you have always been the person I went to, I'm sorry. That was wrong of me.'

'No, it wasn't wrong of you,' I say. 'You'd be talking to Scarlett if she wasn't just getting back on her feet and Maura is very focused on the solution, so if you have a problem, she's determined to have it fixed about four seconds after you tell her about it. It's a very masculine energy, I always think.'

Mum nods, her lips shaking a bit as if she might just cry.

'And Con,' I say. 'Con's too busy trying to find the perfect woman.'

This elicits a laugh.

'Don't think there is a perfect woman for Con. I think he found the perfect woman years ago, but he just couldn't recognise her, what with all the imperfect women he keeps finding,' I joke.

I pour her tea, hand it over to her and our fingers touch. I think it's the touch that does it because suddenly she lets go of the cup, puts her hands on the table, rests her head on them and begins to sob.

'Oh Freya, I can't do this. I, I thought I could look after your father but I'm the wrong person to do it, because I am going to hurt him. He is going to get a pressure sore or he's going to choke on some food because his ability to swallow is going, or something is going to happen that I'm not going to be able to sort out. I was so stupid,' she says.

'You're never stupid, Mum,' I say gently. 'You love him.'

'I thought love could fix everything, but he has medical needs and I can't fulfil them. I've been putting it off but I know there is no other way: he has to go back to full-time care, where they can look after him properly.'

She can't speak for a few moments as the sobs come.

I say nothing but just keep hugging, knowing the story will come out when she's able to go on.

'The occupational therapist was in yesterday and we had a talk,' she says. 'We need so much more equipment to keep him safe here and it would be like turning the house into a hospital and having medical staff on all the time and I could still mess up. He could have another stroke, probably will, and what would we do? The list of things that could go wrong is endless and I don't know what to do.'

'You're going to do what's right for Dad,' I say, holding on to my calm.

'But I thought this was the right thing for him, being with him, loving him.'

'And it was for a while but not anymore,' I point out. 'That doesn't mean you've failed. You have given him everything and you can still continue to give him so much love, but it just won't be here.'

'But I want it to be in our home.'

'And yet it can't be, Mum,' I say. I know my job here – I have to help her through this pain.

'I've tried so hard, I've tried to keep up a happy face and make it look as though I was handling it all but . . .'

I smile at her gently.

'Mum, I was doing that for months after being mugged, pretending it was all fine. I know there's no comparison between that and poor Dad, but the truth is the same: sometimes putting on the happy face isn't the answer.'

Even as I say it, I know this is startlingly true.

'Sometimes, we are powerless and we just have to let go of this false sense of control and say, *no, I'm not coping. I don't feel great today, I can't do this* . . . What helped me was my support group and you don't even have time for that.'

I think of all the people like my mother who are carers, who truly go through tragedy day after day and do it with such courage no matter how exhausted they are. And what helps them most is to be honest and to say when they cannot cope.

'Mum, we have to protect Dad and if that means he cannot be cared for here, then he cannot be cared for here, OK?'

'I thought you'd hate me for saying that,' she says, 'because I told everyone for so long that I would look after him and it would be fine.'

'Mum, you're one person,' I say. 'You can't do everything. Eddie and Granny Bridget were quite enough. But add someone as neurologically and physically disabled as Dad, and you can't manage. Let's all sit down, put our heads together and find out the best place for Dad.

'You gave him time at home in his own home where he's been loved and now he will be somewhere else where he will be loved, but where he will be safe, medically speaking. Because that's something you can't give him anymore, no matter how much you love him.'

'OK,' she's nodding now and I grab some tissues from the table and hand them to her. 'I was afraid you'd think I was a coward.'

'You're far from a coward, Mum,' I say. 'Now, how about tomorrow we talk to Scarlett, Con and Maura.'

'I think Con is going away for a long weekend.'

And suddenly we both laugh in the way you laugh in the middle of great pain.

'Is he ever going to settle down?' I say.

'Probably,' says Mum, 'some day. He has to do his own thing, find his own way.'

'Maybe we all frightened him off relationships with women for life,' I say. And now Mum really laughs.

'He loves the very bones of you all,' she says. 'He's not frightened of marriage for life, he's just being a complete brat, thinking he's the eternal bachelor.'

'I think you should tell him that, Mum,' I say. 'Tell him you expect grandchildren and a proper relationship and none of this messing around anymore. That's your next mission, sorting him out.'

'Freya, I don't do interfering in my children's lives.'

'The three of us managed all right without you, but I think Con is a hopeless case. Now, I'm going to text the other three and we'll set up something for tomorrow night.'

'Fine,' she says.

I text everyone and added for them not to ring, just said briefly what it was about. Mum can talk to Scarlett when she gets home.

'There,' I say to her, 'it's done.'

'Thank you, thank you Freya,' she says.

There's a rattle of keys in the front door and Scarlett appears.

'Hi,' she says, breathless. Her dance class is pure exercise and she says it helps her to sleep. In her tiny T-shirt and footless dance tights, she looks like a blonde Lexi.

'What are you doing here?'

'Just having tea,' I say. 'You look great, lovie. If I get time some night, will you take me dancing or is it such an intense workout, I'd pass out?'

'You'd pass out,' she says, hugging me. 'It's taken me ages to be able to stand the pace but do please come. I'll take care of you if you need a rest.'

'The three of us can go, then,' I said, grabbing Mum's hand. 'You to show us how it's done, me to pass out and Mum to watch and laugh.'

Scarlett sits down and I look at her glowing face and think that her glow comes from more than dancing.

'Tell me?' I say.

She beams at us both.

'He didn't want to come in because he's afraid he wouldn't be welcome but I met Jack tonight.'

Mum reaches out and grabs Scarlett's hand.

'If he still loves you, phone him this second and get him back here,' says Mum.

Scarlett reaches into her pocket for her phone and sends a text.

'He says he left because we weren't people anymore – we were this baby-making unit. Us both swallowing vitamin pills and *we* were lost. That's why he left. But he loves me.'

Mum is calm.

'Of course he loves you, Scarlett. Doesn't mean it's easy though.'

'No,' I agree, 'doesn't mean it's easy.'

September always seems like the beginning of the year to me – it's the beginning of the school year, and once the leaves begin to turn gold, I feel an excitement at the newness of everything.

Lexi's doing important exams this year, so I think she needs a boost with her new family to help her start the year.

Which is code for her not going back into school with no mention of Elisa, who has been off the radar since news broke of her pregnancy.

I phone Adele.

'I gave Adele your number a while ago,' Dan admits. 'I think she's too nervous to use it.'

I laugh so loud I feel an unused stomach muscle ache.

*You must put 'do sit-ups' on your 'to do' list,* Mildred intones. I ignore her.

'How about we have dinner in our house on Friday and Elisa and possibly the new boyfriend come along?'

'We haven't met him,' says Adele faintly, as if she'd met too many of Elisa's men already. 'Do you think that's wise?'

'You could bring your sons and their wives, and their sons . . .'

I let the idea percolate.

'Lexi would have more of your family there. People who want to see her. Let her feel loved, wanted.'

'They'd love that. There's Tony and his wife, Jo, and their twin sons, Michael and Cooper. They're eleven, great boys, high energy. Marcus is the eldest and his wife is Lois, who's pregnant, and she has Joshua, who's fifteen and studies night and day. He's quiet, very gentle. They'll all be at your door happily. Tony and Marcus hated that they weren't allowed to meet Lexi and you all that time in our house. But,' she adds, 'I don't know what Elisa has organised for the week. She's back and is going to parties all the time and meeting up with friends and . . .'

'It's OK,' I say calmly and in the background, Mildred giggles. Mildred recognises the steel inside me. 'I'll invite her and if she can come, she can come. Friday night our house, it will be very casual, very relaxed.'

'I can do casual,' says Adele.

I laugh. 'Promise,' I said, 'because I will be wearing jeans.'

'I have jeans.'

'Good, you could even bring over the dog, that would help. Lexi wants her own dog.'

'Oh, we can get her a dog,' Adele says eagerly.

'No!' I say. 'That has to be a family decision and we are working on it . . .'

'Of course. I'm not trying to interfere,' replies Adele quickly.

'I know you're not. Just leave it all up to me. I'm hoping half six, a quarter to seven. I know that's early for you guys but Teddy is only four, although she behaves as though she's twenty-six and she does need to go to bed earlier or she gets very grisly.'

'No problem, we'll be there,' says Adele.

'That's the spirit,' I say. I hang up. Another thing ticked off my list.

On Friday, the menu planned, food purchased and ready to be cooked, my hair has been blow-dried into enviable and unusual straightness and I've had an actual manicure.

'I don't have manicures unless I'm doing the show,' I say to Lorraine, admiring my nails, a purple so dark as to be almost black. It's funky and fun. It won't last but hey, life's for living.

'Suits you,' she replies, having left the office to assist with turning Chateau Kellinch into a bower of loveliness. 'And you owe me some overtime.'

She'd gone to the flower market early and had enough flowers in Lexi's favourite colours to organise a wedding.

Dan, who thought I was a bit mad what with all this dinner with the entire Markham clan malarkey, had gone off to work as usual, and had taken Liam, still discussing when we'd get our puppy from Patrick and Giorgio, and Teddy, discussing how guinea pigs could actually run very fast when you opened their cages, to their various camps.

Caitlin and Lexi were not, repeat not, going to ballet camp.

'We want to help,' said Caitlin, eyes shining, when I picked them up from ballet the evening before.

'Yes,' says Lexi, looking happier than she had in days.

I didn't know what she'd been saying to my daughter, but I decided there and then that not only were they going to help Lorraine with the beautification, but Caitlin had to stay for the party.

Dan's mother was in our house by the time I was back from all my errands, to help me organise the place.

Sweet, shy and clearly petrified of the wealthy Markham family, I have to sit her down in the kitchen and explain how it was all going to work.

'Betty,' I say, 'you have two sons you love?'

'Yes . . .' says Betty nervously, twisting a duster in her hands.

'They're decent members of society, have good jobs and Zed's going to get married one day and have beautiful children.'

'I hope so.' Betty crossed herself at this plan, which would clearly only work with Divine intervention.

'Do you have any hopeless kids hidden away who've run off from their children and ignored responsibility all their life?'

'Holy God, no!'

'Great. Adele and William Markham have. And it doesn't matter how much money they have in the bank or what sort of car they drive, they have that pain to deal with. That has kept Lexi out of their lives for years. So which of you have the most gifts in life?'

Betty smiled at me. She was a pale woman, gentle and often anxious and I could imagine her being terrified of the Markhams during the whole speed-wedding procedure all those years ago.

'You've been Lexi's gran, and Liam's and Teddy's. That's not going to change. We're opening the door a chink and . . .' I put a pot of tea on the table in front of her, 'we're trying to make Lexi feel better about Elisa telling the world that she's about to have her "first wonderful baby". That is the aim of this. To help Lexi.'

'Tell me what to do,' says Betty firmly, taking a sip of tea, putting it back down and getting the duster out again.

I take it from her.

'Drink that tea slowly and then go out to meet Scarlett. She'll be here in a few minutes and she's taking you to get your hair and nails done,' I say.

'I couldn't.' Betty's worn hand immediately goes to her chest. There have been few manicures in her life. Not that my mother had been a great woman for the beautician's either, but then, my mother chose not to go.

I should have arranged for Betty to have manicures before, I think guiltily.

*You're doing it now*, Mildred points out.

Who are you and what have you done with Mildred? I retort.

By the time Dan brings Liam and a remarkably paint-free Teddy back, our home is utterly beautified.

Lorraine, who has had many careers in her time, did a bit of floristry once and can hand tie a bouquet – with a certain amount of swearing. Every bowl or cup not already in use has been pressed into service and is full of flowers, hiding all the bits of the walls where the plaster is gone and really transforming the place. I've even done a deal with the devil and risked using modern sticky things to hang heavy paintings.

'This one takes four pounds' weight,' reads Lexi slowly.

I hold a giant poster from a Rothko exhibition in New York in one hand. The frame might be four pounds or it might be heavier . . .

*You measure ingredients for a living,* says Mildred. *Are you kidding me?*

Only for baking. I use great skill for cooking and measuring is only for the recipe books, I remind her as the Rothko goes into place, superbly hiding an ersatz Picasso lady with a giant nose and one eye that Teddy must have needed a chair to crayon onto the wall.

Lorraine takes over the hanging up once she's flowered every surface and tells me to finish cooking.

'I want a doggy bag of the scallops to take home,' she says later, peering into the fridge, where scallops lie ready to be sizzled briefly in butter before dropping into lamb's leaf salad with honey dressing.

'Stay,' I say. 'The more the merrier. It's not as if we don't have chairs.'

As we've never had enough room to open up our huge

leaf dining room table fully, we never had enough chairs but Lorraine, used to organising shoots, has called in French restaurant ones along with glassware, flatware, candelabras, ice and magnificent ice buckets that look as if an antique shop will be screaming soon that they've been robbed.

'Oh, do,' says Lexi, who is flushed from her efforts. She and Caitlin are dancing round now, delighted with their party, adjusting the pink lemonade just so in the ice buckets, giggling and discussing the music.

'Yes, do,' I say. 'You've made this special.'

Lexi isn't panicked about Elisa anymore – this is her party. Elisa's just one of the guests.

'But don't bitch at her.'

'Moi?' Lorraine does her picture-of-innocence face.

'Yeah, you.'


At half six on the nail, the Markhams arrive en masse.

First in the door are Adele and William with Coco, the spaniel, who immediately gets taken upstairs by Liam and Teddy with a tin of biscuits.

'She may never come down,' I say.

'Don't care,' beams William, waiting for his turn to say hello to Lexi and Caitlin.

'This is my new granddad, William, ' Lexi is saying. 'This is my best friend, Caitlin, and she's a ballerina like me.'

'I can tell,' says William gravely. 'You both stand in first position. My sister danced.'

'So did I, but I was very bad,' says Adele, her eyes brimming as she hugs Lexi. 'Darling, we are so honoured to be here.'

'Don't cry, Grandma,' says Lexi, who has clearly decided that since she has plenty of Grannys, she now needs a

Grandma. 'Come and see what we did. We've been working all day.'

And the two girls drag Adele off and I stare at her departing form and realise that yes, she is wearing jeans. They are Armani, but still.

'Betty,' says William, stooping to kiss his daughter's one-time mother-in-law. 'You look charming.'

Betty pats her hair which has had the whole works done, with instructions from Scarlett. 'Oh, you know, got to make a bit of an effort, William.'

I wink at her and she winks back.

Before long, the place is full of people: Tony and Marcus, who are Elisa's brothers, and who look so normal and non-nightclubby-fake that I am astonished they are related to her. They are just as lovely as their father.

Twins Michael and Cooper, eleven, a broken window waiting to happen, somehow find a ball, join forces with Teddy, Liam, the dog and the biscuits, and eventually are dragged downstairs to bash balls into the net in the garden, with Coco doing her best to burst said ball.

Jo, their mother, is fanning herself with an actual fan and hugs me, saying: ' I love your show, Freya. It's so cool – this house, so cool . . .'

'But you're hot?' I venture.

'Bloody menopause,' she says. 'It's killing me.'

'You'll have to meet Maura, my sister,' I say, bringing her to an open window and handing her some iced water. 'She says rage is the number one symptom.'

'OmiGod, yes!' Jo screeches. 'Yes!!'

Jo is a screecher and loves jokes.

Lois, who is younger, married to Marcus, and is so pregnant I think we ought to have the ambulance on speed dial, appears mid-joke and asks where the loo is. She also loves my show but says she can't make bread.

'Comes out like cement,' she says sorrowfully.

'Wrong flour?' I suggest.

The only out-of-place person is her son, Joshua, who is very shy, so I show him into the room with the Super Mario yoke and tell him to have a go at it.

'Really?' he says, blinking long eyelashes, as if he can't believe his luck.

'I'll call you for dinner,' I say, 'but the talking bit can be hard, can't it?'

He nods seriously. 'Thank you so much.'

Dan is having great fun as he remembers both Tony and Marcus from school, and soon insults are being traded.

'Keep it down,' says Lorraine, who is passing, 'Betty gets upset if she hears shouting.'

'Sorry,' they all murmur, like schoolboys.

'You've still got it,' I say.

There is no sign of Elisa but nobody, least of all Lexi, notices.

At seven fifteen, I decide we've waited long enough, tell everyone where to sit and with a few helpers, start dishing up my speedily cooked scallops or cheesy garlic bread for anyone young who thinks shellfish is gross.

'I love scallops but I can't have them now,' says Lois miserably. I hand her a plate containing a tiny smoked salmon quiche, small enough not to over-fill a heavily pregnant person.

'You are an angel,' she says, sighing.

By half seven, the plates are clean and my Lebanese shredded chicken salad with pomegranate, and a whole feast of Lebanese sides are on the table. I have made everything myself, put in plenty of simpler stuff for the younger people, and there's even a pile of my own sausage rolls because Teddy thinks these are the last word in entertaining.

There's pink lemonade, sparkling water, wine and orange juice, and Dan clinks his glass for a toast.

'This is for Lexi, our darling girl who has so many new people to love her,' and everyone cheers. 'And to Caitlin, Lorraine, my mother, Betty, and finally, and most of all, to my beloved Freya, for cooking this delicious feast to bring us together.'

We all raise our glasses and toast. Then dig in.

Lexi finally raises the knotty issue at pudding.

It's my masterpiece, the thing Lexi asked for: a huge Black Forest meringue tower filled with chocolate ganache, non-alcoholic cherries for the children's sakes, marscapone cream and dusted with sparkling edible golden dust.

'Where's Elisa?' she asks loudly, as I'm about to cut into it.

The table falls silent.

'Dearest Lexi,' says William and he sounds so sad. 'Your . . .' He casts an apologetic glance at me. 'Elisa did phone to say she might be late but she'd be here about an hour ago. I have rung but nothing. I am so sorry.'

'I'll kill her,' mutters Marcus.

*Can we all watch*, murmurs Mildred.

'Thank you, Marcus,' says a high, wobbly voice and there's Elisa, in through the unlocked kitchen door and looking less than her best. 'My Wearable Chanel Wallet fell into a drain so I had *no phone*! And everyone laughed.'

She begins to cry and against all my better instincts – OK, against the screeching of Mildred: *Leave her alone! She's a nightmare!* – I bring her into the dining room and sit her down in a chair. She has a scrape on one leg, her mascara has run to panda level, something dark and, from the smell, alcoholic has been spilled on her leopard wrap dress and the carefully tousled hair now just looks tousled.

340

'I didn't mean to be late. I was in town, the heel on one of my shoes went and I fell, and the damned wallet fell. It's a collectable!'

'Why were you in town when you were supposed to be here?' demanded Jo, although I can tell Lorraine was just itching to get there.

I hand Elisa some orange juice thinking that she needs sugar and she drinks it down.

'I was meeting Etzu and he was late, and it was so noisy in the pub that I went outside to ring him and then everything went wrong. I had no money then, so I walked here.'

I hear a snort of laughter and just know it's Dan, so I turn and glare at him.

'Come with me and let's get you something to wear,' I say.

I can't hate her, I tell Mildred as we climb the stairs, with Mildred still ranting, and Elisa going on about how far out we lived and how no taxi would take her.

I feel sorry for her.

OK, she has a Chanel wallet and I don't, but apart from that, I am blessed and she is not. She has great muscles, a yoga body, and simply the wrong priorities in life.

In Dan's and my bedroom, I find an old sweatshirt and sweatpants because I know that whatever I give her, I will never see it again.

She changes in front of me, almost forgetting I'm not one of her crew, and she struggles out of her Spanx-style sucker-in garment, leaving her in bra and knickers. Without all the effort, she's got a normal body for a woman of her age, a woman my age.

'Thanks,' she says, balling up her dress and holding it under her arm. 'Er, do you have any tampons . . .?'

I blink. 'I thought you were pregnant?' I say bluntly.

'So did I. Probably why Etzu did a runner. He's safe now,'

she says with bitterness. 'It came on this morning.'

I hand her tampons and let her into the unused avocado suite off the landing.

'This is soo cool,' she says, sounding happier. 'Green is really in. Who did it for you?'

'Andy Warhol,' I reply.

'Is he local?'

'Nah. Not anymore.'

A noise makes me look around and Lexi's creeping up the stairs, eyes wide.

'Is she all right, Mum?' she says, cuddling into me outside the door, as if a monster's inside.

'Fine.' I don't add all the other things I think – that she's silly, interested in all the wrong things. I wonder why I was ever so scared of her?

'Mum, I don't want her to say she's my mother anymore. Is that OK?' Lexi's big brown eyes burn into mine.

'Whatever you say, darling. But you know she's there if you ever wanted to talk to her again.'

She makes that teenage gesture that says 'yeah/no/whatever' and I grin.

'I love our party,' I say. 'You and Caitlin were brilliant helping Lorraine with the flowers and making places pretty.'

'I know.' Her smile gleams at me. 'Can you do that as a job?'

'I think so,' I say. 'You can do whatever you want. Now, get something nice for Elisa to eat. Some of our chocolate cake?'

Elisa sits on the bed and with her feet curled up around her, almost licks the plate clean.

'You can really cook,' she says to me.

'Mum's a brilliant chef,' corrects Lexi.

'I never eat stuff like this,' Elisa says. Then adds: 'I've probably put on five pounds from just eating it. I'll be fired . . .'

Her face falls.

'The contract with Surella . . .?' I ask, somehow knowing the answer.

She nods. 'Stupid bas—'

'We don't swear in this house,' I interrupt just in time.

'Sorry, Lexi. Sorry Freya. They want someone younger for the second wave of publicity, whatever that is.'

Lexi's eyes widen.

'I'm so sorry,' she says, and sits on the bed beside Elisa and hugs her.

I sit on the other side and put my arm around Elisa too.

'You're so nice. I wish I had friends like you,' says Elisa and tears start to fall down her face, not helping the dripping mascara situation at all.

'You do,' I say. 'You have me and Lexi.'

'Yeah,' says Lexi.

'I'm going back to Spain, next week.'

'You can visit, stay with your mum and dad,' Lexi says. 'The house is so big, they've loads of room.'

'Suppose,' agrees Elisa.

And I realise that Lexi has a look of both her birth mother and darling Dan but that her spirit is all her own.

## 24

# *This is the beginning of the life you want*

It's the Monday after our successful dinner party and I am walking on air.

All the Markhams have been phoning to say hello, they adore Lexi, the party was gorgeous and they're really sorry about Elisa.

Oh, and can we do it again soon.

That night, everyone's asleep except Dan and me, and I have a pain inside me at what I must do next. How can I tell him? That I haven't been slowly getting off sleeping tablets, that I've been lying, that I feel devastated sometimes but have hidden it because . . .? Because of what? Because I was afraid of letting all the balls drop?

We clamber into bed and he's about to do what he does many nights, which is hug me, plant a kiss on my mouth, then roll over and say, 'Love you, honey, night night.'

I don't give him the chance.

'Dan, I have something to tell you.'

He sits up and stares at me, those dark eyes watchful in the dim light of the landing, which must be kept on for the children.

He says nothing and I know I've got to come out and say it straight up.

I gulp: 'I'm still taking sleeping tablets and I need to come off them. I need you to help. I've been lying to you. I'm sorry.'

And then he holds me tight, and I've never felt more loved – or more of a betrayer. Sleeping with an entire philharmonic orchestra wouldn't be as bad as hiding this from him. Sure, all partners have secrets, but small ones – how they really look so good (moustache bleaching), that their old girlfriend always asks after you when they bump into her at work events (she says, 'Are you still with what's her name? I know you're not over me'). Secrets that are unimportant to a real partnership.

But this . . . This is different.

How many times has he asked me about the sleeping tablets and I have lied every time. Every single time.

'I know,' he says quietly.

We sit there in utter silence.

'How?'

'I know where you keep them,' he says.

'I'm sorry,' I say. Such a hopeless phrase. 'I thought I could get better myself, deal with the fear, stop taking the tablets but I haven't and now, it's going to be awful giving them up. I feel ashamed. Of staying on them and lying to you.'

Again, he says nothing. Then he sits up, turns on his bedside lamp and reaches for his phone.

This is it, I think. It's over. He's leaving and we are going to be over because he can't take being married to a woman who's addicted to sleeping tablets. A woman who lies.

He spends a few minutes scrolling through his phone and then shoves over till he's beside me.

'Right,' he says in a very calm voice, but the voice he'd use to his mother or even Zed. 'We'll do this. It doesn't sound like fun but if you follow the detox really carefully, titrating down slowly, you can come off them. I'll help. You know I will.'

And then he holds me and I let myself relax against his

chest, shaking, grateful and yet terrified because since I told Dan the truth, he hasn't once said 'I love you.'

Still, I've told him. That's got to mean something.

I lie there, scared, and eventually, let tablet-induced sleep claim me.

The next day, we go to see AJ together and Dan and AJ have a long discussion about how this needs to be done. Dan gets a script for a small amount of an anti-anxiety medicine to help me, which he goes into the pharmacy to pick up.

I sit in the car, shamed, feeling like a Hillbilly Heroin addict who has to be kept away from all respectable people and have my anti-anxiety meds bought for me because I can't be trusted.

'I never meant it to end up like this . . .' I start when Dan gets back in the car.

He pats my knee.

'We'll get you fixed up,' he says, again, as if he's talking to Zed and they're talking about a dodgy knee after a big run. He never talks to me like that. We are intimate, close: his voice changes when he's with me.

Except I've ruined that forever, I think.

This distant Dan is what I've got from now on. It's my fault.

For the first week, I do not turn into a werewolf, but I feel sick, shaky, anxious and irritable.

'Mummy has a bug,' I can hear Dan say blandly to the children. 'Go in for a snuggle but don't stay. The doctor says she has to stay in bed.'

As I'm never sick enough to be bedbound, they decide I am truly ill and creep around the house, making as much noise as usual but telling each other, in stage whispers, to 'be quiet'.

He takes them over to his mother's a lot, and then over to Scarlett and Jack's.

'You didn't tell them?' I ask each time, terrified he would.

'I said you're sick. You've been through enough – you're allowed to be sick. Your mother, Scarlett and Maura are looking at nursing homes for your dad tomorrow.'

I moan with guilt and misery.

'I should be with them.'

'You've done enough,' Dan says firmly. He leaves and closes the door.

Alone, I can cry because I feel alone right now and I've done it to myself. I pushed this wonderful man away.

By day eight, I'm feeling a lot better. I've managed to watch a couple of Netflix series but only funny things – nothing modern or involving drugs in anyway.

Because I feel so shamed.

Dan is an angel: cooking dinners or reheating things my mother has sent over but I feel so terrified that I've lost his love.

My head never stops analysing and over-analysing the situation. Have I lost him forever?

By the second week, I am up most of the time but terribly fatigued because I am barely sleeping.

I've tried hot milk, valerian tea and going for a walk round the block in the evening with Dan.

Once, he'd have held my hand when we walked but now, he doesn't.

Still, he's walking with me and he still hugs me in bed at night, holding me close but briefly.

Like he can't bear to hold me too long . . .?

When he turns out his light at night, he used to say, 'I love you.'

Now, he says nothing.

I still lie in bed at night not sleeping but I don't get up. This is my bed, I've made it and I have to lie on it.

## 25

*When life gives you lemons . . . it's entirely up to you what you do next. Lemonade is good but some days, you do feel like throwing them at someone*

From Freya: Learning to Live With It, *Freya Abalone's new TV cookery and lifestyle show*

Miss Primrose promises to be at the launch for *Freya*, my new TV show, which has been given a one-word title in deference to my newfound fame.

'We'll only come if we can bring Tinkle,' says Giorgio gravely, and he, Patrick and Miss Primrose and I all burst into laughter.

'People will assume Tinkle is called Tinkle because she has no control over her nether regions,' says Miss Primrose. 'Plus, you need to get her fixed, boys. Whisper's totally in love with her and we cannot have another lot of pups.'

'Just one more litter,' begs Giorgio who, now that he has delivered one litter of pups, feels he is at one with nature and wants to do it again.

'We are getting Tinkle spayed,' says Patrick firmly. 'She needs a little pal and it will be a rescue.'

'She's a rescue herself,' points out Giorgio, 'but I never tell her that as she thinks she's a princess.'

'Posie's the same,' I say, referring to Tinkle's offspring,

one of the two pups I took from the litter, both girls. Posie can't quite believe she doesn't have a seat at the table with us. Magic is quite content to sit in her bed.'

'Teddy will soon fix that,' Patrick laughs.

Teddy is a bit of a dog whisperer and all our dogs revere her as their queen. Once Teddy truly begins to teach my two new puppies how to misbehave, all the dog training books will be useless.

My mother has taken another of the litter, although Delilah the cat is quite put out by the little bundle of fur that now roams the kitchen and gives my mother solace now that Dad is in a nursing home.

Mum has a step monitor on her watch and she and Bella walk every morning, something which is putting the colour back in my mother's face.

She visits my father every day, and some days, Eddie comes along and has found a whole contingent of people in the nursing home who also like *Nazi Megastructures*.

'This is my son, Lorcan,' Eddie says proudly to everyone. 'He loves the *Guinness Book of Records* too. Ask us anything. Anything.'

And of course, we took two dogs. Because Teddy insisted and she is in charge.

'What are we all doing?' says Dan, appearing at the kitchen door where Teddy, Lexi and I are working on a recipe.

We are losing ingredients speedily as Teddy is eating the cherries, while Lexi has found my decorating balls and is making a complex pattern on a jam jar lid that will take an hour to recreate on top of the cake.

We have discussed this new cake and Teddy wants to call it *Teddy's Cake*, which may just be its name.

Liam is outside in the garden with the newly vaccinated Posie and her much smaller, and deliciously lazier sister,

Magic, and they are playing ball. Or rather, Liam and Posie are playing ball.

Tinkle, Posie and Magic's mother, is definitely a silky terrier cross while her boyfriend, and therefore father of her many pups, was possibly a Chihuahua. While Posie is all bouncy terrier intelligence with white silky fur like her mother, Magic is very Chihuahua, a doe-like fawn colour and with the air of an exquisitely tiny haughty queen.

She can easily get upstairs on her own but much prefers being carried.

'Will we go for a walk with the mad beasts and the dogs along Sandymount Strand?' says Dan.

Lexi laughs. 'We're not mad beasts,' she says, as he bends to kiss her.

'I know, Squirt,' he says.

'I've grown an inch this summer,' she says.

'I know.'

September and October have been wildly busy what with the children back at school and Teddy's iron will coming up against the sweet but equally implacable iron will of her first big school teacher, Miss Murphy.

I'm hectically busy on my blog which is called The Best You Can Do and looks at recipes for when you're down and has my thoughts – my actual thoughts on life, the universe and everything, rather than fake thoughts.

OK, not all my thoughts.

We all pile into the car and head for Sandymount.

Once there, Lexi runs down the beach with Posie, who likes running, while Liam is left to make do with Magic, who looks as if she wants her own pony and trap to take her further down. Teddy is collecting giant stones into piles and keeps saying, 'Get these on the way back, Daddy,' in her usual imperious tone.

It's a beautifully warm day for late October and I'm wearing a filmy red floral dress Scarlett got for me on one of her vintage shopping trips.

I would never have tried it on because it's clingy but she says it really suits me.

I also have a small rucksack in case of showers and plenty of poo bags because Magic and Posie think that little offerings from their bowels are what the world is waiting for.

I am happy on so many levels. Happy because I have my beautiful family and my career is going from strength to strength. Or, to use a different phrase, levelled out after a lot of turbulence.

Everyone has bad days and now when I do, I say so. And it's given me a whole new outlook on life. Turns out lots of people are like me too: convinced we have to be fake happy to get by when after all, whose life is perfect all the time?

I think of my new happiness as a gift: a gift I had to earn by going through pain in the first place. I think about this a lot in the mornings when I walk the dogs because they came into our lives by accident, and have brought us so much. Pain came into my life by accident via what happened to me in the garage, and yet it's brought me a strength I never knew I had. It's a strange sort of gift – one that has to take root and grow. But it's part of me now, part of the family.

My new TV show, shot at speed after I did so much press and publicity after the article about my being mugged and how I recovered from it appeared, is nearly top of the TV ratings, there's talk of it being bought in the US and it has been bought in the UK. Thanks to more help for me and Lorraine, my cookery book, *Recipes for Happiness*, is to be worked on also at high speed and because I am getting really good at saying no these days (thanks, Mildred!),

I say yes only to the press things I'd like to do.

'Why did you call her Mildred?' is what Dan wants to know when I come clean to him about my inner voice.

We talk a lot more since the early days of my coming clean about lying to him but there's still a tiny wedge between us, to my mind.

'I can't explain it,' I say.

'Should I call you Mildred in bed?' he then jokes, pulling me onto the bed and pretending to moan 'Mildreed, Mildreed, you excite meee,' so loudly that I try to put a pillow over his face and we both explode laughing.

I cherish these moments: when I think we're *us* again, the way we used to be.

He's not laughing now. He looks serious and I feel slightly sick.

It's a long time since we've all managed a walk like this. The kids are all a bit away from us and only the dogs are close by.

'It broke my heart that you hadn't let me help,' he says suddenly, looking into the distance.

'I'm sorry,' I mutter.

Is this it? He wants a divorce? Is this how it's done? Soberly and calmly with the kids running on ahead. No plate-throwing or screeching about how I'd lied to him.

I never thought it would be us. I've tried so hard to make things right these past months but I didn't try when I should have. When I was working so hard at being Freya: Wonder Woman and not letting Dan in.

Nobody's Wonder Woman. We're all mortal, all doing our best, trying to carve out time for relationships in the mass of school and work and have we run out of loo roll, again?

We were so good in bed and I thought that was the deal-breaker for men. If you weren't matched sexually, you were kaput.

But with Dan . . . I thought we were solid and yet I'd messed it all up with my lies. Why did I have to pretend to be perfect to him?

He must have hated it when I told him, hated knowing how much I'd lied to him. But he'd never said a word of reproach to me.

'Dan . . .' I begin, and suddenly the rain decides to give it a good lash and I yell at the kids to come back, start extracting coats from my rucksack and say we'll have to run back to the car.

We're running but the rain is beating us. Now it's a wild tattoo and Dan hasn't moved.

I reach the car with the kids and stow them in, then turning back to where Dan stands about two hundred yards away, raincoat-less, being rained on.

I run back to him, frantic now.

'Please,' I say, 'we can fix it, Dan. Don't go,' I say. 'I am so sorry—'

'I love you,' he interrupts and he looks a little bit haunted. 'But . . .'

I hang my head, feeling the water making this stupid dress see-through. I'm cold now.

'Dan, don't do this,' I say. 'I'm sorry, I love you and I never meant to lie, I simply didn't know how to tell the truth: that I was falling apart. I thought I had to be strong . . .'

'No,' he says,' you don't understand. I can't forgive myself. You went through all this and I never knew. I should have known and I've let you down. That night you told me about the tablets, that was the worst night of my life. I had let you down. I hadn't been there and you weren't able to tell me.'

I turn my head up to the rain and let it flow down my face.

'*You* let *me* down?' I say, loving the feel of the rain. 'I thought I'd let you down. I love you, Dan Conroy. Love you. I thought you wanted to divorce me.'

'No! I love you, adore you. I'd be lost without you, Freya.' He grabs me now and we're both wet from the rainstorm and then he's humming crazily, 'It Had To Be You,' and I'm laughing, trying to dance with him but I've always been a terrible dancer.

'I—' I start, and he starts to say 'I—' at exactly the same time.

'I lied,' I say.

'We all lie sometimes, and you wanted to get strong by yourself, Freya,' he says, his head bent to mine. 'If it had been me, I wouldn't have shared it all. I'd have tried to man up and deal with it all myself. I know I would.'

'Really?'

He nods. 'I love how strong you are, my beautiful wife, but I love all of you. Not just the strong, but the vulnerable, the wet hair . . .'

I laugh. We're both wet, dripping, in fact. The rain is pelting down.

'I love your wet hair, too,' I say. 'I love you.'

'I love you better.'

'Best.'

'Bestest.'

There's a distant banging and I see Teddy with her head stuck out the window like a dog.

'I'm hungry,' she roars. 'Ice cream!'

*Call yourself a chef, you dizzy thing,* says Mildred. *You haven't organised any snacks in the car, have you? Mindfulness is all well and good but you have to think about the future too, you know.*

355

# Acknowledgements

I love acknowledgements in books. Not my own – writing those is a nightmare of enormous proportions because I am scared of forgetting someone. I have a head like a sieve. Just saying.

But other people's . . . thrilling. And there are so many people to thank because contrary to all beliefs, writing is a team effort. Yes, I do the writing but without my family, my friends, my agency, my publishers around the world and you, fabulous readers, this book would be a pamphlet, although I'd have scrubbed the skirting boards and actually knitted (if you can call it knitting) more than a quarter of my light, fluffy blanket. (Thin wool . . . a nightmare!)

So here goes: first thanks goes to my dear friend Marian Keyes, who was first reader, first editor, first person to tell me I am not a moron (we have this conversation every book) and a beautiful human being inside and out.

I would be nothing without the incredible team at Curtis Brown, headed by the ever wonderful Jonathan Lloyd, Lucy Morris, Melissa Pimentel, Hannah Beer, Claire Nozieres, Jodi Fabbri and Sarah Harvey, not to mention all the people who make Curtis Brown such a pleasure to deal with.

In Orion, I could not manage without Harriet Bourton and then Clare Hey, with glorious help from David Shelley,

Katie Espiner, Olivia Barber, Sarah Benton, Virginia Woolstencroft, Amy Davies, Lynsey Sutherland, and the rest of the team. The glorious teams in Hachette NZ and Australia keep these books flying like butterflies into the world and when am I seeing you all again?

In Ireland, the team on the road keep me sane so thank you to Siobhan Tierney, Ruth Shern, Joanna Smyth, Elaine Egan, Bernard Hoban, Breda Purdue and Jim Binchy.

Nobody could have a more brilliant publicity firm than the Communications Clinic, headed by my friend Terry Prone, the utterly amazing Aileen Gaskin and Amy Jordan. Thanks to the wonderful publishers and translators around the world who bring my books into different languages and show that while lives and continents may be different, people are not.

Special mention goes to Caitlin Keogh whose mum, Joanne Keogh, generously donated to the Laura Lynn Foundation to have her dear Caitlin's name in the book.

Also thanks to Janice Ryan, who generously donated to the Laura Lynn Foundation to have her beloved father, Paddy Ashmore's name in the book. As this book deals a little with the non-stop work of the carer, it is only fitting that a hard-working member of the Carer's Association gets a mention, so welcome Lorraine Ryan and I hope you like yourself in the book.

Thank you so much to friend and workmate Gillian Glynn O'Sullivan who is indispensable both as a friend and colleague.

Thank you to chef extraordinaire Catherine Fulvio – who, at time of writing, was nominated for an EMMY! I would still be lying down with the thrill of it all but not Catherine, who is a dynamo. Thanks to Dr Sam Hafford for medical help.

Thank to you all my UNICEF Ireland colleagues because this work is a huge part of who I am. My part is so tiny but the people at the coalface deserve so much thanks for helping give voice to those who have none.

Thanks to darling Margaret Fagan for so much.

I am blessed with so many writer friends, like Ella Griffin (and Womble), Sinead Moriarty, Erica James, Stefanie Preissner, Jennifer Ryan, Sheila O'Flanagan, Claire Hennessy, Louise O'Neill, Jo Spain, and Kate Kerrigan.

Dear friends of my heart are Tricia Scanlan, Gai Griffin, Fiona O'Brien, Julia Kelly, Felicity Hayes-McCoy who also write, and I would be lost without them. More lost-without-them friends include my darling old college mate, Clodagh Finn, dear Stella O'Connell, Fatima, Kelly and her glorious family, Judy, Brenda, LisaMarie; another dynamo - Catherine Lee, Eva Berg, Caroline, Marguerite, Alice, Redika, Libby, Ruth, Denis, Joe, Mary, Gary, Paul, Cathal, Elaine (my eyebrows are fabulous!!!!!), Eamonn and Deirdre. Thanks also to my just-around the corner friends of Barbara, Teresa, Grainne, Claire and Alyson. Thanks for their friendship to Aisling Carroll, Christine and Karen-Maree on different continents, as well as Cindy, Helen, Aidan and Murtagh, Dr Mary Helen Hensley, and Andréa Burke, whose gift can never be repaid.

Thank you to my beloved and vast family including Robert, Katie (and Bailey), Justine, John, Luke, Jessica and Emily, as well as Annabel, David, Andrew, Matylda, Hanna, Hugo and Maulie.

Thanks to my beloved Laura, Naomi and Emer – plus Alice, Hugo and my godpets. I am so proud of you all. You are amazing young women.

To Francis, Lucy, Dave, Anne and Princess Lola, everlasting thanks, none of which can be repaid with anything but love. I would be truly lost without you all.

To Mum, I don't know what I'd do without you. And to the six creatures in this house: Dinky, Licky, Scamp, Murray, Dylan and John – I could not do it without you.

Over a year ago, my dear best friend, Emma Hannigan died from cancer. I go to phone you every day, my love. You taught me so much even though you said I taught you so much. I think one day, in whatever crazy unicorn-filled afterlife you are in, we shall argue about it and giggle and hug. My love and sympathy are always with your beloved Sacha, Kim, Cian, Philip, Denise, Timmy, Hilary, Robyn, Steffi and all your family, whose loss is far greater.

Finally, thank you, the reader, for coming with me on this mad journey of fun, sadness, love and hope that shows us that generally, as Scarlett O'Hara said, tomorrow is always another day.

# Credits

Cathy Kelly and Orion Fiction would like to thank everyone at Orion who worked on the publication of *A Family Gift* in the UK.

**Editorial**
Harriet Bourton
Clare Hey
Olivia Barber

**Copy editor**
Sally Partington

**Proof reader**
Laetitia Grant

**Audio**
Paul Stark
Amber Bates

**Contracts**
Anne Goddard
Paul Bulos
Jake Alderson

**Design**
Debbie Holmes
Joanna Ridley
Nick May
Helen Ewing

**Editorial Management**
Charlie Panayiotou
Jane Hughes
Alice Davis

**Finance**
Jasdip Nandra
Afeera Ahmed
Elizabeth Beaumont
Sue Baker

**Marketing**
Lynsey Sutherland

Amy Davies

**Production**
Ruth Sharvell

**Publicity**
Virginia Woolstencroft

**Sales**
Jen Wilson
Esther Waters

Victoria Laws
Rachael Hum
Ellie Kyrke-Smith
Frances Doyle
Georgina Cutler

**Operations**
Jo Jacobs
Sharon Willis
Lisa Pryde
Lucy Brem

# Help us make the next generation of readers

We – both author and publisher – hope you enjoyed this book.
We believe that you can become a reader at any time in your life,
but we'd love your help to give the next generation a head start.

Did you know that 9% of children don't have a book of their
own in their home, rising to 13% in disadvantaged families*?
We'd like to try to change that by asking you to consider the role
you could play in helping to build readers of the future.

We'd love you to think of sharing, borrowing, reading, buying or talking
about a book with a child in your life and spreading the love of reading.
We want to make sure the next generation continue to have access
to books, wherever they come from.

And if you would like to consider donating to charities that help
fund literacy projects, find out more at www.literacytrust.org.uk
and www.booktrust.org.uk.

Thank you.

*As reported by the National Literacy Trust